HAUNTED LOVE

BY

JOYA FIELDS

Featuring...

Hereafter
Altered Frequency
Sidelined Afterlife

છ

Decadent Publishing Company
www.decadentpublishing.com

Haunted Love
Copyright 2014 by Joya Fields
ISBN: 978-1-61333-591-8
Cover by Tibbs Designs

Published by Decadent Publishing Company
www.decadentpublishing.com

Printed in the United States of America

"What the Critics are Saying...."

"The mystery of what really happened to Angie makes for an interesting read, and the book's paranormal aspects transport readers into a world of possibilities that bring up new questions about the afterlife." ~**RT Book Reviews**

"Fields tale flowed effortlessly and from the first page I just slipped into the story." ~**Kimbacaffeinatte**

"As with her other stories, Joya Fields makes you care so much for her characters and what happens to them." ~**Grace, Sweet Spot Book Blog**

"Their intimate scenes are intense, passionate, and hot enough to spark your e-reader." ~**Lusty Penguin Reviews**

"I have to give serious purrs to Fields for her talent at creating believable characters."
~**What the Cat Read**

"Ghosts, stalkers, true evil, true love, and a bit of mystery all add to the fun."
~**Delphina Reads Too Much**

HAUNTINGS AT INNER HARBOR

DEFLECTED

JOYA FIELDS

Chapter One

Rob jolted upright in his bed, wrenched out of sleep by the sound of weeping. He shook his head. Had he dreamed the sound?

Clad only in boxers, he stalked across the cold hardwood floor and paused with his hand on the doorknob. More quiet crying. The television? Maybe his apartment had thin walls. He exhaled and yanked the door open.

He brushed his hand along the living room wall; his finger flicked the light switch. Nothing. Tried it two more times. Same result. *Damn.* For two thousand dollars a month, he expected reliable electricity.

A muffled, female sob filled the room and his hand froze on the wall. A shiver sped down his spine. He expected to see the blue glow of the television, but the room was shrouded in darkness. Soft weeping followed by a sharp intake of air pierced through the quiet. His breaths came fast and shallow and the hairs on his arms rose.

An intruder. How had she gotten in? An ex-tenant who still had a key? Possibilities scrambled through his brain. Nobody would break into his apartment to weep. They'd take what they wanted and leave. A burglar wouldn't cry. Unless she was on drugs.

The sobbing ceased.

He needed to call the police, but he'd left his phone on his nightstand. He inched back toward the bedroom, mentally preparing to defend himself if the trespasser attacked. Whoever was in his apartment didn't know whether he was armed or not. That might be all the advantage he needed.

Bright moonlight filtered into the small living room and offered enough light to see outlines and shadows—unpacked boxes and neat stacks of files. In the late-night quiet, the only sounds were the muffled intermittent traffic from the Baltimore city street below and his racing heart. He'd had all of one week to unpack and move into the apartment. Tax season took priority over his new living quarters, though, and he hadn't made much progress.

But now, instead of being an annoying reminder that he needed to finish unpacking, the boxes served as a barrier. A hiding place for someone.

A hushed sob from the other side of the small living room broke the silence, and Rob halted. He shut his eyes to force his hearing to compensate. The soft crying began again, and his eyes flew open. His gaze jerked to the black-and-white checkered sofa by the window.

"Who the hell is there?" he asked. He fisted his hands and pulled himself up to his full six feet in case the intruder could see him.

Silence.

Damn. He needed a flashlight. Not unpacked yet. In fact, buried in a box under two other boxes.

The curtains near the sofa fluttered, and he saw her. Medium height, slim, and wearing only a flimsy nightgown. His heart stuttered.

Long golden hair sparkled in the moonlight by the window. Her shoulders shook.

Rob stepped forward. He wanted nothing more than to reach out, touch her pearlescent skin. But it was that very skin that stopped him from getting closer. Almost translucent. As if he could see through her. After rubbing his eyes, he looked again. He couldn't see through her. It was more a feeling that she wasn't all there. Had he lost his mind?

Common sense told him to leave the apartment, call the police. Even shout for a neighbor. But instead of either, he stepped toward the sofa, unable to stop himself. Whoever she was, she was too upset to cause him any harm. He moved closer. "Who are you? Why are you in my apartment?"

Sadness dripped down her face like the tears that tracked to her chin.

Only two more steps and he stood near enough to get a better look at her. "Hey," he whispered. "Do you need help?" He held his hands out, palms up, and stepped closer.

She closed her eyes, took a breath, and then gazed at him.

"What's wrong?" Rob whispered. A million other questions flew through his mind. *Who are you? What are you doing here?*

She took a step back and opened her eyes wide, as if she suddenly realized he was in the room. Hadn't she heard him? Hadn't she seen him? Maybe his near-nakedness scared her.

"It's okay. I won't hurt you." He halted. If he reached out, he half-expected to touch nothing but air. Nothing made sense. Maybe he'd had some bad sushi or something, bringing on a waking nightmare. With a beautiful woman.

She blinked at him. In the dim light, he couldn't see her eye color. A sudden, overwhelming need to comfort her washed over him. The woman glanced around the apartment, and fresh tears slid down her cheeks. Her hunched shoulders made her look like she wished she'd stayed invisible to him. She was trespassing. Still, a part of him that had never quite healed since his teenage years yearned to reach out to offer help. Help he hadn't been able to give his twin brother so many years ago. He forced the memory away.

This woman didn't hold a weapon, didn't even seem to notice him. She wasn't a threat to his safety. He took a step closer and extended his arms. Okay, so this dream was very real. May as well go with it, see where it took him.

At first he thought she'd back away, but when she met his gaze, she bit her bottom lip. She tilted her head as if in question, closed her eyes, and stepped forward into his embrace. Like warm cotton candy straight from the vendor, she melted against him, fitting perfectly. Feeling more real than she looked. What did she need? She laid her head on his chest. So soft, so feminine. Her silky nightgown didn't provide much of a barrier, and he willed his libido to calm.

Her sobs vibrated against his torso. Long, drawn-out weeping accented by gasps for breath as if she'd been holding it in for a long, long time. Sadness ripped at his gut, making him wish he could take her pain away. He wrapped his arms around her, pulled her closer.

"Please," she whispered. Just one word, but it packed a world of meaning. Brought memories of his brother crashing back. This woman needed something. He wasn't sure what it was, and he wasn't sure if he was capable of figuring it out.

"It'll be okay." He closed his eyes, ran his hands over her cool skin, and hoped he could make her better, if only for a few minutes. "Too bad you're not real," he whispered. If she wasn't real, wasn't a dream, what was she? *A ghost*. No. He didn't believe in ghosts. Those days were long gone.

His arms slid toward each other, suddenly empty. He opened his eyes and all the lights came on. She was gone.

He squeezed his eyes shut against the glare. Blinking several times, he squinted to look around the room. No trace to prove she'd ever been in his apartment. What the hell? He panted for breath. Running a hand through his hair, he glanced around the box-cluttered room. Stress overload. A woman in his apartment who disappeared when he told her he wished she was real. *Sure, sure. Way to lose your sanity, pal.*

Her one whispered word reverberated around his mind like an echo. The skin on his chest tingled where she'd laid her head. He bolted to the apartment door. Locked.

How the hell could he sleep after that encounter? Rob frowned at the faint lemon scent that lingered in the room. His imagination. Or was it? There was a time he would have believed what he had seen was real.

03

Angel didn't have to open her eyes to know that the transformation was complete. Her skin prickled with an electric charge. Damp moss touched her legs and the sound of a bubbling brook rippled through the cool air. Her other world.

Angel wasn't her real name, but it seemed to fit because if she had to be a spirit, she liked to think she was a good one.

Tonight, for the first time, someone had actually seen her. Seen her as if she existed in that world, even. That had to mean something, had to be some sort of progress in figuring out where she was and what she was supposed to do. Even now, the pleasure of being touched, of being held by a warm body, heated her skin.

The man. Who was he? How had he been able to see her when nobody else could?

She had no idea how long she'd been between two worlds. There was no way for her to measure time. Days didn't exist in this place. Her lack of memory frustrated her more and more every day. How could she identify objects and places but have no recollection of who she was or why she was in this place?

Standing, she glanced around the tranquil surroundings. Pebbles lined the sides of the brook. She picked one up and tossed it, watching the splash turn into a wave as it swept with the current.

She didn't cry here. Only in the other place.

Across the water, a shadow moved. It didn't scare her any longer. When she'd first arrived, she'd been frightened, alone. Now the shadows brought her peace. Spirits like her, who all walked in their own worlds.

With her nightgown billowing in the gentle breeze, she strolled to her favorite spot under a huge weeping willow tree. Taking a seat in the lush grass beneath the swaying branches, she frowned, but her heart swelled with hope. Someone had seen her. Could it mean she'd finally know who she was and why she traveled alone through two different worlds, going almost unnoticed in each?

Who was this man? Her physical reaction to him confused her. As if her body knew he offered comfort and solace, she had stepped into his arms instead of running away. He'd looked surprised at first and then pulled her into his arms. Peace washed over her. His apartment felt familiar. His embrace awakened emotions she'd never felt before as a ghost. In spite of the dark apartment, she'd been able to make out his sleep-rumpled hair and muscular body. And once he'd held her, his biceps bunched and flexed, locking her into a safe place.

Now the question remained, how could she get back to him as soon as possible?

Chapter Two

The next evening, Rob stepped out of the apartment elevator onto the eighth floor. Despite a fourteen-hour day preparing tax returns at the accounting office, energy still burned inside him.

All day, the same thought had run through his head. Ghosts didn't exist. He used to have an open mind about them; in fact, used to believe that he and his brother chatted regularly on the back porch swing with their grandmother after she passed away. But then his brother died, and Rob's life changed. Ghosts weren't real, and they certainly didn't fall weeping into his arms. The woman had been a dream. A very vivid dream, but nothing more than a figment of his imagination. He'd been working too damned hard lately, and it was taking a toll on him.

Inside his apartment, he glanced toward the window, at the view of the Inner Harbor he'd paid so dearly for in this upscale part of Baltimore. No golden-haired ghost. Of course not.

In the kitchen, he took out a carton of beef lo mein, grabbed a fork, and leaned over the sink to eat his meal.

Tonight, he'd clean and unpack some of the boxes until he was too tired to stand.

To rid the apartment of its stale smell, he walked to the sofa and opened the window a crack. An unusually warm March breeze wafted in, and he took a deep breath. Then he spent the rest of the night unpacking while Deanna Bogart's smoky saxophone wailed on his CD player.

Nodding with approval, he glanced around at the gleaming granite countertops that divided the kitchen from the living room, the neatly arranged framed art on the walls, and books that stood in order by size on the shelves. He gathered the empty moving boxes and piled them by the door. Halfway unpacked. Progress.

At least the woman's appearance had given him something else to think about besides his ex-girlfriend, Sheila. "Good riddance," he mumbled.

With most of the boxes out of the way, the apartment looked livable. But he couldn't shake the memory of him and his brother Mick with their grandmother. Even after her death, she'd visited them, told them stories that made them laugh. At the time, he'd believed it. But now, looking back, he knew it wasn't real, only something his brother had convinced him to believe.

Then Mick died. No matter how hard he tried, Rob couldn't connect with Mick's ghost, couldn't contact Nanna again, either. Proof that ghosts didn't exist.

After a hot shower, he settled himself on the checkered sofa and sighed. An empty bed depressed him these days, reminding him he'd been left alone. Again.

Maybe this golden-haired woman was a handy obsession because his life was hollow now. Her sorrowful expression begged him for something. If only he knew what. He closed his eyes and dug in his memory, willed himself to remember.

The ghost in his dream didn't look familiar, but her expression did. He'd seen those pleading eyes, that hopeless look, in his brother's eyes. Just before he'd died.

He swallowed hard. Fifteen years ago he'd been there for his brother's last breath. The memory drove him to his feet to pace the hardwood floor. He hadn't been able to help his brother that day, hadn't been able to give him blood, or perform CPR. The sleigh-riding accident—the tree he slammed into—left him too broken to fix.

Memories flooded his mind, too strong to push away. The smell of the cold air at the bottom of the hill as he hollered at Mick to hang on, the blood that gushed from his brother's mouth, and his face as he took his last breath before the ambulance could reach them.

Rob's hands shook. He buried that day in his mind deeper than they'd buried his brother's body that cold, snowy winter. He should have told his brother not to go, should have stopped him from sledding down that steep backyard hill one more time. Rob was the wild one, the risk taker, not Mick. But no more. After that day, after the sad, accusing looks from his parents and his own friends, Rob changed. He didn't take chances. He led a predictable life, relying on data and numbers. A safe life.

A life without ghosts.

Exhaustion forced him back to the sofa, worn out by the emotions that swirled through him. He wanted a cold beer and sleep. Or maybe he'd skip the beer and go right to sleep.

Reaching behind his head, he switched off the lamp and closed his eyes. It would likely be a long, restless night.

His mouth tightened into a smile when he smelled lemons.

With each inhale, the scent grew stronger. He breathed deeply, held the aroma before exhaling, like a long pull on an expensive Cuban cigar. The smell conjured a picture of her: golden hair, haunted eyes, and feminine curves.

The citrus aroma grew stronger.

His pulse raced. Dreaming already? He'd only just lain down.

Soft crying sounded from behind him. Weird that his eyes opened since he had to be asleep, right? He shifted to sit and sighed when he spotted her. Her hair blew in the breeze as she gazed out the window. If he had to guess her age, he'd guess early thirties. Tears dripped down her cheeks, and she stared blankly ahead, as if lost in her thoughts, dressed in the same white nightgown.

Rob didn't know what to say, so he kept quiet, watching her, keeping guard over her. *A dream. This is a dream.*

She blinked and then turned to face him. Wet tears sparkled in her eyes.

He pinched himself, and it hurt. Not dreaming. Really? Not possible. People in dreams could probably pinch themselves and feel it. Yeah, that explained it.

The woman stared at him for a long minute. Maybe he was going insane. His brain told him she couldn't be real. What the hell did she want? What if she was some sort of evil spirit who wanted to lure him to the afterlife?

Strangely, the thought didn't scare him as much as it should have. With a dull job, no family, and friends who only called when they wanted to score his company's box seat tickets for sporting events, what did he have to live for anyway? Then he shook the thought away.

"You aren't real. Get the hell out of here and stop bothering me." He groaned, and scrubbed his hands across his face.

When he looked up, she was gone.

☙

Rob woke several times throughout the night, each time thinking of the crying woman. Good riddance. At six o'clock, his cell phone alarm buzzed. He climbed off the sofa feeling like he hadn't slept at all.

Out of habit, he brewed coffee. He folded his arms on the cool countertop and laid his head on them. He couldn't shake the image of his golden-haired visitor.

No woman had ever made him want to sleep on a couch before; when he lived with Sheila, he always crawled into bed and fell asleep within three minutes, even when she was sick or crying in the bathroom after they'd had a fight. She was just one more person in a long line of people to desert him. Well, he'd learned his lesson. From now on, he'd leave them before they left him.

Thirty minutes later, he raced down the hallway as the elevator doors began to close.

"Thanks," Rob said to the bald guy in a suit who held the doors for him, saving him a three-minute wait for the next one. The guy sported a Baltimore City Police Department badge necklace.

The cop smiled. "Ground floor?"

Rob nodded, switched his briefcase to his left hand, held out his right as the elevator doors swished closed. "Rob Morrison, apartment 807."

The man's eyebrows rose as he extended a hand. "J.B. Trueth, I'm in 811. Did you say 807?"

"Yeah," Rob said.

The cop whistled low between his teeth.

"What?" Rob asked.

The blazer strained at the seams as bulky shoulders lifted and dropped. "Isn't that a little creepy?"

The elevator dinged, signaling their arrival on the ground floor. The doors opened onto the lobby and both men stepped out.

A tingle crept up Rob's spine. "Why would it be creepy?"

J.B. leaned toward him, brows raised, mouth agape. "You mean you don't know?" The guy shrugged. "I guess they're not legally required to tell you. Angie killed herself in that apartment. Angie Barsotti." He shook his head. "Such a waste. She was a looker. Blonde hair, worked out in the exercise room regularly...."

"What? Why?" Suicide. In his apartment.

J.B. looked at his watch. "Nobody knows exactly why, although depression ran in her family. Sorry, bro, I gotta split. Early meeting. Nice to meet you, Rob. We'll get a beer soon." J.B. hurried out the revolving door.

ℛ

Angel leaned back against the weeping willow and absently toyed with a blade of fresh grass between her thumb and forefinger. Why did she feel so drawn to that apartment, and why did it make her so sad? She had no memories, no idea what she was supposed to do in either world, but she knew something kept calling her to the apartment.

Frustration built, tightening in her belly. She needed to accomplish something, but what? Ideas and possibilities swirled through her mind.

"Maybe I'm looking for answers." She spoke aloud in hopes of jogging a memory, a purpose. She shook her head. It sounded too vague.

Picturing the dark apartment, and the city lights outside it, she wondered if there was a mystery she needed to solve. "I need to uncover a truth, un-do a wrong." She jolted at her whispered words and frowned. Scary as they were, they carried a sense of realism.

Would she recognize her purpose? As long as she'd been traveling between the two worlds, she'd been asking herself these questions. The man who lived in the apartment. He could be a part of finding the answers.

An unmistakable urge to be close to him filled her. With no memories to rely on, she wondered if she'd known him at one time. He'd been surprised to see her, but she didn't think he knew her.

He didn't want her near him, though, had effectively banished her by saying she wasn't real.

She twirled her hair between two fingers, wishing she knew more about herself, and why she popped in and out of different worlds. "Who am I and why am I here?" She glanced around. Did anyone ever hear her in this world? Nobody had acknowledged her so far.

At least she could speak in this world. When she visited the apartment, it was as if she had no voice. She could barely move her lips, barely express herself except through tears.

Her thoughts drifted to the man who lived there. At first, his strong build and caring nature made her want to trust him. Then he banished her.

Her head snapped up. Maybe he had some sort of power over her coming and going.

A lilac-scented breeze wafted past, billowing her white nightgown. With no control over her visits to the apartment, she'd have to be patient. Thinking back, she wished she'd counted the times she'd been there. For a while, there'd been furniture, but nobody came and went. Then, the place had been empty and freshly painted. She wished she knew how to control her visits back and forth. They just...happened.

Picturing the man's face, she sighed. She'd only seen him at night, in pockets of light. The memory of his light-blue eyes and a nose that was a little too big took her breath away.

She stood and lifted her face to the sun. Always pleasantly warm in this world. And up until the first night she'd met the man, she'd been cold in the other world. The dark apartment that made her cry. She wasn't cold there anymore, not in his arms, but she wasn't welcome there anymore, either.

CR

Rob closed his office door and pushed a pile of receipts to the side of the desk. To hell with lunch. It was the first chance he had to research the woman who used to live in his apartment. He typed Angie Barsotti's name and the address of the apartment into a search engine, sat forward on the edge of his brown leather chair, and then clicked the first link on the list.

A photo filled the upper left-hand corner of the obituary. His hand froze on the mouse, and his body stilled.

Unreal. The woman who'd appeared in his apartment grinned at him from the computer screen. Every muscle in his body tensed. He held his breath. This was some sort of sick joke. He bolted from his chair and paced the area behind his desk.

What he'd seen in his apartment wasn't real. Someone must have shown him a photo of Angie before. Maybe there'd been one on display the first time he looked at the place. Yeah, yeah, that was it. A simple explanation. His tired mind had conjured an image of something he'd seen once.

Tilting his head to the right, and then the left, he cracked his neck and then sat, staring at her black-and-white photo. She'd died at thirty-six. Survived only by a daughter. The death notice listed her workplace as an elementary school. His eyes widened.

He typed in the name of the school where Angie had worked. His heart raced when a picture of her from a PTA newsletter appeared on the screen. Leaning forward, he looked into her smiling eyes. His hands shook and his head pounded.

Releasing a breath, he gazed at the photo on his computer screen. She'd been happy once.

Hundreds of students, their parents, and faculty members turned out for a memorial service to honor Ms. Barsotti. Her easy smile, compassion for her students, and love of history made her popular with kids and parents alike. In lieu of flowers, Ms. Barsotti's family asks that donations be made....

Two quick raps on his office door made him jump. He exited the page.

Mr. Withers, one of the founding partners of the accounting agency, opened the door, frowning. "We're meeting with the new clients in ten minutes. You're prepared, right?"

"Yes," Rob said. "All set."

"Good man." He closed the door.

Hurrying, Rob printed out the elementary school newsletter. He grabbed a folder from the drawer, and jammed the papers inside. He'd complete his work, do what he needed to at the office, but damned if he'd stay late tonight. Finding information about Angie's death took priority now. If he found out more about her, maybe he'd figure out why he couldn't get her image out of his mind.

Chapter Three

Rob's cheeseburger and fries cooled inside the paper bag next to the soda on his granite kitchen counter. He stared into the combination living room/dining room. The folder containing the print-outs about Angie lay on the small, polished table.

A table for two, when all he needed was a table for one. Long, dull workdays didn't leave him with a lot of energy for girlfriend-hunting. Boring days taxed his motivation. Not that there would be a long line to date him—tall, thin...with a big nose. If anyone bothered to ask, that would be how he'd describe himself.

Besides, he'd already been betrayed in the most cliché way possible; his girlfriend and best friend fell in love with each other. Last he'd heard, Sheila and Jonathan were dating. Being alone wasn't half as bad as being hurt by people he'd thought cared about him.

Not that he'd been faultless in the breakup. In fact, he probably deserved more of the blame than Sheila. She'd begged him to stop working so much, to spend more time together. But his father had expectations. Rob was the only son. Long ago, he'd understood his position. He needed to graduate college, pass the CPA exam, and climb the ladder at a prestigious firm. Being engaged to the "right" kind of girl was part of the deal. A predictable life. To make up for the unpredictable decisions that led to his brother's death.

He'd never loved Sheila. Not as a girlfriend, anyway. And certainly not as a fiancée.

Figuring out what happened to the woman who used to live in his apartment helped take his mind off past regrets.

With his hands behind his back, he paced the kitchen floor. The rhythm of his footfalls on the heated ceramic tiles calmed the chaos in his mind. He glanced around the small, upscale living room with its Oriental rugs, plush sofa and matching overstuffed chair. After his breakup with Sheila, he wanted things to be as different as possible. He bought all new furniture and moved from his small hometown, thirty minutes outside of the city, to an historic building that overlooked Baltimore's Inner Harbor. An easy place to get lost in a crowd. At least that's what he hoped.

He leaned his palms on the tabletop and looked over the obituary. The thought of Angie killing herself in this apartment sent chills down his spine. He couldn't imagine taking his own life, couldn't imagine that someone took her last breath in this space.

The newspaper and web articles hadn't mentioned the cause of her death. Probably against their policy to list suicide. He'd stopped by the Baltimore City Police Department and paid five dollars for the full report, surprised to learn it was a matter of public record.

He braced himself, took a deep breath and opened the report. A scan of the top sheet revealed the cause of death and his breath caught in his throat.

An overdose of painkillers.

He lifted his head, pinched the bridge of his nose to ward off the sudden headache, and forced himself to read on. No note, no known reason. His body stiffened. What could make someone so young and pretty, someone with a whole lot of life ahead of her, commit suicide? It took a half hour to scan the remaining seven sheets of paper that listed the details of items found in the apartment at the time of her death, as well as the fact that the coroner's drug test revealed traces of two painkillers, a date rape drug, and sleeping pills. A deadly cocktail.

Slapping the folder closed, he rose from the chair and grabbed a beer from the fridge. He stared at the sofa through the kitchen doorway and took a long gulp. When he finished one beer, he grabbed another.

"Liquid dinner tonight," he said, raising the empty bottle in a mock toast. His words sobered him.

He grabbed the fast food bag and warm drink and sat at the table.

After pulling out a cheeseburger and sleeve of fries, he took a bite, chewed the now-cold sandwich, and washed it down with a gulp of soda. Why was he so obsessed with finding out about her?

Didn't matter. One place to start would be with Officer J.B. Trueth. The guy lived in the building and knew Angie Barsotti. He grabbed two beers and headed for apartment 811.

☙

Angel sat on the cool grass and wrapped her arms around her knees, staring at the brook. Now that she'd had a taste of the other world, now that she'd interacted with someone, she yearned to return. She closed her eyes, concentrating on the man's face, and the apartment, trying to force her thoughts to take her there.

"Oh, it's no use." She stood and paced a small path in the grass.

She'd felt something in that apartment. Not just for him, but a bit of a memory about the place. Part of who she used to be must be in that apartment. But the few fragments of memory that teased her when she'd visited the place were now slipping away. As if the longer it took to solve the mystery, the fewer memories she'd be left with.

She had to get back there, she just had to. Sunshine beamed down on her and she shook her fist at the sky. Why was it always sunny and mild here in this world? Why couldn't there be a goddamned thunder storm once in a while? A storm raged inside her, wanting release, warring with the tranquil world around her.

"I want to go back there," she screamed. Her words echoed around her, but the sun kept shining, and everything remained the same.

☙

Rob leaned back against J.B.'s plush sofa and glanced at the folder on the coffee table between them.

"So was her death ever investigated as a homicide instead of a suicide?" Rob asked. They were on their second beer, and had been discussing Angie's case for twenty minutes.

"At first. But then, when Angie's mother's history came to light, it

23

changed the direction of the investigation. Like her mother, Angie was in counseling—"

"Because of Chloe. She was in counseling to help her daughter, who's a heroin addict, right?" Rob asked. Why would Angie be considered suicidal just because her mother had committed suicide? Besides, his own mother had killed herself shortly after his brother's death. That didn't make Rob suicidal.

"Yeah, but there weren't any suspects or signs of a struggle." J.B. yawned and stretched in his chair.

"The report mentions that Chloe, the daughter, was investigated because she was the sole inheritor of her mother's life insurance."

J.B. nodded. "A cool hundred grand. Yet she still lives in a rundown house with her boyfriend."

"What happened to the money?" What would an eighteen year-old do with that much money?

"She deposited it in the bank. Personally, I thought maybe her mother's death shook her up enough to quit the drugs. But the money was gone almost as fast as it came."

"Heroin?"

"It's a good guess. I wish we had the manpower to tail the girl and her slimy boyfriend, but since there was technically no crime, I could only check the money trail. We know Chloe deposited the money, and withdrew cash as often as she could until the account was empty. If I could pin the crime on those two, I would. What a waste of the inheritance, what a damn waste of life."

"Did you know Angie when she was alive? Aside from the gym?" Rob asked.

J.B. stood and shrugged. "Like I said, she was a looker. I asked her out once, but she turned me down, so I moved on. Kind of snobby, you know? Like she knew she was good-looking." He held out his hand. "Nice of you to stop by. We'll have to do it again soon."

Hint, hint. Good-bye. "Yeah." Rob stood. "I appreciate the information."

"Smart of you to find out everything you can about the person who lived in your apartment. Thing is..." J.B. leaned closer. "There's really nothing to find out. Case closed. Life got tough for the chick, and she took the easy way out."

Rob clenched his jaw to keep his mouth shut. Why the hell did he feel he had to defend Angie's honor? She was nobody to him, and J.B. was entitled to his opinion.

Or was there more to J.B.'s story than he was letting on?

 CB

Rob slammed his apartment door shut. Let the neighbors complain if they wanted. He couldn't sleep, so why should they? He'd discovered a few more details about Angie's death, but nothing significant. Why did he care? It's not like she'd be coming back. Not like she'd ever visited since her death.

As if drawn to the spot, his gaze fell on the black checkered sofa where he'd first imagined her.

With a glance at the kitchen clock, he headed for the pile of boxes lined up against the wall. Unpacking would give him something to do, keep his mind busy for a few hours. Why couldn't his life be uneventful and predictable the way he wanted it? No surprises, no mysteries to solve, just numbers and busy work.

By the third box, one he'd never unpacked at his last apartment, he was breathing easier. It had sat in the garage for a year, taped shut with several others. Maybe he'd find a lot of useless things, but what the hell? He liked this city apartment, liked the way the noise of the busy streets and crowds kept him from thinking.

He lifted out a smiley-cup mug and rolled his eyes. Nothing special, and he couldn't even remember who gave it to him. Goodwill pile. Probably shouldn't have kept it all these years.

Tossing the newspaper liner to the side, he dug out a photo and pulled the paper off the front. Mick. He and his brother with huge smiles on their faces after a July Fourth race they'd won as a team when they were thirteen. Rob squeezed his eyes shut, but heard Mick's voice in his head.

Nobody beats the Morrison brothers. We're unstoppable.

Yeah, until a tree stopped one of them. Permanently.

The memory burned at his skull, and he welcomed the pain. Rob deserved to suffer for what he'd done. He'd place the photo on a shelf and look at it everyday. He yanked the picture out of its layers of wrapping and something fell on his foot.

He stooped to examine it. Mick's black worry stone with a worn ridge on one side where his brother had rubbed his thumb. Rob smiled and picked it up, feeling the weight of the smooth rock in his palm. He sat on the sofa, closed his eyes, and rubbed the stone, wishing it could take his worries.

Oddly, circling his finger on the indent soothed him. He breathed slower, inhaled deeper.

And smelled lemons.

ය

Angel's body tingled. Her skin rippled with electricity, and she recognized the signs that she'd be transported soon.

Yes. Finally. She closed her eyes, wishing she could rush the transition from her world to his. Cool air prickled her skin and she stood in the man's dark apartment. With moonlight shining through the sheers, she could make out his form on the sofa.

He jumped up and faced her.

She wanted to speak, but she couldn't.

"The electricity went off again," he said.

She frowned.

He stepped closer. "Ghosts don't exist."

No. He couldn't banish her again. She needed something in this world. The lights flickered, sizzled, and then went off again.

Please don't tell me to go away; it makes me go away. She might not have a voice in this world, but she could at least think it. She would not go, not when potential answers waited in this place.

The man stepped closer. "What are you doing? Angie, why do you keep coming here?"

Don't tell me to leave...don't tell me to leave. Pictures flew into her mind. People smiling and laughing. A tree in the corner with white lights and boxes under it....

He'd called her Angie.

"You know me?" Her words came out a whisper, but at least they finally came out. Tears tracked down her cheeks. The electricity flickered on, and then, stayed off. The air stopped sizzling. She blinked to adjust her eyes to the darkness again.

"Christ, this can't be happening." He moved his fingers over something in his hand and then pocketed it.

She closed the distance between them and grasped his upper arms, pleading with her eyes because her voice had left her again.

"Yes, I know you." He glanced away and looked out the window, let out a huff of breath, and then gazed at her. "Your name is Angie Barsotti and you used to live here."

No wonder the place felt so familiar. Her spirits lifted. He could help her find out who she was, help her find out what was going on.

"And," he dragged a hand through his hair. "You died and I don't believe in ghosts."

Cold air, cold as ice tore through her, ripping her from the apartment.

Chapter Four

*T*he lights blinked on again, and Rob stared at his arms where Angie had gripped him only seconds ago. He could still feel her touch. Holding Mick's worry stone had reminded Rob of the good times they'd had together. The spirit of their Nanna. Something special the two of them shared. Had holding the worry stone enabled a connection of sorts?

He yanked out the stone and stared at it. Memories flooded his mind. He and his brother had been able to see apparitions as kids. Not just Nanna, but others, too. A child on the playground, the old man in the park.

He didn't know what to believe. The breeze filtered in through the open window and something tickled his arm. He glanced at his forearm. With a frown, he squinted and pulled three strands of long golden hair from between his fingers.

Rob squeezed the rock in his hand, tightening his grip on the memories of his brother, the ones he buried because they were too painful to remember. After his brother died, he forced his ability to see beyond the human plane away, hadn't he? If he couldn't contact his brother, he didn't want to talk to any visitors from the other side.

He paced the hardwood floor. This didn't change anything. If Angie really was dead, he didn't want to talk with her. The only spirit he wanted was his long-lost sibling. But what if she could help him contact his twin?

No. This was all too ridiculous. Entities? He stopped pacing and stared at his hand. The small black stone glinted up at him like Mick winking in his good-natured way.

"Fine. Ghosts exist. There. You happy?" he hollered at the ceiling as if his words would travel to Heaven.

The curtains blew in the wind, and Rob glanced toward the spot where Angie had appeared. He'd told her she didn't exist, and she'd disappeared.

Christ, he was going crazy. There had to be an explanation for all of this, and he knew where to start. He would find out more about Angie Barsotti, and he'd see what she knew about his brother.

He pocketed the worry stone, crossed the room to his desk, and sat at the computer. He pulled out his credit card and typed in the information on a search site. Within minutes, he accessed material most people didn't know they could buy about others. Thank goodness he'd paid attention in his Forensic Accounting class. Angie had a good credit history, and she'd lived in this apartment for five years. He scanned the list of her relatives.

Maybe the teenaged daughter could help him figure things out.

He slept on the sofa—small increments of rest between vivid dreams about Mick, and ghosts. When the sun speared through the window, Rob was glad for the daylight and a chance to investigate Angie's life more thoroughly. For the first time in a long time, he called into work sick.

Mid-morning, with a crisp March breeze against his back, he pushed the city sounds—beeping horns and revving motors—to the back of his mind. He gripped the folder that contained information about Angie's daughter Chloe, holding it tight against his chest in the windy afternoon.

Instead of taking his sports car into a neighborhood where he might come out and find his tires missing, he hailed a cab and slid into the musty backseat. Opening the folder, he read the address aloud.

The mustached driver frowned at him in the rearview mirror. "I ain't promisin' to wait for you in that neighborhood."

Rob cringed and nodded. He'd obtained Chloe's location from his search of a Maryland database. The girl had a criminal record for drug possession and lived in public housing, practically in the ghetto.

The driver pulled the cab to a stop in front of a run-down, end-unit row house with cracked windows and peeling paint around the window and doorframes. Rob passed the driver a fifty dollar bill. "There'll be another one when I come back."

The driver snorted, looked outside the windows, and grabbed the money. "That'll buy ya five minutes and that's it."

Rob opened the door and stepped onto the sidewalk, pulling the collar of his light coat tighter around his neck. The gray sky reflected his dim hopes of finding Chloe or anything useful in this neighborhood.

Halfway up the crumbling sidewalk, the stench of old urine and hairspray hit his nostrils.

"Hey, over here, hon," a voice called from across the street.

He turned toward the sound. Three girls, all with varied bright colored hair, tight outfits, and too much makeup, smiled at him. Prostitutes.

Ignoring them, he glanced at the cabbie, who revved the engine. Rob headed for the door with peeling paint and the faded numerals 501. He knocked and waited. Music pounded inside, shaking the door with its deep bass beat.

Glancing at the cabbie, knowing his time was limited, he rapped again, louder. The music stopped and footsteps thumped against the floor as if hurrying away from the front of the house. In a neighborhood like this, the police probably visited frequently.

He knocked again. "Hey!" he said, cupping his hands against the door. "I'm not the police. I'm looking for Chloe."

Footsteps thudded back to the door. It opened, revealing a tall, skinny man in a faded flannel jacket. He looked to be about twenty-five years old. Rather, his sunken cheekbones and yellowed eyes made him look twenty-five, but Rob's gut told him the kid was likely younger. He didn't know a lot about drug users, having spent much of his college life studying to be a CPA and avoiding the party life, but he'd guess that drugs had aged the man prematurely.

"Why ya lookin' for Chloe?" The kid looked Rob up and down,

making him wish he'd dressed more casually than his pressed khakis and button-down shirt. He probably looked like a cop.

"I want to talk to her...just two minutes." He swallowed, steeling himself against the stench of cigarette smoke and urine wafting from the house.

"Yeah, well, that other cop—that bald guy—already been here plenty of times wanting to talk to Chloe. I think she said what she got to say to all of you." The kid scratched his arms.

J.B. Trueth had been to see Chloe? It made sense if the case was being investigated, but the police report clearly stated the investigation was ruled a suicide and closed. "Look, I'm happy to pay you for your time if you'll let me speak with her."

The man squinted and smiled, revealing stained teeth. "It'll cost ya a hundred bucks. You can do whatever you want. She won't notice anyhow."

Oh, God. Angie's daughter was a hooker. "I don't have a hundred." He dug in his pocket, pulled out two twenties and handed them over. "I just want to talk."

The man grabbed the money, opened the door wide. "That's all that slut is good for, anyhow." He pocketed the money in his baggy, low-slung jeans. "Talk and taking my blow. Made her pay for that one, though." He turned his head toward a long hall with peeling flowered wallpaper and hollered. "Hey, bitch...got company."

The girl who peeked around the corner could have been beautiful. But her oily, stringy hair, sunken cheek bones, and matted old clothes made her look like a poster child for drug addiction. She had Angie's eyes. A sadder, more hopeless, blood-shot version, but still Angie's eyes.

Rob fisted his hands at his sides and swallowed past a growing lump in his throat. The girl had been sent to private schools, been loved by a beautiful mother. How did she end up here?

"Chloe?" he asked, taking a step toward her. He wanted to snatch her up, throw her in the cab, and take her to the nearest hospital.

She stopped, halfway down the hall and curled against the wall. The man stomped toward her, yanked her elbow, and dragged her toward the door. Rob almost intervened, afraid the man would rip

Chloe's thin arm off. But as she got closer, he saw being skinny wasn't the worst part. Track marks—red blotches and lines from needles—covered her pale skin.

The taxi driver honked the horn, alerting him of his deadline. How could he get any information out of this drugged-up, haggard girl?

"Your mom sent me." It was all he could think of to say.

Her sunken and lifeless eyes suddenly lit up and widened. A small flicker of energy transformed her face.

Rob reached forward and held her clammy hands, trying to get through to her. "What happened to your mother? What made her do it?" He hated to be so blunt, but in her state of mind, with his limited time, he had to hurry. This could be the only chance he got.

"Hey!" The scrawny guy pushed Chloe aside, knocking her to the floor. "We already talked to the cops. Crazy runs in this girl's family. Her grandmother killed herself, and her mother killed herself. Pretty soon, this one will probably kill herself, too. Leave us alone." He reached inside his jacket and whipped out a gun.

Rob's mouth went dry. His eyes darted to Angie's daughter's slumped form. "I just want to talk." He held his hands up to show he didn't have a weapon; he wanted to tear Chloe's boyfriend to pieces.

The kid twisted his lips and snarled then shoved Rob backward onto the front porch and slammed the door. He caught himself on the shaky railing and gripped it tight in an attempt to catch his breath.

The taxi driver revved the engine. He glanced at the cabbie and then back at the flimsy front door. Rage made it hard for him to catch his breath. He might be able to break down the door, but then what? Get himself and Chloe killed?

The curtain moved at a nearby window. Rob narrowed his eyes, wanting more than anything to smash the glass and the man's face who stared back at him.

He clenched his jaw and forced himself to stand and straighten. On shaky legs, he stumbled down the front steps. With a last quick glance at the empty doorway, he pulled a business card from his wallet, wedged it in the mailbox, and stomped to the cab.

As soon as he climbed inside, the cabbie floored the pedal and Rob's head jolted back against the cracked vinyl seat. He forced himself to take two deep breaths.

"Up there," Rob said, pointing ahead. "Pull over at that fire hydrant."

"Mister, I already waited for you once in this crappy neighborhood, I ain't—"

Rob yanked out his wallet and thrust a fifty-dollar bill at the driver. "Pull over at the hydrant and we're done. I'll find another ride back."

The man shook his head and grabbed the bill.

Closing his eyes, he braced himself. He couldn't leave Angie's daughter in those conditions. He had to do something.

The cabbie pulled to the curb. "Be careful, man." The driver tapped the steering wheel with his index fingers.

Rob nodded, blew out a breath and stepped out into a muddy strip of brown grass.

The taxi driver peeled wheels and disappeared around the corner. Rob pulled his light sports coat up around his neck and scanned the run-down row houses. Trash and plastic pink flamingos decorated most of the area front yards. A dog barked in the distance, but the street was deserted. He stuck out like a glint of silver in a pile of dull rocks.

But nobody was around to hassle him. At least no one he could see. He narrowed his eyes and visualized Chloe at the mercy of the man who'd shoved her. Anger fueled his footsteps. He'd never been in a fight before in his life, but he'd do everything he could to get her out of that place and to the hospital.

He slowed as he approached the row house where she lived. Even the prostitutes were gone.

If he was going to fight for Chloe's freedom, he should probably have a weapon. At least something to fend off the man with a gun. He halted and leaned against a fence. He didn't have a plan, didn't have a weapon. He could get killed.

He closed his eyes and concentrated on taking deep breaths. He had a weapon. His mind. Would it be enough?

Chapter Five

ℛob carried a milk crate to the side of Chloe's house and situated it under a first-floor window. A crow cawed and landed in a bare tree branch nearby. Rob wished for leaves on the sparse trees to provide him with cover, but it would be another two months before the buds dared to appear.

"No punk kid is gonna get rid of me," he whispered. He stepped onto the crate and grabbed the peeling windowsill for support. Easing himself higher, he looked inside. At first the small room—a dining room—looked deserted except for piles of clothes, liquor bottles, and a stained mattress.

Then he looked closer at the mattress. A small form shivered, curled in a fetal position. *Chloe.* Same blonde hair, same skinny body.

The boyfriend was nowhere in sight.

Anger fueled him. Anger at the fact that a man would treat a woman like this kid was doing, anger with himself for believing in ghosts, and anger that drugs could make a person do horrible things. Even if he got Chloe out of there, how could he force her to go to a hospital? What would keep the punk from going to get her?

He shook his head. It didn't matter. He had to try.

He spotted a rock on the ground and lowered one foot to pick it up, but then he frowned. The window had to be locked. But it would be stupid not to try.

With a quick glance around, he balanced himself on the crate and pushed against the window. It budged. Only a quarter of an inch or so, but it moved.

Rob's heart lightened. Finally, something in his favor. He pushed again and the window creaked open a few inches.

With one final push, he opened it enough to stick his head inside. He had to move fast, had to get Angie's girl and leave.

"Chloe?" he stage-whispered.

She stirred and moaned.

"Chloe, over here. The window."

Shifting to sit, she blinked several times and stared at him.

A dog barked in the distance and his heart ricocheted against his ribs. "Come with me. Your mother needs you." If he got her the help she needed, maybe she could come to his apartment, help him find out why Angie visited.

The girl held a hand to her head and swayed. "My mommy's dead."

"Chloe, it's okay. Just come with me." He reached inside, wishing he could heave himself higher. He'd pick her up and carry her out of there.

"I-I don't know." She glanced toward the hall and her eyes opened wide.

A shadow fell across the room and the punk's body loomed in the doorway.

"Thought I told you to shut up and lay down?" He marched toward the bed, his fist raised.

"Stop!" Rob couldn't hold the word inside.

The man turned, whipped out his gun, and fired at the window.

Rob lost his grip and fell backward into the wet dirt. Shattered pieces of glass rained down on top of him, piercing his face and landing on his coat.

He scrambled to his feet. He needed a better plan. As much as he hated to leave, he ran as fast as he could to the sidewalk and kept running for the next two blocks.

Panting for breath, he bent over, hands on knees, and checked behind him. He worried that the kid would chase him, but aside from the scrawny calico cat that meandered on the curb, the streets were empty.

Spotting a liquor store ahead, he decided to call a cab, formulate another plan.

Twenty minutes later, he sat in the back seat of a taxi, scribbling in his notepad. He desperately wanted to get Chloe out of that house. He'd hire someone.

He sighed, wishing he had someone to talk to. Someone who wouldn't think he was insane. This was a time he needed Mick. This was why seeing ghosts was a team thing. It was their secret, yet a shared secret had made it all seem so sane back then. Now he had nobody. Unless....

Angie. If she came back, he could share things with her. She wouldn't think he was crazy.

He stared at his notes. The police had investigated the girl and her so-called boyfriend, Vinnie. They'd been cleared. Cause of death was a suicide. Had Angie killed herself because she'd tried to help her daughter but couldn't? Taken her own life because her daughter's situation seemed so hopeless? And how was J.B. Trueth involved?

He stared out the window at the litter-cluttered sidewalks and brown grass and wished he know more about Angie and her life before death.

03

Angie buried her head in her hands. The mild breeze and sunlight pissed her off more than soothed her.

Make it rain for once. Match my mood.

The man had banished her again. *You died and I don't believe in ghosts.*

Really? Here's your fucking ghost!

She jumped to her feet and paced the soft grass. At least she knew her name. Angie Barsotti. And she'd remembered little bits and pieces of something in that room, too. Which meant....

She had to get back there. But how? The lights had flickered when she'd refused to let his non-belief chase her away. If she tried harder, could she control it? If she got angrier at him for making her leave, could she stay?

Another day of sitting and thinking in this beautiful world that held her captive. She perched by the stream, staring across at the trees that billowed in the distance, and then closed her eyes, trying to pull back the memories she'd tapped into last night.

Suddenly, her skin prickled and she opened her eyes in the dark apartment that flickered with candlelight.

The man stood in front of the sofa, arms crossed, staring at her. As if he'd been waiting for her. He glanced around the living room and its connecting dining room, and then back at her. "Apparently, your energy cross-circuits my electricity, so I lit candles."

His eyes twinkled in the flickering light. Maybe it wasn't her energy. Maybe it was their combined energy. She'd been to this apartment many times, and the electricity had never gone out.

He cleared his throat and dropped his hands to his side. "I'm Rob, by the way."

"I'm Angie, as you know." Hope rose within her. He was different, subdued, not the hardened cynic she'd met the other times.

"Why do you keep coming here?" he asked, shaking his head, as if ready to deny her existence again.

"I wish I knew." She held his gaze, glad she could communicate. "I don't have any memories." Her ghostly heart pounded hard and warmth spread through her body, making her feel alive even though she knew she wasn't.

She wobbled.

He bolted forward and grabbed her waist, his strong grip and heat steadying her. "Whoa. You okay?"

His hands radiated with strength and warmth. She allowed herself a few seconds to enjoy the feeling, and then lifted her face to gaze at him. "I would be better if you told me you knew something about me."

He nodded, moved his hand to the small of her back, and led her to the sofa. "Let's sit."

She sat beside him and then turned to face him.

"Your name is Angie Barsotti, and you were an elementary school teacher."

"How do you know?" She frowned.

"A neighbor told me your name. I looked you up on the computer." He glanced across the room at a desk.

She peered at the black screen, tickled by a memory of using the device.

"Why do you come here at night?" He spoke softly.

She took a deep breath, blew it out. "I don't know. I'm drawn to this place. Like I'm here to communicate something to you, only I don't know what it is."

"I've only lived here for a little over two weeks. I don't know much about the place." He gazed behind her, out the window. "You used to live here."

"Oh." She glanced around the room. Again, pictures flashed through her mind. A blonde girl, cards at a small table across the room.... "Do you know what happened to me?"

Again, he avoided her gaze. The outside lights reflected on his face and he stared at the sofa. "Well," he hesitated. "Do you remember anything at all before you were...?"

"A ghost?" she finished for him.

He nodded.

With a sigh, she sank back against the sofa cushions. "You're the first person who's been able to see me. I've been here lots of times. First, there were men packing boxes, and people who painted the walls. One night, there was a young girl crying. I was drawn to her, wanted to comfort her." She hesitated, shaking her head. "She stopped crying for a moment, looked around as if she sensed me, but she ran out the door."

"I know some things about you. But they might not be easy to hear."

She shook her head. "I know I must have died—maybe in a car wreck or something. Maybe I need to learn about myself when I was alive."

"I've been investigating your life." He stared at her.

Well, he didn't waste much time getting to the point. Lifting her chin, trying to brace herself for bad news, she nodded. "Tell me what you've found."

"According to the police report, you killed yourself."

A gasp slipped out of her throat and she couldn't find her voice. The room spun and she feared she'd go back. She gripped his hands, hoping for some kind of hold on this world. "I-I couldn't have," she said.

He nodded and held her gaze. "You didn't leave a note; nobody has any idea why you did it. But...."

Her throat clogged with tears and she swallowed hard. This wasn't the time to give in to emotion. She needed to know her own story. Sadness could wait. "But what?"

He knew more, she could tell by the way he turned away and looked behind her, unable to hold her gaze.

She pulled her hands from the comfort of his grip and cupped his chin, forcing him to look at her. "Tell me, Rob," she whispered. "I can handle it. Really I can."

"Your mother committed suicide when you were a teenager. Depression. Apparently you were on prescription medications when you took your life."

Images assaulted her. A woman lying motionless on a bed, sirens, men in uniforms.... She swallowed hard. All of this was information she'd process later. For now, she wanted to know everything he knew. "What else?"

He raised a brow and shifted in his seat. "You had a daughter."

The dizziness smacked her like a bitter wind and she panted for breath. "I have a daughter?" Tears welled in her eyes. Visions of a girl's face flashed through her mind. "Why would I kill myself if I had a daughter? What kind of person am I that I would leave my child?" Tears spilled down her face.

"I'm so sorry." He hesitated, and then laid a hand on her shoulder. She let herself draw comfort from it, half-wanting him to pull her into an embrace, protect her from the knowledge of what she'd done, half-wanting him to take back his words and tell her it wasn't true.

A knock sounded at the door. Angie's body tingled, grew cold, and she left the apartment.

ଓ

Rob jolted on the sofa, more from Angie's sudden disappearance than from the knock on his door.

Shit. Whoever it was had the worst timing ever.

He lifted his palms up to stare at them. She'd felt so real. Not like a ghost at all. How the hell was that feasible? He finally accepted the likelihood that seeing a ghost was possible, and now the ghost felt as flesh and blood as any human he'd ever touched.

"Hey Rob. You in there?" J.B. hollered from the other side of the door.

Rob ran his hand through his hair and shook his head. "Yeah. Be right there."

Finding Mick's old worry stone might have triggered a memory, made Rob believe, but how the hell did it explain how real this ghost appeared? Nothing could explain that.

He crossed the room, and opened the door. "Hey. What's up?"

J.B. lifted a six pack of beer. "Thought I'd see if you wanted to hang. I would've called, but I don't have your number."

With a quick glance at the sofa, wishing he could spend the evening with Angie instead of J.B., Rob opened the door wider and moved to the side. "Sure, come on in."

His neighbor strode past him and stopped just inside the door. "Oh shit, man. You got company?"

Rob shut the door. Dozens of candles flickered. "No. No company. Damn electricity went out."

J.B. flicked the switch nearest him, illuminating the room with bright lights. He grinned. "If you move this little switch thing next to the door, all these lights come on."

"Ha ha," Rob mocked. "Didn't work ten minutes ago." He bent to blow out the nearest candles.

"Yeah, it's an old building; guess the wiring could be quirky in some units." J.B. whistled under his breath. "Sweet place. 'Course all the apartments in this swanky place are plum, aren't they?" He set the beer on the granite countertop. "What the hell happened to your face?"

Rob had prepared himself for the question earlier. The glass from Chloe's window scratched his cheeks. "Sticker bushes at my rental property." Only a half-truth. He had a rental property in the county, and it had sticker bushes. He narrowed his eyes and blew out the last of the candles. Rent topped two thousand dollars a month in these units. How did J.B. afford a place like this on a cop's salary?

J.B. cracked open a beer, took a long swallow, and pointed the bottle at the sofa. "That's where they found her. Angie. That's where they found her body." He shook his head. "Damn shame, damn shame."

Rob took a beer and crossed the room, sat in the white leather recliner. "Have a seat." He motioned to another recliner beside the sofa.

J.B. hesitated, and then crossed the room to sit in the chair, still eyeing the sofa. He took another pull on his beer, and then sat back and faced Rob. "They closed the case. Couldn't find indication that it was anything more than a suicide, but I investigated some stuff on my own."

Rob brought his beer bottle to his suddenly dry mouth. "What did you find?"

J.B. leaned close, over the armrest, his face serious. "She didn't seem the type, man. You know?"

"She was on meds," Rob said.

"Yeah, but I think that was under control. Her daughter stressed her out, but she talked about it with some of her friends. I heard them in the workout room. She was handling it and being very honest about it." He drank again. "It's the people who keep it inside, they're the ones who end their lives."

Rob frowned. The guy had a point. "Why did the daughter stress her out?"

J.B. shook his head. "Chloe was a straight-A honor roll student. Cheerleader, glee club.... You get my drift."

Rob nodded.

"Then she met a guy. A punk who gave her a taste of a different life, and she liked it. I saw Angie and her daughter plenty of times. Good looking girl. Looked like her mama. Then she grew skinnier, got those blank eyes, you know? The drugged-out kind that stare at nothin'."

Rob wanted to pull out a notepad so he wouldn't forget any of this when he told Angie. If she ever came back. He sat up straighter. Of course she'd come back. Wouldn't she?

"Knowing Angie was a city school teacher, I wondered how she afforded to live here. I didn't find out until after her death that she had a trust fund. A life insurance policy paid to her when her mother committed suicide. That's part of the reason the police closed the case so fast," J.B. said.

What? Had he missed something? "What do you mean?"

"Angie knew. She knew the life insurance wouldn't pay out for suicide until two years after she purchased the policy. We checked the purchase date—the policy with Chloe as the sole inheritor—two years and a week before her death."

She'd waited to commit suicide until her insurance was valid? Rob stood, needing to move, needing to shake the confusion from his head. He grabbed another two beers, handed one to J.B. "So Chloe inherited her mother's trust and the life insurance?" Rob asked, pacing the floor.

"Yep, which put her at the top of my suspect list. She lived with her mom still, but she says she spent the night at her boyfriend's house, wasn't here when the suicide took place."

"You don't believe her?" Rob asked.

J.B. shrugged. "Follow the money, that's what I always say. Unfortunately, there's no proof one way or the other about the girl's whereabouts. Her boyfriend isn't exactly the best alibi."

"You were Angie's friend, you know the daughter. Did you ever try to get the girl away from that punk kid?" Rob thought of the house, the way the boy controlled Chloe.

J.B. shrugged. "Can't always help someone until they're ready to help themselves."

Rob leaned back in his seat and studied J.B. as he rattled on about Angie's life. The police closed the case. Why was J.B. so damned interested in what happened? He'd asked Angie out, and she'd declined. And the guy who lived with Chloe had mentioned a bald cop. Did J.B. want to solve a case, or was there another reason he was so interested in Angie? And how the hell did he afford such an expensive apartment?

Chapter Six

*A*ngie stared at the water flowing over the rocks in the brook and inhaled deeply. Thoughts of her former life sent shivers through her body, and she stepped from the stony bank onto the grass that never needed watering or cutting. Everything in this world stayed the same.

And everything in the other world changed drastically.

She'd left a daughter behind. What kind of mother did that? Her eyes filled with tears, and she fisted them away. Cloudy, fog-ridden images of a little tow-headed girl flashed through her mind. Angie closed her eyes, begging the pictures to stay. They disappeared as quickly as they'd formed. Tears stung her eyes again.

Crying wouldn't get her back to her daughter. The key to finding out about her past involved Rob.

"I was a terrible mother."

She glanced across the stream, checking to see if anyone had heard her. Out of the mist, a shadow grew larger, and Angie took a step toward the water to get a better look. Nobody ever approached her in this world, and all she'd ever been able to make out was fuzzy outlines of others.

Never this close.

The shadow emerged.

"Rob?" she asked, leaning forward. She yearned to cross the stream, get closer, but instinct kept her from touching the water.

Rob was a ghost, too?

But the figure that smiled a friendly smile from across the stream was a younger version of the man in the other world. Much younger. A carefree teenager.

"Who are you?" she asked, her voice echoing among the trees and meadow.

The younger Rob waved, looked around, and gave her a 'thumbs up' before turning to sprint back into the mist.

She rubbed her eyes. What did it mean?

A gentle breeze swept past her and blew her nightgown. She lifted her face to the moving air and took a deep breath. She had to get back to Rob. She twirled a strand of hair with a shaking hand. The idea of going back scared her. Not because she might find the truth, but because the truth might be much worse than the world she lived in now.

ᘓ

Rob paced the area in front of the sofa as the midnight moonlight cast a glow on the dark room. He'd lit the candles again after J.B. left, in hopes Angie would return.

If he thought too hard about everything going on around him, he'd go crazy. He thrived on order, specialized in numbers and figures. Ghosts were the things R-rated movies and video games were made of. Ghosts were also the stuff he and Mick used to believe in.

His eyes stung from lack of sleep. Settling himself on the sofa, hoping Angie would come back to finish their conversation, he sank into the plush cushions.

Sunlight on his face woke him the next morning. He glanced at his cell phone. *Shit, seven a.m. already?*

Within a half hour, he'd showered, shaved, and grabbed a cup of coffee. His workload kept him so busy, he only took a ten minute break for lunch. But he didn't eat. He used the time to search the internet, finding odd terms like vapors, ecto-mist, and corporeal.

Corporeal. A ghost with substance. Is that what Angie was? She felt real. But maybe insanity was creeping into his head. The fact that he was even considering the possibility of the existence of ghosts fried his brain.

Then he leaned back in his desk chair, dug in his pocket, and took out Mick's worry stone. He and Mick believed in ghosts once, could he handle this particular ghost by himself?

His desk phone rang, jerking him out of his revelry, but he rubbed the stone before returning it to his pocket.

Six hours later, he exited the automatic doors and walked into the cold March evening.

His cell phone rang and he checked the screen. Sheila. His ex-fiancée. He stabbed the button to send the call to voicemail. She called once a week or so, always apologizing, always wanting to get together as friends. Didn't she get it? He wanted to move on, put her and Jonathan behind him, forget about them.

"Hey. You Rob?" A male voice called.

Rob jerked his head toward the sound. Tall, skinny boy with a skull cap pulled low on his face, smoking a cigarette, and wearing a shabby flannel coat. Chloe's boyfriend, Vinnie. What the hell was he doing outside Rob's office?

He frowned. He'd left his business card, hoping Chloe would look him up. Instead, the punk found him. Rob straightened his shoulders. Fine. If this kid wanted trouble, he'd get it. Anger burned at the angst the boy had brought to Angie and her daughter. Without him, Chloe might be in college. Without him, Angie might still be alive.

Rob stepped closer, his jaw clenched. "Where's your gun?"

Vinnie must have felt his rage. He held up his palms, shook his head. "Gun's at home. Search me if you want." He lifted his arms higher.

Rob looked around, decided against frisking the kid on a crowded city street. "What do you want?"

"You was asking a lot of questions the other day about Chloe. And her mother. I can give you answers." He glanced at Rob's briefcase. "For a price."

"What kind of answers?"

The kid held out his palm. "Five hundred bucks worth of answers."

"I don't carry that much cash."

"How much you got?" The kid pitched his cigarette butt on the sidewalk, and scratched his arms.

If he offered too little, the kid might leave. He didn't want to give him any money, but what if he had valuable information?

"You wonderin' if what I got is valuable? Check into a certain bald-headed cop." The kid narrowed his eyes and glared at Rob.

J.B. Trueth? What did Vinnie know?

Rob dug out his wallet, yanked out two fifties. "It's all I got."

The kid snatched the bills, pocketed them in his droopy jeans. "That bald cop's been over a few times. He's got a damned fancy car for a cop, too, don't he? He's had Chloe alone before. Before I knew he was a cop. She got money after her mom died. Cashed the checks. But I ain't never seen it. Makes me wonder where it went, you know?"

Rob knew very well. He'd wondered where the money went, too. He needed to hire a private investigator to look into Chloe's bank accounts. Wasn't J.B. the one who said 'follow the money'?

ଔ

Angie's skin tingled, and she closed her eyes. When she opened them, she stood in Rob's apartment. He was asleep on the sofa, one hand thrown over his eyes, his brown hair mussed as if he'd been tossing and turning.

Candles lit the room, and Angie knelt beside him. She'd been desperate to get to him all day, dying to know the facts about her daughter. But now she was here, and had a chance to study Rob more carefully.

He frowned, even in his sleep. His lips were parted just enough so a puff of breath escaped as he exhaled. She leaned closer and caught of whiff of something sweet. Mint.

"Toothpaste," she whispered. An image of the white goo came to her mind, an image of herself reflecting back at her as she used it on a brush. *Come on, what else?* Her damn brain needed to unlock these memories of her time in this world.

"Angie?" Rob blinked his eyes and pushed himself upright. "Shit, I must have fallen asleep."

Angie backed away, instantly missing the scent of him. "I just got here."

"Sorry about the interruption last night."

She shook her head and stood, facing the window, hoping the lights outside would quell her sadness. "I must have been a very bad mother."

Rob moved behind her, gently turned her to face him. His hands were strong, yet gentle, and she took a deep breath.

"No, in fact the opposite is true. You did everything you could. She was in trouble. Drugs. And a boyfriend who caused problems for her and for you."

She wanted to believe him, but the emotions she'd swallowed all day in the other world suddenly swelled to the surface, and she hiccupped on a sob.

"We'll get to the bottom of this," he said, running a hand up and down her back.

In his arms, a comfort enveloped her even greater than the other world she lived in. Tears sprang to her eyes and she welcomed the relief. Here, she could let go of the pain; Rob would make it okay.

She grabbed fistfuls of his shirt and let her tension build to a crescendo of sobs. She was the worst kind of monster. She'd left behind her child.

Crying reminded her of the first night she'd seen him in the apartment. He hadn't wanted her there that night, but now he welcomed her. She wept until her head ached; he held her tight and rocked her, whispering soothing words.

Finally, all cried out, she looked up at him with swollen eyes.

He lifted her chin with a finger. "I promise, I'll find out what you need to know. I'll do everything I can to help you."

She smiled, surprised that she could when her heart swelled with misery. If she could find out what happened on her own, she would. But she couldn't. She needed Rob. The expression on his face, the sadness in his eyes told her he wanted to know her story almost as badly as she did.

He smiled and leaned closer. For a second, she thought he might brush his lips against hers. When he didn't, a strange ache washed through her. She wanted a distraction from her sadness, needed someone to make her feel alive.

She took a deep breath, still amazed that as a ghost, she breathed in this world, and glanced across the candlelit room. Her gaze fell on a photo. She gasped, moved out of Rob's embrace, and crossed the room. "What the heck?" she asked, hands on knees, bending to get a closer look.

Rob moved behind her. "That's me. And my brother, Mick." His voice choked on the name.

Angie spun to face him. The boys in the photo were the same age—looked identical—as the boy she saw earlier in her other world.

"I—I don't get it," she whispered.

"What? What's to get?"

Rob didn't look like a ghost. And his heated hands and body certainly didn't feel ghostly. "Are you a ghost?" she blurted.

He flinched and his mouth opened. "What? Why would you think I'm a ghost?" He pinched the skin on his arm as if that were proof of his human existence.

Angie tilted her head to study him. He certainly looked human. Could he be a ghost and not know it? "I saw you today in my other world."

He stared at her, the candlelight dancing in his eyes. She sat quietly and let her words sink in.

"You saw me? In your world?"

"Uh huh."

"I-I don't know how the hell you could have seen me when I was at work today."

"Well, it wasn't exactly you. It was somebody who looked like you. It was like it was you when you were a teenager," she said, frowning at the memory of the younger version of Rob, and then glancing at the photo. Or maybe it was the other boy.

Rob sucked in air, and stumbled backward.

Angie caught his wrists. "Rob? What? What is it?"

His lips moved but he wasn't making any noises.

"Rob, you're scaring me. What's wrong? Are you a ghost? Are you?" She needed to know.

"Mick. You saw Mick?" He clutched her upper arms and pulled her close. His wide eyes searched hers as if her answer would keep him alive. He stared at his hands on her arms, and released his grip. "I'm sorry, Angie. So sorry. Did I hurt you?"

She glanced at her biceps. "I'm fine. Can you tell me who the hell I saw today?"

He took her hand and led her to the couch. "Mick was my twin brother. He died when we were seventeen."

∞

Blood pounded through Rob's head like an ocean wave crashing against rocks in a hurricane. Visions of his brother passed through his mind like an old-time movie. He and Mick on bikes, racing down the hills of their small town, the two of them playing basketball—one dribbling the ball while the other blocked the opposition. They were like two parts of the same person. Ever since Mick's death, Rob had been missing a part of himself. Even now, his brother had some sort of power over him, and the worry stone was proof. Holding the stone that had belonged to Mick opened his mind to the possibility of ghosts.

"You saw him," he whispered.

Angie bent in front of him and clasped his hands in hers. Her cool skin tamed his racing pulse.

"Tell me about Mick," she said. "I'd love to hear about him."

He smiled. Her blonde hair almost glowed in the candlelight. Rob huffed out a gush of air. "We did everything together. And I mean everything." Christ, hanging out with Mick made his adrenaline rush like nothing he'd been able to match since. He chuckled. "We'd jump from roofs onto trampolines, bungee jump from trees...." His mind searched for the memories he'd tucked deep so as not to be hurt by them.

"Your poor mother," Angie said, shaking her head.

Rob's smile disappeared and he pressed his lips together. Yeah. His poor mother. He drove her to an early grave once he got his brother killed with their crazy antics. "She's dead, too." He whipped his head up. "Did you see her? Did you see my mother?"

Angie shook her head and patted his knee. "Just the one who

looked like you."

He nodded.

"What happened to Mick, Rob?" Angie's voice was barely a whisper.

"My idea to go sledding. It was icy, just the two of us, on the hill in our backyard. We'd sped down it at least a half dozen times. I got sick of the long trek uphill. Mick wanted to go one more time. I told him 'go ahead, I'll meet you inside where it's warm.'"

Angie's hands slid over his, and her touch lessened the burden in his heart.

"He took too long to come back. I knew something was wrong. Maybe a twin thing, maybe not. I hiked down the hill and found him bleeding and barely breathing."

Tears ran down Angie's face.

Rob swallowed hard to rid himself of the tightness in his throat. "I screamed until a neighbor called for an ambulance." His chest tightened. He couldn't say anymore, didn't want to think about it.

"It wasn't your fault, Rob." Angie climbed next to him. "I hope you don't blame yourself."

He shrugged. Too many times he'd buried the memory, only to have nightmares about the way things should have happened that day. He should have gone down the hill one more time with Mick. Their combined weight would have kept the sled on track, away from the deadly tree their dad had cut down that next spring.

And his mother. The pills, the heartache, the looks she gave Rob that made it clear she blamed him. It obviously pained her every time she looked at him and saw Mick's face. And then her eventual death.

Chills traveled down his spine and his limbs shook. What did it mean that Mick approached Angie?

"Did he say anything to you?" Rob asked.

Angie stroked her fingers through his hair and glanced out the window behind the sofa, as if thinking. "He didn't say anything. But he seemed happy. Almost childishly so. He waved, gave me a thumbs up, and walked away. I don't know. It was like he approved."

"Of what?"

"I don't know. I just got that impression."

Mick was happy? Rob relaxed his shoulders and let go of the tension in his neck. "If that's what you thought, I'll bet you were right."

"I'll try to communicate with him more if I see him again. Honestly, I was so surprised when I saw him that I don't think I could have spoken. I thought it was you."

He nodded. "Understandable. So what's it like in this other place you go? The place you go when you're not here?"

"It's beautiful. I go to a meadow by a brook. Sometimes I walk in the long, soft grass. The sun shines, but not too bright. And it's warm, but never hot. A Utopia, really."

"Sounds beautiful."

She nodded. "It is. Very peaceful. Time passes quickly. I come here at night, but even though I must be there for an entire day, it only seems like an hour."

"Shorter days?"

"Maybe," she said. "Or maybe time does strange things in that world."

He nodded.

"It's like intense meditation. I see shadows, images of some sort, so I don't think I'm alone there. But it's not scary."

"Purgatory?" he asked, glancing down at her hands holding his.

"Maybe."

"I would have thought you'd go straight to Heaven," he said, running a hand up her arm in a gesture he meant to be supportive. Yet the feel of her silky skin under his palm sent his pulse racing.

She stared at him, her lips parting into a small "o" shape.

This was crazy. Absolutely fucking crazy. He had feelings for a ghost.

Chapter Seven

*A*ngie licked her lips. How could this be happening? Sitting so close to Rob, touching him, drove her senses wild. Impossible, right?

She stood and started pacing on the plush rug in front of the sofa. The soft texture reminded her of the grass in the other world. Yep, other world. As in they weren't from the same worlds and there was no chance for them. So these crazy feelings of wanting to lean against him, snuggle close to his wide, strong chest, had to go. A ghost and a human. Not a good match.

Think of something else, think of something else.

She glanced toward the door. "Do you think I can leave this apartment?" What if she could find her daughter, help her?

Rob stood. "One way to find out."

"No." The word came out harsher than she'd planned. "I mean, maybe later." One step at a time. "Let's sit."

He nodded, but his expression turned serious.

"I can't stop thinking about my daughter. How old is she?" She squeezed her eyes shut for a moment to keep the tears at bay. How could she have been so selfish? "What kind of a mother leaves her daughter?"

Rob tightened his grip on her hands and ran his thumbs over her palms. The motion soothed her, helped her focus. "Maybe you didn't have a choice. And she's eighteen."

"Rob." She braced herself. "Who was her father?"

"You divorced. You were eighteen when you had Chloe. You divorced within a year and your ex-husband moved out of the country. The police report didn't mention a boyfriend, either."

She nodded. She was eighteen when she had Chloe and Chloe was eighteen years old. That meant she was thirty-six. Old enough to know better, old enough to stay alive, no matter what, for her child.

"I think I want to see her. Maybe there's something I can do."

Rob dropped her hands so fast they smacked her thighs. He stood and stared at her.

"How about a photo?" He ran past a few boxes and came back, perched on an armrest with his laptop.

He jabbed the power button and smiled at her. "I can show you—" He frowned and glanced at the black screen. "That's weird," he said, pressing the button again. Then he closed his eyes and shook his head. "Maybe you draw all the current around us in order to materialize. No power. Not even battery backup when you're around." He shrugged. "My cell phone doesn't even work."

She tamped down her disappointment about the photo and managed to smile.

"Tell you what," he said. "I'll print out a picture tomorrow."

She nodded, fear knotting her stomach. "What if I can leave this apartment? Could you take me to Chloe?" Her voice was barely a whisper. "I can't remember her, but somehow I miss her."

Rob sat the laptop on the floor and slid beside her. "It's a shitty neighborhood."

"Please." Her eyes watered with tears. "Even if we don't go to her, can we get close?" Maybe she'd feel a connection, or Chloe would feel her mom's presence. They had to try.

Rob ran a hand through his hair and glanced at the door. "You need to wear more than that. I'll get you some clothes. But no getting out of the car."

"Uh, Rob?" She laid a hand on his chest. Sweet that he treated her as if she were human, but she didn't need clothes. "Nobody can see me, remember? And I'm a ghost...we don't really get cold."

"Yeah." He scrubbed a hand down his face. "True."

56

She took his hand. Instinct fought against her will. Each step toward the door took her closer to something unsure, unknown. Rob led her through the candlelit room. No second-guessing. Her daughter needed her.

Rob paused by the front door, unlatched two locks, and tightened his grip on her hand. "You ready?"

She nodded.

He opened the door. She took a deep breath as he slipped an arm around her waist, and they stepped out the door together.

Cold air smacked her in the face and darkness overwhelmed her. Had the lights gone out in the hallway? "Rob?"

Where was his warm hand? She turned back toward the door, but only cold air and darkness surrounded her. The inky blackness made it impossible to see her own hand. Fear formed a tight knot in her stomach, and she wrapped her arms around herself to ward off the cold.

She turned and lost her bearings. Did she turn all the way around?

A scratching sound, like a trapped animal, echoed from somewhere in the distance. Keeping her right foot planted, Angie stepped out and lunged into the darkness, reaching with both hands, trying to figure out where she was. Her bare feet brushed against cold stone as she took a small, testing step forward into the dark. Left? Right? Forward?

The scratching sounded again, this time followed by a low groan. Something was very wrong in this place. Why had she left?

Her daughter. Was this the way to find her daughter?

"Chloe?" she called into the black surroundings.

Her word echoed back. A cave?

The scratching sounded again, this time closer. "Chloe? It's—it's Mommy." Her voice shook.

A thump followed by something dragging. And then a groan.

Angie panted, trying to keep from screaming. Cold air stabbed at her exposed skin, and she shivered. She'd never been so cold.

Whatever it was moved closer, but this time without sound. She sensed it. Was it possible to die twice?

A gush of cold air whipped past her face. Something reached for her. Something cold and sinister. A scream caught in her throat and instead of the cold presence in front of her, something warm grabbed her from behind.

With a thud, she landed on familiar grass with the sun shining on her face. The younger Rob—no, Mick—knelt down next to her with a smile.

"You-you saved me." She struggled to sit, still reeling from her experience in the land of darkness. What the hell was that place?

Mick smiled, his smooth, young face wrinkling at his big brown eyes. Warmth radiated from him.

Dizziness swamped her, but Angie propped herself on her elbows and studied him. No, it wasn't just warmth and comfort radiating from him, the guy actually had a halo, some sort of aura surrounding him.

"Thank you, Mick," she whispered.

"My pleasure, Angie." His voice had a happy sing-songy quality to it, like a lullaby, and she yearned to hear him speak again.

"Rob misses you desperately." She stared, hypnotized by his gaze.

Mick closed his eyes for a second and sat beside her in the grass. The breeze carried a scent of lilac and honeysuckle, and Angie took a deep breath.

"Will you tell Rob something for me?"

Angie nodded.

"Tell him what happened to me wasn't his fault. None of us has any control over leaving our human existence." He smiled and glanced across the stream. "It was my time. They needed me here, and I am happier than I ever was there."

"Is it...." Angie glanced across the stream at the billowing trees and cloudless cornflower blue sky. "Is that Heaven?"

Mick nodded.

"But this isn't?" Angie gestured at the beautiful surroundings on her side of the stream.

"This side is for those who have more work to do in that world."

"I don't understand," she said.

"You're not supposed to." He grinned, and stood, heading for the stream.

She clamored to her feet. "Wait, Mick. Don't leave yet. I have so much to ask you...."

"I'm not leaving, I'm getting something for you." He bent, reached into the stream, and then walked back.

He stood in front of her, taller by at least a head, and reached for her hand. He still glowed, as if a light shone out his pores. With her hand in his, her hand glowed, too. He moved it, palm up, and placed a cold, wet stone in her palm, closing her fingers over it.

Strong tingles powered through her system, reminding her of the changes she felt when she traveled from one place to the next. *No, not ready to go back yet.* But she didn't go back.

Mick held her closed hand in both of his, and squeezed. The tingles stopped, and Angie looked up at him. "What just happened?"

"Your worry stone. I'll keep it for now, but soon it will be yours. You'll know what it means when the time comes. Your work in the other world isn't done yet. Chloe has an important job to do one day. But she needs her mother. Some things might not make sense when they happen, but know someone higher up," he glanced across the stream, "is in control."

Angie's heart pounded at the mention of Chloe. What did it mean? Did it mean she had the power to help her daughter? "How? How can I save her?"

He plucked the stone carefully from her palm, lifted his index finger to his lips, and then with a running start, leaped the width of the stream and ran into the forest on the other side.

❃

Rob paced in front of the sofa. He never should have let her try to leave the apartment. What now? She'd been gone for twenty minutes; maybe she'd be gone forever. Too risky. Sweat broke out between his brows. Once again, he'd let somebody take a risk, hadn't stopped them.

"Angie, come to me. Please come to me," he begged, calling into the candlelight room.

How could he bring her back? Open the door again? Summon her? *Shit.*

He fell onto the sofa and dropped his head back. Citrus tickled his nose and he jerked his head up. Angie stood in front of him, her fingers covering her mouth. He stood and she ran into his arms.

Her body shook, and he hugged her close, stroked her hair. "Okay, you're okay now." She wasn't human, and he didn't care. To hell with science, and reason.

For a moment, they held each other. He cherished the feel of her skin, the scent of her hair, and her womanly curves. Her breathing calmed, and he rocked with her, side to side, unsure of who he was soothing—himself or her.

On a sigh, she laid her hands against his chest and leaned back. "Mick saved me, Rob. I know this sounds crazy, but when I went out the door, I went into some scary place. Like a dark, dark cave. Cold. Something was after me."

Fear fisted in Rob's chest. She'd gone somewhere different?

"But just when I thought I didn't have a chance, Mick pulled me out, back into the sunshine of my world. His world."

Mick. A hero. Well, wasn't that something?

"God, I was so worried about you. I thought...I thought...." He buried his nose in the crook of her neck, taking her in through all his senses.

"Rob." She dug her fingers into his back, holding him close, her breath warm on his skin. "Mick wanted me to give you a message."

He slid his hands to her upper arms, unwilling to let go of her completely, but wanting to look into her sea-green eyes in the candlelight. "A message?" His heart was doing a crazy flip-flop. Happiness swelled it with relief that Angie was okay, and anticipation that, after all these years, his brother could communicate with him.

Angie smiled and held his waist. Her slim fingers felt tiny on his body. "He said to tell you that the accident wasn't your fault, and that none of us has any control about when we leave this world."

Rob dropped his hands. *No, too easy.* Of course Mick would try to ease the guilt. It wasn't true, it was just his way of trying to make Rob feel better. He turned away from Angie to look at the photo of himself and Mick.

"There's more," Angie said, following his glance. "He said he is in Heaven. He must be some sort of angel or something, because he can go into different worlds—the scary world where I went when I left this apartment, my world near the stream, and his world."

Rob folded his arms on his chest, stared at the picture. He'd like to believe Mick was in Heaven, but he wasn't ready to forgive himself.

Angie laid a hand on the small of his back, stood beside him in front of the photo. Together, they stared at Mick. She cared about his brother, too. And he'd saved her.

"He said he was happier now than he ever was in this world, Rob. And he looked happy. Really happy. He actually glowed."

Rob swallowed past a lump in his throat. His eyes stung with tears he had refused to shed for so many years. Two tears tracked down his face.

Angie wiped them away.

"Mick, an angel?" he asked.

She nodded. "And he gave me a stone, let me hold it for a minute, and then took it back."

Rob froze. "A stone?" He dug in his pocket, brought out the worry stone. "Like this?" His heart slammed hard. He didn't doubt Angie's words, but a stone? Even a scientist or cold-hard-facts accountant had to admit that a stone was proof that Mick was who he said.

Angie leaned forward and studied Rob's open palm in the flickering candlelight. She ran a finger over its smooth surface, and smiled up at him. "Very much like this. Black, smooth, with a little dent in the middle."

Rob took a deep breath and exhaled, letting the grief and the guilt escape with the hot air. A long-carried burden. Time to let it go. Time to move on.

Angie continued to stroke the worry stone, staring at it. "He said something else, too. That Chloe is important, and that she needs her mother. We'll know what to do, he said."

"This is all so fucking weird." Strange, but not as unfathomable as he'd first believed.

"We can find the answers, we can make this work," Angie said. "Hold me, Rob. All I need right now is for you to hold me."

She lifted her face, and he framed it with both his hands and kissed her. They stumbled backward onto the sofa.

ɔઠ

The next morning, Rob raced out of his bedroom, belting his pants as he ran. He'd eat breakfast at the office. He glanced at the sofa, halted, and scratched his head.

Holy shit. He'd acted like a teenager on his first date. He'd made out with a goddamned ghost. He was losing his mind. But damn, had he ever had a good time. She felt as real as any human woman, only better. Because he cared for her more than any woman he'd ever known.

Crazy was his new normal. But, he didn't care. Mick was happy. The sadness Rob had carried all these years, sadness for both of them, had washed away overnight. He stood taller, his steps were lighter, and he wanted Angie's company. Maybe Mick had a hand in putting the two of them together, too.

He grabbed his briefcase and headed out the door toward the elevator. After he stabbed the button for the lobby, he spotted J.B. running, his blue tie lifting as he hurried closer. Rob pressed on the control panel to hold the doors open.

"Thanks," J.B. said, panting for breath. "Gotta be in court today. Can't be late or the bad guy gets off."

"We can't have that." Rob stared at the numbers above the door, his mind still lingering on the feel of Angie's skin, the way she held onto him like she never wanted to leave.

The elevator dinged, signaling their arrival in the lobby.

"Get together for a beer again soon?" J.B. asked, striding out the front door next to Rob.

"Definitely."

"Great. See ya." J.B. turned left and Rob went right into the crisp March wind. He pulled up his coat collar. The cold air might make him think clearer.

Five minutes later, he stopped in front of a small corner business. Black steel bars covered the front glass window and door. A sign overhead proclaimed it to be TKZ, Private Investigator.

He'd passed the spot hundreds of times and never noticed most of the businesses. An investigator could stake out Chloe, keep track of her. Find out more about her life.

Rob looked to the right, and then the left. Fuck it. He could be late for work for once in his life. He stepped to the door and rang the buzzer.

A heavyset guy with graying hair lumbered toward the door, eyed Rob, and then the door made a clicking sound. The man pushed it open.

"What can I do for you?" He kept his hand on his holstered gun.

Rob stood straighter, toying with the impression the guy was an ex-cop. "I need surveillance on someone."

The man opened the door, motioned with his head to enter.

Rob stepped inside. An old rug that might have been nice at one time sported stains and was threadbare in places. The small office smelled of tobacco, and a cigarette burned in an ashtray on an old dented desk in the corner.

"Name's Tuck." The man held out a beefy hand.

"Rob." They shook.

"Come on in, sit." Tuck turned and moved across the room to his desk.

Rob took a seat in a folding chair on the other side. Did the dingy atmosphere mean this guy was a crock? Or did it mean he was too busy taking care of big things to worry about little ones? One look at meticulously lined-up file cabinets behind Tuck's desk made Rob think it was the latter.

"What ya got? Cheating spouse?" Tuck grabbed a pen and leaned over a yellow legal pad of paper.

He shook his head. "Girlfriend's daughter." *Oh good God.* He really was crossing the line into Crazyville. He just called a ghost his girlfriend. Then he realized Tuck would quickly find out who Chloe's mother was and that she was dead. "I mean my former girlfriend. She committed suicide a few months ago."

Tuck raised a brow.

Rob leaned forward onto the desk, looking the man in eyes. "Chloe's into some deep shit. Drugs. Used to be a good kid. I owe it to her mother to take care of things...." He let his words drift off. Pulling the other guy's emotional strings might help win him over.

Tuck's cell phone rang. He glanced at the screen and pressed a button to silence it. "Continue."

Rob told about his visit to the house days earlier, warned him about the gun, and gave him the address.

"You do realize I'm going to check out your story. You lose your deposit if you're lying. And I can't legally take this girl. Not to rehab, not away from this man who lives with her. You know that, right?" Tuck narrowed his eyes at Rob.

"Right now, I just want to know what's going on. Does she leave often, do people come to the house regularly? Is she ever left alone? Take pictures of the people who come and go." Rob swallowed hard. Tuck might not be able to whisk Chloe away to safety, but with the right knowledge, Rob could.

"All right. I'll do it. Six hundred dollars. Half now, the other half tomorrow morning when you stop in to pick up the pictures." Tuck stubbed out his cigarette in a nearby full ashtray.

Five minutes later, Rob stepped onto the city sidewalk. He wouldn't make any decisions about Chloe. That was Angie's call. But he'd give her as much information to base her decision as possible.

He stepped into the expansive lobby of Smythe and Burkett Financial, and his cell phone rang. He pulled it out. Jonathan. Rob shook his head. Couldn't Sheila and Jonathan take a hint? He didn't want anything to do with either of them anymore. Why did they keep trying? The call went to voicemail.

Rob punched the button for the elevator, focused on his next task. He'd make an information folder for Angie, complete with pictures and newspaper clippings, and show it to her tonight.

No matter how much he wanted to help her, how real all of this felt, the fact that he spent time with a ghost, was trying to help her solve a mystery, blew his mind and made him seriously doubt his sanity.

He shook the feeling away. What would Angie do when she saw a photo of her daughter? What would happen when she viewed her own obituary?

Angie opened her eyes. Finally. Neon lights from the city and the water beyond reflected through the apartment widow. She'd been waiting all day to come back here. Weird that she couldn't ever visit during the day, but it was just one more strange part of this life that she didn't have answers to.

"Rob?" she whispered into the semi-darkness. He'd lit candles again, and the flames flickered and danced on the walls.

A door clicked open, and he walked out, pulling a gray T-shirt over his bare chest and rippling abs. Angie licked her lips, remembering how his mouth had tasted the night before, how his strong arms had held her tight, made her forget all her troubles and questions.

"Angie?" He stepped closer and smiled, but didn't close the distance between them.

Inhaling, she took in the scent of him, a piney fresh smell. His dark wet hair hung in tight ringlets around his face.

Rob smiled. "When the lights went out in my bedroom, I figured you were here."

She shrugged. "Busted." Small talk. But they had big things to talk about.

As if he read her mind, Rob pulled an envelope off the dark green granite countertop. "Let's sit."

She perched on the edge of the sofa, and he knelt in front of her, holding out a thick tan envelope. He pressed his lips together.

"Is it that bad?" Angie struggled to catch her breath. She'd long since gotten over the odd fact that ghosts could feel and breathe. She wished, in a strange way, that they couldn't get hurt either. But apparently, ghosts could feel emotional pain as much as any human.

If there was a chance, any chance at all, that the information about how she lived her life could help save Chloe, or solve the mystery of her death, she'd bear anything.

Rob moved next to her and pulled out a single paper. "Chloe."

Angie glanced at the photo and then pressed her fist to her mouth to hold back a sob. A blue-eyed blonde teenager with a sprinkling of freckles across her nose stared back at her. She wore a smile that only a teenager could wear: soft and vulnerable, yet at the same time guarded.

Angie jolted at the thought. A memory tried to poke its way back to her conscious thoughts. She stared at the sweet face in the photo for a long moment, but nothing else came to her.

Tears stung her eyes, but she blinked them back. With a slow, careful stroke, she ran a finger along Chloe's cheek, wishing she could show her daughter how much she cared. Her eyes stung again, and her head pounded with the effort of holding back the tears. Human reactions to all of this. The thought gave her hope. Maybe she had enough human characteristics still within her to be that way again, to be there for her daughter.

She hugged the photo to her chest with both hands, closed her eyes and pictured what it would be like to embrace Chloe, protect her...be there for her.

She swallowed hard and glanced up at Rob, and he rested his hand on her shoulder. She laid the photo on the sofa cushion beside her, placing it gently as if putting Chloe herself to rest. She turned to take the envelope from Rob with shaking hands.

Bracing herself, she opened the flap and tugged out the paper-clipped contents.

The top sheet was a copy from an elementary school yearbook. Angie held the photo close to her face, squinting in the candlelight to see the young faces. With a smile, she tapped her finger on a round-faced blonde. The little girl resembled the photo Rob had given her, yet there was more. Something drew her to the girl. As if she would have found it on her own without knowing what she looked like in later years. A memory? God, she hoped so.

"Here she is." She glanced up at Rob and caught a frown on his face before he quickly covered his concerned expression with a smile.

"She's a cutie," he said.

"First grade." Her mind reeled. "Wait, how did I know that?"

Rob's eyes widened.

She tucked a strand of hair behind her ear, excited now to move on, view the rest of the folder. Maybe it wouldn't be so bad.

She thumbed through old report cards and then pulled out an elementary school newsletter. "Oh," she said, surprised to see a photo of herself on the front page.

"Teacher of the Year," Rob said, leaning over to peek at the words.

"I loved my students." Angie stilled, wondering where the thought had come from.

She turned to the next page. Chloe smiled back at her—a huge, grin with two front teeth missing and adorned from head to toe in pink. A pink leotard, pink tutu, pink tights and pink ballet shoes. "I-I—" The tears she'd been successfully holding at bay leaked out of her eyes and down her face.

Rob wrapped his arm around her shoulders and pulled her close, kissing the top of her head. "You don't have to look at all of this tonight."

She swallowed past a lump in her throat and bit her quivering bottom lip. Rob's touch grounded her. Sitting straighter, she took a deep breath and slowly let it out.

He loosened his grip but kept his arm around her shoulders. She closed her eyes for a second and absorbed his strength. "I'm okay." She'd process the emotions later. Right now, she'd keep digging for information.

She scanned Chloe's report cards from middle school and her first years of high school, frowning when she got to her daughter's junior year.

"This is odd," she said, tilting the paper so Rob could see. "She was an honor student throughout school, but her grades dropped in her junior year."

Rob shook his head and shrugged.

Chills shot down Angie's spine. She turned the page to a copy of the newspaper clipping. Her own obituary.

The room spun. Could ghosts faint? Maybe instead of fainting, she'd just disappear. *No.* She couldn't let that happen. She had to calm herself. Seeing her smiling face looking back at her so closely after reading her daughter's report cards shook her to her core.

"I was weak."

"No, not weak," Rob said.

She squinted at him, hadn't even realized she'd said the words aloud. "I-I left her. Why couldn't I have stopped her from hanging out with the wrong people? Why didn't I help her? Why didn't I keep my daughter safe?" Angie didn't know how she knew that, but suddenly she was sure that her daughter's dropping grades in high school pointed to a bigger problem.

"Don't be so hard on yourself, Angie. In fact, I've been wondering something." Rob rubbed her back and once again she took strength from his touch.

"What?"

"What if you didn't kill yourself? What if somebody staged it to look that way?" He frowned at her.

Was he trying to make her feel less guilty? She relaxed a little, knowing his idea was at least a possibility.

"It's certainly something to think about," she said.

"I hired a private investigator."

Angie frowned. The words sounded familiar, like she should know what they meant, but her grasp of the world of the living was fleeting and incomplete. Some things she instinctively understood, others she knew nothing about.

Rob raised a brow. "He's an ex-policeman. I asked him to keep watch over Chloe for now, take pictures. That way we'll know where she is. I'll have pictures by tomorrow night to show you."

Angie laid her head on his shoulder. He wanted answers as much as she did. Fragments of her past were returning. The more time she spent with Rob, the more things she remembered about her time on earth. Fleeting visuals and thoughts, but maybe they'd grow into more concrete memories.

Rob cared. About her, about Chloe. Being with him gave her hope.

"What else can I do to help you? Do you have any ideas?" he asked.

She lifted his chin with two fingers and stared into his dark eyes. The visual of his bare abs as he'd stepped out of his room moved to the forefront of her mind.

"Yes, I have an idea."

Chapter Eight

Rob faced Angie. Her gentle fingers held his chin captive, and he stared at her sea-green eyes in the candlelight. His gut pinched with sudden need for her. She was as real as any woman he'd ever held, only better.

She was a ghost.

He didn't care. Giving in to impulse, he held out his arms. With a slow smile, she eased against his chest. The subtle glow of her body warmed him from the inside out. He looked down at her pale white face and brushed her cheek. "I'm here for you. I want to help you," he whispered, rubbing a hand up and down her back, elated that he could touch her this way.

Angie searched his face and stared at his mouth.

"Thank you," she whispered. She tilted her head, and pressed her lips against his, warm and feather-light like an intoxicating late-spring breeze.

He held her slim waist with both hands. She wasn't alive, yet she made him feel more alive than he'd been in months. She'd killed herself, yet here he was, kissing her.

It should feel weird.

But it felt right.

Her lips were like nothing he'd ever experienced before. Softer than a rose petal. Even when he'd thought himself in love with Sheila, he'd never wanted to drop everything to be with her.

Angie's cool hands massaged his neck. He closed his eyes to focus on the sensations traveling through his body. Her curves melted against him like a cherished blanket. He tenderly stroked her back, sank his fingers in the light strands of her hair, and enjoyed the realness of it all.

When she withdrew from their kiss, it left him wanting more, needing more. But, he dropped his hands and reminded himself to follow her lead.

She held his hands in hers, staring at him, and then smiled and ran her hands up his arms, stopping at his biceps. With her thumbs, she traced small circles, and he relaxed at her touch. Her cool and delicate skin intrigued him.

With a sigh, she leaned her head on his chest. He inhaled, treasuring each second spent with her, and slid his hand to rest on the small of her back.

She moved her hands to his waist and pulled herself tighter against him. Following her lead, he hauled her even closer.

Rob braced himself, tried to think of anything but the feel of her and the electric pulses that raced through his body, firing a need he battled to control. She was a ghost. One with the substance of a human, but still a ghost. His libido took over and his erection grew. How could he even consider being with her?

Her silky tongue parted his lips and slipped into his mouth, and her fingers freed his shirt from his dress pants. She moaned into the kiss, and he framed her face with both hands. It took every ounce of his willpower to pull away, to make sure this was what she wanted.

As if reading his mind, she smiled, pulled his shirt apart, and brought her lips back to his. Rob's heart beat so fast against his ribs he thought it would flat-line. He panted for breath, yearning to touch her, be touched by her. Desperate to overcome his need for her, he swallowed and cleared his throat. "I want to help you. I don't know how."

She studied him, massaging his shoulders with her hands. "You're so warm," she said, her breath heating the sensitive skin at the base of his neck. "I'm so cold."

"I could get you a blanket." His voice shook as he tried to control his physical reaction to her. "Wait, I thought you said ghosts didn't get cold."

"If it means you'll cover me with your body to warm me, I'm cold."

He gulped. She tilted against him and he lost the last of his willpower. He slipped his hand under her nightgown, traced a finger along her silken skin, past her stomach, and along her ribs. Her breath hitched, and he kissed her neck before reaching to cup a breast. Angie gasped, dug her fingernails into his back, and kissed his shoulder.

He couldn't think clearly with her hands tracing along his spine. Bolts of pleasure raced from his upper body to his lower. He caressed her breast and then brushed his thumb across her nipple, feeling it peak to full attention. She wanted warmth. The heat that pulsed through his body should be more than enough to share.

She ran her hand down his left arm as he kneaded her breast with his right. Her fingers reached the waistband of his pants, and he sucked in a hard breath that left him dizzy.

"You're so beautiful," he said.

"So are you."

Smiling, she tugged at his zipper. He shifted on the sofa, allowing her easier access. After a quick tug, she pulled his pants past his hips, and he kicked them off. This was crazy. He was trying to warm a ghost by making love with her.

Her gaze held his captive and she straddled him. He bent to kiss her again. Passion erupted, and he gathered her close. Her body fit to his as if they were made to be with each other.

He couldn't think straight, couldn't think of anything but Angie. He wanted her to be in charge, let her set the pace. But he could crank it up a bit, let his passion kindle hers. He kissed her lips, dove deep into her warmth as his tongue explored her mouth.

Again she moaned, spiking his desires. He forced himself to think of her needs, not his. Wouldn't be the easiest thing he'd ever done, but it might be the most noble.

Whatever she was, whatever form this woman used to present herself to him, she was more real right now than any woman he'd ever been with. She didn't hide her desire, she responded to his touch as if it were the only thing that mattered in the world. He wanted to be her world, wanted to make her world better.

Slowly, he lifted the billowy gown over her head, exposing her perfect breasts. He glanced into her eyes for confirmation that what he was doing was okay. She smiled and her eyes fluttered closed. He palmed a breast, lowered his mouth and traced a circle with his tongue. With the other hand, he stroked and massaged the rest of her body.

Hearing her lose control, knowing she wanted to be with him, raised his passion and confidence to a new level. He swallowed hard and concentrated on the feel of her hands as they pressed his head closer to her breast, begging him to take more. He nuzzled her soft flesh and inhaled the scent of her skin. Still citrus, but with a musky undertone. Sexual desire poured from her skin, turning him on to an almost painful point.

She dragged her fingers, slowly, like a long caress, through his hair. Pleasure pulsed down his body.

He needed to make her squirm with as much desire as he had. His hands trembled and he traced a path to her panties, caressing as he went. His hand touched the lace edge, and she sucked in a breath. He smiled, turned on anew by her responsiveness to his touch. He slid the lingerie down her smooth, long legs.

Coming back to her mouth, he kissed her hard, taking his time. She tasted like honeysuckle. Everything about her was delicious.

"Yes," Angie moaned.

Rob's worries disappeared. She trusted him. He had to prove that trust was justified. She pressed against him and invited him in. Slowly, ever so slowly, he leaned against her.

Angie moaned again and fell to the sofa, pulling him down with her. "Please," she panted. "I need this. I need you."

She clutched his shoulders. He couldn't last much longer, and yet he didn't want his time with her to ever end.

He kissed the side of her neck and slid out of his boxers. Nudging her legs apart with his knee, he eased against her wet and ready folds, but didn't enter. Slowly, agonizingly slowly, he rubbed up and down.

She gasped. "Oh. Ohhhhhh." She dropped her hands to his hips, forced him closer.

His breath came hot and heavy, and he rocked against her as she wiggled and cried out for release. "Yeah," he said. "Take it, take what you need."

"I-I need you. Inside of me," she panted. "Please." She clutched his buttocks tighter, and he shifted and stroked her again. She yielded against his sensitive tip.

He couldn't last another minute without being inside of her beautiful body. Reaching between their heated forms, he used his hand to guide his swollen need into her, holding his breath to keep from exploding, as inch by inch, he slipped into her, savoring the feel of her.

She pulled him closer and let out a long cry as her body convulsed, squeezing him snug inside as she rocked underneath him.

"Yes. Oh, God, yes," she said, tilting her hips against him.

His gut clenched tight, and he drove into her. In and out as her hands clutched and pulled at him, bringing him closer. He stiffened and orgasm wracked his body, stealing his breath, taking control of every muscle. Her softness surrounded him, and he let go of everything, shuddering and flowing into her.

Angie's body slackened, and she fell back into the sofa cushions.

Moonlight and city lights streamed through the window.

She had a body like none he'd ever touched before. A skinny waist flaring to curvy hips, and breasts that fit perfectly in the palms of his hands. Sweat glistened on her flat stomach and a content smile spread on her face. He smiled back, knowing he'd taken her from tears to joy, at least for a moment.

Sighing, Angie crooked her index finger at him. As if she possessed some magical power, he leaned nearer. When he hovered over her, supporting himself on his arms, she wrapped her arms around his neck, and pulled him down. Her tongue parted his lips. His senses reeled at the feel of her in spite of the craziness that formed their bond. Exhausted, he still held his weight off her. She pulled him on top of her, tight against her as she closed her eyes.

Purgatory...Hell...Heaven. Which was which, where was all of this taking them, and where was he now?

ೞ

The familiar tingling spread through Angie's body and she opened her eyes to bright sunlight in the grassy meadow by the stream. Water gurgled and splashed over smooth rocks. She was back in her other world.

Bolting upright, she checked her hands. When she found them empty, her heart sank. She'd slept with one hand on Rob and the other on the picture of Chloe.

Sadness wracked her. A lump formed in her throat, and her eyes stung with tears. Each photo of her daughter chipped away at a part of her. She couldn't see or touch Chloe anymore.

With a smile, she remembered how she thought she wouldn't be able to sleep last night. But after making love with Rob, she'd fallen into a deep slumber. One she hadn't woken from until landing back in her other world.

Lifting her face to the sun, she thought back to the photo of her daughter and smiled, hoping for a glint of memory about Chloe. But as if a strong steel door shut on her mind, she couldn't tap into anything. Drugs? With fleeting knowledge of the other world, she grasped the evil of the word, but had she tried to help Chloe rid herself of drugs?

Angie stood and strolled to the nearby willow tree. The long, pliable branches hung to the ground like curtains. She parted them and stepped into their shade. Leaning against the sturdy trunk, she closed her eyes, not willing to let go of the vision of her daughter.

And then she remembered.

Chloe on a swing set at the park, laughing as Angie pushed her. Chloe's blonde hair breezed behind when she swung down.

"Higher, Mommy, higher," her voice rang out and echoed in Angie's mind.

She squeezed her eyes to keep them closed, wanting more than anything to hold the vision. It was so real that she reached out as if to stroke her daughter's bright hair. The picture morphed into another, and Chloe stood before her in the pink tutu. "Mommy, I'm scared. I don't want to go on that stage."

Angie swallowed hard. She remembered her daughter. Remembered the things they used to do. Happiness warmed her skin.

"You'll be fine, sweetheart. Just pretend you're at practice." She mouthed the words as if rote memory planted them years ago.

More pictures flashed by in her mind: Chloe at the beach jumping in the waves, Chloe riding a bike. They'd been close. She'd been a good mother.

She opened her eyes when the visions disappeared. Closing her eyes again, she willed the memories to continue, begged for them to return, but her mind remained blank. The shadowy interior of the willow tree now felt cold, damp. She hustled forward, back into the light, rustling the skirt of her nightgown, needing to feel the sun again.

Without Rob she wouldn't have found this treasured memory. She perched by the stream, soothed by the steady current of water cascading over the rocks.

But her need for him transcended the practical. They'd made love last night. A ghost and a freaking human. Had this ever happened before? Did it happen all the time? She couldn't explain anything about their relationship—how it was possible Rob saw her when nobody else could, how she was corporeal to him when she was a ghost....

In his arms, she forgot everything except the way his hands, his mouth, his body felt. He helped her uncover her past and its truths, but more than that, he brought her comfort.

She had to focus on Chloe. Mick said Chloe needed her. But how could she do anything for her daughter when she couldn't even leave the damned apartment in that world?

Chapter Nine

Sun streamed in through the open curtains the next morning. Rob blinked in self-defense at the brightness and rolled over on the sofa. He'd tried to stay awake as long as possible, but holding Angie and making love with her had made that tough. If he'd stayed awake, would that have prevented her from leaving?

He fisted his eyes. Wait a minute. Wait a goddamned minute. They'd made love. He'd had sex with a ghost. *I had sex with a ghost last night.*

All right. He sat and glanced around his apartment. Nothing to prove she'd even been there. Maybe this was like *The Twilight Zone.* Maybe he was caught in some in-between world, and it just looked like his old world.

He could accept that ghosts existed. Mick's worry stone helped him tap into that memory. He could even accept that for some reason, Angie appeared only to him and felt as real as any human ever had. Not a mist, nor a cool figment of his imagination, but feminine curves and substance.

Common sense told him none of it was possible. He stood, crossed the room to the picture of Mick, and the worry stone that lay in front of it on the glass shelf. He palmed it, held it tight. His brother had told Angie strange things would happen. As strange as making love to a ghost?

In the kitchen, he opened the coffee grounds and took a good long sniff, letting the scent bring him awake before he filled the brewer and started it. He shook his head and leaned a hip against the counter. "What am I getting into?" *Is this real or am I going crazy?*

He reached into the cupboard for a mug. Building relationships was not his area of expertise. Every single relationship he'd ever had ended badly. His brother died, his mother gave up on life, and his father still blamed him for his brother's death. His best friend and his fiancée fell in love with each other. Nobody stuck around.

This was beyond crazy. He poured his coffee, walked with it into the living room and stood by the sofa that had become his and Angie's nightly meeting place. He hated to admit it, because it made him feel like a freak, but he was attracted to her. He scrubbed a hand over his face. Was he going insane?

He couldn't ignore her curves and beautiful face.

Still, on a deeper level, he wanted to comfort her so much that his gut twisted when he thought of her pain-filled expression. Tears usually left him unmoved. His mother had cried for so many years, behind closed doors and out in the open. Tears were nothing new to him.

He gulped the coffee, savoring the burn because it gave him something real, a physical response that proved he was alive and awake, and then headed for the shower. There'd likely be a pile of tax returns on his desk. Thank God for that, he needed to keep his mind occupied.

But first, he'd stop at Tuck's and get the information on the surveillance.

Twenty minutes later, he headed out the door toward the elevator. Once inside, he spotted J.B. running toward him, just like yesterday. Rob pressed the door button and held the panels open.

"Thanks," J.B. said, panting for breath. "Gotta be in court today. Can't be late or the bad guy gets off."

"Again?" Rob asked.

J.B. frowned, and stared at the numbers above the door.

Rob narrowed his eyes and studied the bald cop. Tuck needed to run a background check to look into J.B.'s finances today, too.

A dinging sound signaled they'd arrived at the lobby level.

"Get together for a beer again soon?" J.B. asked, striding out the front door next to Rob.

"Definitely."

"Great. See ya."

J.B. turned left and Rob stared after him. Hadn't they had the exact conversation yesterday? His tie was even the same blue one as the day before. Wouldn't he at least change his tie?

Looking down at his dark suit, he realized J.B. wasn't the only one wearing the same outfit. He didn't have any meetings today, and he'd dressed more casually, in khakis and a button-down shirt, hadn't he? Rob's jaw went slack and he gripped the briefcase handle until his knuckles turned white. What the hell was going on?

No. He'd been distracted getting ready. Probably put on the same darn clothes as the day before without even realizing it. Except...he'd tossed those clothes in the hamper.

Okay. It didn't mean anything. His mind was busy accepting that ghosts existed. Not only that they existed, but he'd...he'd fucking made love to one. That put everything else—including his wardrobe—to the back of his mind. Suspending belief obviously took up a lot of brain cells.

He spotted a newspaper stand outside the apartment building and stumbled through the revolving door on shaky legs to drop some coins into the machine.

Yanking out a copy, he read the date. Yesterday's date.

He yanked a passing man's elbow, and the old guy frowned at him.

"What day is it?" Rob asked.

The old man spun out of his grasp and frowned. "It's Thursday." He straightened his trench coat, and with a final glare, stalked away.

In spite of the chilly March air, sweat trickled down Rob's back. No. Today was Friday. Yesterday was Thursday. Laying a hand on his chest over his winter coat, he pressed to ease the pain that stabbed at him, and struggled to catch a breath. Was this what a heart attack felt like?

Angie's words pushed through his worries. Mick said strange things were going to happen. Really? Going back a day in time? *That's beyond strange, Mick, that's downright fucking unbelievable.* Yet, the thought, the tiny chance, that there might be an explanation for all this crap, enabled him to take a deep breath.

Move on. Get the information from Tuck, and then focus on work.

He rang the bell on Tuck's door, and the man lumbered to the front, and stared at Rob.

"What you need?"

Oh shit. Tuck had to remember him. Had to. "I came yesterday. Do you remember?"

He narrowed his eyes. "Can't say I do. What do you want?"

Go with it. Don't freak out. This is all happening for a reason. "I'd like to hire you."

The man buzzed the door open. Ten minutes later, Rob left after giving the man the same instructions as the day before. And just in case any more days switched around on him, he'd requested the information by six p.m.. That increased the price, but it'd be worth it if Tuck didn't remember him come morning.

Rob walked to work, half afraid that when he got there, nobody would know him and it would turn out he'd been wiped off the earth.

Later, as he sat at his desk, staring at the same tax forms as yesterday—the ones he'd completed before he left the office—he glared at the date on the newspaper. What the hell?

He leaned his elbows on his desk and rested his forehead in the palms of his hands. He'd spent half an hour searching the Internet, but every page he pulled up was day-old news. How could everyone around him act so normal as if nothing was out of place? He'd traveled back in time. By himself. Everyone around him experienced the day for the first time.

Blood pounded in his head like an ocean wave crashing to shore over and over again. Why was this happening? It was too real to be a nightmare. Maybe things would return to normal tomorrow. He would go to sleep tonight and when he woke, all of this would be behind him.

Either that or he'd walk to the nearest hospital and have himself committed.

Could he have been drugged?

He lifted his head and glanced around his office. Maybe this was all a bad hallucination. His cell phone rang, and he glanced at it. Sheila. As usual, he let it go to voicemail. After a moment, his phone beeped to let him know he had a message. He scrolled to delete it without listening, but something made him pause.

Instead of erasing it, he listened to the message. "Rob, I know you're mad, and you have every reason to be. Jonathan and I are not going to be together. I thought you should know that. Neither of us would be comfortable knowing we hurt you." She sighed into the phone. "We might not love each other, you and me, Rob, but I care about you. I have a feeling you're deleting your messages, but if you're listening to this, please know we both care. Having you as a friend is more important to both Jonathan and me than any possible relationship together."

She disconnected.

Had she left that message yesterday, but he'd deleted it without listening?

Somehow the anger, the betrayal he'd felt, lessened at her words. He'd call her. Not today.

Today was about finishing his work, and finding out more about Chloe. Was she the key to solving the mystery of Angie's death?

Chapter Ten

*A*ngie opened her eyes to twinkling candlelight. *Finally*. She'd been waiting all day to come to this apartment, to see Rob, and to find out more about her past.

And to find out if he was as freaked out about the fact that they'd made love as she was.

Rob leaned a hip against the kitchen counter, staring across the candlelit room at her. Her pulse—her ghostly pulse—hammered when she looked at him. He wore a tight-fitting T-shirt and jeans that accentuated his athletic build. She could almost feel the way his muscles flexed and bunched when he'd covered her body with his.

He didn't say a word, only smiled at her.

Sheesh. Awkward much? She licked her lips. Okay, may as well be the one to start the conversation. "Last night was...um...fun."

His eyebrows quirked and his baffled look made her want to fall into his embrace.

She raised her arms, inviting him closer, suddenly needing to feel him. Desire sped up her body from her toes to her head with such intensity that she wobbled. Why the hell did she get so turned on around him? Like she was possessed with need for him.

He bolted forward and placed his warm hands on her waist. "Whoa. You okay?"

"Yes." She tried to laugh, but it caught in her throat. All her attention went to the way her skin danced with pleasure under his hands. She wanted them lower, higher, all over her body. She swallowed and tamped down her desire.

"Sorry. I guess this whole popping in and out thing messes with my equilibrium." She smiled, and as much as she wanted his hands on her, eased out of his hold and crossed the room to stare at the photos on his shelf. Mick's picture and the stone caught her attention. Yeah. Mick said weird things would happen. Like crazy attraction for Rob?

She squared her shoulders and turned to face him. "So, uh...last night...."

He stepped closer. "How was it possible?"

She wished she knew. "It's never happened before, if that's what you're asking."

He nodded several times. "I looked it up on the internet. There are people who claim humans and corporeal ghosts can have physical relationships."

"Physical relationships." She echoed his words. Is that what they'd had? She thought it was mind-blowing sex.

"It was, uh, well...." He ran a hand through his hair, and she wanted to push down the strands that remained standing. "Damn, it was something else to be with you like that Angie." He cleared his throat.

She stepped forward with outstretched arms and he pulled her closer. "I don't know how it was possible, either. But it felt so damn right, and soooo damn good." She buried her nose in his shirt.

He held her tight, rocked with her for a minute. Being near him made her believe things could be okay. His strong embrace took away her worries. Her body wanted more from him, but her mind insisted on answers. Reluctantly, she pulled out of his embrace.

"Let's sit," Rob said. "I've got some pictures to show you, and...well, some weird news." He grabbed an envelope from the counter.

Weird news? What did that mean? She'd had enough weird news for a lifetime. And an after-lifetime.

They sat on the sofa and Rob sighed. "No other way to say this, except to say it. I went back a day in time today."

Angie blinked. "What?"

"Yeah. Went back a day in time, as in experienced yesterday all over again today."

"How? Why?"

"I have no fucking idea," he said, leaning back against the cushions.

"Mick said strange things would happen." As in a ghost making love and going back in time? Wow, when the guy said "strange," he really meant it.

"For now, for sanity's sake, that's what I'm telling myself. If I think too hard about all of this, honest to God, my head might explode." He tapped the brown envelope on his lap. "I had the private investigator stake out Chloe's house today. And check into her finances to see what happened with the life insurance check."

Angie tensed, reminded herself to be brave for Chloe, and nodded.

Rob passed the envelope and she held it with shaking hands. He laid a hand on her upper arm, giving her the strength to open the clasp and pull out the contents.

"This is the account of her finances." He tapped his finger on the paper. "She deposited the one hundred thousand dollars as soon as she got it. She's been taking it out, ever since, in increments of nine thousand dollars cash."

"The money is almost gone," Angie said. Money she'd likely meant to keep her daughter from financial trouble in the event of Angie's death.

"Exactly." He pulled the top paper off, revealing Tuck's photo of Chloe's townhouse. "And she isn't using it for rent."

She could do this. She flipped to the next page and froze. Chloe. A gaunt-faced, vacant-eyed teen who barely resembled the little girl in the tutu Rob had shown her yesterday. Dressed in shabby, tattered clothes. Her daughter's once-lush blonde hair stuck to her cheeks as if she hadn't washed it in days. A bruise stood out on her pale face.

The photo caught her blowing smoke out of her mouth with a cigarette—or maybe it wasn't a cigarette—in her hand as she stood on the front porch of an unkempt brick row house.

"Drugs?" she asked, facing Rob.

He closed his eyes and nodded.

She turned to the next photo and bit back a cry. A scrawny, dark-haired man held Chloe by the elbow. Chloe stood on the steps in shabby clothes and wore a helpless frown as she looked up at the man. Did he hurt her, or threaten her? Angie leaned closer, staring at the image. The man looked familiar.

Blinking to clear away the tears that wanted to form, she flipped to the next picture. It was blurry.

"Taken through a window," Rob said.

Chloe's sleeve was pulled up and she'd stuck a needle into her bare arm. Angie cringed. The next photo showed her daughter slumped in a corner. Angie didn't want to see any more.

"When were these taken?" she asked, tears streaming down her face as she looked up at Rob.

"A private investigator took the pictures today."

He ran a hand through his hair, and then looked at the floor again. "I tried to help her that day I saw her." He met her gaze. "I would have put her in a rehab facility, taken her from that idiot's clutches, but the punk—Vinnie—had a gun."

Angie stood, took his hands in hers. "I don't expect you to risk your life to save her, Rob."

He narrowed his eyes and squeezed her hands. "I would have risked it, run with her. Angie, don't you see? I would die for you."

Angie opened her mouth to speak but couldn't find the words.

"But I didn't know how it would change things for you."

"I must have been a terrible mother."

Rob pulled her close, kissed her head. "Listen to me." His palms framed her face, and he looked into her eyes. "I didn't want to show you those photos at first. I knew you'd feel guilty. But that won't help you get her back. You need to know what you're up against."

Angie let the tears run freely down her face and gazed at the tender man before her. "Do you think that's why I killed myself? Because I felt like a terrible mother?"

Rob let out a breath, drew her closer, and kissed her lips. "I haven't known you for very long. But if there's one thing I know, it's that you are and you were a good person. Which means you were a terrific mother, too." He kissed her cheek, brushing away a tear with his lips.

"We'll figure this out, Angie."

She nodded and he pulled her close and rocked back and forth. The motion soothed and relaxed her. He stared out the window and at the harbor lights beyond.

Angie followed his gaze, letting the city lights calm her a bit before she spoke. "Rob, if you die, my chance to help Chloe is gone," she whispered.

Chapter Eleven

*A*t the newsstand the next morning, Rob yanked a newspaper off the stack. Morning rush-hour traffic, complete with honking horns and tires splashing through puddles, bristled in the background. His gaze raced to the date on the paper. He'd gone back in time another four days.

His gut roiled and loneliness smacked him harder than the March wind that chilled the air around him. Dry leaves skittered past him on the sidewalk.

He bought the paper, hunched down against the wind, and strode toward his office building. Another day to hurry through, trying to find out more about Angie's life, ghosts, and now time travel. Then he'd rush home to be with her. They'd made love four more times last night. Five times total since he'd met her.

Wait. He froze in the middle of the sidewalk, and a woman walking a tiny dog almost plowed into him.

When he and Angie had made love the first time, he'd gone back one day. How many times had they made love the night before? Four. And he'd gone back four days.

Recognition spiked. Could that be it? Each time they made love, he went back in time one day. And stayed there.

He snorted, bringing a confused look from the elderly man coming toward him. *Possible?* What was possible and what was impossible here? Would he ever have believed before he met her that time travel was possible? Shit, if he could make love with a ghost, anything could fucking happen.

Oh yeah. He was ready for men in white coats for sure.

How long would he continue to go back in time?

Her death! Maybe if he went back far enough he could somehow prevent Angie's death. However many times they had sex, they went back in time and stayed there.

Quickening his pace, he hustled as fast as he could to Tuck's office. The guy wouldn't have a clue who Rob was. But he needed information on J.B. Why, if the case was closed on Angie's suicide, was J.B. so interested in what happened? And was Vinnie right about J.B.'s visit with Chloe?

After a quick stop at Tuck's, and another request for information by the end of the day, Rob hurried through the wind to his office.

He needed to find out exactly how many days to go back in order to save Angie. He could save her life. He could be with her as a flesh and blood person. The thought of possessing such a power thrilled and scared him at the same time, and he couldn't wait to return to the apartment to share the news with her.

He pulled open the lobby door in his office building. "Shit," he hissed as two thoughts entered his mind. The security guard behind the desk narrowed his eyes. He smiled and nodded at the skinny old guy.

What if, in her human state, she didn't remember him? Just as she couldn't remember anything from her human life right now, what if she couldn't remember anything from her ghost life when she returned to her prior existence? Just another person in a long line of people who left him.

ᚴ

Shortly after nine o'clock, the lights flickered and went out. Fresh out of the shower, Rob pulled a T-shirt over his head and opened the bathroom door.

When he saw her, he sucked in a breath at her silhouette. Her hair flowed around her shoulders, and she stared at him from across the room, a small smile on her face.

"Angie," he said, crossing to her.

She opened her arms and met him halfway.

He didn't realize how much he'd missed her until she fell into his embrace. He ran his hands up and down her, warming her cool skin. He was falling in love with a ghost.

Gently, he held her upper arms, rubbed them. "Let's sit." He motioned with his head toward the sofa. "There's something I figured out today."

Frowning, she nodded. "Okay."

They sat and he exhaled. "Remember how I told you I—or maybe we—go back in time?"

She nodded. "I can't tell the difference between one day and the next."

Reaching for her hands, holding them in his, he leaned closer. "Every time we make love, I go back in time a day. If we make love once, I go back one day. If we make love twice, I go back two days. The days accrue...add up. Once I go back to that day, I stay there. If we make love again, I go even further back."

Her mouth fell open and she shook her head. "How is that...how could that possibly...."

"Don't try to reason it, you'll go crazy." He knew that from experience.

"So...why? How?" she asked.

"Mick?" he asked.

She frowned and nodded. "If we keep making love...." She hesitated. He knew what was coming, but he let her say it. "We'll go back to the day I died." Her voice was barely a whisper.

Nodding, he gave her hands a squeeze. "I think so."

She started pacing in front of the sofa, and then stopped to face him. "How many times, Rob? How many times would we need to make love to take me back to that day?"

"Fifty-one."

She stared at the floor, pensive, first folding her arms on her chest, and then unfolding them. Then she looked at him, smiled. "I'm game if you are."

He laughed and stood, bringing her into a close embrace, reveling in her softness. "Oh, I'm game all right." Fifty-one times might sound like a lot, but just knowing the times might be finite was enough to scare him. How could she mean this much to him, more than any other being on earth had ever meant? And now he might lose her.

"Rob?"

"Yes?" he said, trying to hide his fears and smiling down at her.

"Do you think we'll be able to stop my death?"

೦೮

Angie's heart pounded. Time travel. Time travel tied to the number of times they made love. Tears welled in her eyes. "Do you think we'll be able to prevent it?" She couldn't say the word "suicide" out loud.

He pressed his lips to her forehead and planted a kiss. "Yes."

He calmed her fears, kept her mind off the bad stuff. Helped her make it through the night. "I want to be with my daughter."

"I know."

He crossed the room to the kitchen counter, retrieved a folder. "I hired the PI again today."

Angie frowned. *Please not more bad news about Chloe.* But wait...if Rob went back in time, Chloe was safe on this day.

"On a hunch, I had Tuck check out J.B. Trueth, the cop who lives on this floor. He's very interested in you and your case." Rob fished out a photo. "Recognize him?"

Angie stared at the picture of a bald-headed guy who looked big enough to bust down a solid door. She took the picture, walked across the room with it, staring into the guy's gaze. He did look familiar. Her mind flashed to an image of him, sweaty...a white towel draped behind his neck as he sat and lifted something.

"Yeah...my memory is reaching for something. He's sweaty, a towel around his neck...."

"The workout room? He said he used to talk to you there."

The memory vanished and Angie stared at the photo again. "I'm not sure." She glanced at Rob. "Why is he important?"

"I'm not sure if he is." Tuck had hacked into J.B.'s financial records but couldn't find out where chunks of money, in addition to his salary, originated. "I found out today that he has quite a bit of money in the bank, and his account has been getting bigger and bigger in the months since your death."

ᏮᎶ

Rob closed his eyes against reality. They'd made love again. Twice. She rested, her head on his arm, and he stared at her in the flickering candlelight.

He needed to make the most of his time with her. He steeled himself against the cold truth that each time they made love, he was likely one day closer to losing her forever. He hadn't found traces of a boyfriend in her former life yet, only an ex-husband, but he knew better than to believe in a happy ending for himself. No such thing.

With a resigned sigh, he pulled her next to him, holding her close, still breathless from their lovemaking. Her chest heaved from the exertion, and sweat, cooled by the night air dampened both of their bodies.

"Wow." He leaned across the flannel sheets to kiss her, but stopped when he caught her frowning. "What?" he asked, stroking her jawline.

She had such a strong face. Beautiful and stubborn. She cleared her throat, a nervous gesture, and then looked past him, as if afraid to meet his eyes. "I was just wondering...."

He waited for her to finish.

She raked a hand through her blonde hair, inhaled, and then blew out her breath hard. "Does making love to me feel like a duty, now? Are you just doing this to help me go back to that day?"

He planted a kiss on her head, leaned close, and whispered. "Making love to you could never be a chore." He swallowed against the emotion that rose inside of him. He'd been burned by Sheila, learned to keep his feelings inside. But Angie deserved to know how he felt.

"I love being with you. Holding you makes me feel...." His voice trailed away because he couldn't find the words to explain his feelings.

The corners of her lips rose in a small smile. "Makes you feel complete?"

He nodded. "You're special, Angie. I can't describe to you how different I feel when I'm around you."

Understanding dawned and her eyes widened. "Did someone hurt you, Rob?"

He shook his head. "It's all in the past. It doesn't matter now."

"You're helping me. I'm a good listener and I'm here for you, too."

He shrugged. May as well be honest. "My ex-girlfriend Sheila left me for my ex-best friend Jonathan."

"That sucks," she said, pressing her full weight over him and wiggling against his groin.

Thoughts of Sheila and Jonathan flew out of his mind.

Raising his hips, he nudged his growing arousal against her. "In answer to your earlier question, does it feel like I think it's my duty to make love to you?" He kissed her scalp. "Or does it feel like I need you so badly it hurts?"

She lifted her head, smiled at him and then closed her eyes. Leaning over him, she let her golden hair curtain the sides of her face, falling against his chest. "Rob?"

"Yeah," he moved closer.

"I want to try to leave the apartment again. Maybe I'm stronger now that we've made love, maybe that's what our making love is all about."

"No." Why would she even suggest it? They were on their way to discovering things, possibly traveling back to the day of her death.

"But we don't know that. We can't just wait around for fate. What if I'm okay to leave the apartment now? What if we're supposed to get her? Maybe I'm not supposed to go back to the day I died. Maybe my task as her mother is to save her before she does those things in the picture or spends all of the money she inherited?"

She gripped his hands. "I can't sit around and wait for Fate to take care of Chloe. Time to be a parent. I have to do what I obviously didn't do during my time on earth. What's the worst that could happen? If it gets as scary as last time, Mick will save me."

"No," Rob said. "Isn't going to happen."

"I appreciate what you've done for me, Rob. But a mother has to follow her instincts, and something tells me to go get her now. Whether you like it or not, I'm going."

Stall. If he couldn't stop her, maybe he could stall her. "Tomorrow," he said, reaching for her. "Go tomorrow, and I'll help you."

C03

Rob woke the next morning to an empty bed and boxes all around his condominium. "Wow," he said aloud, knuckling his eyes. He shouldn't be surprised. He knew things would be different when he woke because they'd made love five times last night. He hadn't been that energetic since he was seventeen. His muscles ached when he moved and he yawned, physically worn from their lovemaking.

He had gone back to his first week living in the apartment. Stacked boxes lined the walls and cluttered the center of the living room. He guessed after two more days, he'd be back in his old apartment fifteen miles away in the suburbs.

He froze in his spot in the center of the living room.

He had to stay here. This was their place. What would happen when they went back two more days? The apartment wouldn't be his. He forced himself to inhale, reminded his muscles to relax. He'd stalled her last night, kept her from leaving, and now what could he do? Hold onto the possibility that she would somehow be affected by the time change, and forget that she'd wanted to leave the apartment in search of Chloe?

With a glance at the checkered sofa where he first met Angie, he vowed to get to this apartment by nightfall every night. He'd break in if he had to.

Standing, he stared at the stacked cardboard clutter. He wouldn't bother unpacking anything except the stuff he needed for himself and Angie. Bed sheets, toiletries and a few kitchen items.

He skulked back to his bedroom and picked up his cell phone from the nightstand to check the time. An hour to shower, get dressed, and walk to his office. Then he'd go through a day he'd experienced two weeks ago.

C03

Rob checked the clock on his office wall. Only eight more hours until he'd see Angie. Re-doing tax forms he'd already completed took less time than he thought. He tossed his pencil on the desk and leaned back in his chair. At this rate, they'd be back to the day that had changed Angie's life in a few weeks.

Which meant he had to figure out a way to keep her from leaving the apartment.

His mind drifted to her daughter. If he rescued her himself, he would keep Angie from trying to leave. But changing the past could put Chloe on a worse track. He had no way of knowing. Shit, he had no way of knowing whether their lovemaking was going to change his and Angie's life for the worse, either.

Going back in time was a gift, and he would try his absolute best not to take advantage of it. They had to be going back in time for one reason—to help Angie. So as tempting as it was to play the lottery or invest in stock, he would resist.

He eyed his closed office door and typed "physics, time travel" into his computer's search engine. He believed in numbers and science. Maybe there would be something to help him.

For two hours he scanned information about paradoxes, Einstein's equations and physics. His head pounded with scientific evidence for and against the idea of time travel. Plenty of research over the years supported the idea, so he switched tactics and concentrated on more recent discussions of time travel. Blogs.

All of them suggested time travel was possible and cautioned against changing the past.

At four o'clock, he stacked a tall pile of tax returns on his secretary's desk and left, claiming he had a headache. It wasn't a lie, and nobody would complain, given he'd finished the work of two days in one.

Once outside, he breathed in the crisp March air and his headache lessened. His cell phone rang. Jonathan. Rob didn't love Sheila, never had. But Jonathan and Sheila had something. Kind of like Angie and Rob having something.

For the first time in two months, he answered Jonathan's call.

"Hey Jonathan."

"Uh.... Oh! Rob. I was expecting to leave a voicemail." Jonathan's voice shook a little.

"Yeah. Sorry about that. Want to meet for coffee tomorrow? You, me, and Sheila?" Hell, tomorrow for Jonathan could be three days in the past for Rob if he and Angie made love tonight, but at least for this day, Jonathan and Sheila would feel better. In fact, if he continued to go back in time, Rob would call one of them every day. Ease the pain, if only for the day.

They made arrangements to meet, and Rob headed home.

He'd made his decision. He knew how to stop Angie. It wasn't right, it wasn't anywhere near the right thing to do.

But it would keep her safe.

Chapter Twelve

*A*ngie stood by the window in Rob's apartment, mesmerized by the dozens of candles he'd lit. She sighed and wondered if all ghosts could breathe. In spite of her situation and lack of an earthly body, in this apartment, she felt real.

Footsteps from behind the bedroom door made her smile. Her grin widened when he opened the door, his mid-section wrapped only in a towel.

He arched his back and squinted into the candlelit, cardboard-box filled room. "Angie?"

"Hey." She moved toward him, aching to splay her hands on his chest. "What's with the boxes?"

"I went back in time again. Back to the time when I just moved in."

Part of her wanted to yank off the towel and another wanted to hand him a robe. "You went back as many times as we made love?"

He nodded.

She blinked several times to clear her head. So much to process. All day she'd been focusing on her need to get to Chloe.

"Why don't you get dressed? We need to talk." She smiled up at him.

Even in the flickering candlelight, she caught something like fear flash in his eyes. Had he heard those words before and experienced something bad?

He nodded and turned back into his room and she threaded past stacks of boxes with candles on top and sat on the sofa.

The bedroom door clicked shut. Rob stood in front of it and smiled, clad only in a pair of jeans. He crossed the room and pulled her into his arms.

His embrace warmed her chilled skin like summer heat. He gave her everything. Angie's stomach somersaulted, and she remembered his words last night. He claimed he would die for her.

She closed her eyes, processed the thought. She didn't have specific memories, but guessed that, during her time on earth, she'd never been lucky enough to be with a man as selfless and caring as Rob.

His sorrowful past gave his eyes a haunted tinge. He'd lost people close to him so many times. And no doubt about it, he was falling for her and the feeling was mutual. Unknown territory. They had no guarantees about what would happen when they went back to the day she died. She could be gone forever. She'd be one more person to leave him after he'd loved them.

She had to make him see how special he was. And she had to do it quickly because her time with him could be limited.

"I have to leave tonight, I have to do everything I can to help Chloe. We don't know how I'm supposed to help her, maybe I have to make it through that dark place."

"You don't have to save her, Angie. She's safe. I hired the private investigator again, and Chloe is safely away from the boy who caused her trouble. She's in rehab."

"But if we go back in time again, she'll be out."

"And I'll go back to Tuck, and he'll get her again."

Angie bit the inside of her cheek. It helped her think better. Was Chloe safe without her?

ଔ

The candles in the bedroom flickered and cast shadows on the unadorned beige walls. Rob rested his head on the pillow and stared at Angie as she slept. He wanted to stay awake all night to spend time with her. Guilt ripped at his gut. He'd lied. To keep her safe.

He had done it for her sake, right?

Her blonde curls splayed over her bare shoulder and her perfect lips looked irresistible. He leaned closer and kissed her.

Nuzzling into the pillow against him, she kissed his neck and sighed. "Rob?"

"Hmmm. Yes?" He rested his arm at her waist, so content from her loving that he could hardly move.

She lifted her head, looked at him. Her face was only a shadow in the dim light, but her slow smile warmed his body.

"I thought having sex with you would just be a physical thing—a way to go back to...." her voice drifted off to a whisper and she laid her palm over his heart.

He nodded, brought his hand up to cradle the back of her head and caressed her neck. "I know."

"And I thought it would be a nice distraction from my confusing situation if we made love."

He frowned, wondering what bothered her.

She smiled a crooked smile. "But when I'm with you, I forget about everything except how you make me feel. Safe and needed." She swallowed hard and tears glistened in the corners of her eyes. He hated to be the cause of those tears, but they weren't from sorrow this time.

The covers rustled as he propped himself up on one elbow to face her. He cupped her chin in the palm of his hand. "I want you to be happy more than anything else in this world."

He blinked several times to keep his emotions in check. If only she knew what he'd done.

"You make me very happy," she said.

He leaned close, kissed her lips gently, tasting her. Slowly, he eased away. "I love being with you."

He traced the outline of her full lips with his thumb, hesitating by the sensitive corner before kissing a line of kisses down her chin and her neck.

"Rob," she breathed.

"Uh huh?" he whispered, distracted by his growing need as she squirmed under him.

"I love you."

CC

The sun tinged the sky pink and Rob blinked at the early morning light. He shivered and squinted at the bare window. With a groan, he realized his chills and body aches came from the cold hardwood floor. No bed. No blankets. He'd gone back to the day before he'd moved into the apartment.

He sat and glanced around the empty room. His gaze settled on the only items in the room: his jeans and T-shirt, wadded up like a pillow. He stood, tugged the shirt over his head and stepped into his pants, relieved to find his cell phone, keys and wallet still in the pocket. Without them, he would have to buy a new phone every day. And if his wallet didn't travel back....he shuddered to think how his options, and Angie's options, would be limited.

He took a deep breath, strode to the bedroom door, and twisted the handle to open it before he could hesitate.

He knew this day would come, but the harsh reality of it made him shudder.

The door creaked open. The apartment was completely empty. Freshly-painted walls and polished hardwood floors. Just like it had been the day he'd looked at it when it was available for rent.

He'd expected this, but worry snaked in his gut. He hadn't known the emptiness would cut so deeply. All of his belongings. He guessed they were boxed in his old apartment now.

They'd had sex two times last night. Two incredible times.

With a shake of his head, he glanced around the apartment once more. He'd be back. Every night he'd come back. If he had to buy a sleeping bag every day just to spend the night in comfort with Angie, he'd do it.

He ran a hand through his hair. He was a schmuck. Sleeping with her after he lied. But Chloe was safe. She'd been safe in a time that was now the future, so she was safe now. It made sense.

Dressed in jeans and a T-shirt, he opened the front door a crack and stuck out his head to look up and down the hallway. He'd have to take the steps. He wasn't supposed to live here yet. And a Baltimore cop lived on this floor.

He hurried down the eight flights, rounded the corner to the first floor, and then froze in his spot. If the apartment wasn't his anymore, would his key still work? Had management changed the locks before he moved in?

He raced back up the steps, taking them two at a time. He panted as he opened the stairwell door and checked the hall for observers. After finding the hall empty, he ran to the door and dug his hand in his pocket.

He pulled out the key ring, squinting to find the apartment key. His heart dipped and sweat broke out on his brows. He glanced at his pin-striped pants, pressed shirt and parka. No key, different clothes.

Ↄ

Rob shook his head to ward off the uneasy feeling time travel gave him, and slid the envelope of cash across the desk to Tuck, the private detective. "And remember, I need the results before the end of office hours today." He shifted forward in his chair and stood.

Tuck nodded and stuck out a beefy hand to shake. "For this kind of cash, I can have the information to you yesterday."

Rob raised a brow at the irony of the man's words. "And the professional lock-pick kit, too?"

Tuck nodded.

Rob stepped outside into the blowing snowflakes. The weathermen had predicted merely a coating, but there would be six inches on the ground by evening. Rob pulled his parka hood up and decided the icy flakes that flew at his face would help him wake up if he walked to work.

He smiled as he entered his office, nodding good morning to the staff. With a loud exhale, he closed his office door behind him and leaned against it. Taking a seat in his soft brown leather desk chair, he sped through his work, pressed the print button on his computer and waited for the machine to spit out ten pages of tax forms.

Going back in time had another very attractive advantage—nights were longer this time of year. He'd experience the long, dark nights of February all over again. Angie could come to him earlier and they could spend more time together.

He fired through his files without bothering to stop for lunch. He took a break once to talk with Tuck when he called.

"I got everything you asked for," Tuck said.

Rob leaned back in his chair, watching his office door in case anyone walked in. "Thanks. Good job. I'll be there before five."

He hung up, dialed Sheila's number as he'd been doing every day. They repeated a version of the same conversation, although it was new to her every time.

"Hi Sheila."

"Rob! I've been trying to get in contact with you," Sheila said.

"I know. I got your messages, and I don't want you and Jonathan to be apart. We were friends, Sheila. Nothing more. You know that and I know that. Now we all three need to be friends."

"I'd like that. Want to meet for lunch or coffee tomorrow?" she asked.

"Love to."

He left the office at four o'clock. Many accountants took their work home this time of year. He waved good-bye to the receptionist, and she gave him a woeful look as she spotted his full briefcase.

"Don't work too hard," she said.

He grimaced and lifted his heavy burden. "Don't worry. I won't."

Five minutes later, Tuck opened the office door and gestured toward the billowing snow outside. "Hell of a storm, huh?"

Rob brushed cold flakes off his parka and nodded. He didn't want small talk, he wanted information. Then he wanted to be with Angie.

Tuck must have sensed his get-down-to-business attitude because he scurried back to his desk. He yanked open a drawer in his desk and pulled out a thin metal box. "You sure you're not doing anything criminal?"

Rob nodded. "You have my word."

"Yeah, well, I wouldn't do this for most people, but you have a squeaky-clean record, and I trust my gut about you, too." Tuck opened the lock-pick set and then gave him a five-minute demonstration on how to use it.

After practicing on Tuck's office door, Rob thanked the P.I., handed him another envelope of cash and then stepped back out into the snow.

Three more stops, and then he'd be home to see Angie. Keeping his head down so the blowing flakes didn't blind him, he walked two more blocks to the department store where he picked up a sleeping bag, toiletries, candles and a lighter.

He hailed a cab, read Chloe's address to the driver, and, leaving his purchases in the cab, rang the bell at Chloe and Vinnie's to check on Angie's daughter, who had no memory of him from before. Vinnie chased him away, as usual, but still, Rob had seen her, and she was fine. Eased his guilt just a little.

After one last stop to pick up a meatball sub, a bottle of wine and a corkscrew, he headed back to the apartment building.

On the sidewalk outside of the apartment building, he glanced up at the obstructed setting sun, urging it to set faster to get Angie in his arms. Yet, the lie still burned in his chest.

He took a deep breath and walked into the lobby of his former—or his future—apartment building, and took the stairs again, being careful to slow his pace in hopes that he blended with the tenants around him. Breathing hard from the eight-flight climb, he stopped near the last set of steps and froze in place.

He'd have to go to his old apartment. The one he'd shared with Sheila. All his clothes were there. But not tonight.

He tucked the thought away and started climbing again. That was one day he would rather not relive—the day he found out Sheila and Jonathan were in love.

But it didn't hurt so much to think about it anymore. Being with Angie, seeing what real love was, made him understand he had never been in love with Sheila.

One step at a time. He'd wait and see how tonight went, see where in time he'd end up. Lifting his chin and straightening his shoulders, he put thoughts of his old apartment and the issues it presented off until tomorrow. Or yesterday. Or whatever the hell day it would be when he woke up.

He shook his head and chuckled. If he didn't take this situation with a sense of humor, he'd end up in the loony bin for sure. Then he sobered, remembering his lie.

At the top of the stairs, he opened the door a crack. Nobody in the hallway. He scurried out, heart hammering against his ribs. He propped the two shopping bags against the hallway wall and pulled the lock-pick set from his coat.

Sweat broke out along his brow and dripped down his back. For someone who had never broken the law before, he'd have to break it on a daily basis in the coming weeks in order to see Angie. He couldn't help but think how Jonathan would get a kick out of seeing his straight-laced buddy breaking and entering.

Tuck's lesson paid off. Rob finessed the tool in the lock and it clicked. With another glance to the left and right, he opened the door, pulled the bags inside, and shut the door behind him.

He didn't know if it was a good or a bad thing that he'd been able to get into the building so easily.

He dropped the bags by the door and glanced around the empty rooms. The apartment had been vacant for the months between Angie's death and his move-in day, so he didn't have to worry about another tenant. But J.B. Trueth lived nearby. He'd be the type to question someone he'd never seen in the building.

Rob shook the thought away, shrugged out of his parka, and bent to spread the sleeping bag on the floor in the living room. No black-and-white checked sofa any more.

He unloaded a few candles, lit them and then stood. How long could he hold this lie inside, and what would Angie do if she found out he'd kept the truth from her?

Chapter Thirteen

"*W*ow, this place is really empty," Angie said, walking around the almost-dark apartment, feeling her way as Rob unpacked a bag and lit more candles.

He nodded, focusing on the candles.

Why wouldn't he look at her? She moved to stand beside him in the kitchen. "Is something wrong? What happened today, Rob?"

He smiled, but it was the type of smile that only lasted for a few seconds. "Just tired, that's all. Look what I got." He opened another paper bag and brought out a small tin box. "Lock pick set."

"Oh. Yeah. I guess your key wouldn't work if you didn't live here. I didn't think of that." She sidled next to him and cupped his chin, forcing him to look at her.

"How's Chloe?"

He clasped her hand in his, and kissed her fingers. Something was wrong. Terror built inside her.

"I went back in time again," he said.

"Yes. But Chloe. How's Chloe? You saw her, you got her into rehab again?"

"Chloe is fine. I'm sorry. I just didn't sleep much last night."

She blew out a breath. Thank God. She nuzzled against him. He wrapped his arms around her, and her worries lessened. His heart beat fast, and he swallowed hard. Something was wrong.

He kissed the top of her head.

"You're sure Chloe is fine?" she asked, glancing up, willing his gaze to meet hers. In the dim candlelight, his eyes flickered away from hers. She slid her hands to his biceps and held him close. "Rob. You took Chloe to rehab again today, right?"

He turned toward the sink, filled a paper cup. With his head and shoulders slumped, he emptied it again.

"I checked on her. She's at the house with Vinnie. I never took her to rehab, I only told you that to keep you from risking your life—your unlife—whatever the fuck it is that makes you the woman I love."

Angie gasped and fought for breath, watching the liquid he poured circle down the drain like her hopes and dreams for her daughter's safety. Chloe wasn't fine, wasn't safely in rehab. And never had been.

Rob swirled and faced her. "Chloe was alive in the beginning, she's alive now. We know she is, for the simple fact that she exists in the future. I've checked on her today and every day. I can't let you risk yourself again, Angie. I love you."

Fire burned in her gut. Love? She didn't know how things worked in his world, but in her world, lies equaled the opposite of love. Rob didn't love her.

Adrenaline coursed through her ghostly veins, making her feel more human, more alive than she'd ever felt. The lights flickered on, blinding her for a few seconds before flickering off. The air around her charged with energy greater than the charge she felt when she changed worlds.

She spun around, raced out of the kitchen, and out the apartment's front door.

03

The electricity—everything from the overhead lights, to the television and stovetop flickered on and off in a crazy voltage symphony. Rob backed against the counter and stared through the flashing lights for a split second, and then raced to the door. Flung it open.

The power flashed on, lights blinding him as he stared out into the hallway.

"Angie!" he called.

His words echoed back to him in the empty, carpeted corridor. He ran up and down the hall, and then checked the stairwell. Empty.

With slow, somber steps, he climbed to the top stair and sat, elbows on knees, head in his hands. He never should have lied to her. Feeling like a man twice his age, he dragged himself back to the apartment with heavy, plodding steps. How could his world have turned so completely around, given him a taste of what goodness felt like again, and then snatched it from him?

He loved Angie, wanted to protect her, just like he should have protected Mick from harm. But just like with his brother's accident, he failed. He hadn't saved her. And maybe because of his mistake, he lost the best thing in his life.

CB

The inky blackness surrounded Angie again. Bolts of fear sprinted down her spine and cold air, such cold air, prickled at her skin like icicles.

"Chloe? Mick?" What made her try this again?

A deep growl echoed in the distance. She pulled in a long, deep breath to calm herself. Maybe she could make it through the darkness to the other side. Like the hallway outside the apartment, when she reached the end, she'd be in the stairwell where she'd be able to leave the building and get to Chloe. Take care of her like only a mother could take care of her child and keep her safe.

A deep groan again, and she forced herself forward, running a hand along a cold, smooth wall. A few more feet.

A gush of cold air whipped past her face. Something behind her grabbed at her nightgown. She swallowed a scream and ran forward, full force, as she forgot the wall, and forgot one step at a time. Blind rage sent her flying forward, feet barely touching the floor, trying to get to the end of the void.

Another slice of cold air cut toward her, like the cold blade of a knife on the back of her neck. Her feet left the ground, or the ground ended, and she spiraled through the darkness, nothing underneath.

Her stomach pitched. She flailed her arms and legs, met only with cold air.

A flash of warmth touched her skin, yanked her hard, and she crashed to a grassy, sunlit area. Her other world.

Mick. Where was Mick?

Still shivering, in spite of the intense sun, she glanced around. Catching movement on the other side of the stream, she sat. "Mick?" she hollered.

He was on one knee, bent over as if catching his breath. His head lowered as if disappointed in her.

"Mick, I'm sorry. I didn't know what to do."

He glanced at her, his hand over his heart, panting to catch his breath, and signaled with his index finger. *Wait.*

Oh God. What had she done? Saving her had taken a toll on him. She was so stupid to try it. So crazy to think that she'd be stronger this time. Rob was right. Chloe was alive in the future, she would survive the rest of the days it took to get back in time to her. She'd tried it her way, out of desperation. But now she needed to do it Rob's way. If he'd have her.

Mick stood, hands on knees, still gasping for breath. He pointed to his throat several times, and shook his head. Then he crossed his arms, resting his hands on his shoulders and rocked, as if in a lovers' embrace.

He didn't have a voice. He must have used every ounce of whatever kind of energy he possessed to save her again. And the lovers' embrace. What was he telling her?

Rob. Making love with Rob was the answer.

"I'll go back to him, Mick. I'm so sorry you had to come for me. I won't do it again." Tears stung her eyes. He was just a kid, really, a kid who risked everything for her once. And how did she repay him? By asking him to do it again.

He smiled, hugged his arms on his shoulders again, nodded, turned and walked away.

ભ

Rob woke on the floor of his apartment to the smell of fresh paint. Fully dressed, he stretched and groaned because his joints ached from lying on the cold hardwood floor.

He scanned the bare and basic room devoid of furniture and pictures. For the first time, in a while, he'd gone forward in time.

Angie!

Bolting to a seated position, he scanned the room, hoping for a sign that she'd come back during the night. Nothing.

Maybe she was gone forever.

What did he do now? If he left the apartment, it would be the day after whatever the hell day yesterday was.

Without Angie, he didn't care. He wished there was furniture in the place, if only to give him something to hurl at the wall. He needed to vent, to let out his anger.

"I'm beyond help. Not even the psychiatric ward could fix me," he said aloud to the empty apartment.

With a sigh, he yanked his polo shirt over his head and lay down on it, using half of it as a pillow, and the other half to cover his face. He didn't understand how this time travel worked, and when he tried to think about it logically, circuits in his brain went haywire, but he appreciated the fact that somehow, some way his clothes traveled back in time with him even when they weren't on him. Maybe it had something to do with the things his body touched, and maybe that was why Angie traveled back in time with him.

Would he ever have answers to all the questions that raced through his mind? Would he ever see her again after lying to her?

He'd stay, waiting for her, praying for her to return. She never appeared during the day, and neither of them understood why, but he would wait all day and all night. He fished Mick's worry stone out of his pocket, rubbed it. The stone made him believe in ghosts again, maybe it could bring Angie back. So he could explain.

Hours later, he staggered to the bathroom. He flicked the switch, amazed when the light fixture over the sink turned on. He guessed the building supervisor kept the electricity on so it would appeal to potential renters.

Splashing water on his face pulled him awake.

He shook his head and stared at his reflection. So he was in love with a ghost.

"Yeah, that would be my luck." He had finally found true love and it was with someone he couldn't be sure would stay in his life for much longer.

Even if she came back to him, if his calculations were correct—and they'd damn well better be because if he was off by one day their whole plan would fall apart—they had thirty-one more days before they were back to the day Angie died. At the rate they made love some nights, that could be less than a week.

"Angie," he whispered, his breath fogging the mirror, reminding him that she might disappear like mist when the time was right.

He closed his eyes and gripped the sides of the sink. He couldn't afford to feel sorry for himself; his focus had to be on Angie. Feelings could wait. Yes, he loved her. In a way he'd never felt before. He had thought that he loved Sheila, but he hadn't known what real love was back then. Those days seemed like forever ago.

Is that what Sheila and Jonathan had together? Was their love real? He owed them huge apologies. If their feelings were anything close to Rob's for Angie, he understood why they had to be together.

"It doesn't make me a sap to understand that they belong together, it makes me...." His thoughts drifted, searching for the right word.

"Compassionate."

He whipped around, heart slamming in his chest.

"Who said that?" he hollered, leaning out of the bathroom and searching the empty bedroom.

But he knew that voice. Angie's voice.

This couldn't be a dream, couldn't be his stressed-out mind playing tricks on him.

Could it?

He stood tall and lifted his chin. He had a choice. He could trust his gut and ignore the little voice in his brain, or he could catch a cab to Sheppard Pratt Psychiatric Hospital and check himself in as a patient.

"My gut wins," he said. "I'm staying."

In the living room, the lack of furniture and wall decorations tugged at his heart. Someone was erasing Angie's existence.

"I love the smell of fresh paint."

Rob whirled around. Angie stood by the window, beautiful as ever, gazing at him. Her smiling face, slim shoulders, cascading blonde curls and shapely body made him want her every time he saw her...heck, every time he thought of her.

He raced across the room with open arms, his gut clenching. She was okay. She had come back.

"I'm so sorry."

"Shhhh," he whispered in her hair. "Thank God you're okay."

"I wasn't okay," she murmured against his chest, squeezing her arms around him, pressing against him. "Mick saved me again, but it took a lot from him."

Rob stilled, and Angie moved her hands to his waist, putting some distance between them, but holding tight. "He's okay. But I think he loses energy or something when he goes into the dark place. I don't know what made me think I could make it through that to Chloe. But I had to try. I'm sorry. I love you, Rob. I love you and I trust you."

He nodded. "I love you too, Angie, and I don't blame you. I shouldn't have lied to you. I couldn't bear the thought of losing you. Selfish."

Angie ran her hands up and down his bare back. "Not selfish. Practical. And doing the best you can with the information we have."

She stood on her toes and kissed his lips, and then parted his mouth with her silky tongue, exploring, bringing all parts of him to attention. Yes, she was beautiful and enticing, but his desire for her was so strong it surpassed anything human. She obviously felt it too. Divine intervention that created strong sexual urges.

He kissed her earlobe, trailed a line of kisses down her neck, and tasted the soft spot at the indent of her shoulder. "You know," he whispered. "It's an earthly tradition to have makeup sex after a fight. I hear it's pretty good."

ᘓ

Angie leaned against her favorite weeping willow, lost in her thoughts. They were getting close, so close, to the day of her death. After her voyage into the Dark World, she let go of her need to hurry. It wasn't easy, not at all, especially in this world where she couldn't do a darn thing about getting to Chloe.

This world brought her closer to Chloe in memory, though. In these peaceful surroundings her mind quieted enough to let her past out of the part of her mind that locked it tight. Little by little, as if her psyche couldn't handle it all at once, the memories seeped out. The more time she spent in Rob's world, the more times they made love, the more memories escaped to her conscious mind.

She smiled and ran her hand along a nearby delicate willow limb that bent, but didn't break. Kind of like her daughter, Angie hoped.

She breathed in the clean air, and closed her eyes. An image formed of Chloe in a long, peach dress, with sparkly earrings and an updo that made her look like a princess. A handsome boy beside her placed a bouquet on her wrist.

Angie smiled at the memory, and then the handsome boy morphed into a skinny, pock-faced man with greasy hair and a syringe in his hand, holding it to Chloe's neck while blood trickled from her jugular vein. Angie gasped, opened her eyes, and then raced away from the weeping willow.

Please Rob, bring me back there soon, bring me back to help my baby.

Chapter Fourteen

The days passed in a blur as Rob relived time. He sped through tax returns and made appointments with Tuck for information and lock-pick sets, and spent long, wonderful nights with Angie.

Now the day had come to make the final arrangements. Once he got back to the apartment, he wouldn't be leaving until Angie was back to the day she died.

He could be facing possible death. Even with Tuck's help, they hadn't been able to find out where Chloe's life insurance money had gone. If Angie's death wasn't a suicide, he could die along with her.

Which meant he had to make things right with Sheila and Jonathan. Today. If he lived long enough to go back in time, he'd have to make things right all over again, because they would go back to an earlier date, but at least he set his affairs in order if his life was at risk.

Rob strummed his fingers on the pine kitchen table at his old apartment in Baltimore county. The one he'd shared with Sheila before she'd returned from a business trip and told him she was leaving him. They'd ended the fight as enemies.

Rob expelled a shaky breath, wondering if he was doing the right thing.

No hard feelings. Not this time, anyway. It wouldn't be the knock-down, drag-out fight like they'd ended things the first time around. He wanted Jonathan to be his best friend again. He missed watching football games with him, going out for beers after a tough day.

And Sheila. Well, she deserved to be with someone she loved.

Smiling, he traced the grain patterns on the table, circling the smooth wood. The action reminded him of how he'd glided his hands across Angie's smooth curves the last time they'd made love.

He froze as a key turned in the apartment door.

Sheila walked in, prettier than he remembered—her shoulder-length red hair shined in the hall light, and her quick smile reminded him why they'd been friends.

"Hey, you're home," she said, dropping her purse on the hall table and parking her wheeled suitcase by the door. She didn't approach him, didn't kiss him. The realization jolted him—things had been going downhill for them for a while. How long had they gone without making love? Sure, things were bound to cool off after a year-long relationship, but had they appreciated each other? Had he appreciated her?

Gone were the days when they'd greet each other with a tight embrace and a long lip-lock. And he hadn't even noticed. They'd settled into complacency. His fault...maybe hers a little too, but he could have been more attentive, more aware. Instead, he'd been busy climbing the ladder at work, neglecting his relationship.

"Hey yourself." He smiled at her, genuinely missing her smile, her friendly face. "Welcome back. How was Tucson?"

"Good." She stared at him. "In between meetings, I had a lot of time to think about...well, about other things."

"Yeah? Let's sit for a minute. I got your favorite wine," he said, gesturing to the bottle and two glasses on the table. He wanted to talk before she told him she planned to leave.

She crossed her arms. "You bought my favorite wine?"

He raked a hand through his hair and stood. He deserved her suspicion. Closing the distance between them, he draped his arm around her shoulder and walked her to the table.

"What's going on, Rob? Is something wrong?" she asked as he guided her to a chair and poured merlot into a glass. Her brows folded into a frown.

He shook his head, and then took a seat across from her. May as well dive right in. "Sheila, I'm not being fair to you."

She held her wine in the air, frozen. "What?"

Rob took a deep breath and leaned toward her. He took the glass from her hand and placed it on the table. Reaching for both her hands, he noticed how cold they were...and that they shook.

"I've been working a lot of hours, trying to get ahead." He gave her a squeeze and then let go, leaning back in his chair. Picking up his wine, he took a long drink. Then he leaned forward on his elbows and stared into her dark green eyes. "You deserve more. I'm hardly ever here, I focus too much on work."

Tears started to gather in the corners of her eyes. "It's okay. I know you're—"

He had to rip off the band-aid. "Sheila, I want you to be happy, and I don't think I'm the man to make you happy."

Her expression changed. Relief, he was sure of it, and tears freely ran from her overflowing eyes.

He grabbed her hands again, and she didn't try to pull away. She loved him, he realized that now. She cared about him as a friend and had never meant to hurt him. But her relaxed face told him more than words. Relief that she didn't have to keep living a lie.

But there was something else, too. Concern. For him?

"I-I don't know what to say." She leaned toward him.

"You don't have to say a thing."

"Rob...." She sniffed through the tears, and bit her shaking bottom lip. "Are you going to be okay?"

"I'll miss you. But I know we wouldn't be happy if we forced things. You deserve better, Sheila." He could lose two women he cared about within the span of a few hours...or days in real time. His gut reeled at the thought of being alone again.

Sheila paused and a tear dripped down her cheek. "We had some good times."

He nodded, freed her hands and passed her glass to her. "Some people talk about staying friends." He raised his glass, and she lifted hers. "We'll actually do it."

She smiled through her tears.

For over an hour, they talked—talked like they hadn't talked in months. He helped her pack some things after she insisted she would be the one to leave—she wanted to stay with her sister.

He loaded the last of her four suitcases into the back of her compact car and then closed the trunk. Wiping his hands on the sides of his jeans, he turned to face Sheila. Her lips quivered and she blinked back tears.

He held out his arms and she fell against him. "We'll see each other soon. It's 'so long,' not good-bye."

She sniffed, let out a shaky breath and then stood back to look at him. She brushed a hand several times at the top of his dress shirt. "You got dusty when you dug those suitcases out for me."

He chuckled.

She pulled him in for another hug and then, without another glance, hurried to the driver's side, pulled open the door, and got in.

He moved to the sidewalk and waved, and she rolled down the passenger window. "So long. See you soon." She drove away.

So different from the way they'd parted originally. This time, there was no slamming door, or hurtful words, and no cutting the ties forever. This time, he knew he'd see her again.

He pulled out his cell and dialed Jonathan's number.

"What up, Rob?"

"Uh, I thought you should know that Sheila and I broke up."

"What?" Jonathan's voice raised two octaves. Surprise, Rob thought. But he heard something else too. Hope?

Rob held the phone tight, choosing his words carefully. "It's all good. She's moving in with her sister for now. We parted as friends."

"Yeah, well, that's good."

"I know she'll want to start dating soon. I probably will, too. You know, now that I think about it, you and Sheila have a lot in common. You both love golf, for one thing."

Jonathan coughed, a spasm of choking sounds. "Er, I—"

"I'm just saying that if it happens, we can make sure it isn't weird for all of us."

"Uh, yeah."

"Gotta go. See you soon."

Rob hung up and fist-pumped the air.

Now, time to get a gun.

Thirty minutes later, Rob stuffed his hands in his dress pants' pockets to keep from fidgeting. Tuck's late-model Civic smelled of old coffee and a recently-smoked cigar. The private eye hadn't even blinked when Rob had made his request for a gun this morning. Tuck told him to return after four o'clock for his purchase, and they'd head to a field behind a local deserted warehouse to practice.

Now Rob had second thoughts. He prayed he wouldn't have to use the weapon. But tonight could be the night that he and Angie traveled back to the day of her death, and he needed to be prepared for anything.

He and Angie had made love an average of five times each night. He should be sore, or at least tired. But instead he wanted more than ever to be with her and get finished with this part of his day.

He'd learned so much about her in the short time he'd known her. She wouldn't have taken her own life. If she hadn't, who had killed her and staged it to look like suicide? J.B. the cop? Chloe on drugs? Vinnie the punk? A stranger?

Tuck put the car in park and set the brake. "Okay, there are your targets. I set 'em up earlier." He pointed to a spot by a row of bare trees with a shallow stream that ran behind them.

"I appreciate this, Tuck," Rob said, opening his door.

"Yep. A man needs to be able to protect himself, that's what I say. Just don't tell anyone where you got this gun. Since the serial number is filed off, it's illegal. But it's only temporary until we get you a registered one, properly. If you really feel your life is in danger tonight, I'm not going to keep you from arming yourself." Tuck frowned at him.

"I know. Thanks. And you have my word I won't use it unless I have to defend myself or a loved one."

Tuck nodded and exited the car. Rob took a deep breath and followed the private detective across the frozen brown grass.

"Okay," Tuck said, raising his brows and studying Rob for a few seconds. "Here's the gun." He pulled a two-shot derringer out of a paper bag and passed it over, handle-first.

The weight of the gun surprised Rob and his hands shook. He pictured himself aiming it at a human being and firing it, and his gut twisted with real pain. *Get a hold of yourself,* he ordered.

"First things first. You need to learn about gun safety. Then you learn to shoot." Tuck squinted at him as if doubtful he was up for the task. "You ready?"

Straightening his shoulders, Rob nodded. "I'm ready." For Angie's sake, he had to be. As long as he didn't leave the apartment between the time he got there and the day she'd died, the gun would stay in his pants. In his heart, he knew he could use it.

ങ

Later, as night fell, Rob stood at the apartment window, glancing at the city lights but not seeing them. Wet snow whipped against the glass and stuck. His mind whirled with possible scenarios for the way this night would end. His hands shook and his heart beat so fast he was afraid he'd pass out.

"They sure cleaned this place out quickly after your death." He looked around at the bare walls beyond the granite countertop to the empty kitchen cupboards. Would someone walk in on them any minute? Painters, or cleaners who'd originally been there after Angie died?

"Come on," Angie said, patting the quilt on the floor. "Worrying isn't going to change anything."

Forcing himself to take a deep breath, he crossed the room wearing only his boxers and sat next to her. "I know. I can't stop shaking."

She smiled and her eyes sparkled in the light flaring from the small fire he'd made. But her lips quivered enough to show her nervousness. "You know, drinking all that coffee probably made you jittery."

With a glance toward the kitchen at the almost-empty, now-cold coffee pot, he nodded. "I know. I have to stay awake tonight. I can't fall asleep." They'd already made love once since she'd arrived at dusk. Three more times and they'd be back to the day of her death.

He had to stay awake and be ready. Jittery or not, he'd be sucking down cold coffee tonight.

Angie moved closer and he wrapped an arm around her shoulder and then buried his nose in her hair. How much longer would he get to breathe in the scent of her? After this night, she might be a distant memory for him. And after this night, she might not remember him at all.

She maneuvered to her knees and moved in front of him, cupping his face with her hands, forcing him to meet her gaze in the dim light of the candles and fireplace.

Her green eyes swam with tears. He wanted to close his eyes and turn away because it hurt too much to see her unhappy.

"Rob, I love you." She bit her bottom lip between her teeth. "Whatever happens, please remember that."

He nodded, unable to speak because emotion clogged his throat. What had he done to deserve her? How could he live without her?

"It doesn't have to be tonight."

"Yes it does, Angie. You want to be with Chloe, and she needs you."

She shifted onto his lap and he cradled her, lost himself in the feel of her soft skin against his. In spite of his concerns, his body responded to hers. Unbelievable how strong their attraction for each other was. As if a greater power deemed them irresistible to one another.

"I want you to know something, Rob."

"Mmmm. What's that?" He kissed her collarbone, needing to feel her skin, breathe her scent. He had to take in as much of her as possible in these next few hours.

Placing two fingers under his chin, she lifted his face until he met her gaze. "You're really good in the sack."

He chuckled. Her words and compassion eased his concerns enough that he could let go. If only for a little while.

"No, I mean it. We never really talked about past relationships—not that I would remember any of mine—but, Rob...." She kissed his lips. "I would have remembered any man as special as you, I know I would...." She shook her head slowly. "But nobody compares to you. You're caring, compassionate, and a really good lover."

"Thanks." The word wasn't adequate, but he didn't think there was a word written in the English language that would convey how her words made him feel. All his adult life, he'd struggled to let go of his inhibitions, to get over the fear that being spontaneous and past the idea that letting himself enjoy life would bring him and those around him pain. But he'd taken a chance with Angie. Believed in what she was. And now, freedom filled his lungs like fresh mountain air.

She kissed him again and then snuggled in, wiggling herself against him seductively. "I'm just saying we don't have to do it three more times tonight if you don't want to."

As if he could ever resist her? With a deep inhale—to smell as much of her citrus scent as possible—to remember her by it if all else was lost—he kissed the top of her head. "I think it's time we take you back to that day."

For all of her confidence and surety, Angie's eyes widened. "I'm not sure what to do."

He pulled her closer, gathered her in his arms, and kissed her. "Then we won't let our minds be any part of the decision. Our bodies will rule the night."

"I like that," she whispered.

"I love you," he whispered back, lowering his mouth to hers. He drank in the sweet candy taste of her and yielded to the power of her kiss.

Drawing her closer, he lowered his lips to her jawline.

She groaned and clasped her arms tighter around his neck and rested her head on his shoulder.

Rob tugged the blanket around her, wrapping both of them in its softness.

"You found this in the closet?" she asked, stroking the edge of it.

"Um huh." When he'd awoken this morning, he was on a rug in the sparse bedroom—but suddenly there was a dresser and a few things in the closet, linens in the bathroom. Someone had taken anything of value—most of the furniture, clothes, food from the kitchen. Like a vulture...someone had cleaned her out just four days after her death.

As if reading his thoughts, she shivered. "Anything else of interest in the closet?"

He didn't blame her for being afraid. After all, the closer she got to the truth, the closer she got to her death. "Want to go look?"

She stared into the flames, took a long, deep breath, and then turned to face him. "Yes."

Wrapping herself in the blanket, she followed him toward the bedroom. He carried his pants—didn't bother putting the rest of his clothes on—and led the way to her barren bedroom.

After lighting the two candles on the high dresser, he stood against the wall, allowing her full access.

His heart ached for her as she opened and closed drawers, finding almost nothing—just a battered old T-shirt, a few pair of socks. Holding the shirt against her chest, she closed her eyes, probably trying to picture what it felt like to wear it, who she had been, or even if it had belonged to her. Then she sniffed it, again with her eyes closed as if trying to pull out a memory.

She shook her head and then glanced at him. "Nothing." Her head hung low in the candlelit room as she folded the shirt neatly, placed it in the drawer. "If I wore it, I don't remember." With a sigh, she walked to the double-doored closet, placed her hands on both knobs and then hesitated.

With a glance back at him, she took a deep breath and yanked, opening both doors at once. The spacious closet held only a few pair of sneakers and a robe.

Dropping the blanket, she reached for the robe, wrapped herself in the white fabric. "Ahh." She turned toward him and smiled. "This might not bring back a memory, but it feels so good."

She crossed the room, slid her arms up and over his chest and shoulders, and laid her head against his naked chest before resting her hands behind his neck. His pulse soared and he wondered if his body would ever be immune to hers.

"Take me away from here. Take my mind off this awful stuff, this empty apartment." She held onto him, but leaned around him to blow out the candles. "It's as if everything about me is erased."

"No," he said, his voice a whisper in her ear in the near darkness. "You are too special to be erased." He guided his hands across her buttocks, rested them in the small of her back, letting her feel his arousal. "Let me show you how special you are."

ଔ

"Oh...holy...cow, Rob," Angie whispered, panting. "I think I forgot my name. You shook it right out of me." She smiled, hoping her stab at humor calmed him as they lay on the rug in front of the fire.

She'd felt his stress all night. Not that she wasn't worried, too. Her life—or chance at living again—could be destroyed or changed by morning.

Her stomach twisted with pain when she wondered if she'd forget him, worried he'd forget her. She ached to see her daughter again, to help her get out from the dark place drugs took her, but she wanted Rob to be happy, too.

It saddened her to think she might go on with a life she once had but without him.

She'd leaned on him enough these past weeks, taken so much from him. And she needed to give back. More than sex, more than love. She needed to give him a chance for complete happiness. How could she say it without hurting him, though?

Rob kissed her mouth, slowly, gently, and it stirred her ghostly heart. She blinked back her tears. If he saw her sadness, he'd worry about her. He shifted to lie beside her, and she snuggled close.

"I love you, Angie."

"Oh, Rob. I love you." She kissed his neck.

Earlier, she'd been honest when she told him how special he was, how cherished he made her feel. She'd meant it as a thank you, a good-bye. But she'd also meant for her words to assure him that any girl would be lucky to have him. She couldn't say it, couldn't express it in a way that would make it sound as if she were pushing him into another woman's arms should something happen when they went back to the day of her death.

He'd told her about his ex-girlfriend, and she'd sensed the hurt he was trying to avoid. What if she hurt him? She had to be prepared. If something happened to her—if she still died, or if she didn't remember him alive, he had to know many women would be happy to be with him, and that love was worth taking a chance on. Not predictable like tax return forms.

She ran a hand over his chest, hoarding the sensation of his skin.

"Two more times," he whispered.

"Two more," she echoed.

"You cold?" he asked, pulling the quilt over them.

Her entire body shook. Terror built within her. What would they face in the morning? How could she go on without him? For a moment, she considered never making love to Rob again in order to stay together forever. But there was too much at stake.

Instead of burdening him with her worries, she simply nodded.

ଔ

With Angie's head snuggled against his chest, Rob reached in the darkness to find his khakis, just to make sure they were there. The candles had burned out over an hour ago. They'd made love two more times. Daylight would bring the truth. And possibly an end to his time with her.

He swallowed hard and willed himself to stay strong. He'd find a way to keep Angie from killing herself and then the rest would be up to fate.

But until dawn, he would stay awake, cherish the way her soft curves relaxed against him, the way her blonde curls spread across her face. He'd study her and keep her in his heart and memory if he couldn't keep her for real.

And he'd stay awake to prepare for her attempt at her life.

"Wonder if I need another pot of coffee," he mumbled aloud. He rubbed Angie's back, content in the knowledge that the two pots he'd made on the camping stove earlier would keep him from falling asleep.

Reaching for his pants again, he pulled them closer, felt for the gun. Although if she attempted to overdose, he had no idea what good a gun would be. They'd both checked the apartment thoroughly for pills, finding none.

Rob kissed her head when she moaned in her sleep, and switched positions, wrapping her arms around his waist.

Yes, he'd stay up all night. Between the coffee and the adrenaline that coursed through his veins, he'd probably be awake for days to come.

Smiling, he savored Angie's hand on his skin. She'd wanted to stay up all night, too. But he wouldn't wake her. The rhythmic in and out of her relaxed breathing brought him comfort.

They'd said their good-bye without words as they'd loved each other tenderly, passionately and let themselves linger on the feeling of holding one another.

Because it could be their last time.

Chapter Fifteen

*R*ob woke with a start when the pink hue of morning sun splayed through the parted curtains into the bedroom.

He bolted up in a four-poster bed and glanced at the white dresser, cheerful purple curtains, and clothing-covered chair in the corner. Angie's clothes.

Shit! He'd fallen asleep.

Shit. Where were his pants?

Shit. Shit. Shit. Where was Angie? How the hell had he fallen asleep after all that coffee?

Twisting, he threw his legs over the side of the bed and almost tripped over his khakis on the floor. Grabbing them, he thrust his hand in the pocket, searching for the gun. His shaking fingers touched the cold metal of the two-shot derringer, and he blew out a relieved breath.

His pulse raced as he stood at the bedroom door and listened. The derringer shook in his hand and he swallowed hard to regain control of his muscles. His heart pounded so hard his whole body vibrated.

Laughter in the next room. A deep, hacking baritone that sent chills down Rob's spine.

He eased the bedroom door open a slit, turning the knob slowly to keep silent. Crouching, he glanced through the crack in the door.

He hadn't realized he'd been holding his breath until he expelled a gush of air when he spotted Angie.

She was alive—missing that glow or slight translucence she'd had around her skin at night—she stood in the middle of the living room. Even her white nightgown looked different, more in-focus somehow. He wanted to scream at her, or run out to hold her in his arms.

He opened the door wider, trying to find the source of the sick laughter.

"Fine," Angie slurred. "W-whatever it t-takes." Her words dragged as if she had a swollen tongue or....

Rob shook from the top of his head to his feet. He leaned his head against the doorframe to get a better view. Three glasses of orange juice sat on the coffee table. Could they have been laced with drugs?

Slowly, he opened the door wide enough to fit his head out. Chloe's skinny boyfriend held a syringe to Chloe's neck. He wore clear latex gloves. Rob squeezed his eyes shut to ward off the pain in his chest. The pain Angie must be feeling that her daughter's life was in danger.

Chloe slumped against the wall with bloodshot eyes, lethargic to the point where drool spilled out of a corner of her mouth. He couldn't tell if she was part of the problem or not.

Taking a steadying breath, he raised the gun to test his line of vision. No way could he get off a shot at the kid. Chloe's body blocked the way. Even if he just tried to hurt him, not kill him—although seeing the effect his actions had on Angie made Rob want to kill the kid—he wouldn't be able to. He was no sharpshooter.

He lowered the gun, kept it at his side.

The kid laughed again.

Angie took a step forward, staggered and held onto a chair for balance. "Please...let Chloe g-go."

Her daughter giggled, suddenly more alert. "Momma...gimme," she slurred, laughed, and then her laugh turned into a coughing fit.

Angie grabbed the back of a chair with both hands and lowered her head. Rob wanted desperately to lunge forward, pull her into his arms. She swayed and he was afraid she'd pass out any second.

"Uh, uh. Stay right there," Vinnie said, pressing the syringe against Chloe's neck, pressing into her flesh.

Angie looked up and lifted a hand in front of her in a motion of temporary surrender. She wobbled, and Rob thought for sure she'd fall. Her eyelids fluttered closed, and she panted for breath.

Rob brought the gun up again, hoping for a better shot. Nothing. Now not only was Chloe in the way, Angie was between him and the daughter, too.

"M-money?" she said, her voice a whisper as her shaking hands held the chair. "If you need m-money, I'll get you some."

Vinnie smiled an ugly smile. "Yeah, sure I'll take your money. Soon as you take your pills like a good girl."

"What?" Angie asked, her body straightening as if a bolt of adrenaline pulsed through her.

Atta girl, Angie. Fight to stay awake. Give me a chance....

The kid tossed a bottle of pills toward her. They rolled to a stop by her bare feet. Angie's eyes widened. "Are you crazy? Why would I—"

Vinnie yanked Chloe's head back further. "I got a vein here, and enough of this shit to kill her. You or her, momma." Chloe moaned and her eyes rolled back in her head. If she was lucky, she'd pass out. Rob clenched his jaw, barely able to keep his temper in check.

He had never in his life had to work so hard at staying still. He wanted to jump out, fling Angie and Chloe out of the way, and shoot to kill. But Chloe would be dead before he reached the punk. Rob had to wait for the perfect moment. He could only pray his hesitation wouldn't get Chloe killed.

"Pick up the pills," the kid ordered.

"No, don't touch it," Rob whispered. He didn't want her anywhere near the drugs.

But he watched in horror as Angie held onto the chair and bent toward the pill container. In her shaky hand, the chair crashed to the floor, and she staggered, regained her balance and then bent to pick up the pills. Her entire body shook and her eyes rolled back. Then she dropped, limp, to the hardwood floor with a thud.

Vinnie scrambled to her, leaving Chloe in a heap against the wall. Within seconds, he took the lid off the bottle, poured the pills into Angie's mouth.

Angie spit the pills in his face, kicked out with her bare feet, catching the kid in the gut. He stumbled backward.

Rob opened the door.

"Mommy?" The listless girl suddenly blinked, focused.

"Shut up!" Vinnie regained his balance, pointed the syringe at the weak girl.

"Don't touch her," Angie screamed.

The kid lurched toward Chloe.

Rob aimed his gun. "Stop right there or I'll shoot."

Vinnie's head snapped toward Rob, his attention diverted just long enough for Chloe to gain strength, balance herself.

Eyes blaring, the punk aimed his body at Rob and ran toward him, syringe outstretched.

This guy cannot be reasoned with. Rob took two steps back. Angie's would-be killer laughed and lunged at him. Rob squeezed the trigger. A deafening roar filled the room.

The bullet grazed Vinnie's shoulder. He staggered back and his eyes flew open in pain or disbelief as he clutched at his bleeding shoulder. Rob stepped forward on shaking legs, steadied his right hand with his left as Tuck had taught him. He trained the gun on the kid and readied himself to fire again.

Chloe pulled away from the wall, moved quickly but awkwardly with outstretched arms toward her mother. "Mommy."

Vinnie glanced at the gun and then reached for Chloe, grabbing her long hair as she stumbled away from him. But she yanked harder and pulled out of his grasp.

The punk dove for Chloe, but Angie kicked the overturned chair toward him, and he tripped on it. Rob aimed the gun, ready to fire again, but Angie's daughter was too close to Vinnie.

As if in slow motion, the kid's eyes widened and he writhed, flailing his arms to catch himself before he hit the floor. He stumbled, couldn't find footing. He fell on his own syringe, piercing his chest with a sickening crunch.

Rob's hands shook, but he held the gun as steady as he could. Vinnie's mouth dropped open but no sound came out. Keeping the gun trained on the him, Rob glanced at Angie and Chloe, who both lay inert on the floor, then back to the kid.

Vinnie glared at Rob with narrowed, bloodshot eyes. His body convulsed.

"I said don't move. I'll shoot to kill." Rob's heart beat so hard that he could feel it in his neck. He didn't think the kid needed a bullet; he was slowly dying.

Rob steadied his grip on the gun, faced Angie.

She struggled to open her eyes, reached out to lay a hand on her daughter.

"Angie, don't worry, you and Chloe will be fine," he said, stepping toward her.

Vinnie went limp.

It was over.

"Police! Open up."

Banging on the door jolted Rob from his trance. He stumbled on shaking legs, still dazed and holding the gun, to the door, opened it.

"Drop the gun!" J.B. Trueth aimed his gun at Rob. "Toss it over there." He pointed with his head to the corner.

"Thank God you're here, J.B. That kid—"

"Shut up. I said toss the gun."

Rob pitched the gun toward the corner. It clattered and landed against the wall. Of course J.B. wouldn't remember him. They'd never met in the elevator. He was too far back in time.

"Get on the floor! Get on the floor, now. On your knees with hands behind your head," J.B. hollered, keeping his gun on Rob while he shot a glance at Angie.

Rob scrambled to his knees and locked his hands behind his head.

"Now on your stomach with your hands and legs spread out from your body."

Shit. Would he go to jail for manslaughter? Rob obeyed the order.

"Stay put. Angie, is there anyone in these other rooms?" J.B. asked.

"No, it's just the four of us," she said, her voice strained.

Rob stared across the room. He'd shot a kid. His legs shook and chills ran down his back, making him glad for the support of the floorboards.

"I called for backup when I heard the shot," J.B. said, keeping his gun trained on Rob.

Angie pushed herself from the floor on her forearms.

"Don't move," J.B. said.

"J.B., that boy broke into my apartment, hurt me and my

daughter," Angie said.

J.B. glanced at the kid and then over at Rob. "Are you okay?" he asked, directing the question back to her.

"Yes," she said, looking at Rob, a slow smile spreading over her face. "Thanks to him. My daughter needs a paramedic, though."

"I'll put in a call." The officer lowered his weapon and glared at Rob. "Why'd you have a gun?"

Rob held Angie's gaze, captivated by her, in spite of a dead body and a hurt girl in the room. Did Angie know who he was? Did she remember him?

As if on cue, the officer faced Angie and asked, "Who is this man and why did he have a gun?"

Rob held his breath. His head pounded from the tension that had built in the last half hour but that pain dulled in comparison to the reality of his situation. If she didn't know him, he'd probably go to jail. But worse than that, he might have lost Angie.

Suddenly, the apartment grew cooler, and a cloud-like mist formed between Angie and Rob.

His heart hammered. *Mick.* The mist formed into the see-through form of his brother at seventeen. First Mick touched Angie's hand. Rob couldn't see why. Then he turned and smiled, giving a thumbs-up before he vaporized.

Rob's throat clogged with emotion. Mick, looking happy and content, had finally visited him. At the moment he needed him the most.

"Angie, I asked you who this man is and why he has a gun."

Angie opened her hand and stared at her palm.

Rob had no idea what she held.

"He's my boyfriend...Rob." Tears sparkled in her eyes and her voice shook. Her quivering lips turned up at the edges in a small smile.

Rob heaved a sigh. He hadn't dared to hope she would remember him. How on earth had she when their timeline of existence changed?

Angie sat, and then pulled her daughter's head in her lap. With a shudder, she glanced at Vinnie's body on the floor.

"Rob saved our lives." With a smile, she lifted something dark and shiny between her thumb and forefinger. "And I have his brother's worry stone to prove it."

That wasn't Mick's worry stone. Rob's eyes widened and he smiled. The stone Mick had Angie hold in the other world. He'd waited to give it to her until she needed it. That stone was her connection to the other world while she was in this one.

The policeman knelt next to the kid, felt for a pulse again, and then shook his head.

Rob struggled to find mercy in his heart to forgive Vinnie. Not now. Maybe one day, though. Then his eyes met Angie's over Chloe's relaxed and breathing body.

"Thank you, Rob, for giving me another chance at saving my daughter."

She was safe. They could build a life together.

"Okay..." J.B. said, taking out a notepad. "What happened here this morning?"

Epilogue

Two Weeks Later

*A*ngie smiled across the table in the rehab facility as Chloe screwed the lid back on the bright pink nail polish.

"It looks great, don't you think, Rob?" Chloe asked.

Angie wiggled her nails as if to show them off.

"Don't even think about painting mine," he said, tucking his hands in his pockets.

Her daughter laughed, warming Angie's heart in a way she wondered if she'd ever feel again. Two weeks in this place, and Chloe was healthier than she'd been in months. Angie knew about those months now, had all her memories. Sometimes she wished some of the worst ones had stayed tucked away forever.

But no. Those awful times gave her a barometer to contrast this Chloe to the lost one. The bad crowd that seemed so cool at the time. As the counselors here reminded Angie, sometimes addicts had to hit rock bottom before they admitted they needed help.

Once she regained her full memory, she realized that even J.B. Trueth, with his badge and experience, hadn't been able to talk sense into Chloe or scare away Vinnie. Rob suspected him of being part of Angie's suicide, but once the facts came out, turned out J.B. was a hero. Even the most suspicious part—increments of cash in his account—attributed to a relative who owned several rental properties passing away and leaving them to J.B.

And the life insurance money...well, this time around, it wasn't needed. But while they were going back in time, Vinnie had been taking Chloe's cash to start his own drug business.

Thank goodness Angie had the chance to be there when her daughter hit rock bottom, and Rob to stand by her side through the worst of it.

Chloe glanced at the wall clock. "Group meeting time. I'm going to announce that I'm signing up for horticulture classes at community college." She grinned. "Sorry to kick you two out, but...."

Rob smiled back, and the skin around his eyes crinkled. "We can take a hint,".

They stood, and Angie pulled her daughter close for a hug. For so long, Chloe had resisted affection. God, it felt good to hold her.

Chloe glanced at Rob. "Take good care of my mom until I'm home for good, okay?"

"I promise," he said, draping an arm around Angie's shoulders.

Chloe walked away, an unmistakable lilt to her step that hadn't been there for a long time. And in a few days, she'd be graduating from the in-patient program to an outpatient day program. Mick had said Chloe had a purpose, she'd do great things. A purpose so great, someone had interfered with the life...death...Angie had been dealt and had given her a second chance. Why Chloe? Only time would tell.

"I think she's nurse's pet. An inspiration to the other patients here, too." Rob took Angie's hand and they headed for the exit.

Warmth filled her heart and spread through her body. She didn't know she could be this happy. Still, one more question lingered between them. They'd yet to make love, to find out if they'd travel back in time. Since it had only been two weeks, they had no ideas what, if any, negative effects the various changes Rob made in the future, would have. So far, the only snag in their plan was the unregistered gun he had used to defend them. He wouldn't divulge where he got the gun. He couldn't snitch on Tucker. Besides, the private detective had no clue who Rob was now.

Since the gun was used in self-defense, J.B. called in favors and helped convince the D.A. not to press charges.

At the apartment, Angie closed the front door, leaned against it, and crooked a finger at the man who had saved her and her daughter.

He hesitated, but then stepped forward to pull her into his embrace. "Are you sure you want to try this tonight?"

"We can't keep hiding from it. If making love still takes us back, we need to know now." She pressed her hips against him, loving his instant, and undeniable reaction. "I've missed you, too." It was true, she'd missed being with him, but they both admitted the crazy hard-to-satiate need for sex had disappeared. They wanted each other, but not with the strong pull that was almost like a spell cast over them.

"That obvious, eh?" He kissed her full on the mouth, stirring her desire as his hands cupped her bottom, holding her against him. "Bedroom?" he asked, trailing a line of kisses along her neck and sliding his hands inside the waistband of her jeans.

She gripped his shoulders to keep her balance. "How about the sofa?"

He planted a tender kiss on her lips and scooped her into his arms.

"Oh," she whispered, wrapping her arms around his strong neck.

Within seconds, they shed their clothes, with only the lights outside the window illuminating the room as they lay together on the sofa.

His lips fused with hers and he covered her body with his, sending sweet warmth along every inch of her skin. The familiar feel of him took her breath away. She never wanted to go another day without being held by him, touched by him.

"I love you," he whispered, his breath hot on her neck.

"I love you, too."

ଔ

Angie woke with a start. Rob shifted beside her on the sofa. With a down quilt wrapped around them, they shifted to sit.

"I'll take my cell outside the apartment." Rob pulled on his jeans, chest and feet bare, and strode toward the door.

Angie nodded and, like the kids she taught, crossed her fingers and stared at the desktop, her back and muscles rigid with tension. *Please don't be yesterday's date, please don't be yesterday's date.*

Rob opened the door, stepped into the hallway, and pulled his phone from his pocket. When he poked his head back inside, a grin split his face. "We didn't go back in time."

She clasped her hands in front of her face, prayer-like, and smiled. "So we can make love as often as we want?"

"We can be together forever in every way we want."

HAUNTINGS AT INNER HARBOR BOOK 2

ALTERED FREQUENCY

JOYA FIELDS

Chapter One

*M*issy Prescott shoved her key into her apartment doorknob and turned it. *Nope.* Once again, the stubborn old lock didn't open on the first try. Working till midnight had its advantages—no beltway rush-hour traffic and an awesome view of the Baltimore city lights on her drive home, to name a couple—but having to wake up the superintendent at one in the morning wasn't at the top of that list.

She tried the key again. Cool air—a sudden, subtle breeze—surrounded her, and she shivered.

"Jiggle the knob to the left while you turn the key, dear," a woman said.

Missy jumped and whirled around with her heart thundering and keys spiked through her fingers. How many times had her policeman father warned her to be aware of her surroundings? To be ready in an instant to flee or defend herself?

A white-haired woman with bright lipstick stood in the middle of the hallway. Where had she come from? As quiet as the building was, even the carpeted hall floor wouldn't have muffled footsteps that much. Would it?

"Where did you—how—" Missy lowered her hand and stared at the woman, who was dressed in pink sweats and wearing flamingo earrings. She had to be at least ninety. No threat there.

"I'm sorry. Didn't mean to scare you. Tell the super to squirt some WD-40 on it for you. It'll fix it right up." The woman smiled and then tipped her head toward the apartment door across the hall. "Have you met Blake yet?" Her grin grew larger, crinkling even deeper creases around filmy blue eyes.

"Uh, no." After a long day at the radio station and a string of intensely personal—and draining—conversations with her listeners, all Missy wanted was her feather pillow and bed. But a combination of habit and courtesy made her extend a hand. "I'm Missy Prescott. I moved in about a month ago."

The woman ignored Missy's hand and tilted her head. "I know who you are. You and Blake should meet. He's a great guy." Then she winked, walked to a nearby wall, and rested her hand on the red fire alarm.

"Oh my gosh! Don't—"

An ear-piercing siren split the air. Missy covered her ears. The woman disappeared. *Holy shit*. What the hell was going on? The woman had just freaking vanished into thin air. Was Missy's mind playing tricks on her? No. Someone had set off the alarm, so it wasn't her imagination. The high-pitched wailing continued. What was she supposed to do now?

The door across the hall swung open to reveal a bare-chested man. In spite of the screaming alarm, Missy's gaze lingered on his washboard abs before she hurriedly glanced down—gray sweatpants— then upward to take in his messy, dark hair, a chain tattoo on one of his broad shoulders, and stubble around his jaw line. A pair of tennis shoes dangled from one hand and he held a black shirt in the other.

"Fire. Take the steps. Go outside and cross the street. I'll knock on doors to get the others." He dropped the shoes from his hand to the hallway carpeting and stepped into them.

"It's not a fire." Missy blinked away her awe of his physique and the blaring siren took over her world again. "Some old lady just pulled the lever. No fire!" She shouted over the sound, but he must not have heard her.

The man from the apartment across from her—what was his name? Blake. Blake raced up and down the hall, banging on doors and then shuffling people toward the stairwells at either end of the corridor. Sleepy residents in robes and pajamas wandered into the brightly lit hallway, rubbing their eyes.

Blake raced back to her and held a hand to the small of her back, heating her skin through her cotton T-shirt. "Come on...let's move."

Seriously? How many times was she going to have to tell him there wasn't a fire? His warm hand sent her blood rushing through her veins. Or was it building anger?

"Listen to me." She yanked away from him. "There isn't a fire. I saw a woman pull the alarm."

"No fire? False alarm?" He ran a hand through his dark hair. "Need to get to the control room."

Ten minutes later, standing across the street from her new apartment building, she spotted Blake again. The chilly late-night June breeze lifted tufts of his dark hair. Red-and-white fire truck lights bounced off his face. He'd donned the black beater and now stalked toward her. Everything about him screamed control freak. Everything about his build, from his dark hair and eyes, to the way his sweat pants fit loosely over what she imagined after the up-close view of his torso were muscular legs, exuded strength and power.

"You were right. False alarm. Fire captain checked the control room and said the alarm malfunctioned in the eighth-floor zone."

Why was he looking at her with such intensity, and why did she suddenly feel like she needed to defend herself? And where the heck was the old lady who dashed away after she pulled the alarm? *Cripes. This guy doesn't think I pulled the alarm, does he?*

"I'm Blake Decker." He extended his hand, reminding her that the elderly lady had neglected to introduce herself. Maybe because she'd planned to pull the alarm and didn't want Missy to know her name?

"Missy Prescott." She shook his hand, not a bit surprised by his strength.

"How did you know it was a false alarm?" The noise of the fire engine leaving filled the area and halted their conversation for a full minute.

Missy glanced at the apartment building entrance. The residents were filing back into the lobby. She cleared her throat and straightened her back as the big truck disappeared around the corner.

She had nothing to hide. "I saw the person who did it. An elderly woman. White hair, about five feet four inches. She was wearing pink sweats and dangly flamingo earrings. She helped me—"

"Wait. Back up." Blake's eyes widened. "Pink sweats and dangly flamingo earrings?"

What now? Was this woman a known criminal or something? Why did Blake act like he knew her? Hold on...that woman knew him. She'd said something about Blake being a great guy. Could it be his grandmother? Well, for crying out loud, Missy didn't want to get his grandmother in trouble, but she didn't want the blame, either.

"Do you know who the woman is?" Missy stepped closer to him.

Blake stood, wide-eyed, lips pressed together but didn't answer.

"I've only lived here for a little over a month. I've never seen her before." So now Mr. Bossy didn't want to say a word.

Fine. Time for bed. A soft drizzle fell, sending chills down Missy's back. She wanted to crawl into bed and sleep until noon. She'd process this fiasco of a night tomorrow. When her brain was working again.

"Okay, well...nice meeting you." Missy blinked against the raindrops.

Blake stared at her.

Whatever. She stepped into the street, intent on the comforting promise of her apartment. Maybe she'd even snag the superintendent to help with her doorknob, now that he was awake.

At the apartment lobby, Blake caught up with her and grasped her arm. "How could you know that? How could you know what Betty McAllister was wearing?"

⋈

Blake stared at the brown-haired woman in the bright lights of the lobby. The stubborn lift of her chin and her full lips, set in a firm line, made him want to lean closer. How could she know about the pink sweat suit and flamingo earrings? Impossible. Unless....

No! He wouldn't go *there*.

And how was it Missy had lived here for over a month, and he'd never seen her? With her looks, there was no way he would have missed her.

"Who is Betty McAllister, and why are you gripping my arm?" She raised both dark brows, an enticing move that made him stare even harder at her eyes.

He loosened his hold on her arm and gazed at the brown flecks in her hazel eyes. "Oh. Sorry." *Shit.* He'd been so busy stopping her, needing answers, that he'd practically accosted her. "Really sorry." He stuck his hands in the pockets of his sweats as a reminder to keep them to himself.

So she wanted to know who Betty was, huh? Well, he was the cop. He'd do the questioning. "Why were you in the hall at one a.m.?" Party animal? The local downtown bars were full of good-looking women like her. Her casual T-shirt and jeans could be construed as bar attire.

She hiked her purse, looked around the empty lobby, and crossed her arms. "Why do you want to know?"

The corners of his mouth wanted to lift into a smile at her reply, but he got it under control. Too bad she lived across the hall. She'd likely be a load of fun in bed. She lived too close to be his usual one-night stand. He'd have to see her again and again. Tempting as it was, he'd have to keep his hands off this one. "I'm a cop. It's my nature."

Her eyes widened and she jolted. Just a little, but enough for the alarms in his head to go off. Running from the law? On probation? What was her story?

She shrugged. "Not that it's your business, but seeing as we're neighbors and all.... I work until midnight every weeknight."

Waitress? Could be. Lots of diners stayed open till midnight. "Where's work?"

"Wow. You really like to ask questions, don't you? Fine. I'll answer one question for every one question you answer of mine." She stalked across the marble floor of the hundred-plus-year-old lobby toward the elevator. He caught up with her as she stabbed the button.

The doors swished open and they stepped inside. "I'm a deejay on a local radio show," she said.

The doors shut. He pressed the button for the eighth floor. "Which station?"

She wagged her pointer finger at him. "Uh-uh. My turn to ask, your turn to answer. Who is Betty McAllister?"

Lie. His brain screamed for him to keep the full truth under wraps. "She used to live on the eighth floor."

"So why was she here tonight?"

Now it was his turn to wag his finger at her.

She sighed and rolled her eyes as the elevator dinged their arrival.

He stepped to the side to hold the door while she exited. Perfect opportunity to check her out from behind, too. And damn, those faded jeans fit her shapely ass well.

She pulled her keys out of her coat pocket. Nope, he wasn't ready to leave her yet. Why not? Must be the mystery of finding out who she was and what she'd seen.

"So." He moved closer, standing a full six inches taller. "Which station?"

Her gaze searched his for a few seconds and he caught a whiff of her perfume. Something spicy. Like cupcakes. Vanilla. He wanted to see if she tasted as good as she smelled.

She looked him up and down and again his lips quivered. This time, he couldn't hold back a grin. Was this a power contest? She obviously wasn't intimidated by the fact that he was a cop, so he shelved his theory about probation or criminal activity.

"WLOV."

"Huh?" *Damn.* The radio station call letters. He'd been so focused on her delicious smell, he'd forgotten the question.

"That's where I work."

Wait. That voice. That hypnotic, soothing voice. He knew it well. Most of the guys at his precinct listened to her. "You're Misty till Midnight."

She smiled and her whole face lit up. "You've heard of me? You don't seem the lovelorn type."

He frowned. Lovelorn? Hell no. Not him. "I like the music you play, that's all." And her voice. The voice that made him feel like everything would be okay. Like a warm chocolate-chip cookie with a glass of milk. Soothing. Oh, great. He'd just met her and already he'd compared her to a cupcake and cookies and milk. Maybe he needed a sugar fix.

Missy stared at him. "My turn to ask a question."

Fair was fair. He lifted his shoulders and dropped them. "Go ahead."

"I'll ask the same question again because I don't think you told me the whole truth. Who is Betty McAllister?" She jingled her keys.

Well, she might as well know everything. All she'd have to do was power up her computer and do a search and she'd know. "You're asking the wrong question. It's not who *is* Betty McAllister. It's who *was* Betty McAllister."

Chapter Two

"Okay. Who *was* Betty McAllister?" Missy stood in front of her door with her hands on her hips. What difference did it make if the woman still lived there or not? She'd pulled the damn alarm. No malfunction in the system. Missy wanted bed, not drama. And damn it, she'd been so distracted by her neighbor that she'd forgotten to knock on the super's door.

"She lived right here." He nodded at Missy's door.

Missy shrugged and inserted the key in the lock. "That doesn't explain why she set off the alarm. Does she come back often to visit in the middle of the night and wake her old neighbors?" She jiggled the knob, but the key didn't budge.

"Jiggle the knob to the left while you turn the key, dear."

At the memory of the woman's words, Missy froze with her hand on the knob. Slowly, she twisted the knob to the left and the key turned, unhitching the lock with a *click*.

"She lived here. In my apartment?" Missy faced Blake, studying his deep brown eyes, remembering the way he'd looked shirtless. Too bad he was a cop. He'd probably be a lot of fun in the sack with all those muscles and strength. His dark brows would probably furrow with intensity while making love. But she'd never date a cop. Never. The reality of the dangers of that profession had already hit home for her.

He stepped closer as Missy opened her door. "She lived here." He nodded toward the inside of the apartment. "And she died here."

Chills raced up Missy's spine. "In my apartment?" She slid her hand off the door and backed up a step.

"Brain aneurysm."

Someone had died in her apartment? *Creepy.* Was that why she felt like someone had been watching her ever since she'd moved in? Did she have a ghost? "Uh...that sort of invalidates the theory that she was the woman I saw."

"Yeah, maybe you saw a picture of her or something." He stared as if he wanted to add more, but he didn't.

Not really a possibility, but she wasn't exactly prepared to go with the ghost theory. She needed to be alone with her muddled thoughts. Staring at this muscled guy was messing with her brain cells. Especially since she kept picturing him without his shirt. Bare-chested. Taut abs. Or maybe her brain fuzziness could be blamed on the fact that she'd been awake for almost twenty hours now.

"Well, if I see her again, I'll certainly let you know." She took a step toward her open doorway with a renewed sense of eeriness now that she knew someone had died inside. No way she'd let him see her hesitate, though. She didn't need some knight in shining armor to butt into her life. "Nice meeting you, Blake."

"Yeah. Nice meeting you, too." He crossed his arms, but didn't make a move toward his apartment. "I'll have to call in to your show sometime soon."

She faced him and smiled. "That'd be cool. I love to hear from listeners." Her cell rang and she tugged it out of her jeans pocket. "That's my mom. I texted her when we were outside the building. She's checking to be sure I'm home safely. See you soon."

He waved and turned toward his door and Missy entered her apartment, closing the door behind her.

She tapped the phone screen to accept the call. "Hey, Mom."

"Hi, sweetie. You're home now? Door's locked? " Her mom's voice sounded more sing-songy these days. Thank goodness her sister Deborah's wedding planning was keeping Mom so occupied.

Missy turned the two deadbolts on the door. "All locked in and safely home. No fire, just a false alarm."

"Good, good. I won't keep you. Just checking in."

Missy smiled into the phone. A month earlier when she'd moved here, her mother's calls had annoyed her. Yes, she called out of love and concern, but one of the reasons Missy had left California was because she was tired of feeling suffocated. Her mother had good reason to be overprotective—she'd lost her husband fourteen years ago and lost her only son just last year. Both were cops who'd died in the line of duty. Their deaths left her mother fearful for the lives of all of her remaining loved ones.

But, a month later, now that loneliness had crept in—living in a new town with no friends and no real feeling of belonging—Missy treasured the calls from her mom.

"I appreciate it, Mom. How was your day?" Missy yawned, tossed her purse on a red chair, kicked off her boots, and plopped onto the sofa.

"Good. Deborah and I looked at two reception halls. But I'll e-mail you tomorrow about it. I heard that yawn, young lady. You need to get to sleep."

Her mom's teasing tone brought a smile to Missy's lips. Nobody...nobody understood her like her mom. Maybe she'd made the wrong decision by moving so far from home. Being lonely sucked. But it sure was nice to hear her mom so happy.

After signing off, Missy stretched and yawned again. Maybe she'd sleep on the sofa instead of getting up and moving to her bed. *Nah.* As tempting as the thought was, she'd end up with a kink in her neck and a sore back tomorrow.

She padded across the carpeting—making a mental note to buy a coffee table and a few side tables—toward her room.

With heavy lids, she flicked on her bedroom light and then stared at her bed. The pillows were fluffed and arranged near the headboard, and the patchwork quilt was partway turned down. Like a maid had come in. Except she had no maid. And she'd left the bed a rumpled mess that morning. Hadn't she?

Moving closer, her breath caught in her throat. The oversize black T-shirt and yoga pants she'd shed at eight in the morning lay neatly folded at the foot of her bed. Only she'd left them in a heap on the floor. Right?

She rubbed her eyes, trying to focus, and the scent of apple pie made her lift her head and sniff the air. It was the same scent she'd noticed the first time she'd looked at the apartment. The superintendent had told her the lady who lived in this apartment used to bake a lot. 'Course he'd very cannily never mentioned that she'd died here, too.

Missy took three steps down the hallway toward the kitchen. The scent grew fainter. Really? Shouldn't it grow stronger? Moved back inside her room. Apple pie. As if it had just been taken out to cool.

She took a deep breath and blew it out. Could Betty be haunting this place? Ghosts. Missy had never seen one—had tried séances with her friends as a teen and even saw a medium once, all in hopes of contacting her father, seeing him again. But it never worked.

After brushing her teeth, washing her face, and donning the previous night's T-shirt and yoga pants, Missy stood by her bed. Well, if Betty was haunting the apartment, she certainly didn't mean any harm. In fact, it felt pretty good to have the company.

She climbed under the covers and reached to turn out the light. "Good night, Betty. Thanks for making my bed."

Cold air touched her hand as she flicked out the light. Missy laid her head on her pillow with sweet aroma of apple pie tingling her nostrils and the image of a dark-haired, muscled guy from across the hall in her mind.

ℭℨ

A domestic call had turned into an assault on a fellow officer.

Blake slid behind the wheel of his patrol car, waving to two other uniforms as they strode past to their cars. This was his family. These were the guys he could count on. And they could count on him. Within a minute, five patrol cars showed up at the scene downtown. The idiot who'd threatened the safety of that cop was headed to jail. Blake would do everything he could to keep his brothers safe. Not brothers in blood—he'd never had siblings—brothers by the bond of the police force.

A check of the dash clock showed him his shift was nearing the end. An early shift today. He smiled and merged into the evening rush-hour traffic. Meant he could listen to Missy's show from the comfort of his apartment. He'd been so busy today, he hadn't had time to think about the hazel-eyed beauty from across the hall. *What? Oh hell no.* Not staying in on a Friday night. The weather was warm, which meant the Fells Point bars would be full of good-looking women.

The guys would expect him to be there. Just like they'd expect him to leave around midnight with a girl on his arm. A different girl from last weekend, and not the same one he'd be with next weekend.

Suddenly, the thought of small talk and the whole pick-up game made him tired. Maybe he needed a Friday night off from the bar scene. Missy's full, pink lips, along with the way her jeans had hugged her bottom last night, crept into his mind. Why the hell did he think of her when he was figuring out his weekend plans? Damn it to hell, she was a neighbor. Not someone he could easily avoid after some fun in the sack. No matter how hot the body, how pretty the face, he wouldn't get involved with someone who lived across the hall.

The idea of a weekend night at home sounded good. Felt wrong—a single, thirty-year-old guy should be out on the town, right?

Besides, it would give him time to work on his puzzle. A three-thousand-piece jigsaw of the world that had covered his dining room table since he'd moved in to the apartment in early February. Yeah, what did it say about him that he was more excited about putting together a puzzle than going out on the town on a summer night?

With a chuckle, he couldn't help but think Betty would approve of his puzzle plan. Whenever she had caught him escorting a girl from his apartment, she would roll her eyes and tell him he needed to settle down soon.

Two hours later, after an intense gym workout, with a large pepperoni pizza in one hand and a six-pack of beer in the other, he strode to his granite kitchen counter and laid his dinner there. He couldn't really afford this place, but J.B., a former cop who'd inherited enough property from a relative to quit his job, was subleasing the place to Blake for a year while he traveled.

The memory of why he couldn't afford a place like this made him clench his jaw for a few seconds. He couldn't force the hurt of Claire's deception from his mind. She'd stolen his credit cards and racked up the bills, and before he'd noticed and been able to report it, she'd stolen his identity, too.

Yeah. One-night stands beat relationships any day of the week.

He hauled the six-pack to the fridge, but stopped as he opened the door. Apple pie. He smiled and took a deep inhale. This wasn't the first time he'd smelled the sweet aroma that reminded him of Betty. They'd become fast friends after he'd moved in. She missed Stanley, her husband who'd passed a few months earlier, and Blake had felt protective of her. He'd check on her often, knowing elderly people who lived alone needed looking after, and often took her trash out on Sunday nights. She'd always repay him with an apple pie.

The other day, he could have sworn he smelled pie after he walked into the room to find a pile of change on a nearby table. Coins he had no memory of leaving there. Coins that had likely come from between the sofa cushions. Just when he'd needed some extra cash for the soda machine, too.

Blake slid out a slice of pizza and leaned over the open box to take a bite. What did these unexplained events mean? His mind teased him again and again with the idea of a ghost. Betty's ghost. But common sense told him otherwise. He'd never seen a ghost in his life. Didn't believe in them. Not even in this hundred-year-old building.

Yet last night, when Missy had mentioned seeing an elderly woman in pink sweats and flamingo earrings—the very outfit Betty had been wearing when he'd found her dead on her apartment floor six weeks ago—he'd almost believed it was possible.

He took another bite of the gooey pizza, and stared at the jigsaw puzzle. *Nah.* Ghosts didn't exist except in movies. But the woman with the golden radio voice existed. Damn right, she did. And what was with that funny jolt she'd done when he told her he was a cop? He needed to run a background check using Maryland Case Search tomorrow to make sure his new neighbor wasn't hiding something.

But for now....

He crossed the room, flipped on the high-quality stereo J.B. had left behind, and tuned it to WLOV. Some love song was playing, but at least it was a classic love song. Not one of those techno songs that blasted at the downtown bars every weekend.

With a cold beer in his hand, he settled at the table, ready to take on the world. His puzzle of the world, anyway. He snapped a few outside pieces into place, hopeful he'd have the perimeter done by the time he went to bed. Probably only needed another ten pieces or so to reach that goal, but finding them in the mix of jumbled pieces would be the challenge.

The song ended, and Missy's sultry voice filled the room. Sitting back in his chair, Blake lifted the remote and turned up the volume. He glanced out the double windows at the night sky that was partially lit by the Inner Harbor lights, even this high up.

The only light he'd bothered to turn on was one in the kitchen. The rest of the apartment was shrouded in darkness, making him feel alone in the room with Missy.

She took a call from a listener whose girlfriend of two years had just walked out on him. With a soft, whispery tone, she consoled the guy and then played the song he requested. Music filled the room again, and Blake lifted the beer to his lips and glanced back at the puzzle.

The perimeter pieces were neatly pinned into place. All of them.

Chapter Three

"*S*o...Betty. Would you like a glass of merlot?" Missy smiled as she poured wine into a glass at her kitchen counter. No response. Not even a whiff of apple pie. Maybe the ghost was haunting this place, maybe not. But company was company, and the idea of someone, anyone, keeping her company these days was comforting.

She and Diane—another deejay from a different station in her building—were getting to be friends, but after years of hanging out with her siblings and the people she'd grown up around, Missy couldn't help but miss the good old days back home.

She rolled her neck to get the kinks out. All night, she'd rushed around the studio, taping listeners who called in dedication requests, playing songs, and editing the parts that played on air. She had another hour of work to do before she'd call it a night. She remembered her daily blogs for next week. If she wrote some of them tonight, she'd have less to do this weekend and next week. Between blogging and social networking, the station kept her busy at home as well as at the studio.

With a sigh, she powered on her laptop and took a seat on the padded maple kitchen chair she'd bought at the secondhand shop. Taking a sip of wine, she leaned back to think. What could she write about this time? Hot, sexy men? A vision of Blake as he looked when he opened his door last night filled her mind.

Damn. She needed to stop thinking of him that way. "Not dating a cop. Not getting even remotely involved with *anyone* in a dangerous profession. Ever." Her words echoed around the kitchen. The hurt squeezed her gut to this day. Losing her brother Jeff—who had only been twenty-four—hurt in a way she knew would never heal. She'd missed him every day since that awful night when he'd been shot during a routine traffic stop.

Scooting closer to the table, she stared at her laptop screen. *Focus on work.* Staying busy would keep the painful thoughts from taking root in her mind. A blog about how love songs can heal heartache. *Yeah. That'll be good.*

She positioned her hands on the keyboard and started to type. Suddenly, the lights went out, the refrigerator stopped running, and the apartment went completely quiet. *Damn these old places and their ancient electrical wiring.* At least her cell phone and laptop were completely charged.

With a shrug, she felt her way to the kitchen drawer where she kept her lighter. Good thing she was a candle freak. A dozen candles perched atop various tables, and she lit them all. The room flickered with a pleasant ambiance. *Hey, maybe this will make for better writing conditions.*

Smiling, she sat at the table again. Her smile turned to a frown. *What on earth?* The laptop battery—which had registered full only moments earlier—now blinked empty. Ten seconds later, the computer shut itself down.

Three knocks sounded on her door. She jolted, accidentally smacking her wine glass with her hand.

ය

Something crashed inside Missy's apartment and Blake put his ear against the door. What was going on in there? His cop-trained mind instantly flew to worst-case scenarios—an intruder, a serial killer....

His thoughts made him want to bust down the door to get to her, but common sense prevailed and he pounded harder instead. "Missy. It's Blake from across the hall. You okay?"

He'd only wanted to check on her. She'd just moved in, so she might not even have a flashlight. At least that's what he told himself.

Now, in the hallway lit by dim emergency lights, glancing at his hand that held the extra flashlight, he wondered if he wasn't making excuses to see her. *No. Not me. And certainly doing anything more than being neighborly with her.*

Two locks clicked on her door and she opened it. His mouth went dry. With candles flickering behind her, he almost heard a chorus of angels. Her brown hair hung loose past her shoulders and tight black yoga pants made him want to twirl her around so he could check out her ass. She wore a loose black T-shirt. Casual beauty.

"Hey." She tilted her head. "Power's out."

He cleared his throat. "Yeah. Thought I'd check to make sure you had a flashlight, but looks like you've got the lighting under control."

She smiled and he stared at her sexy lips. What would they taste like? *Get a grip. Too complicated to get involved with her.*

"I tend to overdo the whole candle thing a bit."

"Hey, if it keeps you from tripping over chairs in the dark, it's a good thing." He shrugged.

"Very nice of you to think of me. I have a flashlight stashed in about every room, though. You know...being from California and that whole earthquake-preparedness thing." She checked over her shoulder and for the first time it hit him that she might have company.

"Well, okay. If you ever need a spare flashlight then...." He tapped the light against his palm, suddenly wanting to get the hell out of an awkward situation.

"Thanks. I appreciate you checking on me."

The scent of apple pie drifted past his nose.

Missy opened the door wider and moved toward him. "Do you smell that?"

Play dumb. Turn and leave. Avoid the awkward moment when you have to explain you think ghosts might exist.

"Smell what?" he asked, shifting his stance. He wasn't a good liar and hated dancing around the truth.

She sighed and her shoulders slumped. "Oh, never mind. I guess it's just me."

No way. He couldn't let her feel alone. "Apple pie."

Her head snapped up. "Yes!"

He sniffed the air. "Damn, she made the best apple pies."

Missy stepped to the side. "The closer you get to the kitchen, the more intense the aroma. Last night, the smell was strongest in the bedroom. Come in, smell it."

No. Stay right here. Being alone with this woman in a candlelit room was just asking for trouble. He moved inside and she shut the door behind them. After setting the flashlight on a table, he followed her heart-shaped ass toward the kitchen.

"Be careful. I spilled some wine by the table and there might be glass—" She froze by the counter, staring at a small wooden kitchen table with a computer on top. "No way."

"What?" When her eyes widened, Blake instinctively moved his hand to the spot on his hip where his holstered weapon usually perched. He carried no gun tonight, though. Just delivering a flashlight.

"The mess...it's gone." She turned to stare at him. "I knocked over my wine. There was wine and shattered glass...." Shaking her head, she moved a hand to cover her mouth and glanced from the clean floor to his face.

His puzzle. Her mess cleaned up. Apple pie.... He didn't believe in ghosts. Never saw one in his life. But damned if this didn't have the earmarks of Betty coming back to keep an eye on them.

"Is this apartment haunted?" Missy thrust her hands on her hips and lifted her chin.

The scent of apple pie grew stronger. A burst of cool air moved past him and all the candle flames blew out at the same time. The hairs on the back of his neck stood.

Missy gasped.

The room was pitch-black. No moonlight, no lights from the city refracting through the window. Flashlight. He needed to get back to that flashlight. He took a step toward what he thought might be her front door and crashed into her.

Moving his hands to her waist to steady her, he willed his body to calm. Touching her sent off crazy signals to his body, and all he wanted to do was pull her closer. His hands itched to travel from her small waist to the curve of her hips. He swallowed hard and kept his hands in somewhat safe territory, but the reality of it was that no place on her body would ever be safe for him. Like nobody he'd ever held before, this woman—her body, her sassy attitude—called out to him. Like fire on gasoline.

Her body shook and his protective instincts kicked in. Carefully, willfully, he moved his hands to her upper arms. Nothing sexual about that, right? "It's okay. I don't know if this is place is haunted or not. I can tell you one thing, though. If it's Betty, you couldn't have a nicer ghost."

She expelled a sigh, and he leaned closer, beckoned by the fruity scent of her long hair. He wanted to bury his nose in it, work a line of kisses down her jaw to the crook of her neck....

"Would you think I was a wuss if I laid my head on you for half a minute?"

Her body shook, and he pulled her closer to rest against his chest. His instant hard-on left no doubt she could tell his body's reaction.

"Not a wuss. Strange situation we have here." *Concentrate on the idea of a ghost, not her body pressing near yours.* He ran a hand up and down her back over her soft T-shirt. No bra. Great.

His erection grew and he shifted his hips away from her, guarding her from his libido.

"I've never seen a ghost."

She moved her hands to his arms and he closed his eyes and swallowed hard. Every touch sent fireworks through his body. But he couldn't give into it. Not with somebody like her. He could already tell she was the relationship sort, and he wanted nothing to do with that.

"Me either."

Missy cleared her throat and pulled off him. He missed her heat instantly. "Okay. Better now. Thanks. Let's find that flash—"

Cold hands gripped his shoulders and shoved him forward with so much force he crashed into Missy and they both tumbled to the floor. Midair, he clutched her, flipping his body so he'd take the brunt of the fall.

They landed on the hardwood floorboards near the kitchen table and his breath whooshed out.

"Sorry. I...shit. I don't know what happened." He panted for breath. With his legs spread, and her body lying atop his, there was no doubt she could feel his desire for her.

Her breath came in short pants, and the smell of wine danced across his nostrils. He didn't think. Didn't plan. Simply cupped the back of her head with his hand and brought her mouth to his.

Those full lips he'd been fantasizing about softened against his mouth, uniting them. With a moan, she parted his lips with her tongue and he moved a hand to her back, pressing her small body against his, needing to feel her.

His mind whirled with passion as he worked his hand up the soft skin of her back. She arched against him and the world spun. He drank in the taste of her—wine combined with an undertone of sweetness. Everything, from her smile to her feisty attitude and her cute, little body, called out to him.

Alarms rang in his head, warning him of the dangers of getting involved with her. He could stop now, and they could remain friends. Maybe. But if he went any further, there'd be no turning back, no way to stop the freight train that could take them into dangerous territory known for him as relationship chaos.

He couldn't do that. Not her. Too nice. Too kind. Not his type at all.

But when she shifted, allowing room for his hands to slide inside the front of her shirt, he silenced the warning bells and skimmed along her tight stomach, past her rib cage, and cupped her breasts.

She groaned and her silken tongue explored his mouth, going deeper, dancing with his. He ran a thumb over her nipples and arched her head back, exposing her neck to him. With small flicks, he lapped and kissed the base of her neck.

The lights flickered on and he froze—his hands in her shirt, her lower body pressed against his. Missy's hair curtained the sides of her face and she squeezed her eyes shut, and then opened them, staring down at him.

"This is crazy," she whispered. Her pink lips were swollen from their kissing and he wanted nothing more than to flip her over, finish what they'd started. She climbed off, panting for breath, and sat beside him.

Which crazy was she talking about—the fact that a ghost was haunting her apartment, or the way her pushy neighbor had practically attacked her on her kitchen floor?

Chapter Four

𝘔issy smiled and handed the autographed WLOV bumper sticker to the middle-aged couple in front of her at the grand opening of the Inner Harbor bookstore. Her first personal appearance as Misty from *Misty till Midnight*. "Thanks very much for coming out today. Great to meet you."

The woman grinned and her green eyes sparkled in the sunlight that filtered through the glass storefront. "Honey, you're such a pleasure to listen to. Keep up the great work. I knit while listening to your show every night, and Frank here plays with his Civil War toys."

The man gave his wife a mock angry look. "Not toys. Collector pieces." He turned to Missy. "Welcome to Baltimore, Misty. Love your show."

Missy laughed at the couple. They made her a little homesick because they had that sort of relationship where friendly, teasing banter was considered conversation. Just like her parents once had.

With a wave, the couple strolled away from the promotions table where Missy hawked free bumper stickers, contest entry forms, and a few other station goodies. Luckily, there'd been a steady stream of avid listeners all afternoon. Lucky, because the action kept her mind off last night's heated action.

After a glance around the store, she stared out the window at the tourists and locals strolling around the Inner Harbor promenade. The boats and ships docked at the harbor rocked in a gentle wake and the sun sparkled off the water while hordes of people walked along the paved brick pathways. She huffed out a breath that sent her bangs flying and took a seat near the giveaway table.

Sliding her fingertips to her lips—swollen from Blake's stubble and demanding lips—her stomach did a funny flip. He'd crashed into her and they'd both gone flying to the floor. Before he scrambled out the door, he claimed he'd been pushed. Betty?

Yeah. Fine. But Betty hadn't been the one kissing her. Couldn't blame that on a ghost. If only his lips and muscular body hadn't made her crazy with desire. If only he wasn't a goddamned cop.

She shook her head. And neighbor. *Don't forget that little fact.* If they got into a relationship and it didn't last, it would be mighty awkward to run into him due to their proximity. Didn't matter. Nothing more could happen between them. It was a fluke. A one-time thing. Because she didn't date cops.

But his hands.... Those hands had sent desire to the very marrow of her bones. Nobody she'd ever been with affected her like that. Why? *Who knew?* Maybe Betty put some sort of a spell on them. At this point, anything was possible. Ghosts. Making out with a sexy neighbor she'd known for less than twenty-four hours....

The bell jangled on the bookstore door and she stood, prepared to welcome the customer and hand out some free stuff from the station.

Blake stood in the doorway in full uniform. He exuded power in his creased black pants, matching crisp short-sleeved shirt, and a hat that cast a mysterious shadow over his forehead and eyes.

Her mouth went dry, and her heart dropped to her toes. *Damn it all to hell, why does he have to look so hot?* If she had to fall for a man in uniform, why couldn't it be a waiter who wore a tux? At least then he wouldn't be risking his life every time he went to work. But it wasn't the uniform. It was the type of man. Strong. Take-charge. Brave. Like her father and brother. The type she needed to avoid because they put the safety of others before their own. No way she'd live her life under that shadow.

He strolled closer, a slight smile on his face. Another uniform—his partner—turned to browse a bookshelf.

"Hey," Blake said, moving closer. He kept his expression neutral. Like nothing had happened between them.

Fine. She could act natural, too. "Hey. How's it going?" She used her softer, on-air voice. Business. She was a deejay welcoming a customer to a store that was paying her for a public appearance.

Blake moved closer and stared at the table of goodies. He ran his hand over a stack of pens. "Good. Going good. How about you?" He lifted a pen to examine it like it was the most interesting thing in the world.

Keep staring at the pen. Avoid eye contact. Makes it easier to pretend we didn't practically rip each others' clothes off last night. Her heart pounded. Tough to stay professional when her eyes focused on the way his hand held the pen. And all she could think about was the way those hands felt as they held her waist, broke her fall, and massaged her breasts. *Oh shit. No.* She could not go there.

"So, what are you doing? Stalking me?" She leaned a hip against the table, trying to appear casual even though she suddenly found it hard to take a normal breath.

His gaze darted from the pen to meet her gaze. "Stalking you? No." He held the pen toward her, used it as a pointer as he accentuated his words. "You're in my territory."

Inner Harbor was his beat? That had to be pretty safe for him, right? Baltimore city had its crime problems, but everyone from the mayor to the beat cops worked hard to keep the harbor a safe area. She might only have lived here for a month, but she already knew this area was Baltimore's bread and butter.

Still. A cop was a cop. Not a safe job, no matter where he frequented.

The bell above the door jingled. Missy glanced at the balding guy and his slight paunch. His wrinkled button-down shirt and khaki pants had seen better days. He glanced around the entrance and then grinned when he spotted Missy. With an internal grimace, she noticed the guy's hands were behind his back. She'd been around enough cops to know they didn't like it when they couldn't see someone's hands.

"Hey, feel free to keep the pen," she said to Blake, hoping the offer would distract him. "I gotta do my song-and-dance thing here."

Her subterfuge didn't work. Blake took a step to stand between her and the new customer.

She elbowed past and shot him a look.

She strolled toward the customer. "Hi! Welcome! I'm Misty from WLOV's Misty till Midnight show. We're helping to celebrate today's grand opening—"

"I know!" The man grinned and his face turned red.

Blake glared at the man and Missy gave him the slightest shake of her head. *Back off, Blake.*

The man pulled out a bouquet of roses from behind his back and thrust them toward Missy.

Blake crossed his arms, his body less rigid, but he kept his gaze on the customer.

"These are for you. I'm Kurt...you know, from the show. I called you twice this week."

Missy backed up a step, giving the man her full attention now that Blake had calmed down. *Wow. A fan. Cool!* She took the proffered bouquet of roses and inhaled the sweet scent. "This is awesome. Nice to meet you, Kurt." She'd had dozens of callers last week. Her mind scrambled to place his voice or name, but she came up empty.

He nodded several times and turned a deeper shade of red as he wrung his hands in front of him. "I hope you like them."

Cute! Too awesomely cute. She'd never had a fan before. Most of her voice assignments in California had been behind the scenes—advertising work and phone "hold" messages. It paid well, but she didn't exactly glean a following in that line of business.

"I love them. Thank you!" She motioned with her hand to the table with giveaways. "Come on over and get some freebies before you browse this awesome new store." As she was being paid to help garner more traffic to the store, the least she could do was encourage people to make a purchase.

Blake moved to the side and tapped the WLOV pen on his palm. He probably thought he was acting nonchalant, but his narrowed gaze followed the fellow's every move. The guy scrambled toward the table and then glanced back at Missy. Sheesh. Her paranoid neighbor was going to scare off her one and only fan.

Missy glanced over her shoulder at the other cop, who was reading the back cover of a paperback. "Blake, you never introduced me to your friend." She strode toward him—an older guy whose silver hair poked out from beneath his cap. In pretty good shape for an older guy, too.

"Hi, I'm Missy," she said, choosing to use her real name since he was Blake's friend.

"I know. Blake makes us listen to you every night." His eyes crinkled and he sent a shrug at Blake, who hurried to join them. "Not that I mind. You've got a great voice. I'm Larry. Welcome to Baltimore, by the way." He held out a hand and Missy shook, not a bit surprised by his strong grip.

Blake stood by her shoulder, sending off a crazy reaction in her body. He nodded at the flowers she held and glanced at the fan, who loaded a pen and bumper sticker into his shirt pocket. "Those flowers aren't cheap. That guy spent an awful lot of money on you, and he doesn't look like the type who has a lot to spare."

Missy wanted to roll her eyes. Typical cop. Everybody was a bad guy. Everyone acted suspiciously until proven otherwise. For years, she'd lived it with her dad and then later with her brother. "Let him be. He's a fan."

"Fan...stalker. Could be the same thing."

This time she couldn't halt the eye roll.

The man wandered closer, turning red again when he spotted the uniforms. "Well, very nice meeting you, Misty. I'll be sure to call in next week again." He glanced at Blake, then Larry, and then hustled out of the store.

"Let's see where he goes," Blake said, glancing at Larry.

"I wanted to get this book for the wife." Larry tapped the book with his finger.

"We'll come back later to buy it. You can't carry it around with you for three hours anyway." His gaze riveted to the man who'd left the store.

Missy jabbed her fists on her hips. "Do not follow that man. He didn't do anything wrong."

"See you soon, Missy." Blake took off for the door.

"Nice to meet you. Don't worry. I'll make sure he doesn't scare your fan. We'll probably get a call that will divert us from this mission soon, anyway." Larry hustled out the door and jogged to catch up with Blake.

She ran a hand through her hair and stared out the glass doors at Blake's back. *Damn, his ass looks fine in that uniform.* The holstered gun. The way his cap pushed strands of his dark hair over his face. *Shit.* She needed to stay away from him, needed to stop thinking about him. But the memory of his lips on hers made it hard to contemplate pushing him away.

෪

Blake pulled open the door to the bookstore and Larry walked inside behind him. Without Missy's continued presence, the place had lost some of its earlier energy.

"Ha. You were hoping she was still here. I was right. You have the hots for her."

Larry flashed a grin and disappeared around a shelf display to pick up the book for his wife before Blake could answer.

No. He had come back at the end of their shift to keep Larry company. His gaze lingered on the spot where Missy had sat earlier. The memory of the way her body fit so well with his last night, and the feel of her soft lips and mouth....

"I'm gonna pay for this." Larry tapped the book in his palm and indicated the cashier at the back of the store.

"Yeah. No hurry. I'll look around some." Look around? No. He needed to get out of here. His mind kept wandering to the sassy woman who'd been here earlier. What was it about Missy that had him wanting more of her? Wasn't like him. He loved women, for sure. But like oil and water, he tended to separate from them after a short bout together.

Blake glanced toward the cashier and leaned a hip against a table display of cookbooks. Short unions were all he wanted to know, for crying out loud. He figured out long ago he wasn't relationship material. Not with his messed-up life. Messed-up childhood—a mother who left claiming she'd be back, and never returned—and a father who paid more attention to the dog than to Blake. Fine by him. As he grew, he found his family. His brothers on the force.

Larry, for instance. The guy—in spite of his pushy, nosy nature—was like a brother to Blake. Without Larry, he'd probably spend holidays alone, or working a double shift. In Larry, he had someone to confide in, and someone to trust. He smiled and glanced at the linoleum floor. His uniform pants covered the tops of his dress shoes, just like his brothers' did.

He chuckled, remembering how the guys had baffled a hospital worker. Gilbert—a beat cop who'd been shot in the head by a bank robber twenty years ago and ended up blind—needed bone marrow a few months back to fight the cancer that had crept into his body.

Gilbert's wife, daughter, and son had been first in line. And behind them, forty-five men from the Baltimore city police department volunteered. When the hospital worker asked each man what his relationship was to Gilbert, each and every one of them said they were his brother. After hearing the same answer several times, the poor woman sat back, looked at the line of men, and quipped, "Oh yes, I'm definitely seeing the resemblance."

Blake loved being a part of that. His marrow wasn't a match, but one of the other guys' was.

All the family he would ever need. Who needed family when he had a band of brothers with a bond stronger than anything as weak as mere blood?

"Ready?" Larry strode toward him with a white bag in his hand.

"Yeah. Sure you don't need to stop for chocolates and flowers on the way to the car?" They moved outside into the early evening sunshine. A throng of people filled the brick paths around the shops at Inner Harbor. The scent of crab cakes and seafood filled the air, making his stomach growl.

"Ha. Make fun all you want. Love is like that, buddy. When you find the one, it changes you. Makes you do things you never thought you would." Larry raised a brow. "Maybe I should stop for chocolate. You know, get Tina in the mood tonight...." He elbowed Blake.

Blake shook his head and laughed.

"That Missy woman sure is fine. Maybe she's the one who'll change you."

"Not likely. Too messy to get involved with a neighbor."

"Yeah. Awkward." Larry stalked to the drivers' side of their patrol car and then got in.

Blake sat inside the car and pulled his seat belt over his chest.

"Too bad you've already fallen for her, though."

Oh no. He wasn't falling for anybody. Larry and his imagination. "I haven't fall—"

"Oh look. A red SUV. Wasn't there a missing elderly man who was last seen in a red SUV?" Larry pressed the button to speak into his radio.

Typical. Larry's favorite way to get out of conversation he wanted to end. Distraction.

Too bad the guy didn't know what the hell he was talking about.

An hour and a half later, Blake exited the elevator on the eighth floor of his apartment building with a bag containing a cheeseburger and fries. Add a beer, and he had his favorite dinner.

A shadow moved from the other side of the hallway. Blake froze, and his fingers moved to his weapon. He blinked. Nothing there. He dug in his pocket for his keys and glanced at Missy's doorway.

Betty—wearing her pink sweat suit and flamingo earrings—stood grinning at him. She winked, raised her hand, and then knocked three times on Missy's door.

Blake's mouth opened and then closed. Betty disappeared. He closed his eyes for half a minute and then opened them when he heard Missy's door open.

Missy stood in the doorway wearing the same clothes as earlier. A white T-shirt, a pair of jeans, and a simple necklace that hung between her breasts, spiraling the memory of her body to the forefront of his mind. He knew exactly how those curves felt under his hands and he craved the feel of them again.

"Hey. Thanks for stopping by the bookstore today." Missy pocketed her hands in her jeans, pulling them down just enough for him to get a glimpse of her lower belly. He swallowed in order to concentrate.

"You—you should look out your peephole before you open your door." There. He'd be the concerned policeman who lived across the hall. But how the hell had Betty...no, it couldn't have been Betty. What was going on?

Missy frowned. "You feeling all right?"

"Yeah. Of course."

"'Cause I did look out my peephole and I saw you." She tilted her head. "I sort of thought it was okay to open up since it was my neighbor, the cop."

How had he gotten in front of her door? He'd been several feet away when Betty...when.... *Oh shit.* He really needed that beer now. Time for a change of subject. He'd process the other stuff later.

Her hair hung loose, and her exposed neck made his mind wander to the way she'd tasted last night. One more taste...that wouldn't be a relationship. If one time together on her floor hadn't made things awkward, maybe one more time with her would be okay. They were adults. If she could handle it, he could.

"Listen," he said, taking a step closer, wishing his heart wasn't beating so fast. *What? That never happened to him.* He didn't get nervous around women. He shook the thought away. "I'm sorry about the way...sorry about last night."

She waved a dismissive hand in front of her and shrugged. "It wasn't one-sided."

Good. Promising attitude. So maybe she was up for a little fling, too. One time with her and then she'd be out of his system. A little fun between two neighbors who could keep it casual and be civil after.

"Yeah. So I was thinking to make it up to you, I could take you out for a beer tonight." Wow. *Real smooth.*

Missy's gaze dropped to the red hallway carpeting between them and she ran a tongue over her lips, probably having no idea how that tiny move sent his body into overdrive. That tongue had explored his mouth last night. And damn it, he wanted it exploring him again. Now.

"I can't, Blake." Her gaze fixated on a spot on the carpeting and then lifted to meet his. "I mean it when I say you don't need to apologize. I liked what happened last night. Liked it a lot."

Good. This is more like it. Maybe she was trying to tell him that she was a one-night-stand kind of girl. Perfect. If she had other plans, they'd get together tomorrow. Or the next day.

"It can't happen again, though." She sighed and crossed her arms on her chest.

He held her gaze, unsure of what to say next, while his heart thundered.

"My brother died in the line of duty last year. My father died in the line of duty when I was fourteen." A tear trickled down her cheek and she knuckled it away. "Blake, I can't risk having feelings for someone whose job puts his life at risk."

"Okay." His strong voice belied the fact that his gut clenched. *Must be hunger.* "Friends." He forced a smile and extended his hand.

She took it and her lips curved into a small smile.

With her hand in his, he set his dinner bag down and covered her hand with his other one. "I'm so sorry about your brother and father."

Nodding, she pressed her lips together. Probably to keep them from quivering. God, losing a parent and a sibling. She was obviously close to her entire family. Good thing she blew off his invite, then. Turned out she wasn't the one-night-stand person he thought she might be.

"We could go out for a beer. As friends." He bent to pick up his dinner bag. "I could even split my burger with you."

She laughed. Well, good. At least he'd been able to help her shake her blues. Seeing her upset affected him more than he wanted to admit. He liked her happy. Liked hearing that smooth, relaxing voice of hers.

"Thanks. I promised a friend from work I'd go to Federal Hill with her tonight, though."

"Another time," he said, turning toward his apartment door.

"Yeah. That'd be great."

He shoved the key in his lock and opened the door. Glancing behind him, he watched as her door shut.

Inside, he laid his bag on the counter, no longer hungry. What did it matter if Missy didn't date cops? Who cared? Not him.

The newspaper on the coffee table fluttered and opened. No open window and his door was shut. And what the hell had he seen in the hallway? Not Betty. Ghosts weren't real.

His gaze fell to the kitchen sink where, that morning before his shift, he'd left it full of dishes. Now, to the right of the sink sat a neat pile of plates, a small stack of silverware, and clean glasses lined up in a formation as tight as a group of soldiers.

"Betty?" he whispered.

The newspaper fluttered again and the room grew cool.

Inhaling a deep breath, he stepped toward the coffee table and glanced at the paper. Missy's smiling face—her professional headshot—stared up at him in black and white, advertising today's bookstore appearance. Closing his eyes, he blew out the breath he held.

"Betty. It won't work. Give it up. She doesn't date cops, and you know I can never have what you and Stanley had."

☸

Missy closed her door, slumped against it, and then placed her hand over her fast-beating heart. She had never wanted to say yes to someone as much as she had wanted to say yes to Blake.

Those intense brown eyes. That serious face. And the memory of the way his hands felt on her....

Grief for her brother and father, and the risks they'd taken to keep others safe, always fogged her emotions when she thought of them. The loneliness—the hole in her life that had gotten bigger when her brother died—was likely what made her feelings so raw, her heart so exposed.

Exactly why she couldn't be around Blake. No matter how badly she wanted to.

Her phone rang, and she pulled it out of her jeans' pocket. Diane. They were supposed to meet in twenty minutes.

Missy cleared her throat. "Hey!"

"Girl, you're not going to believe this. Petey just threw up on me." Diane's clear, throaty deejay voice was about two octaves higher than usual.

"Oh no. Poor little guy." Guess their night on the town was postponed. "You take care of him and yourself. We'll do our girls' night another time."

Diane sighed into the phone. As a new mom, she could probably use some "me" time, but apparently that wouldn't happen tonight. "Sorry, Missy. I was looking forward to it."

After setting a new date with her friend, Missy disconnected and plopped onto the plush red sofa she'd bought second-hand from the same consignment store as the kitchen chairs. She had plenty of money in her savings—the voice work she'd done in California had paid well—but she couldn't bring herself to pay full price for anything. An old habit from the days after her dad passed away and money was tight.

The room grew colder, and Missy shivered and rubbed her arms. When would June get warm?

The rocking chair to her left began to creak back and forth. Not a chill from the weather. A ghost was changing the temperature in this room.

Tilting her head and narrowing her eyes, Missy studied the chair. "I'm not afraid, Betty. In fact, I could use some company tonight."

A shadow formed in the chair and Missy swallowed hard. What was she doing? Calling on a ghost? That could open up all sorts of scary things, couldn't it?

The shadow morphed into a white-haired woman in a pink sweat suit. She sported a huge smile.

"B-Betty?" Missy whispered.

"Uh-huh." She beamed, flashing white teeth that Missy was pretty sure were dentures. Oh great. Not only did she have a ghost, her ghost had gone into the afterlife with her dentures intact.

"Umm...well, thanks for making my bed the other day." What did one talk to a ghost about?

"You're welcome, dear." Betty stood. "Since you're staying in tonight, let me make you a cup of tea. And then let's chat." She moved into the kitchen.

Missy nodded, only because she couldn't exactly speak. Her mouth went dry and her heart hammered so hard that Blake could probably hear her across the hall.

"Your neighbor across the hall is a nice young man." Betty said, her soft voice rising above the noise of the faucet as she filled the teakettle with water.

This was so crazy. Missy was sitting in her own living room while a ghost made her a cup of tea. Like something a grandma would do. So why, when she should be freaked out and running for the door, or at least a local psychiatric hospital, did she feel comforted instead of scared?

Maybe partly because she'd wanted for so long to see spirits—to see her dad or her brother, to know they were doing okay wherever they were.

Missy stood and walked to the breakfast bar that divided the kitchen from the living room and leaned her elbows on the granite. "Do you know my father? He died fourteen years ago. Bob Prescott. Or my brother Jeff?" A lump formed in her throat at the thought of him alone and scared on the other side.

Betty set the kettle on the stove and turned on the burner like she did such a thing every day. She moved around the counter, across from Missy, and stared. Missy smelled apple pie, and the scent relaxed her, made her breathe deeper.

"I haven't crossed over yet, I'm afraid." Betty shook her head. "My Stanley has...." She closed her eyes and smiled with her lips closed as she looked heavenward. Then her eyes opened and she stared at Missy. "I tried to cross over, but my guide—a nice young man who looks like the fellow who lives down the hall here on the eighth floor—told me I couldn't go all the way to the light...to Stanley...until I earn it."

"Earn it?" In spite of the circumstances, Missy couldn't help relaxing in Betty's presence. As if she were real. Heck, she looked as real as any human.

Betty shrugged. "I'm new to this whole death thing. My guide told me that ascension is earned." She strode to a cabinet to the left of the stove and then opened the door.

Missy straightened before walking around the counter and joining Betty in the small kitchen. Instinctively, she opened a cupboard to the right of the stove and took out a box of tea and two mugs.

Betty smiled. "I kept them here." She pointed to a spot where Missy's spices and canned goods stood.

Missy laughed and plucked two tea bags out of the box and set one in each mug. "Well, I guess I'll have to rearrange that tomorrow so it's arranged the way you like it." *Holy crap! I'm standing here having a conversation with a ghost.* It should feel weird. It should feel wrong. But this was the least homesick Missy had been in over a month.

"Sugar?" Betty pointed to the lidded bowl next to the stove.

"None for me, thanks," Missy said. When Betty pulled the milk glass container closer, Missy opened a drawer, took out a spoon, and handed it to her.

"I have a bit of a sweet tooth. Maybe that's part of why I can't ascend yet. I always tended to indulge in things I loved." Betty heaped two spoonfuls of the sweet granules into her tea and stirred.

Missy pressed her tea bag against the side of her mug with a spoon. "I don't think a sweet tooth would keep you from going to...well, is ascending the same thing as Heaven?"

"Oh sure. That's what it looked like, anyway. I just couldn't get there. Not yet. I have a little more work to do. That's where you and Blake come in." After Betty rinsed her spoon and set it on the drain board, she inhaled the steam coming from her mug.

She walked—or almost glided, really—back into the small living room and sat in the rocker again. Missy followed, cup of tea in hand, and perched on the edge of the sofa.

"Blake and I can help you ascend?" She'd love to help this sweet woman. But how the heck could she?

"Well, eventually, we'll probably have to involve Veronica, the pretty gal who lives on the first floor. She's a psychic-medium, and she knows about vortexes and all that ascension stuff. Problem is, because of something that happened a while back, she's not real happy about seeing ghosts any more. I try not to bug her. She's in Europe for a few weeks."

Missy nodded, although her head was spinning from information overload.

Betty relaxed into the chair, cupped the bottom of her mug with her left hand while holding the handle with her right, and peered at Missy. "I know what I need to do to get the energy to cross over." She took a sip of her tea, while gazing at Missy over the rim of the mug.

Suddenly, Missy didn't want to hear about it. This couldn't be good.

"I need to be sure you and Blake find true love like my Stanley and I had."

Missy choked on her tea, splashing hot liquid onto the old

hardwood floors.

"Oh dear." Betty set her mug on the table and dashed into the kitchen with speed that defied her age. Ten seconds later, she was back with a towel. Pretty damn fast for an old lady. A ghostly old lady.

Betty squatted to blot the spill, and Missy put her mug on the table and kneeled across from Betty. "Here, let me. I'm the goof who spilled it." She reached for the towel. Brushing Betty's hand in the process, she jolted from a slight electrical shock.

"Ooh. Sorry." Betty stood. "I always forget about that whole energy thing when I touch stuff." She winked. "Like I didn't mean to turn the lights on when I left you and Blake last night. I plan to leave you two alone whenever you're together from now on."

Betty beamed a huge smile.

Memories of the way Blake's calloused hands had felt as they'd glided over her skin made her heart skip a beat. How could Missy let the woman down gently? This relationship wasn't going to happen, but Betty was intent on playing matchmaker.

"And I didn't see anything you two were doing. I kept my back turned last night, just so you know."

More memories of the way it made her feel when Blake touched her flashed through her mind. "Betty, it's nice that you think Blake and I should be together. I'm flattered. I mean...he's a good-looking guy—"

"And good. That boy has a heart of gold." Betty sat back in the rocker and leaned forward, putting both hands on her knees. Her blue eyes sparkled with so much life, it was hard to believe the woman wasn't alive.

It was probably time to explain about her father and brother. Make Betty understand. And then maybe they could figure out a way for her to find the light...or whatever the heck it was that meant she would move on to be with her departed husband.

"Blake checked on me every day." Tears filled Betty's eyes, threatening to overflow.

Missy's throat clogged with emotion. This lady had been a good person during her living years. She couldn't be this kind as a ghost and not have been the same person as a human. Somebody like her deserved peace and happiness in the afterlife. Missy's own grandmother lived happily with dozens of friends in a retirement community in California, and she couldn't help but think how well her grandma and Betty would get along. Probably even cause some trouble.

Betty smiled and blinked the tears away. "He not only checked on me, he brought me groceries, took out my trash every Sunday night, picked up my medications."

Missy nodded. Tough on the outside, caring on the inside.

Betty took a sip of her tea, set the mug on the table, leaned back in her chair, and started rocking again. "He's the one who found me—" Betty glanced toward the door. "Well, you know...found me...splat, kaput...dead." She clapped her hands once as if portraying her own fall to the floor.

Oh shit. He'd come to her apartment, probably expecting to take out her trash or something equally mundane, and found her dead. It must have been very difficult for him.

"I know it sounds crazy because I only knew him a few months— but he was like a son to me. The child I never had." She gazed off into space, smiling, as if picturing something. "I would have been a proud mom if he'd been my son." Then her smile dropped away. "I think he had a rotten mama, though. He never opened up about it, but he isn't close to his family. Doesn't think he needs people."

Yeah. Pretty much the same thing Missy had deduced from her time with him. Not big on relationships. Her mind slammed back to the way he'd looked earlier as he stood at her door. Sexy. Reeking of testosterone. Making every molecule in her body want him.

"He seems like a nice enough guy, but I don't date cops, Betty. What I'd like to concentrate on is you. How can we help you get to where you need to be?"

Betty's brows rose. "Kicking me out already?"

Missy laughed. A nice, from-the-belly laugh that released some of the stress she'd been carrying. Between ghost visits and trying to tamp her desire for her sexy but never-going-to-happen neighbor, she'd been tense for days.

"Honestly?" Missy took a sip of tea, enjoying the spicy sweetness. "I feel a little crazy sitting here talking to a ghost. I've always believed in ghosts but never knew how to summon one."

"Not sure you can." Betty rocked back and forth. This was feeling more and more like a grandmotherly chat than a ghostly encounter every minute. "And I'm not exactly sure what I have to do to get to my Stanley. My guide—the kid who looks a lot like that guy who lives in apartment 807—said something about needing to *earn* ascension. To me, that means I need to help Blake find true love."

Missy opened her mouth, ready to interject.

Betty held up a palm. "Sorry, darling. I didn't know what it was I had to do until you moved in. It's you. You're his true love. And I can't move on until you and Blake realize that you have what Stanley and I had."

After taking in a deep breath, Missy expelled it. *Concentrate on helping Betty, not her misguided plan to push two people together.* "Apartment 807, you say?"

Betty nodded. "Uncanny. I haven't seen my guide for a while, but he hangs out in the hallway near that apartment."

Missy made a mental note to learn more about apartment 807. She'd seen the couple that lived there once or twice, but nothing stood out about them other than the woman was very pretty.

"I want to help you, Betty. I want to help you get to Stanley." Missy stood and paced the hardwood floor in the small living room. She needed to research helping ghosts cross over. Maybe even find a different psychic if the one on the first floor was out of the country.

"That's great! It's not too late to go over and knock on Blake's door. He's a night owl. He loves your voice. All you have to do is talk to him, and he'll be putty in your hands."

"I'm sorry, Betty. Truly, I am. I wish I could help you." Missy stood in front of the elderly lady. "There has to be another way to help you. We'll figure it out. I, well, I have my reasons. I can't get involved with Blake." She should tell Betty why, but right now she didn't want that particular pain to fill her heart.

"Honey...." Betty stood and then cradled one of Missy's hands with both of hers. "You're going to have to trust me."

Chapter Five

*M*issy leaned forward in her swivel chair at the control pad and pressed the button to set up six songs in a row. She'd play a bit of uninterrupted music for the listeners from seven to nine before she started playing her show's dedications.

At the station, she could forget about missing her mom, and the heartache of her brother's and father's deaths. She could listen to other people, get so tuned into their lives that she could forget about the complications in her own life. Like her sexy neighbor.

She had knocked on his door before she'd left for the station, but no answer. Not that she wanted to see him or anything. But after researching ghosts, afterlife, portals, and vortexes, she realized she needed to talk with Blake. He was the only one who could help her figure it out. Anyone else would think she was crazy. But he'd known Betty. He'd want to help her again. Missy had even knocked on the door at apartment 807, hoping to find a clue about why the guide, as Betty called him, looked like the man who lived there. Had the couple had a teen who'd passed away?

She slid the pot lever lower to turn down the volume as the phone lit up, indicating a caller phoning in a dedication.

She cleared her throat to ready her radio voice and then connected with the caller. "Hi, you're on Misty till Midnight on WLOV. What can I play for you tonight?" Sometimes she had to edit the length of the calls before they aired, so she taped all of them.

"Misty, it's me Kurt. Remember, we met at the bookstore?"

"Hi, Kurt. How's it going tonight?" She used a softer voice than her normal tone to keep the mood casual. The name sounded familiar, but she'd met at least a dozen fans that day. *Come on, give me a hint...were you with your wife?* If she couldn't figure it out, she'd have to tell him she met a lot of wonderful listeners and ask him to remind her who he was.

"Are the flowers still fresh? I could get you some new ones."

Bingo! The guy with the flowers. "They're so beautiful, Kurt. I really appreciate them. What can I play for you tonight?" The other phone buttons would likely be lighting up soon, so she tried to make the dedication calls as quick as possible and yet connect with her listeners, too.

He chuckled. "Thanks to your show, I'm feeling like a happy song tonight. My girlfriend of two years left me last week. Last week, I requested sad songs. This week, I'm feeling a little better. Can you play 'Ready to Love Again'?"

"I sure can. Thanks for calling, Kurt. I'm sorry to hear about your relationship, and I hope things work out for you."

"Thanks, Misty. Thanks a lot!"

"My pleasure. You have a great night, okay?"

"You, too."

She disconnected just as two buttons on the phone lit up. With a glance at the computer screen, she double-checked how much time she had before going live again and then took the calls, putting one listener on hold and taking a happy-anniversary-dedication love song from the other.

The rest of the night passed in a blur as her phone stayed lit. She recorded and edited calls to play back later and played the songs that kept the nice people of Baltimore feeling happy and listened to.

With a final good night to her listeners, at midnight she stretched and put the station on automation. No live deejay until tomorrow morning's rush hour.

With a final glance around the studio to ensure everything was tidy, she grabbed her backpack and strode toward the lobby. It wasn't far to their cars, but she and Diane always parked near each other and walked to the lot together.

Heck, she was a policeman's daughter. She knew danger was real. Especially for a woman alone at night. Anyone who said different was just plain in denial. Her dad had taught her the best self defense was to think smart and avoid being a victim. Forget being a black belt and using pepper spray. Her dad constantly preached about being smart about safety.

"Hey!" Diane sprinted around the corner from her section of the building. "Sorry about the other night. Maybe we can get a drink on the way home tomorrow night?"

"Sure thing. How's Petey?" Missy punched a code into the box on the wall and the glass doors to the lobby slid open.

"No more vomit, thank God. That puke stuff...." Diane made an exaggerated shiver and wrinkled her nose.

Missy chuckled. "Well, glad he's doing okay, and that you don't have to deal with throw-up."

They marched through the lobby and past the reception desk. The night security guard got up and joined them at the door. He insisted on watching the late-night employees as they walked to their cars.

"Thanks, Dan. Have a great night."

"You, too."

They paused by the front door where Diane keyed in the code. The door clicked open and they pushed on it and walked out. One perk of working for a radio station, everything was very secure. Nobody was allowed inside after business hours, and each door needed a different code.

Missy hesitated on the brightly lit sidewalk in front of the lobby. "Diane, this might sound weird, but do you believe in ghosts?"

Diane shrugged. "We live in Baltimore. Lots of history. I've heard lots of ghost stories." She tilted her head. "Are you asking for a reason?"

She'd stuck her neck out. *May as well go for it.* "I think there's a ghost in my apartment building. A nice one. I'm looking for an honest medium to help the ghost cross over. Does that sound crazy?"

"No. It doesn't. My mom is into that sort of thing. She gets psychic readings all the time. I'll ask for you." She laid a hand on Missy's shoulder. "Lots of people see ghosts. I think it's cool that you're helping one."

It felt good to confide in someone. And even better to have Diane believe her. They walked side by side to their cars.

Safety first. Her dad's motto. Her mind flashed to Blake. He helped keep people in this town safe. Too bad nice guys finished last.

CS

Blake shoved the key into his apartment doorknob and turned. Or tried to turn. No dice. The lock wouldn't budge. He yanked the key out and tried again. *Great. Maybe I should open the six-pack of beer I went out for and drink the whole damn thing right here in the hallway.*

He set the brown bag on the carpeting and used both hands to wrangle with the key.

The elevator dinged, and he glanced down the hall. Misty exited, her long legs taking strides toward him. Her long, brown hair billowed as she walked. Dressed in faded jeans and a breezy white top, she did things to his libido he couldn't control.

"Need to borrow my WD-40?" she asked.

Good God. This woman was always gorgeous. In the afternoon...and also at one in the morning.

"Yeah. That would be great. This has never happened before." He scratched his head and glanced from the knob to Missy. *Betty's doing, or a freaky coincidence?*

"Okay. I'll be right back." She unlocked her door easily and disappeared into her apartment.

Crazy. He'd been thinking about her as he walked back from the liquor store. Good thing she didn't know that he'd waited to leave his apartment until after her show. He didn't want to miss a minute of her sultry voice...the way she always seemed to know what to say to someone, whether they were in a troubled relationship or celebrating a happy one. Even the ads for local sponsors sounded better when she was the one hawking them.

"Here you go." She passed him the lubricant.

"Thanks." He adjusted the spraying tube, aimed, and fired into the lock. A few seconds later, he inserted the key and it turned smoothly. "Well, that worked great. Gonna have to pick up a can for myself." He handed the canister back, and their fingers brushed. Pleasure ripped through his fingertips and traveled all the way to his groin. "Great show tonight, by the way."

She grinned and he couldn't take his gaze off her full lips. He'd kissed those lips and wanted to kiss them again. "Yeah? You listened? Thanks."

He chuckled. The way she said it made it seem like she was surprised anyone listened to her. Didn't she know how talented she was? Heck, the sheer number of callers each night should tell her she was doing something very right. "Yeah. I had the early shift today, so I worked on some stuff. Your show was on in the background." Couldn't let on that he'd tried to hang a shelf in his bathroom but kept returning to the living room when the songs ended to hear her voice. A job that should have taken a half hour had taken a full one instead.

Missy's phone beeped, and she pulled it out, tapped into it, and then slid it back into her pocket. "My mom. She checks on me every night."

"She sounds like a great mom." Nobody had ever cared enough about Blake to check on him. Except Betty. And his partner Larry.

"I knocked on your door earlier, but you weren't home." Missy nibbled her bottom lip and worry snaked up his spine.

"Why? What's wrong?" Instinct kicked in and he forgot about the way her voice soothed him, made him feel less lonely, and instantly wondered what put that worried look on her face.

"Nothing's wrong." She glanced up and down the hallway and then met his gaze. "I was wondering if we could talk. It's about Betty."

What had Betty done this time? "Sure." He hefted the bag from the floor. "How about a beer?"

"That would be great." Her voice belied her cautious gaze. She obviously didn't want to be alone with him. Whatever bothered her was enough to overcome her caution, though, so it must be important.

He tilted his head toward her apartment and opened his door wider. "Your door locked?"

"I'm a cop's daughter. What do you think?" Her narrowed eyes sparkled.

"I think you're smart." He did, too. Smart and pretty. And way too much fun to be around. Friends. They could do this friend thing. It could work. "Come on in."

He set two beers on the glass coffee table in front of the sofa and headed for the adjoining kitchen.

Missy gave a slow whistle and glanced around the apartment.

"Don't be too impressed." He threaded the four remaining bottles between his fingers and clinked them into the fridge. "None of this is mine. I'm subletting from my friend J.B., who's traveling for a year."

"Wow. Nice." She bent to pick up a beer bottle from the table and barehanded the twist top off.

Gotta love a woman who can take care of herself.

He strode into the room, grabbed the other bottle, and opened it. "Have a seat." He gestured toward the sofa and then sat a safe distance away in a matching recliner.

Missy took a swig of beer and then stared into the bottle. "Betty needs our help to cross over."

Blake choked on the beer he'd started to swallow.

"I'm not kidding." She leaned toward him, beer on her knee, and pleaded with him with her expressive hazel eyes. "Betty thinks of you as her son."

A dagger to the heart. He swallowed hard and steeled himself. He'd never had a real family. But Betty...not a mean bone in her damn body, and she gave her love so freely, so fast. Everything he'd ever wished someone in his own family would have given him. "You mean she *thought* of me as her son. How would you know, anyway?"

Missy sat back into the sofa and crossed her arms. *Good.* The more distance from her, the better he could think. She sighed, glanced away for a long moment, and then stared at him.

"Do you believe in ghosts?"

He lifted the beer bottle to his mouth and took a long swig to buy some time. How the hell did he answer that question? A resounding no to prove his sanity? Or fess up and tell her about the two times he had literally felt the life go out of a dying person's body? Felt the cold of it on a hot summer's night. Saw the shadow that lifted and took off from the form.

Play it safe. Find out what she believes in first. He shrugged. "Let's say I have an open mind."

Missy narrowed her eyes at him. "I had tea with her in my apartment."

Guess I don't have to worry about being the crazy one in this room. "Tea? Really?" His tongue pressed hard into his cheek as he tried to hide the smile.

"Ha-ha. Go ahead and laugh. I expected you to. She's probably tried to show herself to you, and you weren't open enough to see her."

Blake frowned. The scent of apple pie, the puzzle pieces, the coins from the sofa. Last night in the hallway.

Nah. The guys would have a field day with that one. "So what did Betty tell you she needed?"

Missy rolled her eyes. "Okay, you know what? I don't care if you believe or not, but she's appeared to me twice now. She's done a bunch of helpful things around my apartment, too."

Blake's mind flashed to the clean dishes on his drain board. *Yeah. If Betty was a ghost, she'd be that kind of ghost.*

She rose and jabbed her hands on her hips. "Look, I thought you might be the only one I had a chance with. You knew her, you took good care of her...and you found her the day she died. Obviously I made a mistake to think you would want to—"

He pushed himself out of the chair and stood face-to-face with her. "How did you know I was the one who found her?" Only a few people knew. He'd wanted to keep Betty's passing dignified, not a sideshow for gossip from other tenants.

"She told me." Missy lifted her chin and held his gaze. "Can you take your hands off me now?"

Shit. He hadn't even realized he'd gripped her upper arms. "Oh. Sorry." He dropped his hands to his sides. She didn't move away. Held her ground and stared stubbornly at him in spite of the fact that he had a six-inch height advantage over her.

They stood so close he felt her warm breath on his skin. Those lips...those damn lips. He needed to taste them again.

Her chest rose and fell, and his gaze dropped to the skin exposed by the V of her shirt. He could lay a kiss there...right there near her collarbone....

"Listen," she said, her voice almost a whisper. "I guess I was wrong to confide in you. You obviously think this is all crazy. I figured you'd want to help, but I guess I figured wrong." Her hazel eyes glowed with passion, or maybe it was anger, and she whirled away and started for the door.

"Wait." She turned to face him. Some of the guys might laugh if they caught wind of this. More importantly, if Betty really did need his help, he needed to be there for her. God help him, he was probably crazy to agree to this. "What can I do to help you?"

Chapter Six

*M*issy ran her hand through her hair as sunlight streamed through the bathroom window. Blake would be at her door any minute. He had the day off, and she didn't have to be to work until three. She felt the need to look her best even though they were only going down the hall to chat with the people who lived in apartment 807. Her fluffing wasn't for Blake. No way. *Yeah...go ahead...deny it.*

Three knocks sounded on the door and Missy's heart beat a little faster. It wasn't just the excitement of helping Betty.

After peeking through the hole, she opened the door. Blake wore a dark tan shirt that stretched the width of his broad shoulders and clung to his expansive chest. He hadn't bothered to shave, and dark stubble shaded the sides of his face and upper lip. Her hand itched to reach out to see what it felt like.

He couldn't have looked hotter if he'd tried. She wanted to yank him inside her apartment, have hot monkey sex, and get him out of her system once and for all. This physical craving would likely go away after one time with him.

"'Morning," he said.

"Hey." May as well get down to business. Staring at him wouldn't help Betty. "Did you get in touch with Angie in 807?"

"She's happy to meet with us. Making coffee right now, I think." Blake grinned, glanced down the old hallway decorated with framed paintings of Baltimore, and then held out his elbow.

Missy plastered a smile on her face. "Great." After locking her door, she threaded her arm through his. Felt good. Like a couple. Her heart skipped a beat. She really needed to find someone to date in this town. Someone who wasn't a cop.

They stood in front of 807 and Missy shivered. "Damn. It's colder here than it was down the hall."

Blake frowned. "Are the hairs on the back of your neck standing right now?"

She met his worried eyes and nodded twice.

He shook his head and rapped his knuckles under the numbers.

Missy crossed her arms to warm herself.

A few locks clicked, and the door opened. The pretty blonde Missy had seen a few times wore a simple T-shirt, and jeans. Her hair was in a ponytail as if she was ready to workout. "Hey, Blake. I appreciate you bringing Missy by to introduce us." She opened the door stood to the side. "I made coffee. Come on in."

"Hi, Angie. I'm Missy Prescott."

Angie shook Missy's hand and gave her a wide, welcoming smile. Missy liked her instantly.

"I'm curious about some things with the building and its recent history," Missy said.

A worried look flashed across Angie's face, and then she smiled. "I've lived here a few years. I'm happy to share what I know." She waved them into the upscale kitchen-dining room area that was almost an exact replica of Blake's apartment. Beige wall-to-wall carpeting, plush sofas, and granite countertops in the kitchen. A silver-filigreed coffeepot, three cups, and saucers sat in the middle of an oak table.

"Gorgeous pot," Missy said.

Angie laughed. "Not many occasions to bring it out, so I thought today would be a good time. Belonged to my grandmother."

Blake grinned and leaned a slim hip against the counter. "To think I've settled for instant roast in a dollar-store mug all these years."

Angie and Missy laughed.

"Want to grab coffee and sit in the living room?" Angie nodded toward the window.

"Great. Thanks. You really didn't have to go to all this trouble, though." Angie poured the brew.

"If you don't mind me asking, what exactly happened in this apartment last winter?" Blake asked.

The saucer and cup Angie held rattled so hard she set them down on the table again. She looked at Blake, then at Missy, and took a deep breath. "Most people know. And it's been in the media. Scares me to think about it all even to this day, though."

"Of course," Blake said.

Oooh, he was smooth.

Angie leaned her hands on the back of a dining room chair and stared at a spot across the room. "My daughter got involved with someone very bad. A heroin dealer. He corrupted her." She bit her bottom lip and tears sparkled in her eyes. Then she straightened her shoulders and walked to a chair.

Missy followed and perched on the sofa. Blake sat beside her, his leg touching hers. Missy took her cue from Blake, saying nothing, giving the woman time to collect herself.

"Vinnie—my daughter Chloe's boyfriend—drugged my orange juice, tried to kill me, and make it look like a suicide for my life insurance money. It almost worked." Angie glanced at the wall near the sofa. "He died right there. My fiancé, Rob, shot him, but that's not what killed him. He died when he lunged at me and tripped and then he fell on his own syringe full of heroin."

"That's when J.B. came in? After the kid was dead?" Blake asked.

"Yes. J.B. heard the gunshot."

Missy leaned forward. "I know this sounds strange, but have you ever felt like this place is...well, haunted?"

Angie's brows rose. "Why do you ask?"

Missy couldn't tell her about Betty. Not yet. Too unbelievable. Better to keep asking questions. "The kid that died...did he look like a younger version of your fiancé, Rob, somehow?"

The woman blinked and gasped. Was the drug-dealer kid her fiancé's son? Could that have been something that wasn't common knowledge about the case? Missy had looked up the report online, but only found out basic facts about a stabbing and shooting that resulted in death in the apartment. Nothing more specific than some gossip and speculation in the local newspaper blog comments. Hard to sift the truth from the rumors that hinted at a drug deal gone wrong.

"Angie? You can tell us. We're curious, that's all." Blake's voice was low, soothing. Keeping his cool like a cop, while Missy's heart pounded at the woman's reaction.

Angie stood and moved to a nearby bookshelf. "This is a younger version of my fiancé." She turned a revealed a framed photo of a smiling teenaged boy. "Have you seen him?"

Blake and Missy shook their heads.

"Looks like your fiancé a little bit," Missy said. What was the woman getting at? What was with the childhood photos?

"This isn't Rob. It's his twin brother Mick, who died when he was seventeen." Angie caressed the frame as if the photo was a treasured item, and then glanced at Missy. "You asked about ghosts. I'm going to be straight with you because I think there's a reason you're asking."

"There is," Missy whispered.

The woman nodded and reset the frame. "I've seen his ghost. He's a helpful, kind ghost. But there's something bad—something supernatural-bad—outside in the hallway. It's colder there. Creepy. Not enough to make me move...only enough to make me cautious. I never stand out there too long."

"Care to tell us when you saw Mick last?" Blake asked.

"It's been a while. A few months." She sat in the chair again, glancing from Missy to Blake, clearly curious.

"Why did he appear? Was he...I don't know...haunting you?" Missy asked.

"No, no. He wouldn't do anything to hurt anyone." Angie leaned back in the chair and crossed her arms on her chest. "Listen, I'm not great about sharing this stuff. I think eventually I'll open up more, but it's very fresh in my mind. I might even try to chat with a gal from the first floor—Veronica's her name—who is a psychic, one day in the future. For now, all I can tell you for sure is that Mick was good as a human and he's good in the afterlife. And there's something bad in the hallway on this floor." She stood.

Visit over. They wouldn't get any more information here.

Missy and Blake stood at the same time.

"Do you mind if I ask one more question?" Missy asked.

Angie shrugged. "Go ahead."

"Have you seen any other ghosts around here?"

"No. And I hope I don't. But something tells me you have." She fidgeted with her pony tail.

Missy nodded. "Thanks for your time."

The woman led them to the door. "Nice meeting you, Missy. Nice seeing you again, Blake. Good to know there's a cop on this floor. Makes me feel safer."

Blake nodded a good-bye.

Missy and Blake stepped into the hall and Angie closed the door.

"It's really cold here." Missy rubbed her arms. Blake moved closer and warmth radiated from him.

"I feel it, too." He frowned. "I'll deny it if you ever repeat this, but I'm getting a strange feeling that someone, or something, is watching us."

♋

Blake pulled into the underground garage at his apartment building and turned off his truck. Two burglaries, one domestic dispute, and over a dozen other calls while on patrol that night. At least he'd gotten to listen to Missy's show in between calls. If she hadn't become a deejay, she would have made a good shrink because she always knew what to say to her listeners, and her calming voice could convince a dog to give up a bone.

His footsteps echoed on the deserted cement floor, and his handcuffs clinked on his belt as he made his way to the elevator and inserted his key into the panel. It was a security measure meant to keep outsiders from entering the complex.

The elevator motor whirled into motion, and the sound of a car approaching made him turn around. A blue Honda Accord rounded the corner and parked across from his truck. Missy? At one fifteen in the morning, it was about the right time for her to arrive home, he supposed.

Sure enough, the first thing he spotted was the top of her head and then her smile.

"Fancy meeting you here," he said. "I'll hold the elevator." The doors opened, and he held the button.

"Hey! Great. Thanks." She beeped her car locked and jogged across the lot toward him.

He scanned her body as she took off, unable to resist a lingering gaze at her long legs and a loose, navy blue blouse. It was enough to give a hint of the curves below. Blake swallowed the lump in his throat. *Damn.* Maybe he should stop listening to her show. Hearing her voice, and then seeing her in person—knowing the person behind the voice—made him want more from her. And she'd already made it very clear that wasn't a possibility.

She stepped into the elevator, keys in hand, and he pressed the number eight.

"Good show tonight." He stood in one corner of the elevator and she stood in the other.

"Yeah? You caught it even though you were on patrol?" She fished her phone out of her pocket and held it in her hand with her keys.

"Parts of it. Busy night...but what night isn't?"

"True. Baseball games must make it even more hectic." She leaned a slim hip against the hold bar and yawned. Was it his imagination, or was she staring at his uniform? Her eyes fixated on his badge, then his weapon.

"Yes, ma'am." May as well pour it on thick. The whole cop routine. *That's what she wants, right? A reason to keep him away from her.*

His words did the trick. Her gaze flickered to his and held it. *Anger?*

The elevator dinged, announcing their arrival on the eighth floor. Neither of them moved.

"You must very good at your job. Very observant to notice me taking in your cop attire." She exited the elevator and strode toward her apartment.

Yep. He'd pissed her off all right.

She turned toward him as he stepped off the elevator. "Have a good night."

His gaze swept behind her. Something wasn't right. A shadow. A dark shadow had moved, as if the door had closed. "Don't move!" he commanded, pulling his weapon and running toward her apartment.

She froze in her spot with eyes opened wide.

He stood between her and her door, both hands on his weapon as he aimed it at her entrance.

"What is it?" she hissed from behind him.

He reached out, tried the knob. Locked. "Give me your keys."

Without hesitating, she passed her keys to him. "Should I call 9-1-1?" She kept her voice low, obviously trusting him, and not shrugging off his reaction as if unnecessary. *A cop's daughter. A smart woman.*

He reached forward, inserted the key, and twisted the knob before slamming the entry open. "Police. Come out with your hands up."

A strong odor wafted to his nostrils, stinging them. "Stay here," he ordered. Stepping inside, sweeping his gun from side to side, he spotted something in the middle of the living area. Moving closer, he lowered his Glock and lifted his undershirt to cover his nose. A flea bomb. *What the hell?*

With a quick check of the other rooms to be sure they were empty, he hurried back to the hallway where Missy stood with her cell phone at the ready.

He closed the door behind him. "A flea bomb. You can't go in there."

"What?" Her brows shot up. "Is that what that smell is? Why the hell would there be a flea bomb in there? I don't have a pet. I'm allergic to cats."

"Betty." They both said it at the same time.

"Seriously? You think she'd do that? Like I wasn't already freaked out enough about the caller who asked for naked pictures tonight? I didn't need this." She pocketed her phone and rubbed her temples.

"What caller?" Alarms went off in his head. She was too nice, too friendly. Apparently the phone calls she aired weren't the only ones she was receiving. The image of her naked in a picture flashed through his mind, though, making him feel as dirty as the perverted caller.

She waved a hand in front of her face. "Some jerk. It's nothing. We get those kinds of calls all the time. But now I'm calling the superintendent. I don't care how late it is. Maybe it wasn't Betty who set that flea bomb off."

"May as well check." It could have been Betty, but the more he thought about it, the more he wondered if it was something she'd do.

Missy tapped numbers on her phone. "Kevin? It's Missy Prescott from apartment 812. There's a flea bomb going off in my apartment. Do you know anything about it?"

Her full lips parted, and she shook her head and closed her eyes for a few seconds before opening them again. "Seriously? How could you put it in the wrong apartment?"

She listened a few beats and then sighed. "Fine. Good night."

"He put it in the wrong apartment?" Blake asked. *What a pain in the ass.*

"He sounded drunk. And yes, the wrong apartment." She glanced at her neighbor's door on the left side.

"Stay at my place tonight." *Shit. No. That won't work.* Hard enough being near her as they figured out this ghost stuff. Besides...he needed a shower after his sweaty shift, and he had a hard-and-fast rule after having his identity stolen. Nobody allowed by themselves in his apartment unless he was right there with them. She was a cop's daughter for crying out loud.... But he'd been fooled before.

Missy studied him for a moment, her hazel eyes searching his.

In spite of his worries, more words tripped out of his mouth, needing to convince her to stay. "It's after one in the morning. You can't stay there, and a hotel would be a pain. I have a perfectly good sofa. You can have my bed." Great. Now he was visualizing her naked in pictures and in his bed. Stupid to offer her a place to stay. Better to offer to drive her to a hotel.

"You're right. I appreciate it. Thanks." She nibbled her bottom lip and glanced toward his door.

Too late to take back out of his invite. He'd need willpower to get through this night. Betty's interfering had thrown them together, and their need to help her was keeping them together. Problem was, the more time Blake spent with Missy, the more he couldn't get her off his mind.

He couldn't blame Betty for that.

Chapter Seven

$\mathcal{M}$issy cracked open a beer and leaned against the granite countertop in Blake's kitchen. The sound of the shower running through the thin walls made her picture him naked and wet. The sheer force of his take-charge personality in the hall had turned her on. *Damn it!* She needed to date safe guys.... The problem was, when she did, they did nothing for her.

Blake was the type of guy she wanted. Maybe she could get him out of her system. No Betty to push them together this time. Missy wanted to be with him, wanted those strong hands on her again. Her need came from deep within.

Why not have him? One time. Nothing would change except they'd get each other out of their systems and move on with being neighborly as they helped Betty.

Missy took another swig of her beer and glanced at the counter where one of Blake's clean T-shirts and a pair of his boxers lay. His loan so she could sleep in comfortable clothes.

She glanced toward his open bedroom door and the bathroom within where the shower water halted.

She wasn't a one-time sort of girl. She'd been brought up to think sex was something you did when you were committed, part of a relationship. Time to make an exception. Being around him fogged her mind. One time, and they'd move on to bigger and better things. Like helping Betty.

She scooped up the T-shirt and boxers and made her way to the small half-bath across from the kitchen. Not exactly a slinky nightie, but if she donned them now, he was sure to get the hint that she wanted him. Standing on tiptoe, she eyed herself in the mirror above the sink. His navy blue shirt smelled like clean detergent and hung loose past her hips, almost to the hem of the boxers.

Swallowing hard, she closed her eyes and leaned forward with both hands on the sink. Maybe she should just grab a blanket and go to bed.

Missy opened the door at the same time he strolled out of the bathroom and into the bedroom. She had a clear view of his room.

His back faced her. Wearing only black boxers, he opened a dresser drawer. Dark hair hung in wet ringlets against his neck. Broad, tanned shoulders rippled as he rummaged through his drawer. She wanted to trace the chain tattoo on his shoulder with her finger. Or her tongue. Droplets of water trickled down his spine and Missy dropped her gaze lower. Her hands itched to find out how muscular his butt was. She wanted to rest her head against his strong chest.

He stopped as if realizing she stood nearby, but didn't turn. Instead, he glanced over his shoulder. His gaze swept from her eyes down to her bare toes and then back to her eyes. With a look, he sent passion firing through her entire body. Her breath hitched and her heart went into a wild beat that rivaled tribal drums.

Holding her gaze, he turned to face her.

Oh, holy shit. Her gaze dropped to his muscular pecs, down his taut abs, and to the trail of dark hair that veed into the black boxers and lower. There was no doubt in her mind that he wanted her.

Forcing her gaze higher, she stared at his tattoo. A part of him. A mystery about him. She couldn't wait any longer. She needed to touch him, have him touch her.

"Want me to show you where you'll be sleeping?" His voice was husky.

She'd already turned him down once. That meant she had to be the one to make the move this time. "I'm not really tired." On shaking legs, she crossed the carpeted room and stood in front of him, breathing hard.

He smelled like clean soap and Blake. Mostly he smelled of Blake and that was a damned good scent.

God. Why is it so hard to breathe? She'd had sex before. She'd been with a few men. Never like this. Never with an overpowering need to be close, to be touched...to be one.

He didn't budge, as if letting her make the choice. Somehow that turned her on even more.

Aching to touch him, almost afraid of the fire she'd start if she did, she reached out and laid her hand on his arm, just below the tattoo, and then traced it with a finger.

He sucked in a breath.

"What do these chain links mean?" Her voice came out a whisper as she traced the three links and the two end links with edges that faded into heated skin.

"Protection. Strength."

She nodded. "I like it." One step closer, and she'd be able to lay her head on his chest, hear his heart beat.

"You look pretty hot in that shirt," he said. His chest rumbled with the words, and she gave into the temptation to lean against him. Her head met hard muscle and soap-scented skin. Something in her core liquefied.

"Say something else," she whispered, splaying a hand on his pec.

Instead, he chuckled. The sound sent spirals of desire through her body. Standing so close, knowing he wanted what she wanted made her weak with desire. Every limb trembled, and liquid fire bloomed between her legs.

He cupped her chin in his palm and she glanced up at his brown eyes. A thin stream of light from the open hallway door arrowed inside and threw a shadow on one side of his face, conveying an aura of mystery.

Her gaze searched his, and her breaths came in short pants. His eyes asked a hundred questions, but she only had enough breath to answer one.

"Kiss me. Please." She had to have him...had to taste that mouth again, feel his hands on her body, touch the rippling muscles of his form.

His hand moved to the base of her neck, and his lips touched hers.

Heat spiraled from the tip of her skull to her toes and she moaned into his mouth and dug her fingers into his strong shoulders.

He kissed the seam of her lips, gently licking until he found an opening, and then his warm tongue probed deeper, searching and exploring as he moved his hands lower, to the sides of her waist.

Missy's legs grew weak and she held on to him, not just to be close to him. She needed his strong body to balance against.

His erection pressed against her middle and his warm hands stroked her sides, lifting the light T-shirt. He skimmed her skin. Gently, stirring a passion deep in her belly, his fingers trailed a heated line to the sides of her breasts as his tongue explored, going deeper, searching, stirring a passion so strong in Missy that she couldn't think about anything else except this man. This sexy man who held her close.

His strong body made her feel feminine in comparison. He groaned and kissed the corner of her mouth and then trailed a line of hot kisses from her lobe to her collarbone. Missy tilted her head back, giving him complete access as his hands moved inward, cupping her breasts with his palms and using his thumbs to tease her pebbled nipples.

Torture. Sweet torture. Moisture pooled between her legs and she ground against his erection.

"So soft," he murmured into her ear as he nuzzled his nose into her hair and massaged her breasts.

"So hard," she said, her words coming out choked as she moved a hand to the outside of his boxers and massaged his cock over the cotton fabric. He moaned and grew even harder. This powerful, sexy man was responding to her touch, answering her needs with the same level of need as hers. She needed him on top of her. Under her. Any damn way she could get him.

It didn't matter how they'd gotten to this point, all that mattered right now was that she couldn't go another minute without being with him in every way possible.

His hands traced from her breasts and left a hot trail as he slid his fingertips down her spine, vertebra by vertebra, to the elastic of the boxers he'd lent her. She gasped as his fingers shifted the fabric and his hands moved inside to cup her buttocks.

"Damn, you've got a hot body," he said, kissing the corner of her mouth. His warm breath skimmed her cheek and she smiled, enjoying the feel of his cock in her palms and the way his hands explored her ass globes.

She laid her head on his chest, closed her eyes, and sighed. Passion so raw, but something else, too. A connection. Heat soared inside and she knew he felt it, too.

"Blake...." She struggled to catch her breath, trying to tell him in words what her body was already signaling to him. She wanted to make love with him.

Before the words formed, she opened her eyes and the first thing she saw was the chair where he'd neatly laid his clothes before getting in the shower. Like a bucket of ice had been dumped on her head, everything inside of Missy froze and her breath hitched.

A bloody police uniform...a half-dozen bullet holes...her brother's unmoving form.

Blood rushed to her head, pounding between her ears. This was a mistake. She had to get out of there before she fell for this guy and lost him...and her heart.

Blake turned his head, followed her gaze. His hands moved from her ass to her waist and he backed up a step, replacing the heat of his body with the air-conditioned room air. Part of her wished he'd take his hands completely off her, the other part begged him to hold on.

His uniform lay like a dragon waiting to breathe fire and swallow them whole. She couldn't do this. No matter what her heart and her body said, she could not go through the grief of losing another person to a dangerous job. This wouldn't work, and she could never be with him.

Besides, he'd hate her now, right? Label her a tease. They'd taken each other to a level where the next step was bed and sharing their bodies in the most intimate way possible. But now....

He leaned his forehead against hers. Not mad...not upset. "I guess I should leave."

He got it. He understood why she had freaked out and he didn't seem to hold it against her.

A giggle rumbled from the deepest part of her throat at this, the most inopportune moment. "Uh, Blake. You're not going anywhere. This is your apartment."

He pressed his lips together, held her an arm's length away, strong hands gripping her shoulders as he glanced around his bedroom. "So it is." He nodded a few times as if coming to grips with the situation.

Good that *one* of them could come to grips with it, because her head spun with indecision. She'd gone from lust-filed, weak-legged passion to a flashback of Jeff's sudden death.

Emotional whiplash.

Blake cleared his throat. "Listen...I'm going to take a shower." He glanced between them at his erection. "A cold one this time."

Missy bit the inside of her lip. This whole situation was so fucking unbelievable. She wanted him, but couldn't have him. So not fair. Why couldn't he have been a waiter? Or an accountant? Or another deejay?

"Okay." How exactly did one apologize for giving a man a rock-hard erection and then slamming on the brakes? "I'm sorry, Blake. I—"

"Do you like puzzles?" He crossed his arms and stared at her with narrowed eyes.

Puzzles? Was he saying her hot-then-cold antics puzzled him? Then she remembered his dining room table and the world map.

She attempted a smile and then shrugged, the lump in her throat preventing her from answering.

"Why don't you get us two beers and we'll work on the puzzle and figure out some ideas for helping Betty?" He massaged the back of his neck with one of his hands as if working off tension.

"Good idea." Relief flooded Missy's overworked system. He wasn't mad, didn't seem to think she was a tease. He was willing to be friends. All the more reason she wished he had a different job.

He headed back to the shower, and her gaze fell again on the black uniform folded on the chair.

It represented so much: respect, duty, strength.

Pain...grief...death.

ᬃ

Blake yawned and rolled the sausage links in the frying pan. He hadn't slept well knowing Missy was in the next room, knowing what those soft curves felt like in his hands. At least she'd insisted on taking the couch. Picturing her in his bed would have driven him all kinds of crazy.

Didn't help that she was currently in his shower and he couldn't shake the image of her naked and wet only a few feet away. Grease splattered from the pan and he welcomed the shot of pain on his hand. A distraction.

Cooking breakfast for two. A first for him. Usually, he was long gone before the light of dawn. Easier to cut any perceived ties that way. A good-bye in the dark was easier than a good-bye in the light of day.

The bathroom water shut off and he cracked an egg into a bowl and then grabbed another one. Great. Now he was picturing her naked...toweling off those long, lean legs...that firm ass. Maybe a towel wrapped around her long, brown hair.

His cock hardened and the egg cracked in his hand, its insides seeping out of his palm. He shook the liquid and shell pieces off his hand into the kitchen sink and washed his hands. He needed to get laid soon. Tonight would be a good night to hit the bars and find someone fun.

Just one problem: suddenly, the only woman he wanted was the one who didn't want him. Must be some sort of ego thing. He didn't fall for women. He was too smart for that. Long ago, he'd learned that lesson. And had it hammered over his head again and again, too. Women couldn't be trusted. His mother had proved that years ago, and then Claire confirmed it when she stole his identity.

He wanted Missy because he couldn't have her. That had to be it. Made her more attractive...a challenge. No. He had to be honest with himself, even if he couldn't be honest with her. Being around her made him happy and he had no idea why.

"Mmmm." Missy rounded the corner. "Something smells good." At least she had her clothes on. Her wet hair hung past her shoulders and her face was free of makeup. Seeing her earlier that morning in his T-shirt and boxers had filled him with desire. Fully clothed, he could picture her sitting in the studio with her microphone in front of her. Nothing sexy about that. Unless her warm breath on the microphone reminded him of the way her mouth might feel on his cock....

Shit! Get a hold of yourself.

"Sausage and scrambled eggs okay with you? Breakfast is the only meal I cook." Small talk. He could make small talk and forget about what almost happened last night.

"Awesome. Can I help?" She moved beside him and he caught a whiff of his soap. *Damn, it smelled much better on her.*

"Want to refill our mugs and grab plates and forks?" He shoved his empty cup down the counter, closer to the coffeemaker.

She filled the cups and set them on the breakfast bar beside each other. This was all too cozy. No wonder he'd never done this before. He liked to fly solo. Hated this whole host thing. Yet a part of him ached when she set a plate by each mug. What might that be like? To trust someone enough to live with them, let down your guard?

Missy rounded the breakfast bar and sat on a stool, lifting her mug with both hands toward her lips. Those luscious lips he couldn't seem to get enough of. Yeah, the sooner he got her out of there, the better off he'd be. He plunked two pieces of bread in the toaster and pressed the lever.

He grabbed the skillet and scooped scrambled eggs onto each plate. "Hope you like lots of cheese."

"Oh yeah. The more cheese, the better."

Great. One more way they were in sync. Turning, he grabbed the other skillet and forked two sausages onto each plate. The toast popped and he plucked the butter from the fridge, and then slathered some on each piece before setting the toast between the plates.

Missy eyed the toast and then laughed. "You don't worry much about fat content, do you?" She forked a bite of the scrambled eggs.

"What? You got a problem with the menu?" He liked this. Neighbors bantering. Not lovers. Friends. He could handle this.

"Hell no. I never criticize a free meal I didn't have to cook." She cut a piece of sausage and guided her fork to her lips.

Blake grabbed a piece of toast and loaded scrambled eggs onto it. "Well, more for me if you don't finish."

She laughed and they ate in relative quiet.

After, Missy insisted on doing the dishes while Blake checked his e-mail.

"That was fun working on the puzzle last night." Missy hung the dish towel on the stove handle. "I appreciate you letting me crash here and for breakfast. I called the super and he said the apartment is fine now. He took out the flea bomb and opened the windows first thing this morning."

"Well, at least you know your apartment is flea-free."

Missy chuckled, a warm sound. That voice that made listeners open up about their lives every night sounded pretty damn good in the morning, too.

She grabbed her purse off the back of a stool. "I'll wash the shirt and boxers you loaned me and bring them back, okay?"

"Sure. Great." He stood and walked to the door behind her. May as well get one more look at that heart-shaped ass that felt so good in his hands last night.

She walked into the hallway, jingling her keys in her hand.

Yeah, her firm, shapely ass looked good in those jeans.

Blake's gaze was on Missy's butt, so when she stopped suddenly, he almost plowed into her.

Missy gasped. "Betty! What are you doing?"

He followed her glance to the end of the hallway, and spotted a dark shadow.

Missy took a step.

The shadow moved and the hairs on the back of his neck stood as if the air were filled with electricity. Why did she think it was Betty? All he could see was a dark form floating outside of apartment 807.

Shit! The bad vibes Angie had spoken about.

"Betty, you need to get away from there." Missy strode closer to the shadow. But how did she know it was Betty? It could be the awful thing, if he believed in that sort of thing, that Angie had mentioned.

"What makes you think it's Betty?" Blake hissed, putting himself between her and the entity at the end of the hall.

"Don't you see her?" Missy grabbed his hand, held it tight.

And suddenly, the black, shadowy form morphed into Betty McAllister, her blue eyes shimmering with tears, her flamingo earrings dangling. He'd smelled Betty before. Sensed her, even. Why could he see her so clearly this time? Because he was touching Missy?

Blake's heart slammed. A swirling, fog-like mass filled the corridor behind Betty outside of apartment 807. A passageway into another world? But was that world good or bad?

"Betty, you have to get away from there." Blake stood in front of Missy, one hand holding hers, the other blocking her from passing. He glanced over her shoulder at Missy.

"We need to get her away from that vortex," Missy whispered.

Blake cleared his throat, shaking off the disbelief that he stood in front of a ghost that looked like a human. "Betty. Come toward us. Please." He reached a hand toward her.

She frowned, as if just noticing them, and then smiled. "Did you two both come out of the same apartment?" She took a few steps closer to them and Missy let out a sigh and moved beside Blake. He gripped her hand, unsure if he'd lose the ability to see Betty if he let go. Didn't matter. He liked the warm feel of her small hand in his.

Betty stopped when she was almost to them and turned to look at the other side of the hall. "I wanted to see Stanley. I wasn't going to go in. I know better than that." Tears shimmered in her eyes, but she smiled.

"I think you need to stay far away from that area of the hallway, Betty. Until we figure some things out." Unreal. He was having a conversation with someone who'd been dead for almost two months. If Missy hadn't been standing beside him, seeing the same thing, he'd have chalked up the entire experience as a waking dream.

"Why don't we talk about what Blake and I are trying to do to help you get to Stanley, and what we've found out?" Missy gestured with her hand toward her apartment.

"Tea?" Betty asked, as they all turned as a unit toward Missy's door.

"Sure...tea."

Missy shot Blake an I-told-you-so look. He'd teased her earlier about having tea with a ghost, and now he was about to do it. Fine. *May as well take this whole ghost thing to a new level.* What the hell, maybe they could all put a puzzle together, too.

Missy unlocked the door and stepped inside.

True to his word, the super had opened all the windows and the apartment smelled like a warm city breeze. Complete with exhaust fumes. Missy started closing windows.

"So...Betty..." Blake said. "Any chance you had anything to do with a flea bomb in Missy's apartment last night?"

Betty smiled and looked at the carpeted floor, wringing her hands together. "Well, Kevin was so drunk, all I had to do was give him a little push from the door of that apartment next door to this one."

Blake gazed over Betty's silver-haired head at Missy who nodded and rolled her eyes.

"Should I make some tea?" Missy walked around her breakfast bar into the kitchen.

"No thank you, honey. Come sit with us." Betty took a seat in the rocking chair, and Blake perched on the edge of a side chair, staring at her.

"This is the first time you've really seen me, isn't it?" Betty asked, leaning with her hands on the armrests and rocking back and forth. She looked like anyone's grandma on an ordinary day.

Missy took a seat near Blake.

"I thought I caught a glimpse of you once. But...now.... You look so *real*." Blake glanced toward Missy. "I've felt you...I've smelled apple pie...."

Betty smiled and stopped rocking to lean toward him. "Really? You smelled apple pie? Like the ones I used to make you?"

He nodded.

Betty glanced at Missy and then back at Blake. "This whole supernatural thing has too many layers to it. I'm ready to move on. I want to see my Stanley. I was hoping that if I stood by that portal at the end of the hall, my guide would come. I can't figure this out on my own."

They needed to solve this problem for Betty, help her move on to be with Stanley. But how?

"Did you find him?" Blake asked.

"Nope. Nobody there. Just some creepy fog." Betty rocked again and looked toward the door as if picturing the fog.

Blake frowned. How could they help this special lady find what she needed in the afterlife? He could sit here and deny her existence—deny the existence of ghosts—but he'd known Betty lingered. Knew it in his gut, from the little things she'd done, the odd things he'd experienced since she'd passed away.

It took Missy's acceptance of Betty to help him accept Betty.

He settled into the plush chair. "Missy and I talked with the woman who lives in 807."

Betty's eyes widened. "Angela Barsotti. Such a pretty young lady. A nice daughter, too." She smiled. "I heard Angie and that handsome accountant got engaged." Her smile faded from her lips and she leaned forward. "The daughter's boyfriend died. He was bad news."

"That boyfriend might be the evil presence outside of apartment 807," Missy said.

Betty gasped.

Better for Missy to reveal the information than Blake. All this hoodoo-ghost stuff made him feel like he was living in a parallel universe. One he'd never believed in.

"Angie said something...." Missy glanced at Blake before gazing at Betty. "Well, she actually showed us something that makes us think the guide you mentioned—the good spirit—is Rob's twin brother, who died as a teen."

Betty tilted her head as if processing the new information. "What a nice young man he must have been."

Part of Blake wanted to jump off the chair and run out of this apartment. They were sitting here—with a spirit—discussing ghosts as if it were an average everyday conversation. What the hell? In for a penny, in for a pound.

"Have you heard anything about a psychic who lives on the first floor?" Blake wondered if it was too early in the day for a shot of whiskey. After a night of pulse-hammering almost-lovemaking that had his blood pumping even now and then, for a morning of conversation with a ghost he could use something to calm his thoughts.

Betty waved a dismissive hand. "Veronica. Let's wait to talk to her. She won't be back for a week or so. Don't get me wrong, she's a very nice young lady...but I know what to do to earn my chance to cross over and see Stanley." She winked at Blake and then smiled at Missy.

Matchmaking. Yeah, well that plan wasn't going to work, so they'd better have a backup plan. He'd treat this like an investigation. He'd pretend for a moment that sitting here talking to a ghost wasn't the craziest damn thing he'd ever been involved in, and figure out what Betty needed to get to the other side. *Don't overthink this.*

"Maybe the nice young lady can help speed up the process. You know...get you to Stanley faster." Blake glanced at Missy for help and she nodded, picking up his cue.

"I'm sure she'd have something useful that would help us help you. We're pretty new at this whole spirit-world thing." Her mouth curved into a smile and her entire face lit up. Blake's mind flashed back to the way those full lips had swollen under his greedy mouth last night. He shifted in his seat and angled his feet at the door. He had to get out of there. Between the ghost stuff and the crazy thoughts that ran through his head when he was around Missy, he needed distance.

Betty took a sip of her tea, gazing at Missy over the edge of the cup as if she had all the time in the world. Well, of course she did. She had eternity. But he had to be at work by three.

"Maybe we could hire a psychic. Or a ghost hunter or something. Aren't there people who do that for a living?" *Damn.* Word about his involvement had better not leak out to the guys at the station or he'd never hear the end of this.

"No hurry, dears." Betty smiled at them and then stood. "I know not to get too close to that energy vortex—whatever it is—again. I was just peeking to see if I could find my guide. Ask him some questions. But I think I have to wait for him to find me. I need to be patient."

She nodded at each of them, a twinkle in her eyes. "Good to see you both come out of the same apartment. I might be old, but I'm not old-fashioned." She giggled and held her chin high. "I'm going to leave the two of you alone now. We'll figure things out when Veronica gets back. That will be enough time to finish what I need to do."

Betty faced the door, but instead of opening it, she disappeared.

Blake's heart dipped to his size-twelve feet. Ghosts. Vortexes. Evil spirits. *I am not cut out for this shit.*

"What do we do?" Missy asked.

Blake shook his head and glanced up at Missy's kind, hazel eyes.

Even without makeup, her skin glowed and her eyes shone with passion.

"Let me make some calls. Maybe we can find an expert who can help her get to Stanley."

The faster they helped Betty move on, the faster he could stop being tempted by the beauty who had a hold on his thoughts—and heart.

Chapter Eight

$\mathcal{M}$issy highlighted three songs on her computer screen and then clicked the option to play. That would give her at least ten minutes to take listener calls.

It had been a week since she'd last seen Blake, but the memory of their almost-sex haunted her. No matter what she did, she couldn't shake the thought of him. Watching a movie didn't work, although having Betty as company in her living room made her feel less lonely. Especially when Betty giggled like a little girl at the romantic comedy they'd chosen.

She and Blake texted a few times. They kept their conversations neutral. Always about Betty. After some back-and-forth about reputable local psychics, they decided Veronica would be the best person to help them. If there was something evil and Veronica knew about it, they'd need to beware.

A light blinked on Missy's studio phone, and she cleared her throat, readying her radio voice for the caller.

"Hi, this is Misty till Midnight. What song can I play for you tonight?" She kept her voice warm and friendly.

"Nothing, babe. Just get naked and text me your photo." The caller kept his voice at a husky whisper. Probably to make himself sound creepier.

Missy took a deep breath. Didn't matter that she'd received dozens of calls like this. She still hated it. Hated that people thought she was some sort of dumping ground for their boredom, or their freaky desires. He'd blocked his number, so it didn't show on the caller ID. Even though she felt like hanging up on him, it would probably make things worse.

She inhaled slowly and then blew out a quiet breath. "Let me remind you that calls are being recorded, sir."

Click.

Ha! A small victory. At least she'd shut him up and gotten the last word. Her thoughts flew to Blake again. Maybe she should mention this guy to him. She had lots of regular callers now, talked all the time to people she only knew from phone conversations. Almost counted them as friends, they called so often. But the few crank calls she got creeped her out.

The phone lit up again, and she braced herself. Another creep, or a real caller?

"This is Misty till Midnight. What can I play for you tonight?"

"Misty! Can you play 'In the Mood' by Glenn Miller?" The phone crackled with static and she almost dropped it.

"Betty?" Missy whispered.

"Yes, honey. 'In the Mood' was Stanley's and my song...." The rest of her sentence got lost in the static, and then the line went dead. Missy stared open-mouthed at the receiver.

Betty was probably sitting in the rocking chair, listening to the show. How had she gotten a phone? A landline, possibly?

She chuckled. She'd search for a copy of the old song and play it. Betty deserved a little fun. She needed to move on, of course, to be with her Stanley, but a selfish part of Missy liked having her company. A new town and the slow process of making new friends, made coming home to Betty, watching movies, and having tea with her...made Missy less lonely.

Her phone lit up, and she glanced at the computer screen. Plenty of time to take more calls and then edit them.

She lifted the receiver and spoke her standard line, hoping she sounded sincere since part of her kept dreading the naked-picture guy being back on the line. Lucky for her, a nice young woman who had just gotten engaged wanted to send out a love song to her new fiancé. After a friendly chat with the happy caller, Missy edited the call to play back later on the air.

She smiled and searched for the song, and added it to the play list for the evening. This was what she loved. Hearing happy stories and helping people celebrate. Or hearing sad stories and helping people get through a rough time. Sometimes she felt like she was healing through music. And why not? She'd always loved music, and one of the things that got her through those rough months after her father died—and then again when Jeff died—was listening to her favorite songs, or banging them out on the piano in her mother's living room.

Yeah, those years of lessons hadn't been totally wasted.

She caught movement at the studio window and smiled at Diane, who wiggled her fingers in a wave. Missy gestured her inside and her friend poked her head in the door.

"I've got a three-set playing. Thought I'd see if you were up for a last-minute date. Jason got a babysitter, and his friend is in town this week. I'm meeting them in Federal Hill for a drink after I get off." She grinned. "Andrew's cute...and single. Want to join us?"

Why not? "What does he do for a living?" Better to make sure he had a safe job before getting in any deeper.

"Stockbroker. Some sort of finance whiz. Jason knows him from college." Diane glanced at the hall. "Text me. I've gotta hit the ladies' room and then get back to my studio."

Don't hesitate. Just do it. "I'll go." A stockbroker was a nice, safe profession. Probably lucrative, too. Couldn't hurt to meet the guy. Maybe he'd jolt her thoughts off the handsome guy who lived across the hall. Maybe he'd be hot enough to quell the desire she couldn't shake since she'd made out with Blake.

"Yes!" Diane pumped her arm. "Oh! I almost forgot." She yanked a slip of paper from her pocket. "The psychic my mom uses. In case you still want it."

"Thanks." Missy tucked the paper in her jeans. They'd probably use the psychic from the first floor. It didn't hurt to have a backup.

"Sure thing. Off to the ladies' room." Diane hurried out of the studio.

Ten seconds later, Missy potted down the volume and turned on her microphone. She ran down the list of dedications she'd just played and reminded listeners to call in with their requests. Then she clicked the link to play two advertisements.

Her phone lit up, and she took a call. "It's me again. Kurt. I know I call a lot, but your songs, and the way you talk to your listeners...well, it's like you're a friend. I know you're just being nice, but it helps me feel better."

This was what she loved. Really making a difference in someone's life. Kurt had been distraught over his girlfriend's leaving when he'd called the first time. Time had been the main healer of his heart, but heck, a little music could finish the healing process sometimes.

"What do you want to hear tonight, Kurt?"

"How about you pick for me? Let me dedicate one to you for being such a good friend. I'm ready to move on now. Maybe I'll even ask out this woman at work I've had my eye on."

Missy chuckled. Nice that he wanted to reward her with a song, but that felt too self-serving, selfish. She couldn't play a song to herself on her show. Better for him to play a song that gave him the confidence to move on to a new relationship. "How about a great song about keeping your confidence high? 'I'm Still Standing' by Elton John?"

"Perfect! Thanks, Misty. I'll call you next week and let you know if she said yes."

He disconnected and Missy edited the call immediately. That would be a fun one to play back. Maybe the woman at his work would even recognize his voice, and be flattered that he'd gone to so much trouble for her.

The advertisements finished playing, and Missy went live again, then played the edited dedications and clicked on the songs that accompanied them.

Huffing out a breath, she leaned back in her chair. Busy night. Being her own producer kept her hopping, and she liked it that way. Her shift flew by. A glance at the black-and-white clock on the wall showed she only had a half hour left. Time for a few more dedications, and then she'd sign off.

Needing a stretch, but not wanting to leave the phone, she stood and strolled around the studio. A TV with the volume off showed the baseball game and the Orioles were winning. She glanced closer at the screen as a news alert crawled across the bottom.

A Baltimore city policeman was shot at the Inner Harbor. Currently at University of Maryland, Shock Trauma. Condition unknown.

Her breath caught in her throat and her lungs refused to allow a breath. Her heart pounded. On shaking legs, Missy stumbled to her purse. *Get a grip, get a grip. He's fine. There are hundreds of Baltimore city cops. Chances are it wasn't him.*

With trembling fingers, she scrolled to Blake's name on her phone and tapped it to connect. After three rings, it went to voice mail.

Shit!

She exited the screen to text him. But her damn fingers shook so badly she kept missing her intended letters.

"Come on. Get it together. Deep breaths." Hearing her voice—even though it sounded shaky and scared—calmed her enough to concentrate. She typed out a message.

She'd give him one minute to respond, and then she was out of there. She could try the police station, but they wouldn't give out information to the public. Hurrying to the computer, she quickly scanned in a block of songs to finish out the night. Her listeners wouldn't be happy, but she'd make it up to them.

Missy stared at her phone, willing him to text back. "Light up, damn it!" she growled at her phone. It didn't, and she wanted to hurl it across the room.

Images of Jeff—the blood on his uniform, his pale, white skin at the crime scene...his lifeless body—raced through her mind. She glanced at the TV again, but the news crawl had ended.

Panting for breath, she closed her eyes and leaned on the counter that held her microphone. She couldn't sit here wondering if it was Blake. He had to be okay; he just had to be. One way or another, she had to know. She grabbed her purse and ran out of the studio. This time of night, most offices were empty.

Near the end of the corridor, she skidded to a stop, checked to make sure Diane wasn't on-air, and opened the door.

Diane turned from her computer and jolted. "What's wrong?"

"I've got to go." It sounded like someone else's voice, not hers. Deeper. Shakier. Scared shitless. "Hospital...cop shot...can you cover?"

"Yes." She crossed the room and laid a hand on Missy's shoulder as she turned for the door. "Are you sure you should be driving? I could call a cab."

"I'm fine." Deep breaths. Keep taking deep breaths.

She'd hold it together and get to the hospital. Then she'd find out it wasn't Blake. It would be okay because it wasn't Blake.

She sped down the side street, glad it was almost midnight and there was virtually no traffic. She hit the beltway and pressed the gas pedal to the floor. What the hell, if a cop pulled her over for speeding, at least he might be able to give her an update about the policeman's name. It wouldn't be released to the public yet, but other local cops would know.

Ten minutes later, she swerved into a parking spot in the hospital lot. With her knuckles pressed to her lips, she raced inside, bracing for the worst...praying for the best.

The emergency room was packed. Black uniforms filled the area so there was barely enough room to stand. Had to be over two hundred of them, but only a low murmur of voices filled the room.

Missy fought to pull in a full breath, but her lungs wouldn't cooperate. Short gulps of air were all she could get. She'd been in a room like this a year ago. Brothers helping brothers and so many shoulders for her to lean on when Jeff....

She couldn't think about that right now. She had to find Blake in this sea of black uniforms. Making her way inside the room, she glanced to the right and left, searching for his dark hair, his muscular body, his brown eyes that held so much passion. Damn, she wanted that passion. She'd had her chance. Why had she passed it up? He did something to her. Something no other man had ever done. Made her forget her worries with his kisses, took her to new highs with his hands.

Her heart pounded as she neared the desk. She spotted a name tag. A sergeant. She'd ask him if the man who'd been shot was Blake.

She needed to know. Had to know. But the words wouldn't come out of her mouth.

"Missy?" Blake's voice. Or in her frantic need to hear him, was she hallucinating?

She whipped around toward the sound. With furrowed brows, Blake threaded his way through the throng of officers. The handsomest, loveliest, most wonderful furrowed brows she'd ever seen in her life. He was okay. He was alive. He wasn't hurt.

Tears filled her eyes and she raced toward him, plowing into his chest and throwing her arms around his shoulders.

Chapter Nine

*B*lake caught Missy midair as she leaped at him and held her close. He'd been so worried for Chad, who'd been shot in his midsection. Kevlar protected strongest at the chest...shots to the midsection produced unpredictable injuries.

Holding Missy, drawing in a deep breath of her peach-scented hair, calmed him almost as much as the news that Chad would be okay. He'd been so scared. Even with his brothers surrounding him, he'd felt alone.

It wasn't until Missy sprinted across the room and into his arms that the bad washed away. He buried his nose in her hair, holding her close, not caring that every man around probably gawked at them.

Her body shook, and she clutched his shoulders. Slowly, he lowered her feet to the floor. He leaned forward to keep her head in the crook of his neck.

"I saw the news. I thought...I thought...." Her husky, warm breath in his ear made his heart skip a beat. She cared about him. Cared so much that she'd left her show early and wouldn't let go of him. A new feeling. Nobody had ever cared that much before. His gut stirred with emotion.

"Shhhh. It's okay." She'd heard this type of news before. Twice. Both times it had ended horribly for her. Why hadn't he thought to call her? The fact that she'd been avoiding him for a week shouldn't have kept him from easing her mind. "Chad's going to be okay. Flesh wound and a broken arm."

She sniffled.

"Did you bring your car?" He rubbed a hand up and down her back, treasuring the feel of her. "I could use a ride home. I jumped in Larry's patrol car when we heard the news."

She leaned back, her hands on his shoulders, and nodded. Black mascara tracks trailed down her cheeks.

She'd cried for him? He swallowed hard. Worry was one thing, but tears? Nobody had ever cared enough to cry for him. He used his thumbs to wipe her tears and then cradled her face. "Come on. Let's get out of here."

With his hand on her back, Blake guided her through the crowd. His thoughts turned from his comrade, who would be okay, to the woman next to him, who likely was in shock after seeing the news.

Outside, the night air surrounded them. A welcome relief from the crowded waiting room. Missy stared straight ahead but made no effort to move out of his hold. Her warm, slim body next to his was just what he needed after the scare he'd had. Companionship. Company. His brothers inside the waiting room had a bond. The connection he felt with Missy was different.

"Over here." She pointed to a spot across the parking lot.

Her voice, that voice he loved so much, was serious now. Pissed. Who could blame her? Her worry for him made her worst nightmares slam back at her.

So maybe all he had with her would be a car ride home. After that, neighbors. Neighbors who worked together for a little while to help a nice lady ghost. Then, she'd likely avoid him forever.

They approached the driver's side of her car and he reluctantly took his hand off her back. "Want me to drive?"

"No. I'm fine." She didn't look at him, just unlocked the car with her fob and got in.

He strode to the passenger side and entered, huffing a breath as he clicked on his seat belt. Should he try to get her to talk about it? He wasn't good at that sort of thing, but he should probably try to help her, talk her through it.

She started the engine and peeled wheels out of the parking spot. *Yep. Pissed. Best to keep quiet.*

Her cell phone chirped, and she yanked it out of her jeans pocket as she turned out of the lot. "It's my mom checking to see that I made it home safely. Text her back that I'm with a friend and my friend will make sure I get home safely."

He took it, entered the text message, and sent it, glad for a distraction from his worries and from her anger.

She made a sudden turn behind a row of businesses and then maneuvered into a small fenced-in parking lot and pulled between two eighteen-wheeler trailers. After throwing the car into park, she cracked the windows open and locked the doors.

Only a thin stream of moonlight filtered into the car. She turned to face him. So she needed to talk this out. *Fine.* He unclicked his seat belt and turned to face her.

She took off her belt, stared ahead, and toed off her shoes. *Well, guess we're going to be here a while if she's getting comfortable.* She took a deep breath and blew it out and then braced her feet on the floor and arched her butt off the seat and unbuttoned her jeans.

He froze. *What the hell?* Just when he thought he understood, she threw in a curveball.

With a quick glance at him, she pulled her jeans and underwear down her legs and kicked out of them.

He swallowed hard as his heart ratcheted into high gear and his breaths came faster and faster.

Turning to face him, she maneuvered over the emergency brake and straddled his lap. *Holy fucking shit.*

His hands moved to cup her ass and heat sizzled through his torso straight to his dick. Her skin was soft and warm, and he massaged her ass, fighting to catch his breath as she leaned closer and her lips touched his.

Yes. This was what he needed. He teased the seam of her lips with his tongue and delved inside, yearning to taste her, get inside her as far as possible. So many emotions spiraled through him: fear, relief, passion. He could let his emotions rip with Missy, give in to this connection he felt with her.

He knew what she was going through, and she understood how he felt right now. Needed her. Needed her bad. Like he'd never needed anything in his life, as if his very survival depended on being with her. And maybe it did.

She broke the kiss and leaned back, panting. "Do you have other uniform shirts?"

"Uh-huh." He moved a hand from her ass to the small space between them and ran a finger along the wet folds between her legs.

She gasped and then tugged the hem of his shirt from his pants and yanked at the fasteners so hard that half the buttons flew. With another forceful rip, the rest of the buttons flew off and she leaned back, gasping as his finger moved inside her. His cock hardened and a slow moan escaped her lips.

"Off," she said, tugging at the shirt. He moved his hands to help her take off first one sleeve and then the other before she crumpled the garment and tucked it in the backseat.

After the turmoil she'd felt, she obviously needed to feel an element of control. Fine, he'd give her that. In fact, he liked letting her take the lead.

She wiggled her naked crotch over his pants-covered erection. His mind went blank with lust and she ripped at the Velcro fasteners on his Kevlar vest, and then tugged it over his head and tossed it in the backseat. *Damn. The woman knows what she is doing.* Within seconds, his T-shirt was off, too.

Needing to touch her, needing to feel her closer, he cupped the nape of her neck and pulled, burying his head in the crook of her neck, tasting her salty skin, pumping his hips against her core.

She reached to the side and he heard something click. The seat back slammed down. With his hands around her waist, and her body atop his, he scooted them backward.

Missy leaned back, straddling his thighs.

"Hold on...just for a second." He unclicked his gear belt and lifted his hips to pull it out from under him. Gently, he lowered it to the backseat floor. Her nimble fingers unfastened his pants. Lifting his hips again, he helped her move his pants to his ankles. Now nothing stood between them. No inhibitions...none of the worries they each carried around each day. It was the two of them, nearly naked and hot....

"Missy...." He wanted to tell her how badly he wanted her. Wanted to let her know how often he thought about her when she wasn't around. But the words wouldn't come. Maybe he could show her instead. He pulled her in for a kiss, tasting her, wanting the connection to her. He trailed a line of kisses from her lips down her chin. Part of him wanted to savor the moment. Another part wanted her right here, right now. Fast.

"I want you, Blake. Want you like I've never wanted anyone in my whole damn life." She reached to the side, dug in her purse, and came out with something in her hand. With her teeth, she opened a packet. A condom.

Leaning back, she slid her fingers to the base of his dick and rolled it, inch by agonizing inch, down his length. He hadn't thought he could get any harder. Her touch...the feel of her hands on him. Knowing this smart woman with the smooth voice and caring disposition needed him as much as he needed her right now...it drove him wild with desire.

His chest rose and fell with short, panting breaths. He held Missy's waist as she positioned herself above his cock and lowered herself onto him. *Oh, sweet Jesus!* Her wet and ready folds parted and he slid inside as her warmth clenched around him He tensed, holding still the best he could, keeping his hands to himself for now to let her guide the pace. She wasn't going to take this slow.

He cupped her ass, helped her rise and lower as her hair fell forward and curtained his face. His head spun with so much at once. The worst thing possible, the fall of a comrade, had almost happened tonight. Now, the best thing possible. Missy. In his arms. Taking him inside of her again and again. Surrounding him with her warmth.

"Missy...." He needed to say her name. Needed her to know it was her he wanted. Not just sex. Sex with her.

What had he done to deserve her? Didn't matter. He had to have more of her. Pumping his hips, he met her thrusts and moved one hand between them. Sliding two fingers to her clit, he stroked her wet folds.

"Blake...yeah." She moaned, her hot breath warming his neck.

His mouth sought hers and their tongues explored deeper.

She pumped harder, faster, and he stroked her to the rhythm she set. He couldn't last much longer. It took all his willpower not to explode inside of her right away.

With a small cry, she arched away from him, taking him deeper, lifting her torso off him by clutching his shoulders, digging into his bare skin. Her passion turned him on as much as her body. He fingered her clit, rubbing, stroking...little flicks.

Her body throbbed, thrusting him deep inside of her, and then she let out a long moan as her body convulsed and writhed with orgasm. He moved his hands inside her shirt and under her bra, cupping her breasts as she rode the climax.

The feel of her pebbled nipples responding to his touch and her body shaking with release sent him over the edge. He gasped for breath and arched against her, thrusting inside, letting go.... The orgasm emptied his head, emptied his emotions, drowned out everything except the feel of Missy.

CS

Fifteen minutes after their hot, crazy sex in her car, Missy stood beside Blake as the elevator doors opened to the eighth floor. What now? Being with him hadn't sated her desire for him. It had made her want him more.

She swallowed hard and pulled her keys out of her pocket. He waited for her to exit and then followed. Good thing. Because one glance at him—carrying his Kevlar, belt, and his ripped uniform shirt, his rippling muscles and a hot shoulder tattoo, she wanted to trace with her fingertips—might have driven her to hit the Emergency button in the elevator and take him all over again.

What was it about him that made her want to do things she'd never done before? Like sex in a car. Part of her wanted to run inside her apartment and hide until next year, hoping he'd forget about the way she'd jumped his bones and taken him in a wild, animalistic moment of need. The other part wanted to lean against him, feel those strong muscles against her and be with him. Again and again.

As if sensing her indecision, Blake cleared his throat and moved beside her, cupping her chin in his palm, taking her breath away as she stared up into his brown eyes. He swallowed so hard his Adam's apple bobbed and her gaze fell to his lips. Those warm, passionate lips.

"Do you think I could come inside?" His voice was husky and he leaned against the old hallway wallpaper while he stroked the side of his fingers along her check. A simple move, but sensations rippled through her body, tapping into her need to be close to him.

She nodded, suddenly unable to find the words.

Inside, she locked the door and turned. He dropped his Kevlar and shirt to the floor and moved both his arms overhead, pinning her to the door. Hot, molten desire tore through her body.

"You do things to me, Missy." His gaze bore into hers, and he leaned his hips against her. His steely length pressed against her stomach and she struggled to catch her breath.

How could he find the energy to speak? All of her effort was on keeping control, finding a way to tamp this need to get him naked again and running her hands over him. This wasn't her. This was some sex kitten with an out-of-control libido. Her chest rose and fell with quick, small breaths.

Nibbling on her lip, she widened her eyes, excited about the opportunity to be with him again. "What kinds of things?"

He grinned. "Why don't you let me do some things to you...things we didn't have time or space to do earlier?"

Oh, God. The image of his mouth, his body, and his strong hands on her again formed in her mind. Moisture pooled between her legs. She tilted her head. Fine. He wanted to play. She'd banter with him. "There's a lot of space in my bed."

His grin widened and he leaned closer, so close his lips almost touched hers. Almost...but not quite.

"Hmmm.... You. Naked on a bed. Me kissing you, finding out what that soft spot between your legs tastes like...."

Her knees went weak.

Before she could fully process what he offered, he kissed the corner of her mouth and then laid a hot trail of kisses to her ear, where he sucked gently on her lobe.

She angled her neck to give him better access and slid a hand into the front of his pants, delighting in the trail of coarse dark hair to his cock. With a slower pace, she could savor his skin, his muscles, his everything. He hardened and she enjoyed the power of making this strong, muscular man's desire grow. He moaned against her ear, the sound of his deep baritone rumbling through her body and ending at her core.

With a swift move, he bent, placed a hand under her knees, and scooped her body against his chest.

"Blake!" She loved it. Loved the feeling of being held so close, loved being literally swept off her feet, and relished the fact that they would be together again. She kicked off her shoes.

"Let's find that bed you mentioned earlier."

With closed eyes, she leaned her head to his chest. This wasn't supposed to happen. She'd fought so hard to keep away from him. Tonight. They had tonight. She'd think about the repercussions tomorrow. Tonight would be the time of no thinking...just doing.

They stood by the side of her bed. Still holding her, he lowered his lips to hers, a slow touch where he worked his lips from the corner of her mouth to the seam of her lips. She gripped his shoulders tighter and slid a hand behind his head, dragging her fingers through his thick hair.

She opened for him, welcoming his warm tongue as he flicked and explored. Slowly, with his mouth on hers, he lowered her to the bed. The soft quilt against her back contrasted against the hard, muscular body that covered hers.

Bracing his arms by her sides, he kissed the area below her jaw, flicking his tongue in little beats of pressure. She squirmed with need and raked her fingers under his shirt along his taut abs. Nobody had ever made her forget the world like this before. All she wanted was to be with him. His body, his strength, his goodness. She wanted it all.

His hot breath caressed her collarbone before he planted a long, lingering kiss there and sucked her skin just enough to send bolts of pleasure to the tips of her toes.

"I want to feel your body against mine." The words tumbled from her mouth before she processed them.

"Ummm." He leaned back enough to grasp the hem of her shirt and tugged it over her head. Cool air filtered across her torso and he grinned a crooked smile in the dim light that speared in from the hall.

"I like this red bra a lot."

She reached to pull at his shirt, but before she could, he yanked it over his head. Incredible. Fucking incredible. Even in the shadowy light, his muscles rippled as he tossed the jersey to the floor.

Wanting to feel him, needing to feel that body, she reached for his pecs, but he leaned forward, and her hands slid to his strong shoulders instead.

Hot breath steamed over the lace cups of her bra. With one hand, he caressed her breast over the thin fabric. His lips and wet tongue worked at her other breast. She gasped at the feel of both sensations at once.

"Mmm, yeah. I really like red-lace lingerie." His words rumbled his chest again, vibrating right to her crotch as his mouth wet her bra and his words heated her, inside and out. Instinctively, she spread her legs, making room for him.

"Yes...get ready for me, beautiful. I want a taste of you." He slid lower, kissed her ribs, massaging her breasts with both hands as he worked his way over her tummy.

Her breath hitched and a sigh slipped through her lips. She knew where he was heading, and the anticipation of his mouth *there* was almost too much to bear. This was Blake. The hot, muscular, testosterone-laden guy who was supposed to be off-limits. And his mouth was working magic on her.

He unsnapped her jeans. Panting for breath, she lifted her ass, and he slid her denim and underwear past her knees and ankles, before tossing them on the floor. Naked now, except for her bra.

"Beautiful...just beautiful." He spread her legs and ran the ends of his fingertips along the sensitive skin on the inside of her thighs. Moisture pooled, and she moaned.

"Blake...." she whispered. "Let me touch you, too."

"Uh-uh." He shifted to his knees and scooted back on the bed, settling his face near her belly. "You got to pick last time. My turn to pick what we do this time." His breath flittered across her stomach, and her muscles clenched and tightened, her passion building with each touch, each word he spoke.

He kissed the skin over her hip bone and every nerve ending danced with desire. His fingers swept ahead of his mouth, teasing her with the hint of where his lips would go next.

Slowly, with only a whisper of a touch, his fingertips touched her wet folds, while his warm mouth moved to the inside of her thigh.

She cried out and gripped the quilt, clutching it to channel the tension that built with each flick of his hands and tongue.

"I love the taste of your skin. Soft...so soft." His mouth moved closer to her core as his he worked magic on her labia, massaging, making way. "Do you like it when I touch you here?" He slid a finger inside as his tongue lapped gently at her clit.

"Oh! Ohhh, yes." Her husky voice came out a loud whisper and she arched toward him, begging him to go deeper, to keep going.

He used two digits to slide in and out of her and she pumped against him, clutching the blanket with more force as his heated mouth circled her clit and then stroked a slow line along her nether lips. She ground against him, needing the heat of him, wanting more, taking everything he was giving her.

His fingers worked in and out in perfect rhythm with his tongue as it flicked her clit, slowly at first, building her desire. Then as she arched and cried out, he flicked faster, exploring her body even deeper.

Her mind went blank and he moaned, vibrating her clit and all the surrounding sensitive areas. She tensed and bolts of pleasure flashed through her, melting her bones, making her forget everything except the feel of his hands and mouth as she convulsed with orgasm, shaking the bed as he held her in place and relentlessly devoured her in the most perfect way until she finally stilled, unsure if she'd ever be able to move again.

Who cared if she couldn't? It would be worth it.

Chapter Ten

Blake blinked against the morning sunlight that poured in through the lacy curtains. Not his room. Memories of last night filtered through his mind and he glanced beside him. Missy lay sleeping peacefully, a smile on her lips. The light quilt had slipped past her waist and she wore only a thin, long T-shirt that did nothing to conceal her curves. The curves he knew so well now.

Thrusting a hand through his hair, he shifted to the side of the bed and sat. He didn't spend the night with women and they didn't spend the night with him. He always made that clear up front. Spending the night meant more than a sexual encounter...it promised something else. He never made promises he wouldn't be able to keep. Saying good-bye in the middle of the night was a lot easier than saying good-bye in the light of day. Yet somehow, he hadn't been able to force himself to leave Missy's side in the middle of the night.

Missy had caught him off guard. She'd offered him what he'd craved after the scare for Chad's life. Relief and passion had made a powerful union. So now what?

He shouldn't look at her. Shouldn't even let his gaze fall on her sleeping form. Yeah. He needed to grab his clothes and go. He'd text her later. His body must have craved sadistic punishment, though, because he turned to gaze at her. The subtle way she curled into herself, the way her brown hair cascaded behind her on the pillow. His hands had skimmed that small waist last night and ended on her pert breasts. Her reaction to his touch had made him want to give more, take her higher, and be the one who made her feel good.

She'd been damn good at making him feel terrific, too. His gaze swept down the sway of her back, lingered on her bare ass, and then trailed down her long legs, remembering their strength as they clamped around him when she rode him hard, took him deep.

"Morning."

He jolted at her voice. Damn. Busted, looking at her almost naked body. Cue to leave.

"Good morning. Sorry...didn't mean to wake you. I was just heading back to my place." He shot her a smile and meant to take his attention off her so he could get going. But he couldn't. Her hazel eyes locked with his as she stretched and his gaze fell to her full lips. Swollen from his kisses. He raised a hand to his jaw, felt the stubble. Knowing his rough face had given her those glowing lips turned him on all over again.

He had to get the fuck out of there.

She cleared her throat and yanked her shirt hem lower over her bare ass and then swung her legs off the side of the bed. "Want some coffee first?"

Coffee? No. Cold shower? Probably a good idea.

This was all wrong. All wrong. He wasn't supposed to feel anything now. Their time together was supposed to get her out of his system. It only made him want her more. Distance. He needed to put distance between them to think properly.

"Uh...no thanks. I'd better get back to my place...check on Chad, the officer who was shot. See if his family needs anything."

He shoved his feet into his work pants and stood, forcing himself to keep his attention on his clothes, not the almost naked, gorgeous woman behind him who was sliding into her clothes. Fighting the urge to whip around, pull her back into bed for another time with her, he reached for his T-shirt and tugged it over his head.

"Looks like it's going to be a nice day today, doesn't it?" Well, shit. Awkward, much? He'd just spent the night getting to know her body, enjoying every aspect of being with her, and now he made small talk about the weather? He had to get away from her. She was messing up his routine. Have fun, have sex, and move on under friendly terms. He usually handled it well.

Must have been the whole spend-the-night thing. He'd been tired. That was it.

"Yeah. A nice, sunny one." She kept her head down as she zippered a pair of shorts. Her brown hair fell to the sides of her face, so he couldn't see her expression. She wasn't used to this, was she? The awkward good-bye, the morning after.

He picked up his gear belt, vest, and shirt from the carpeting, intent on holding them tight because it gave him something to do when all he wanted to do was touch her. Should he kiss her? Shake her hand? Damn, why hadn't he escaped during the night and left a note? Maybe he'd been too worn out. Or maybe she wasn't the type of woman a man could leave in the middle of the night. He shook the thought away.

"I thought I'd check out that used book store on Pratt Street before work today. See if they have any books about vortexes and portals. Maybe we can learn something ourselves that will help Betty." She stared at him, with only the rumpled bed between them. The bed where so many good things had happened last night.

Good. The subject of Betty was neutral territory. Missy wasn't going to try to talk about what last night meant. She wasn't going to make him figure things out. Maybe because she regretted it?

Didn't matter. They could work together to help Betty, then remain friends.

"Good idea. Veronica gets back in two days, and we should wait to do anything until we talk to her. She might know more about this building. But it wouldn't hurt to be prepared so we know what she's talking about." He couldn't believe he was talking about ghosts and portals and psychics as if it were something he did all the time, but Betty did that to him. He wouldn't have believed in ghosts if it hadn't been for Betty. She wouldn't steer him wrong, wouldn't lie to him like so many people through his life had done. With her, there had been instant trust.

"I agree. I'll call you if I find anything. Maybe Betty will show up today, and we can go over the books together." Missy strolled around the bed and he made his way toward the doorway. He should be a gentleman and let her go through first, but if he had to look at that round, inviting ass again, he might slam the door and stay there all day with her.

Couldn't happen. Had to move on.

"All right, well I'll talk to you soon then. Thanks for the ride last night." Damn. That was about the stupidest exit line ever. She'd taken him on a ride, all right. Not just home from the hospital.

"I hope Chad and his family are doing well. Good luck." She moved behind her kitchen counter toward the coffeemaker. Her morning routine. Part of him yearned to be a part of it.

"Thanks." He turned toward the front door and his gaze fell on an envelope mixed with some other mail. His breath caught in his throat and his heart pounded. His address on the front. A utility bill. And it had been opened. Couldn't be. Missy wasn't like Claire. Missy wouldn't take something that belonged to him. Missy was different....wasn't she?

Clenching his jaw, he reached for the envelope. She not only had his mail, she'd opened it. Angry daggers of hurt stabbed at his chest. He tamped it and took a deep breath. He had measures in place now, safeguards from having security or identity issues.

"I see you have my utility bill." He relied on his cop voice, maintained control of his emotions like he was talking to a suspect.

She glanced over her shoulder and smiled. "Oh, shoot. Sorry. I meant to get that to you. It was in with my mail and I wasn't paying attention and opened it. Meant to slide it under your door yesterday but was late for work and forgot." She poured water into the coffeemaker as if she didn't have a care in the world.

Could she be telling the truth? Or was it Claire all over again? He'd been let down way too many times. Finding this letter was perfect. Perfect, because just when he'd started to let down his guard, the open bill was a reminder to protect himself. People couldn't be trusted. They said one thing and did another. Missy was a friend...a neighbor. Being with her last night meant nothing. Only that they'd had fun together.

"You okay?" Her furrowed brows as she turned, coffee scoop still in her hand, made her concern look genuine.

"Yeah. Perfect. See you later." He shoved the envelope in his pocket, flipped the locks on her door, and stepped into the hall.

"See you." Her voice trailed off as he closed the door, the click of the door latch acting like a reminder of the steel doors he needed to keep around his heart. Nobody could hurt him. He wouldn't let them close enough.

ભ

Missy strolled down the busy downtown Baltimore sidewalk. Usually the storefronts and sale signs drew her attention, but not this morning. Her mind whirled from last night with Blake. He'd left in a hurry that morning, like his freedom depended on it. So different from the man who had touched her so tenderly all night long.

She didn't regret being with him. It was too damn good to regret. The scare—that gut-wrenching feeling that he'd been hurt, or worse, last night—was enough to remind her they didn't have a future together, though. A roller coaster of emotion, and she would worry every time he went to work. Who could live like that?

This morning, though. Wow, that had been different. For one thing, she didn't casually hop into bed with men. She had been in a relationship with every man she'd ever slept with. Sure, she had friends who did the occasional booty call with an ex or a one-night stand with a friend of a friend. Not Missy. Not that she judged those who slept with someone they weren't committed to, it just...well, it wasn't her.

Apparently, it was now, because Blake wasn't someone she planned on seeing again. *That damn shooting.* She'd been so relieved to see him, so relieved he was okay. Twice before, she'd gotten news of a police shooting, and twice before it had ended horribly. Seeing him when she had been thinking the worst made her lose her senses. All she had wanted was to be with him in every possible way.

The crosswalk light illuminated, and she made her way across the busy city street with her bag of books in hand. She had a few hours before she needed to be at the radio station, and reading would help distract her from her thoughts about Blake. The woman at the bookstore had recommended three different ghost books and had written down some good Internet sites to visit, too.

They could make progress with Betty like they'd promised, help her get to Stanley. And then she and Blake could go their different ways. Out of sight, out of mind...except for the whole living-across-the-hall thing.

Ten minutes later, Missy keyed open her apartment and smelled apple pie. After a night like last night, she could use some company, and she and Betty could read the books together.

"Hi, Betty." Missy shut the door behind her. Betty stood on the sofa, holding a small painting to the wall.

"Hello, dear. I thought this beautiful ocean scene would look much better over the sofa than over that dresser." Betty's earrings dangled and she climbed down from the cushions and smiled. "What do you think?"

"I like it. In fact I like it a lot." Betty had a knack for decorating. "My mom painted that."

"Oh, my. She's good."

Missy had been hot outside—summer was apparently here to stay in Baltimore—but inside her apartment, the temperature was much lower. And not only because of the air-conditioning. Betty's presence kept things cool. After speaking to the woman in the bookstore, Missy understood that was something most humans felt around ghosts. Cool air, and an electric charge.

"You remind me of my mom a little bit." Missy lifted the paper bag of books and pamphlets. "If you have time, we can look through these research materials before I leave for the station." She moved to the kitchen counter and settled on a stool.

"Oh, honey, all I have is time." Betty winked and took a seat at the counter next to Missy.

"I'm hoping these books can help us find a way to get you to Stanley." Missy flipped to the index of the paperback and scanned for a section on crossing over.

"I can't do that until you and Blake are happy together." Betty smiled and tugged a book closer, fanning through the pages, not really stopping to read. "Speaking of which...what did the two of you do last night? Did you get together because you had to take his mail to him?"

That had been Betty's doing? He'd looked so pissed when he found that piece of mail. She'd mindlessly opened her stack of bills and flyers, and once she'd discovered it was his, she'd laid it by the door to take to him. But the look on his face when he'd found it....

"You put it there? I thought the postman put it in my box by accident."

"Nope." Betty grinned. "All me. You two seemed like you needed a little push. I gave you an excuse to see him. Did you two make a connection?"

As much as she wanted to read the books and find out more about the Betty's world, Missy jolted at the word *connection*. Sure, they'd connected...in many, many ways. Tears stung at the corners of her eyes and a lump formed in her throat. All morning she'd succeeded in keeping the hurt buried. She had feelings for Blake. Feelings she'd never be able to act on because of his dangerous job.

"It doesn't matter. We could never make it work. He's a cop, Betty. I can't be with a cop because my father and brother were cops and they were both killed in the line of duty."

Betty tilted her head and placed her cold hand over Missy's. Even with its cool temperature, Missy welcomed the contact. "There's always a way to make it work, dear."

Missy closed her eyes and forced the tears back. She wouldn't cry. She needed to move on, not mourn. The faster they found a solution for getting Betty to her Stanley, the quicker she and Blake could go back to their own separate lives. The air around her warmed and she opened her eyes. Betty was gone.

೮ర

Missy let out a long breath and strolled through the front door to WLOV, happy to have her work to distract her from her personal life. No matter what kind of day she was having, she could walk into the studio, leave Missy behind, and become Misty till Midnight. Like an actor, she shed the day and smiled at Kathryn, the receptionist.

"Hi, Missy. Want your messages printed out, or do you want me to e-mail them to you?"

"E-mail would be great. Thanks, Kathryn."

Kathryn buzzed the second set of doors and Missy entered, comforted by the familiar surroundings. Her apartment might be different from her place in California, but this state-of-the-art radio station was almost identical to the one she'd left behind. Dozens of colorful wires ran the distance of the long, carpeted hallway ceiling, providing a strong signal and clear broadcasts for the five stations housed in the building. She walked past windowed studios, waving at another deejay who was inside recording promo spots.

After a quick stop to grab a cup of coffee from the snack room, she headed for her studio, fired up the computer, and opened her Facebook page. She posted a photo of a Maryland crab and reminded listeners to call in during her show in a few hours, asking for comments about their favorite summertime food.

A few e-mails later, she clicked on one from an address with letters and numbers. Spam? The subject line read My Request. Sure sounded like something a listener might write. She hated to delete it unread...didn't want to disappoint a fan. She clicked to open it and a photo of a penis with a hand around it filled her screen. The words below it read: *Now you send me a photo of you naked.*

Instinct made her want to hit the Delete button. Instead she forwarded it to the station manager. Let him deal with it. Could be spam...or a coincidence. After the call from the listener who'd asked for naked pictures, though, better safe than sorry. She typed a message for her manager, reminding him that a caller had been harassing her about naked photos. Time to have this guy checked out. His number hadn't appeared on caller ID because he blocked it, but maybe someone who knew more about computers could trace the e-mail.

She sent a quick e-mail to Blake, too, letting him know that Betty had left his mail on Missy's table on purpose. Yes, she'd opened it...absentmindedly, but no she hadn't stolen his mail. The look he'd given her implied all sorts of options ran through his head. *Really? After what they'd shared together?*

Stretching the kinks out of her neck, she moved on to post her blog, again thankful for a busy afternoon and evening because she could shelve her personal life for now.

Six hours later, she neared the end of her show. An unusually busy night of dedications, most of them with young couples falling in love. Summer romance...young love. She smiled and put the phone on speaker as she set up a song to play for the young man who had just called in a song for the woman he'd become engaged to tonight.

"All the best to you and Sheila, Tom. I'm so glad she said yes. I'll play your song in just a few, okay?"

"Thanks, Misty! We love listening to you."

Missy smiled at the energy and happiness in his voice. *God, I love my job.*

She disconnected and the phone lit up again, almost immediately. She hit the Record button. "This is Misty till Midnight. What can I play for you tonight?"

"It's me, Misty. Kurt. I'm feeling better these days about my breakup and it's all because of you. In fact, I think I'm better off without L—I mean my ex-girlfriend. Can you play 'I Feel Good' by James Brown? I think it says what I'm feeling right now."

"That's great, Kurt. I'll play that song for you and for everyone who's ever had a broken heart. Glad you're feeling better and thanks for calling." Misty pulled in a deep breath and let it out, glad that people could find solace and hope through songs.

"Thanks, Misty! You're the best."

Misty lined up the song to play. It would be the last one of the night. And then home to her apartment. Where she'd what? Read some more about ghosts? She seriously needed a social life.

Twenty minutes later, she and Diane met in the hallway, per their usual routine.

"Damn air conditioner is set too cold in my studio. Good set tonight?" Diane asked, shrugging off her sweater as Missy tapped the code into the security pad by the inside door.

"Great set! How about you?" The door clicked open and Missy held it for Diane.

"'Night, Dan," they said as they passed the security guard behind the desk.

He gave them a friendly wave and walked around the counter. "I'll watch you get to your cars. You gals be safe, now."

"Thanks, Dan," they said in unison.

"Good set for me, too. I guess people stay up later in the summer. Lots of listeners." Diane pecked the code for the outer doors and pushed them open, shooting a glance at Missy. "Speaking of which, we totally need to reschedule that meet-up with Andrew, Jason's friend. He really wants to meet you."

"Do it." Exactly what Missy needed. New people. New surroundings. "I'm free this weekend if he is...and if you can get a babysitter."

"Sounds great! I'm on it." Diane unlocked her car and waved good night.

Missy waved back and climbed into her car and started the ignition. After Diane passed behind her, Missy backed out and headed for the parking lot exit, where she halted at the stop sign.

Movement in the car made the hairs on her neck stand. Her emergency brake cranked on by itself. No...not by itself. Fear shimmied up Missy's spine. Something cold and wet covered her mouth and nose and the world went black.

Chapter Eleven

Blake switched off the stereo in his apartment. He shouldn't have listened to Missy's show. A clean break. Not this vacillating back and forth. *I want her. I don't want her.*

Just when he thought he'd found an excuse to keep his distance from her—the open envelope in her apartment—he found out that it had been Betty's doing. Her effort to push them together.

Fuck! Didn't matter. Missy wasn't what he needed.

But why, suddenly, when he thought of her did he wonder what it would be like to wake up next to her every morning? Like this morning. To linger in bed...to come home to her at night....

Other women didn't get to him like this. What was it about her? Damn. He'd been doing okay, pushing thoughts of her to the back of his mind while he'd visited Chad at the hospital, practiced at the firing range, and then met some of the guys for a beer in Fells Point.

Now he was alone. Just him and his puzzle in a quiet apartment. This time last night he'd been in her car, in a dark lot with his hands on her body.

He grabbed a pillow from the couch and threw it across the room. It bounced and skidded toward the bedroom.

Stomping back toward the stereo, he punched a button and found a hard-rock station. No more love songs. He'd pound the thoughts from his head with some Black Sabbath. Cranking the volume high enough to pulse through his apartment but low enough to keep the neighbors from complaining, he plopped into the dining room chair and concentrated on his puzzle. Getting lost in the tiny pieces with their various edges was better than getting lost in the memories of what it was like to be with Missy.

The scent of apple pie drifted toward his nostrils and he lifted his head. How long had Betty been here? Enough to witness his tirade?

Movement by the front door caught his eye and his hand instinctively went to his weapon, still at his hip.

Betty stood by the front door, wringing her hands, a worried look on her face. Why? Did she think he'd be mad that she left his mail at Missy's?

He lifted the remote control for the stereo, shut it down, and took a half-dozen steps toward her.

"Betty? What's wrong?"

"You can see me?" Her blue eyes lit up with hope. "Oh, thank God, Blake." She closed the distance between them and grasped his hands with her cold ones. Her grip was much stronger than he expected. "I think Missy's in trouble."

Great. Like he wasn't driving himself crazy enough with thoughts of Missy. Now Betty wanted to try to talk him into being with her. Couldn't she see their relationship wasn't the same kind she and Stanley had enjoyed? They were too different, and he wasn't the right person for Missy. Too much crap in his past, too many hang-ups, to be a good match for someone as steady as Missy.

"Look, Betty. I appreciate that you want me to be happy, and it's cool that you came back to look after me, but—"

"This isn't about you." Betty yanked her hands off his and put them on her hips, glaring at him.

In all the time he'd known her, Blake had never seen such a serious expression on her face. Had she become possessed by that vortex? Had she gotten too close? Shit, this whole paranormal experience could take a quick turn for the worse.

"Okay, tell me what's going on." His cop voice. *Maintain control. Rely on your training.*

"Missy's not home yet and I think something bad has happened." Betty's usual smile was gone, making her look older.

Blake's gut clenched and he pulled out his cell to check the time. 1:00 a.m. "Maybe she went out with some friends after the show." His heart did a weird shuffle when the thought crossed his mind that she could be on a date.

"Uh-uh. Her home phone is ringing every few minutes. Her mom, probably." Betty relaxed her stance, but now her lips quivered like she might cry.

"Okay...let's call her cell." He laid a hand on Betty's shoulder, again surprised by how real she felt. With the other hand, he punched the button for Missy. Maybe this was a ploy to get them talking again, but right now he just needed to get the concerned look off Betty's face.

Missy's phone went straight to voice mail. He disconnected and tried again. Didn't mean she was in trouble. She could be in a loud bar, deep in conversation. He huffed out a breath, sent her a text, and gazed at Betty. "I sent her a text."

Betty shook her head. "Follow me." She whirled, opened Blake's door, and walked out into the hallway. He followed, and they stood outside Missy's apartment. Missy's home phone jangled inside.

"Maybe she's in the shower." Blake forced that image away.

"Nope. I checked."

The phone continued to ring. Worry snaked up his spine. Maybe Betty wasn't overreacting. "I don't have a key."

Betty rolled her eyes and then disappeared through the door. Two seconds later, the locks clicked and Betty pulled Missy's door open from the inside. *Damn.*

The phone in Missy's kitchen stopped ringing and her voice mail kicked on. Blake's gut clenched. Was it Betty's concerns rubbing off on him, or was there something seriously wrong here? Suddenly, Betty's fears didn't seem so far-fetched. Blake raced to Missy's bedroom, into the open master bath, and then into the hall bath.

His scalp prickled with fear. *No. Stay in cop mode. Panic later.* He checked his phone, hoping she'd returned his text.

The landline rang again, making him jump. Betty was right. Missy's mother called every night to be sure she'd arrived safely. He picked up the receiver. "Hello?"

"Oh...uh...is Missy there?"

A woman's voice. Very similar to Missy's smooth sound, but a little older. "Mrs. Prescott?"

"Yes, this is Missy's mom. Is she there? I've been worried about her. Who is this?"

"I'm a neighbor...." How exactly did he explain how he'd gotten into Missy's apartment?

"Oh! Blake?" Blake wanted to celebrate the fact that Missy had told her mother about him, but his distress overtook any temporary glee.

"Ma'am, have you spoken to Missy tonight?"

Betty stood beside him, wringing her hands, eyes wide as she waited for information.

The woman on the other end of the line hesitated. "You mean she's not there with you?"

"No, ma'am, I'm afraid she'd not." Blake's heart pounded. Something was definitely wrong. The parking garage? He needed to backtrack over Missy's steps.

"I've been calling her cell phone and texting her. This isn't like her." The woman's voice grew shakier.

"Ma'am, I'm going to find out where she is." He yanked a piece of paper from a notepad on Missy's counter. "Give me your number. I'll call you as soon as I have information."

"Oh, my God. Oh, my God. She's okay, isn't she?" Blake couldn't imagine the worry the woman must be feeling. She'd lost her husband and her son. But he needed to get off the phone and find Missy. Now.

"Ma'am, your number."

He scribbled it down, gave her his number, and shoved the paper into his jeans pocket, promising to call her as soon as he found anything out.

Maybe Missy's phone was malfunctioning and she was perfectly safe with some friends. He'd take that. Even if it was with another guy. All he wanted was for her to be okay, and until he found out otherwise, he'd assume she was.

"She would call her mother. She wouldn't cause her mother anguish like this. Something is wrong." Betty laid a hand on Blake's upper arm. "What are we going to do?"

"Her phone might be on the fritz. I'm going to check downstairs in the garage." He patted his jeans pocket, glad his keys and wallet were there, along with his weapon at his side. He thought about stopping in his apartment for his Kevlar vest. No time.

"I'm coming with you," Betty said, right behind him as he dashed for the door.

"You're able to leave the building?"

"Sure. I sit by the harbor all the time."

Blake shook his head. "You stay here in case she comes home. Lock the door after I leave, please." He didn't wait for her answer, just ran out the door and down the hallway to stab the elevator button.

A minute later, he exited into the underground parking garage. Over a hundred spaces. He ran past her usual spot but didn't see her car. With a glance left and right, he figured he'd make quicker time circling the lot in his truck, so he keyed it open and got in, then gunned the engine out of the spot, peeling wheels as he checked the garage.

"Damn!" He banged the steering wheel. He'd head to the radio station. Maybe she had to work late and her phone was turned off.

"Double damn," a high-pitched voice beside him said.

He almost veered into a parked car. "Betty! I told you to stay at the apartment."

She stared straight ahead, ramrod straight in her seat. "I'm coming. You might need me."

She had a point. Her little trick of opening the door sure had come in handy. "Fine. At least put your seat belt on."

"Really? What do you think is going to happen? I'm going to die again or something?" She pulled the restraint and snapped the belt into place.

Glad it was the middle of the night and traffic was light, Blake kept the accelerator pressed to the floor, driving much faster than he should, but reaching the radio station in half the time he should have.

He skidded in front of the entrance and threw the truck into park.

With a quick glance of the almost empty parking lot, he didn't see Missy's Accord.

He ran to the front doors of the studio and yanked. Locked. No surprise there. Movement inside caught his eye as a bald security guard frowned at him from behind a desk and then stood.

Blake scowled when the man didn't approach him but then he noticed an intercom. He pressed the button. "Missy Prescott. Is she still here?"

"Who wants to know?"

"Her mother. I'm her neighbor, a cop from the Twelfth Precinct in the city, but her mother is worried. Missy never came home."

The man moved closer to the door, his bulky body moving slowly and methodically. A retired cop. Cops never lost that beat swagger, even after retirement.

The guard pressed a button on the interior wall by the door. "She left with another deejay right after their shows ended, like usual." His voice came through the intercom and his brows furrowed.

Blake glanced up, spotted an enclosed security camera. "Do you have this lot on surveillance? Can you check to see if she made it out okay?" Maybe someone waited for her by her car.

"I could go in there, open the doors, and you could check the security camera yourself." Betty stood beside him.

"No. Let me handle this." Blake glared at Betty.

The guard glared at Blake and glanced to the spot where Betty stood. Of course, he saw nothing. He pressed the button again. "No need to check. I watch those two ladies every night to make sure they get to their cars safely. They both made it to their cars just fine and left the lot."

"Did they say anything about going out after work? Could you call the other lady to see if they're together?"

The guard shook his head. "Look, buddy. We get some kooks here. Misty's becoming popular. I can't give you any information unless she tells me I can." He sighed and folded his bulky arms. "Twelfth Precinct you say?"

"Yeah. The twelfth." Blake's hope rose. Maybe this guy would help them after all.

"You know a guy named Tommy Maloney?" The guard stared through the glass with narrowed eyes.

"Bubba? Yeah, I know him. He's retired now, goes fishing a lot—"

"Good enough to prove you're who you are without a bunch of phone calls downtown. Let me call the other deejay, see if she knows where Misty is." The guard moved away from the door and pulled out his cell.

Blake pressed his lips together, hopeful the guard would have good news.

After a quick conversation, the guard returned. "Sorry. She has no idea where Misty is." Concern etched the man's face.

"Thanks. I appreciate your time."

The guard nodded. "Let us know when you find her. Now you have everybody worried."

"I will."

Could the guard be lying? Blake would need a subpoena to obtain the security video if he had to go that route. Damn. A dead end. Where could she be? Where else could he look? The stalker guy had called her show again, talked about moving on. And the naked-pic guy she'd mentioned. Were they the same person? It might take hours to wake the station manager, trace that kind of information. Hours they didn't have.

He crossed the sidewalk, heading back to his truck, and yanked out his cell. He'd keep trying to contact her. He willed her to pick up, be in a loud bar where she was safe, or even drunk, and hadn't heard it ring earlier. Rounding the back of his tailgate, he stilled as the call connected.

And a phone rang nearby at the edge of the parking lot.

Betty moved beside him. "Her cell," she whispered.

They both took off running toward the sound. A cell phone lit up as someone called. Blake skidded to a stop next to the phone. *Blake Cell.* So much for the theory that it wasn't working.

Betty fidgeted beside him, staring at the lit device. It stopped ringing.

"We can't afford to get fingerprints on it." He glanced at his truck. "Let me get gloves. I'll be right back."

He grabbed a flashlight, a pair of gloves, and a plastic bag from the area behind his seat and ran back to the cell. Betty stared at it as it lay on the dark parking-lot asphalt.

His fingers itched to scroll through her recent calls, see if there was evidence of a meeting. But it could ruin any prints. Maybe he'd do it anyway if nothing else worked. Using his flashlight to scan the area, he didn't see anything else out of the ordinary. The words *foul play* came out of the back of his mind and into the forefront and cold chills skittered down his spine.

"I have an idea." He nodded toward his truck. "Come on."

He'd written down the stalker's license plate that time at the Inner Harbor when the guy had visited the bookstore where Missy made an appearance. On a hunch, he dug in his glove box and yanked out the notepad he carried while on duty. His fingers shook—just the tiniest bit—and he took a deep breath, forcing his mind to stay in cop mode. He'd worry later, work now.

"There!" He tapped the page from a few weeks ago where he'd written the make and model of the guy's car.

"What's that?" Betty asked, peering around him at the notebook. He'd forgotten she was there.

He tore out his phone. "I'm calling my buddy to have him run this tag. It belongs to an overly friendly fan who came to see Missy at the Inner Harbor."

"Oooh." Betty laid a cool hand on his upper arm. "If anyone can find her, you can, Blake."

He called a beat officer who was likely in his patrol car with quick access to his computer. Adam answered on the first ring. "What's up?"

"Need you to run a tag for me. You in your car?"

"Quiet night here. I'm ready. Give it to me."

Blake read the combination of numbers and letters and waited, tapping his fingers on the roof of his truck as he stood by the open door. Betty stared at him with wide, worried eyes. Even after death, she couldn't get away from worries. He needed to help her find peace soon.

"Guy named Kurt Bishop." Adam read the address and Blake scribbled it into his pad. A county address. He'd wait to call the county police. See if he could get this Bishop to talk. Technically, the guy had done nothing wrong, but one suspicious word...one inclination that the guy might be involved would have Blake calling in favors from the dozens of county cops he knew. He wasn't playing by the rules and he knew it, but to hell with regulations when Missy's life could be at risk.

"Got the address. Let's go." He put one foot in his truck and looked around. Betty had disappeared. *Good, I can concentrate better if I'm alone.*

Blake gunned the engine and took off out of the radio station parking lot toward Bishop's address. *Please be there. Please be safe.*

Is this what she'd felt like when she had feared for his life? This painful, gut-wrenching worry? Why she couldn't be with him? No wonder she couldn't deal with it.

He peeled wheels around a corner, wishing he had lights and sirens on his truck so he could run the traffic signals. Instead, he looked both ways and ran them anyway.

Being with Missy made him feel all sorts of things he'd never felt before. Staying the night with her, wanting to be there by her side in the morning, made him think of things he'd never wanted before, too. A real relationship. A family one day. Someone to come home to.

He'd have to think about it later. Right now, he needed to find her. Alive and well.

With lips pressed tight together, he made the last turn into a cul-de-sac where Bishop lived.

Without a search warrant, he worried the man wouldn't answer questions or let him inside. Especially if he didn't identify himself as a police officer. Instead, as Blake skidded to a stop in front of the house, his headlights hit Bishop as he stood in boxers and a white T-shirt, staring with wide eyes at his house.

"Oh thank God. Are you the police?" Bishop padded in bare feet across the lawn. It was the middle of the night, and a few neighbors had porch lights on, but the neighborhood was quiet otherwise.

"I am." No need to tell the guy this wasn't his beat. "I think we met before. I'm Blake Decker." He extended his hand toward the stout guy, but Bishop only stared at his house. What the hell? And why had the guy asked if he was police? "Did you call the police?"

"Yes. Somebody's in there." He pointed to his small house. "I was asleep. First the doors started opening and closing, then when I turned the lights on, they all went off." The guy was breathing so hard he was having a tough time getting out his story.

"An intruder?" Shit. Maybe this was a dead end and he'd stumbled upon a break-in. He didn't have time for this.

"And then a woman screamed 'get out!'"

The front porch light flickered on. Betty walked through the closed front door, hands on hips, and stood on the steps. "She's not in here. I checked everywhere."

Blake swallowed his disbelief. Betty must have read the address from his notepad and materialized inside the house. He wanted to laugh, and maybe if she'd found Missy alive and doing okay, he would have. Instead, fear bunched like a fist in his stomach. If she wasn't here, where the hell could she be?"

"Mr. Bishop, have you seen Missy Prescott?"

"Look, the light's on. Did you see that? The burglar turned the light on." Bishop stared at the porch. Sirens echoed in the distance. Then the man turned to face him. "Missy Prescott? Who's Missy?"

"Misty. The deejay." Blake glanced at Betty as she moved beside him. She smelled like burned apple pie. Odd.

"Misty. I love her show. Just tonight she—"

Blake didn't have time for this. "Listen, pal. If you know where Missy is, tell me right now. She never got home and if you took her, I swear I'll rip your limbs off and—" Betty's cool hand rested on his upper arm. He blinked, remembering his training. Easier to get more information from the guy if he acted nice. But the fact that Bishop could be involved in Missy's disappearance....

"I understand you're friends with Misty."

The guy nodded several times. "She's helped me through a tough time. She cares about her listeners. I know she does." The guy stared at the grass and then jerked his head to gaze at Blake. "Wait. Did you say she's missing? Misty's missing?"

"Correct." The sirens grew closer. *Come on, buddy, spit it out, spit it out. I know you have something to say here.* Blake clenched his jaw to keep quiet, keep the pressure on the guy, and did his best to force a friendly smile.

"Lynn." The guy frowned. "But she wouldn't have. Not really."

"Who's Lynn?" Blake yanked out his notepad.

"My ex-girlfriend. I'm over her. Finally. In fact, I'm better off without her and I know it now. She's been messing with my head lately, and she blames Misty because I won't get back together with her. She said she'd get rid of Misty."

Two patrol cars rounded the corner and pulled to a stop, headlights and red-and-blue lights bouncing off the neighborhood as porch lights and interior lights switched on all around them.

"Give me Lynn's address," Blake said.

"Three miles from here. Over on Loch Raven." He spat out the numbers. "But she wouldn't—"

"Talk to the officers. Tell them about the doors and lights. I'll be in touch." Blake looked beside him, not a bit surprised to find that Betty had once again disappeared.

Chapter Twelve

*M*issy blinked her heavy lids and then closed them again. *Tired. So tired.*

"Missy, wake up!"

Something cold touched Missy's arm, and she wanted to brush it away. When she tried to move her hand to do so, she met resistance. Something was holding her hands together behind her.

"That's it. Come on, honey. Open your eyes."

She knew that voice. Like her grandmother...someone who'd been kind to her. Betty!

Missy forced her eyes open. Betty's stared back at her. They were nose to nose.

"Oh, my lands. Thank goodness you're okay."

"Betty..." Missy whispered. Her voice was scratchy and her throat burned. Chloroform? Could someone have reached forward, yanked on the emergency brake, and chloroformed her? Betty? No. That wasn't possible.

Forcing herself to stay alert when all she really wanted to do was go back to sleep, Missy shifted. She sat on cold dirt and her hands were tied behind her back to a pole that felt like steel.

"What happened?" Missy grunted. "Why are you here?" A lone, low-watt bare bulb cast a yellowish light around a small cellar.

"Blake is on his way. He's been going crazy. He loves you. Whether he admits it or not, he does. I saw that look on his face when he realized something bad had happened to you." Betty moved behind Missy. "Let me untie this rope...."

Missy leaned back, hoping to slacken the tie. Her head pounded as if she'd been hit on the head with a rock. More likely, the chloroform, or whatever it was, was still affecting her. Blake was on the way? "Where am I?"

"Lynn's house. She's Kurt's ex-girlfriend. You know...that guy who calls your show. She probably thinks if she gets rid of you, she'll get back with Kurt."

"What?" None of this made sense. She needed to get out of there and find Blake. Why, when she was scared, cold, and her life was in danger, did she want Blake? Not just a cop...Blake. Being around him felt right. Suddenly, her concerns for his safety felt ridiculous. Here she was—enjoying the safe, comfortable job of being a radio deejay, and she was the one who'd been kidnapped and whose life could be in danger. Go figure. Thank God for her guardian angel, Betty.

"Well, darn...." Betty's soft voice, softer than usual, like the volume had been turned down, whispered behind her.

"What's wrong?" Missy asked, leaning farther back, hoping to loosen the knot enough for Betty to get it loose.

"Hmmm, I...." The ropes around Missy's wrists remained tight although Betty crouched behind her. "I can't seem to hold on to it. My hand is slipping through it. Like a ghost."

"Like a ghost?" Well, of course. Betty was a ghost. Did she mean like a ghost that wasn't corporeal?

Betty moved in front of her and swayed. Was it Missy's imagination, or was Betty less whole...less solid? *Must be the chloroform messing with my head.*

Betty stared at her hands. "I can't seem to grip anything. My hand goes right through it." She glanced toward a set of shabby wooden steps a few feet across the cellar. "I'm sorry, Missy. Let me see if I can open the trap door. I didn't see her up there, and there's carpeting over the...."

Betty grew see-through. Her lips continued to move, and her eyes opened wide, but Missy couldn't hear her. More chloroform effects? A sad look crossed Betty's face.

Then Betty was gone.

"Betty!" Missy's cry rang out of her scratchy throat, barely a loud whisper. Something was wrong. Why had Betty disappeared like that? It was so different from other times when Betty had wanted to disappear on her own.

Betty would be fine. Missy had to hold on to that thought. Right now, she had to get out of there. The sooner she got out, the sooner she and Blake could work together to find Betty and help her. No crazy ex-girlfriend was going to keep her from the man she loved.

Wait...what? This drug was doing a real number on her. Crazy thoughts.

A carpet over a trap door. Okay...good to know. Up the steps and through the door. Missy worked at the rope behind her and glanced around the small cellar. Cinderblock walls. Lots of spiders. Maybe she could climb out the small window near the stairs. Or was it too high off the cellar ground for her to reach?

Footsteps overhead.

Missy froze and then worked harder to untie the ropes. Blake? Had he found her? A scraping noise followed by a creak. No. The movement was too sure, too confident. Someone had moved the rug and opened the trap door. Betty? She prayed it was.

Another squeak and something closed. Footsteps on the wooden steps.

Missy would pretend to be unconscious. She slumped, letting her head loll to the side as if she were passed out. The movement intensified the pounding in her head.

Through slitted eyelids, she spotted first one boot and then another. Definitely female. Betty had been right.

In the dim light, Missy risked a glance at the woman. Tall. In good physical shape. Strong. She held a gun in her hand.

Missy's heart pounded. No! She'd come too far, been through too much for her life to end like this. She'd survived the grief of losing two people she loved. She could get through anything.

The woman kicked Missy's tennis shoe with her boot. "You still out, bitch? Wake up. I want to see the look on your face when I kill you for stealing my man."

"What...huh?" Missy slurred her words and squinted up at the woman. Keep her talking. Get these damn ropes off. "Who—who are you?"

The woman's lips curled into a sneer. "Your worst nightmare. A woman wronged. Whores like you don't get to live."

"But I don't even know you." The ropes loosened enough for Missy to slip her hands out. Now all she needed was the woman to get close enough. Whether from the effects of the drug or the cold cellar floor, Missy didn't trust her legs to support her. Her toes tingled with half feeling. Sure, she could run, or crawl if she had to, but she'd only get one chance. Better to get the woman closer. Behind her back, she wiggled her hands, forcing the blood to circulate.

The woman snorted. "Don't even know me and I'm the one whose boyfriend you've been screwing? Typical."

"I have a boyfriend. I don't need another one."

"Oh, really? Then I'm doing him a favor by getting rid of you. I'm sure he's better off without you." The woman's eyes narrowed.

No, Blake wouldn't be better off without her. And she wouldn't be better off without him. Why couldn't she have realized that before she was confronted with a gun? "I can't see your face. It's all blurry...my head...everything is so fuzzy. I think I was drugged." Missy made her voice as pathetic as possible, as unthreatening as possible.

"Oh, yeah? Like chloroform, maybe?" The woman laughed and then went into a coughing spasm. A smoker. Probably not as strong as she looked if she had a smoker's lung power. "I came down here to get rid of you. Would have shot you before, but I wanted you to know why you're dying. No more screwing with my boyfriend or anyone else's. I'm doing womankind a favor tonight."

"Please...I don't want to die. And I don't even know you. If I could see you, maybe I'd know what you're talking about. I've done some bad things. Let me at least apologize."

"Oh. Very nice. Now that it's time to die, you want to repent." The woman moved closer, though, even if she probably wasn't aware of it. "Plenty of time for you to repent in hell, sugar."

A noise upstairs. Knocking. Pounding on a door. The woman

frowned, looked toward the steps.

She leaned closer, aiming the gun at Missy's chest.

Now or never.

Blood pulsed through Missy's veins and sweat broke out on her brows. With her right hand, she swung out and knocked the gun from Lynn's hand. With her left, she jabbed her palm full force at the tip of the woman's nose and jammed her hand upward. She heard a crunch and blood spurted from Lynn's nose as she moaned and fell to the floor.

On shaky legs, Missy shuffled to the gun and picked it up, held it in hands that quivered so hard she thought she'd drop it.

Pounding again from upstairs. Could it be Blake? Betty had said Blake was on the way. The relief that washed through her, knowing he could be near helped her grip the gun tighter. Like a teacup in a saucer. One hand holding the gun, the other bracing it. Just like her father had taught her years ago.

"You bitch. You broke my nose." The woman moved to her knees.

"Stay on the ground." Missy blinked, trying to clear her vision. Her head pounded so damn hard it blurred her sight.

"You won't shoot me. I haven't done anything to you." She used her T-shirt to wipe the blood from her upper lip and leaned forward.

"I said stay down!" Missy's scratchy voice didn't have the impact she wanted it to.

She needed to run up the stairs and out the door. If only her damn legs didn't feel like they were embedded in cement. Like in a horrible nightmare, she needed to run, but couldn't.

"Blake! Blake I'm in the cellar," she hollered. But her hoarse voice hardly traveled across the small cellar.

The woman sneered and started crawling. Her nose lay at a strange angle and blood gushed down her chin and neck onto the dirt floor.

"Stay down or I'll—"

Missy couldn't finish her sentence. The woman lunged toward her like a hungry tiger after its prey.

℘

Blake jolted at the sound of a gunshot. Somewhere toward the back of the house. He whipped out his weapon and jumped over the porch railing, wishing he'd followed procedure and called for backup.

Fuck procedure. Missy was in there.

Blake clenched his hands and raced around the house. Another shot. From the cellar. He crouched by a small window. Missy held a gun in her hands, pointing it shakily at a muscular woman on her hands and knees. The woman had blood on her face and shoulder.

With a hard kick, Blake shattered the glass window and then fell to the ground. He aimed his gun at the woman. "Police. Don't move."

The woman sneered and narrowed her eyes. He'd seen that look plenty of times before. She had nothing to lose.

The window was small, but his shoulder, arm, and head fit through. He had a clear shot of the woman, too.

"Missy, I need you to back up slowly." He willed her to be okay. Blood speckled her face and chest. Splatter from when she'd shot Lynn? God, he hoped so.

Missy backed up a step, and then another, holding the gun on the woman. *Damn, she impresses the hell out of me.*

"Is there anybody else in the house?" He shifted his peripheral vision toward the steps. If anybody else was here, they should have come running at the sound of a gunshot. Didn't mean he'd assume the house was empty.

"I don't think so." Her voice was scratchy.

"Stay there, honey. Hold the gun on her just like you're doing. I'm going to lift you out this window." He grasped his weapon with one hand and pulled his cell from his pocket, keeping his gaze on the woman as blood trickled down her face and shoulder. Broken glass ripped through his bare skin, but he didn't care. All he cared about was making sure Missy was safe.

He dialed 9-1-1 and quickly gave the address and details.

He couldn't fit all the way through the window, but maybe Missy could. He could tug her through. But that would mean they'd both have to put down their weapons. With that animalistic look on her face, no way could he trust Lynn to stay still.

He wished Betty was there. She could have searched the house to let him know it was empty. Then he could have sent Missy upstairs to safety. He couldn't let her out of his sight until he knew it was safe.

Lynn growled and lunged toward Missy, hands extended.

"Missy, get down!" Blake fired at Lynn's midsection. The deafening shot echoed through the cellar. Sirens blared in the distance. Lynn fell to the dirt floor and lay immobile.

Missy glanced at Lynn's inert body and then gazed at Blake with wide eyes.

"Are you hurt? Do you think you can climb out this window if I pull you?" *Blood splatter...please be blood splatter on her face and clothes.*

Missy glanced at her shirt. "I'm fine. This isn't my blood."

"Give me your gun." She passed it to him, and he laid it in the mulch. His gaze fell on a small rug at the bottom of the steps. Good enough for protecting her from the shards of glass. "Grab that rug first."

She snatched it from the dirt and passed it to him.

"Take my hands." He holstered his gun, wanting her out of the cellar as quickly as possible, and wanting out of this vulnerable position, too.

She grasped his wrists and he was so happy to be touching her, so thrilled she was okay. He never wanted to let go of her again. "Okay, try to get a grip on the wall with your shoes." The window was at head height for her. He changed his hold to grip under her arm, holding her hand tight with his other and pulled.

His chest tightened when he heard a growling sound. A dog? He pulled harder, but Missy didn't budge. Sirens wailed closer. Help was almost there.

"It's Lynn. She's pulling me back in." Missy's body shifted and wiggled in his arms. A few more feet and she'd be safe.

Blake held tight and gave a final yank. Missy slid toward him and he stumbled backward, holding her tight. He caught a glimpse of Lynn as she fell to the cellar floor.

Police lights bounced off the surrounding houses and tree. Beams of light flashed around the corner as three uniforms rounded it.

Blake lowered Missy to the ground and kneeled next to her, pulling out his shield and ID.

"Hands up!" one of the cops hollered.

Blake raised his hands above his head. "I'm Baltimore Police. Officer Blake Decker. The one who called. In the interests of police safety, I am armed with a Glock. I'm holding my badge and ID in my left hand. I have secured the attacker's weapon. It is on the ground to my right. This is the victim, Missy Prescott." He hated saying her name and the word *victim* in the same sentence. "The attacker is inside."

Procedure was a bitch sometimes. All he wanted to do was comfort Missy, but he knew the cops had to secure the scene, keep themselves safe.

"Keep those hands in the air," the cop ordered.

Blake obeyed. He kept his gaze on Missy as her chest rose and fell quickly and she stared with wide eyes at him.

"Ma'am, do you have a weapon?"

"I did. I shot my kidnapper. She's in the cellar there. The gun is in the mulch." Her voice shook and Blake wanted to hold her close and comfort her. He'd have to wait. Each second ticked by like an hour.

One cop moved forward. "Keep your hands up. If you're a cop, you know the drill. I'm taking your weapon from your holster and I'm going to verify your badge number with dispatch." He unholstered Blake's weapon and passed it to the other cop and then took the badge and ID out of Blake's hand. The faster they figured out he and Missy weren't a threat, the faster he'd be able to hold Missy.

More cops raced around the corner.

He kept his gaze on Missy. She was quiet. Too quiet. Cops moved behind him to the cellar window holding their weapons on Lynn.

"Blake Decker. Okay. Sorry. Had to check. You can put your hands down. Anyone else in the house?" the cop asked.

Blake read his name tag. *McDowell.*

"Just the woman in the cellar, as far as we know," Blake said.

"She was in the backseat of my car...and then I woke up here." Missy blinked in the bright light as the cop shined his flashlight on her.

The men hollered orders, but Blake tuned them out. "Did she shoot you, Missy?"

"No."

Blake moved beside her. "She's hurt. We need an ambulance."

"I already called it in," the cop said.

"Missy, are you okay?" Blake dragged over a nearby cement planter and propped her feet up. No wounds, but she had to be in shock. Blood splatter covered her face, her white shirt, and the front of her legs. No! Not his Missy. This wasn't supposed to happen to someone like her.

Missy lifted her hands in front of her face to stare at them. Her breaths grew shallow and fast.

"Missy, listen to me. You're okay. It's just a little blood splatter. Everything is okay. Take a deep breath and look at me."

She blinked, took at deep breath, and then met his gaze.

"That's it. You're doing great." He kept his voice low, controlled. He could freak out later. For now, he needed to help Missy.

"Is Lynn...dead?" Missy whispered.

"I think she's hurt, not dead. You did good, Missy."

"Betty! Where's Betty?" Missy tried to move to her elbows, but Blake gently pushed her back to the ground. "She tried to help me with the ropes but she didn't have the energy."

Officer McDowell jolted. "There's someone else involved?"

Oh, shit. How exactly did he explain a ghost to the cops? "She meant thinking of Betty gave her the strength to get the ropes undone. A friend of ours who would never go down without a fight." Time to change the subject. "Did you find anyone else inside the house?"

The ruse worked. McDowell shook his head. "House is empty except for the woman in the basement."

A man in a suit rounded the corner. "Ms. Prescott, this is Detective Ramirez. Do you feel up to answering some questions?" McDowell nodded toward the detective, who carried a small spiral notebook.

"We can move to the car if that makes you more comfortable," the detective said.

Missy nodded, and Blake moved beside her, hooking her arm over his shoulder, and holding her waist. Damn it felt good to hold her, to know she was okay. The fear of losing her had gone so deep, deeper than any fear he'd ever experienced before.

"Wait." Blake paused and dug in his pocket for his cell, handed it to Missy. "First, call your mom so she knows you're okay."

An hour later, after the detective finished his questions and the

EMTs treated Missy when she refused to go to the hospital, she looked more like herself. The medics had given her wipes to get rid of the blood on her skin, and her voice sounded almost normal again.

Finally, they were alone together, leaning on the back of Blake's truck. Missy stared at her hands. "I shot somebody."

Blake nodded. "Self-defense."

She glanced at him, tears in her eyes. God, he hated that she'd had to go through this. Not her fault. She'd done what she had to do. "Had you ever shot someone before tonight?" she asked.

He shook his head. "Yes. I'm always ready to if I have to, and I've had to do it a few times. Including tonight."

"Why did she do this?"

He'd had some time to do a search while the detective was questioning Missy. "She had a history of mental issues. Served two years in jail for setting a woman's house on fire—a woman she thought was trying to steal her boyfriend."

Missy's eyes widened.

"I'm sure it wasn't easy to do what you did, and it's going to bother you for a while. I know lots of guys who sought professional help dealing with the aftermath of something like this. I hope you'll at least think about seeing a shrink."

"Yeah. Sign me up. I'm ready right now." The corners of her mouth lifted into a smile as the sun rose behind the trees, casting an orange glow on the early summer morning.

Her smile faded. "Have you seen Betty?"

It was the first he'd had time to think of her. "She came to my apartment when you didn't come home from work."

"You saw her?"

"Yeah. She broke into your apartment, and your phone was ringing and ringing."

"My mom."

He nodded. "After we checked for you at the radio station, I called your phone and we heard it ringing at the end of the lot."

Missy frowned. "Must have fallen out when she moved me out of the driver's seat." She glanced to a spot in the open garage where her car had been partitioned off with crime scene tape.

"I remembered I had Bishop's license plate written down—"

"Wait, what?"

Blake sighed and casually rested an arm over her shoulder, bringing her closer. He had to touch her, remind himself she was okay. His mind couldn't get past the image of her covered in blood.

"That day at the Inner Harbor. He seemed a little stalker-ish to me. I followed him and wrote down his plate."

"Was he involved?" Missy's hazel eyes met his.

"I don't think so. I think you genuinely helped him get over his breakup, and he was ready to move on. Lynn didn't like that so much." Blake kicked at a stone in the street with the toe of his shoe. "Police are questioning him."

She frowned and shook her head. "I know I locked my car door. I always do. How did she get in the backseat?"

Good question. He'd like the answer to that one, too. "She's a computer programmer, and there's a chance she has access to a program and device that, if she's adept at computers, can capture a key fob code. Not easy to do these days, but someone who knows about computers can do it."

"So Betty...." she said, burrowing closer to him, leaning her head against his chest.

God, what a feeling. Holding her close, knowing she was okay. It made him think all sorts of things he had never thought about before. Making her his wife. Having a family. None of that was *him*. But suddenly he wasn't himself. He was somebody different...better...more alive and accepting. Betty'd had something to do with that, too. The first person he'd ever truly trusted in his life. He trusted her so much that he'd even trusted she was a ghost when he didn't believe in ghosts.

"Yes, Betty. She read Bishop's address from my notepad." He let out a chuckle and it felt good after the crazy night they'd had. "She turned off his lights, opened and closed doors, looking for you. Scared the shit out of the poor guy. He ran outside. That's where I found him when I pulled up."

Missy laughed and then started coughing. She reached behind her into the bed of Blake's truck, grabbed the water bottle he'd brought her, and took a sip.

"Then when Bishop gave us Lynn's address, she disappeared again. I figured she came to you. Haven't seen her since."

"She did come to me. She wasn't herself, though. Kind of see-through. Not all there. One minute she was trying to loosen the ropes, and the next, she stood in front of me, like a hologram, and then disappeared."

"We need to find her." Blake rubbed up and down Missy's arm. Because of Betty, Missy was okay. But at what cost to Betty?

Chapter Thirteen

*M*issy lifted her head from Blake's rock-hard chest and swept her wet hair behind her shoulder. Morning sunlight speared in through the windows, casting a bright spotlight on the sofa where they sat, yet she shivered. She'd headed straight to the shower as soon as she walked in the door. The red water circled down the drain as she washed off the blood, making her muscles shake all over again. Even now, she could feel the cold cellar dirt against her body.

Blake stroked her hair and pulled her closer. In spite of the ninety-degree heat outside and the sweatshirt and jeans she wore, she couldn't stop shaking. She snuggled closer to Blake, trying to absorb some of his strength and warmth. This was exactly what she needed. To feel his heart beating. Let herself enjoy his steady and strong and arms that held her in a tight cocoon.

"I hoped Betty would be here waiting for us," Missy said.

"I know. So did I."

"It was weird. She's always been so real—heck, I mistook her for a human when I first saw her. In that cellar, when she crossed the room, she was different. Like a ghost. I could even see through her."

"And when she came outside of Bishop's house, she smelled like burned apple pie. I didn't think anything of it at the time. I was too busy searching for you."

Missy lifted her head just enough to glance around her small apartment. "It's like she used up all her energy on us."

"She'll come back. You'll see. We'll help her cross over and find Stanley. I'll check to see if Veronica is back from Europe. She'd due back any day."

His baritone voice echoed in his chest against her ear and she smiled, savoring the feeling. So strong. So alive. She'd saved herself. Her dad and brother would be proud of her. All of their advice had come spiraling back to her as she needed it. She'd shot someone, and that didn't feel so great. No doubt Missy would have been killed if she hadn't acted, though. And that, that she felt good about. Her ability to protect herself.

Here, now, hours later, though, what she wanted was to be weak for a little while. To lean on Blake. To let him hold her tight. He'd made her tea. It sat on the table in front of them, the steam jutting toward the ceiling and then disappearing.

"I don't want to move from this position at all." She meant it, too. The way he held her tight against him, the way his arms circled her waist and back, and the way he kissed the top of her head every once in a while. She loved her family. The love she'd been missing, though, was the love of a partner.

She shifted just enough to glance up at him. "You have the risky job, and I was the one whose life was in danger because of my job."

The corners of his mouth lifted into a small smile. An I-told-you-so smile.

God, she loved that mouth. Wanted to kiss it every morning for the rest of her life. How deep did his trust issues with women go? In spite of his protests about relationships, wasn't that what they had? A relationship?

She let out a breath. "Nobody knows what will happen to them— good or bad—on any given day." Her mind shifted to friends of her dad's, cop friends, who were still alive and going to work every day. What stroke of bad luck had made her dad and brother a target? The same stroke of bad luck that made Lynn make Missy a target.

"Missy." Blake shifted his arm and trailed the back of his fingers up her jaw line. "I understand your fears completely. A vision of what my life would be like without you flashed before my eyes." His hand stilled and he clenched his jaw. Fighting back emotion? "A lonely and empty vision."

What was he saying? Her heart hammered, and she clutched his T-shirt, needing to hold on because she wasn't sure if he was letting her go or begging her to stay.

"My friends are my family...my brothers. I never had a real family. Never thought I could want one—"

Now that she'd finally gotten over the fact that his job was dangerous—and any job could be dangerous—how did he feel? She almost didn't want to know, would rather hang onto the hope. When her life was at risk, it was Blake she didn't want to leave. It was Blake she needed.

"When I'm with you, I want all sorts of things I never wanted before." His chest heaved. "I have trust issues, Missy. My mom left, saying she'd come back. Only she didn't. I thought it was ancient history until I got involved with a woman I thought I could trust a while ago. She stole my identity."

"Is that why you freaked out when you found your open bill on my table?" It made sense now. He'd acted on experience.

He nodded. "You're not like that. It took almost losing you for me to realize that."

Missy held her breath.

He ran a hand through his hair. "I want...I want to be with you. I want a relationship." He spat the words out fast, as if he was afraid they'd get stuck if he didn't.

No longer shaking, in fact glowing with happiness from the inside out, Missy cradled his face and pulled him nose to nose with her. "I'd love to be in a relationship with you."

His breath came out in a rush, feathering over her lips, and then his cell phone rang.

"Maybe you should get that. It might be one of your brothers."

With a shake of his head, he tilted her chin upward and lowered his mouth to the corner of her lips. "Let it wait. Whatever it is, you're more important."

Heat seared through her limbs. His lips pressed against hers and his tongue searched for the seam of her mouth. She opened, welcoming him, needing to get lost in the taste and power of him. The walls he'd built around his heart were weakening and he was letting her in.

His phone beeped, indicating a message. Five seconds later, the text alert went off. In spite of her happiness for their newfound connection, the noises from his phone distracted her enough to pull away.

He loosened his hold, and Missy took a deep breath.

"Sounds important," she said. "You'd better check your phone."

With a nod, he leaned to the side and tugged his phone from his pocket. His eyes widened and his lips parted.

"What is it?" Missy leaned to view the screen.

"Betty. She's in Angie and Rob's apartment."

"Thank God." She'd been afraid to admit it, but she'd been so scared that Betty had disappeared, or even moved on, without a good-bye. "Let's go."

Missy grinned and leaned forward to kiss him. God, it felt freeing to let herself love him like she'd been wanting to from the day she'd met him.

Love? No...that took time. This was something else. At least for now.

"Rob says Betty's a little weak." Blake tapped on his screen to send a reply to Rob. "Can't even hold objects."

Missy stood. "Well, I need a hug, so I hope she still has substance."

Blake stood, tucked the phone in his pocket, and they hurried together from the apartment, hand in hand. A team. A couple.

The door to 807 opened before they could knock. A man with light brown hair, blue eyes, and a serious look on his face opened the door.

"Hey, Blake." He opened the door and nodded at Blake and then turned to Missy. "Hi, I'm guessing you're Missy. I've heard a lot about you. I'm Rob."

Missy shook his hand with her right while holding hands with Rob with her left. She instantly liked Rob. A trustworthy face. But why so serious?

She stepped inside the spacious apartment. Betty sat on a black-checkered sofa by the window. Angie perched beside her. A huge smile lit Betty's face as she glanced at Missy and Blake and then at their joined hands. Blake squeezed her hand as if noticing and signaling for them to hold tight so Betty could see her job here was done.

Angie nodded hello and Missy smiled back at her and then glanced at Betty.

"Betty!" Missy headed for the sofa with Blake by her side. "I was so worried." She faced Blake. "*We* were so worried about you."

Betty waved a hand in front of her face. "Fiddlesticks. Don't worry about me. I lost of little of my ju-ju powers by being so far from this apartment building, I think. I'm better now."

"Or maybe close to the vortex," Rob said, glancing at the front door.

Rob could be right. Maybe the vortex gave Betty the energy she needed to do what she did. She didn't look like her usual self, though. Her expression was positive, and she sounded the same, but it was almost as if Missy could see though her. She dared not ask for a hug, because her arms might go right through her and right now she wanted to appreciate that Betty was still in their presence. That was enough for now.

"Betty, thank you so much for letting me know Blake was on the way." Missy kneeled in front of Betty with her hand clasped in Blake's and tried to force the memory of the cold dirt floor and the danger that presided there from her mind.

Betty's smile grew even wider, and was it Missy's imagination, or did she suddenly gain more substance? Betty glanced at their joined hands. "I'm glad you made it out alive, honey. And I'm glad you two have figured out you're in love."

Blake's eyes opened so wide that Missy almost laughed. One step at a time. But maybe he'd reach the same conclusion about the two of them as she already had.

Blake cleared his throat. "It's time, isn't it, Betty? Time for you to go to Stanley."

Betty nodded several times, her smile firmly in place.

Rob leaned on the edge of the sofa near Angie.

"Any ideas?" He turned to face Rob and Angie. "I know you said last time that you couldn't open up to us about how you know about the paranormal stuff that goes on in this building. I don't want to press you, but Missy and I would love your help."

Inside, Missy's heart swelled with pride. The team thing again. Damn, she liked it.

The smile dropped from Rob's face and his jaw tightened. He laid a hand on Angie's shoulder and then faced Missy and Blake. "I'll help you, but I want to get Angie far away from here. One of these days, we'll tell you the whole story, but I can't risk that Angie is anywhere near that vortex."

"Rob, I'll be fine, I—" Angie said.

"Please, Angie. For me." Rob pulled her hand into both of his.

Angie sighed and then turned to face Missy and Blake. Whatever she'd experienced, Rob definitely didn't want her going through it again. Missy's curiosity was piqued, but her concern for Betty overshadowed everything else.

"Veronica Matthews lives downstairs. We used to work out together in the gym. She's a psychic-medium, not by profession—she's a photographer. Something bad happened a while ago. She never talked about it, but it changed her. She started traveling more and doesn't want anything to do with her abilities. I don't know why." Angie bit her bottom lip. "I should have tried to help her...get her to talk about it." She glanced at Rob.

"I can ask Veronica for help. I've met her once or twice," Rob said.

"Rob looks just like my guardian angel," Betty said, breaking the tension that filled the room.

"That would be my brother Mick." Rob glanced at Missy and Blake. "Let's give Angie time to get out of the building, and then we'll visit Veronica. She came back early. I saw her this morning. Let's see how she can help."

Ten minutes later, Missy, Blake, and Rob stood outside apartment 105. Betty opted to stay in the apartment. The longer she sat, the more energetic she felt. Angie took a trip across town to visit a friend.

"Ready?" Rob's jaw was set as he lifted his hand to knock.

"Ready," Blake and Missy said, together.

He rapped on the door. Loud music thumped from inside, but nobody opened the door. Rob knocked again, this time louder.

Within a few seconds, the door swung open and a petite woman with red, curly hair and a beautiful heart-shaped face stood staring at them. A nose ring glittered. Missy guessed the woman was in her late twenties.

"Hey, Rob." She used a remote to turn down the music, fixed her gaze on Rob, and then raised a brow at Missy and Blake.

Missy had no idea what she'd expected Veronica to be. An older lady, maybe? This woman had her rethinking what a psychic-medium would look like.

"This is Missy and Blake from the eighth floor," Rob said.

"Hi," Missy and Rob said in unison. *Seriously?* Like they were in sync or something. Why did warm, gooey feelings travel through her when she thought of being so connected to him?

"Hey, nice to meet you." She didn't look happy to meet them. In fact, the way she kept her hand on the doorknob made her look like she wanted to say good-bye and shut the door.

"Welcome back. I heard you were out of the country," Rob said.

Veronica nodded. "Thanks."

Rob glanced at Missy and Blake and then huffed out a loud breath. "Listen, Veronica. We need your help. We have a situation on the eighth floor. A woman who used to live there...who died there...is stuck. She can't cross over. We need—"

"No." Veronica straightened, lifted her chin, and started to close the door.

"Wait, Veronica." Blake stepped forward and put a palm on the door. "Please. We don't know how else to help her. She was—she was like a mother to me. The mother I never had. When she was living, and also as a ghost. She stayed here for me. Waiting for me to find...." Blake swallowed hard and swept his gaze over Missy.

Warm heat traveled through her bloodstream. The soft look in his eyes, the tender set to his mouth. So different than the night she'd met him.

"Well, she was waiting for me to find someone to trust. Somebody I could be with...for...well, for a long, long time."

Missy smiled. That was enough. More than enough, really. One step at a time and their relationship would bloom.

Veronica pressed her lips together and for a moment, Missy's hopes rose. She would help them.

"I'm sorry. I can't." She started to shut the door again and Missy's heart dipped. Something cold brushed her shoulder and she turned. A breeze?

Veronica stared at the spot behind Missy, her gold eyes widening and her lips parting. She smiled as if seeing an old friend, and it changed her expression completely. Suddenly, the hardened look she apparently worked so hard to hide behind slipped away and a friendlier version of Veronica unmasked. Her eyes grew teary, and she stared at the spot over Missy's shoulder.

Missy turned again, expecting to see Betty. Maybe she'd lost so much energy that she was now invisible and only a psychic-medium could see her.

"Betty?" Missy whispered, turning to face Veronica.

Veronica opened her door wider to let them in and kept her gaze on the spot behind Missy. "No. It's Stanley."

C&#x08;

Blake swallowed the fear that built in his gut as they stood in the hallway outside of 807 with Missy, Rob, and Veronica. Not criminals or danger, the kind of fear he faced every day. No, this fear went deeper. Loss. He had never had the chance to say good-bye to Betty when she had died. Now he could. Problem was, he didn't want to.

Apparently Stanley had disappeared as quickly as he'd presented himself. Only Veronica had seen him. In the elevator, she'd mumbled something about payback being a bitch and that she owed him.

Missy edged closer to Blake, pressing her side to his as she reached an arm around his waist and hooked a finger through his belt loop. Comfortable together. They hadn't known each other long, but he knew her better than women he'd known for months. These new feelings, this weird opening up, would take a while to get used to. Instead of dreading that task, he found himself looking forward to the challenge of throwing out his old mistrustful feelings and latching on to a newfound trust.

Betty gave Rob and Veronica a quick hug and then crossed the short, carpeted area to stand in front of Missy and Blake. She smiled and nodded several times, her flamingo earrings bobbing with her head. "Warms my heart to see you two like this. I wasn't sure you hardheaded kids would figure out you were meant to be before I had to go."

Blake swallowed past a lump in his throat. She was already dead. This wasn't a funeral. Betty reached up and laid a hand on his chest. She was at least a foot shorter than he, and her touch was cool on his shirt. He wanted to ask her to stay, yet he knew it was time for her to go.

"I'm going to miss you, Betty." He clenched his jaw to ward off the stinging in his eyes. Cops didn't cry. At least not in public. *Hold it together, man.*

She patted his chest with her cool hand. "Think of me when you have apple pie." She winked at Missy. "I gave Missy my recipe."

He couldn't help it. As miserable as he was, he couldn't keep the chuckle from rumbling out. Just what he needed to relieve the tension. Missy slipped her arm from around him, allowing him to step forward and pull Betty into a firm hug.

With his eyes closed, he savored the strength and love that flowed from the woman. He could have gone his whole life without feeling accepted or truly loved. Instead, Betty made him feel loved. Twice loved. She'd found Missy for him.

She patted his back and stepped away, winking at him. Yeah, he'd miss that twinkle in her eye, too. Didn't matter. She'd always be a part of his heart.

Betty stepped in front of Missy and placed her hands to the sides of Missy's face. Tears glistened in Missy's eyes. She was the force that had brought Betty out, she was the reason Blake had a chance to see Betty again. Missy's belief had made all of this possible. Including Betty's chance to cross over.

"You are a special, woman, Missy. Not just to this lug over here." She gazed at Blake and winked again and then back at Missy. "Your listeners depend on you, too. You've been given a gift. Your voice...and your caring nature."

Missy's bottom lip quivered and tears streamed down her face. "I'm so glad I got to meet you, Betty." She pulled Betty in for a hug and ran her hand up and down the back of her pink sweat suit.

Betty eased away, keeping her hands in Missy's. "I'm going to look up your dad and your brother after Stanley and I have a good, long hug."

Missy smiled. "Tell them I love them."

"I will."

Thunder rumbled outside. "I love the rainbows after a summer thunderstorm." Betty looked upward as if seeing the storm.

Veronica stepped forward. "The timing couldn't be better. A storm will provide even more power for the vortex." She held out her hand to Betty. "I think it's time."

Betty let go of Missy and Missy reached for Blake as he reached for her. With their arms wrapped around each other, clasping tight for strength he knew he could count on from her, they watched the older woman take Veronica's hand.

Veronica glanced over her shoulder at Rob, Missy, and Blake. "Move to the end of the hall. Only one entity goes through the vortex today."

Blake hated moving farther away from Betty, wanted to stay close and send her as much strength as he could. Would it hurt while she crossed over? Would she be happy on the other side? The three of them moved toward the elevator.

"Stay to the right," Veronica said, her words gentle to Betty. The woman sure put on a show to act tough, but the way she coddled Betty, held one of her hands and placed another on the older woman's back, she must be a softie on the inside.

The electricity in the hallway flickered and then came back on and then a rumble of thunder shook the building. The hallway grew blurry, almost shaking.

"Do you see that?" Blake asked. He wasn't the only one, was he?

"It's like the air is moving," Missy whispered.

"The vortex?" Rob asked.

Betty turned, kissed her fingertips, and then bent her palm to blow a kiss toward them.

Missy sucked in a loud, shaky breath and Blake pulled her closer. Her body shook with sobs and her tears wet his shirt.

"Stay to the right and go straight. Mick, Rob's brother, is waiting for you. He's your guide and he'll take you to Stanley, Betty. You'll be just fine. Can you walk the rest of the way by yourself? I need to stop right here. Only a few more steps...." Veronica patted Betty's shoulder.

Blake tensed. From Behind, Betty looked so fragile, so small. Her white hair blew in an unseen breeze. She nodded, stood straighter, and marched forward.

And then she was gone.

ℛ

Missy's ponytail fluttered in the humid late-afternoon breeze. The storm lasted only a half hour or so. Just enough to clear people off the downtown Baltimore streets. Blake strolled hand in hand with her along a residential road in Federal Hill.

Maybe the hilltop view of the water would relax them and shake away the bad stuff.

"I know we should be asleep right now, but I can't seem to settle down enough." She'd been kidnapped...and then shot a person. No, she shouldn't be dozing. She should probably be in a state of shock.

And maybe she was.

"Mouthfuls of downtown air are enough to make anyone tired," Blake said, giving her hand a squeeze.

Missy laughed. "Would that be the truck fumes or the humidity that does that trick?"

He turned to face her. They'd walked for fifteen minutes and now stood at the edge of Federal Hill overlooking the Inner Harbor. Quaint, historic row homes loomed behind them and the waterfront and all of its attractions spread below them.

"I didn't know Betty very long." Missy turned to face Blake. "Not nearly as long as you did. I loved her, though, Blake. Is that possible?"

Blake grinned and took her other hand. Bolts of pleasure traveled up her arms and headed to her core. How could simple contact with him do so much?

"It's possible. You knew Betty as long as I've known you and I...." He pressed his lips together. Those sexy lips and that wicked set of his mouth that made him look like he was laughing at a joke only he'd heard.

Those lips she loved in so many ways. "Well, I have...feelings for you."

She shouldn't laugh. She really shouldn't. He was baring his soul. In typical Blake fashion. But laughter bubbled up inside her chest until she couldn't hold it back anymore. She knew what he meant. And she'd get an "I love you" out of him one day. Hopefully one day soon. For now, she'd settle for *feelings*. Laying her head on his chest, she released his hands and hugged his muscular body close, then ran her hands up and down his back.

"I love you, Blake. I'm glad you think a few weeks isn't too short of a time to really fall in love with someone. And I'm glad you have feelings for me. That's all I need."

He didn't say anything, simply laid his chin atop her head and stroked her hair with one hand and her upper back with the other.

Something caught her eye across the street and she narrowed her eyes, squinting.

"A rainbow! Look at that."

Blake glanced up. "Well, what do you know. Betty said there would be a rainbow after the storm and—" His body tensed and Missy tore her gaze off the colorful rainbow to glance at him.

"What?"

"No way..." he whispered.

She followed his gaze. The rainbow arched across the narrow city street, shedding colorful light as if in a fog at the end of the block. And the rainbow faded to an end in a set of flower pots.

Flower pots with two flamingos that bobbled back and forth in the slight breeze.

"She made it," Missy said, her heart swelling with joy. "She's with Stanley."

"Yeah, she made it." A slow smile spread across his face as he lowered his lips and touched them to Missy's. Apple pie and a matchmaking ghost might have brought them together, but in the end, their willingness to look past what they each thought should keep them apart had brought them together.

He grinned and draped an arm over her shoulder while the rainbow faded into the sun that broke through the clouds. "She's with Stanley and now I want to go back home and be with you."

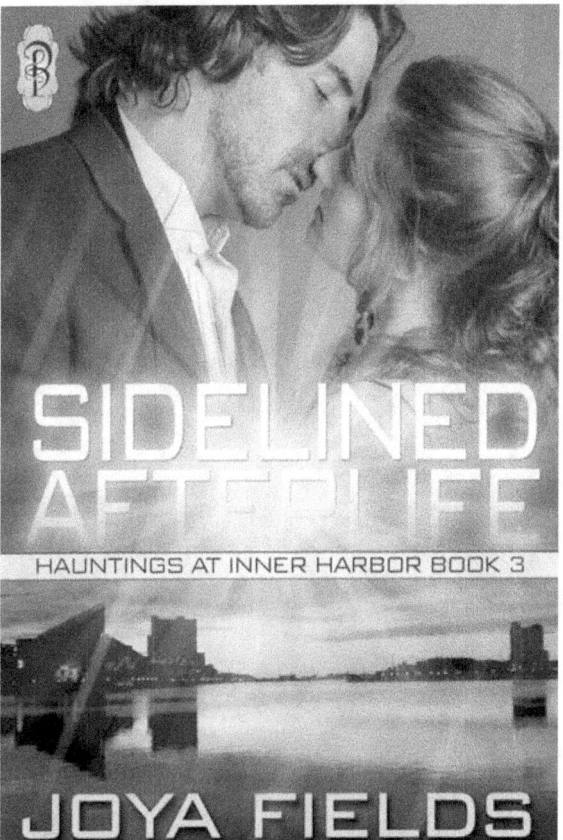

SIDELINED
AFTERLIFE

HAUNTINGS AT INNER HARBOR BOOK 3

JOYA FIELDS

Chapter One

*H*elping a ghost cross over to the other side always upset Veronica Matthews. She needed to walk. Or have a good cry. Needed to get the hell outside and take some deep breaths of fresh air. She stepped off the elevator and into the marble-floored lobby of her apartment building.

"Hi." A handsome, dark-haired man with searing blue eyes nodded at her as they passed each other.

"Hello." She nodded back to him, and at the young black man in a red football uniform next to him. "How's it going?"

The man spun and clasped her upper arm. His baby blues were wide and hopeful. "Oh my God. You see her, don't you?" The man looked to his right where the young black man had stood earlier, but the kid had moved behind him now.

Does that guy think the ghost with him is a woman?

The kid tilted his head and narrowed his eyes, studying Veronica. He moved his mouth as if to speak, but no words came out.

Shit. She could usually tell the difference between the living and dead. She'd trained herself so well. She should have felt the signs. Like skin that looked pearlescent...a light that shined outward from within the body. The cold...the slight glow to the football player's skin. Not sweat from the humid, rainy day. Other-worldly.

With a pointed glance at the spot on her arm where the man gripped her, she forced herself to stay calm. "You can release me now."

He blinked and stared at her, almost mesmerizing her with those eyes, before he glanced at his fingers digging into her arm. "Sorry." He snatched his hand away and stared at it as if he hadn't known what he'd done.

She didn't need this. Didn't need people pressuring her about what she saw. Veronica hated her so-called gift of being able to connect with the dying and the dead. Hated it like an enemy. Where had it gotten her in life? Nowhere. Worse than nowhere. It had given her nightmares and headaches. Pain. Made her feel like a freak. Facilitating a ghost's cross over made her feel slightly helpful, but the other stuff...well, she could do without it.

The man who'd gripped her lowered his brows. His face radiated hurt. "You see someone with me, don't you? Please.... Nobody has ever seen her before. I need to know."

Pretend you don't know what he's talking about. Pretend you don't care. Veronica was a photographer by trade, not a psychic-medium. The gift brought too many complications and this ghost apparently came with a demanding man begging to know more about the entity.

She glanced at the kid, who stared at her with wide eyes. Had nobody addressed him before? How long had he been dead?

"I don't know what you're talking about. I'm late. I have to go." She whirled away from the man and the kid. *Exit now!* Guilt over the hopeful look in this man's gorgeous blue eyes threatened to overwhelm her. She shoved it down.

Free of his grip, she ran across the lobby and headed for the glass doors that led to the downtown Baltimore sidewalk. So what if rain gushed from the afternoon sky, interrupted only by a bolt of lightning and the following blast of thunder? At least she'd be free of ghosts.

Outside, she lifted her face, welcoming the pounding water on her skin, letting it wash away everything she felt. After a few blocks of speed walking through the storm, her breaths came easier but her old friends, guilt and remorse, kicked in. She should have helped that man and the young man beside him. They had both looked at her with eyes that pleaded for answers.

But it could lead to disaster.

The mystical powers she'd received after a drowning accident ten years ago weren't something she could easily handle. Each time, the headaches got worse, and each interaction opened her up to the supernatural world even more. Let the handsome guy figure out who was next to him on his own. She'd rather walk in a storm than deal with more drama from a ghost.

Warm summer rain poured down on her, plastering her thin cotton T-shirt to her skin and making her jeans feel heavy as the water soaked her long hair. Her flip-flop-covered feet splashed in puddles. Instead of making her uncomfortable, she savored the feeling and slowed to stroll down the empty sidewalk.

She'd moved to Baltimore's Inner Harbor because of a photography magazine's editor job offer and a free place to live while she worked on her photography book, but she knew Baltimore's history...knew there were more ghosts here than most places. The rain calmed her as she marched forward. The ghosts weren't the biggest problem. It was the dying beings that haunted her—the "psychic" side of her psychic-medium powers.

Veronica had led police to dozens of bodies over the past five years, in four different states, including two months ago in Baltimore. She'd been so close to finding that three-week-old baby girl alive...had *felt* that infant was still breathing. Holding the pacifier in her hand had given her the connection she'd needed. But she lost contact and feared the worst. They'd been too late. Little ashen lips and a tiny body wrapped in a small T-shirt, with a shock of dark hair that contrasted against her pale skin. The bitty thing had looked asleep. She was dead.

Regret and grief choked her throat.

She could never go through that again. But ghosts were already dead...and maybe helping the handsome dark-haired man who was being haunted by a dead football player would be a way to use her gift for a good purpose.

If only each time didn't exact such a toll.

ᑯ

Hunter Anderson hurried across the lobby and opened the heavy glass door to the sound of pouring rain. It fell from the sky so hard that it splashed back up from the sidewalk. He wouldn't follow the auburn-haired woman with the pierced nose as she raced out into the storm. He was the one who'd chased her out there. He'd even grabbed her in desperation. She'd rather be in the elements than near him. Her long, curly hair straightened in the downpour, and her green shirt—the one that played up her haunting golden eyes—was plastered against her trim shoulders and waist.

Who could blame her for running? He'd come on too strong. In his defense, she'd taken him by surprise. Shock, really. She was the first person who had ever noticed the ghost with him, his constant companion since his wife's death almost two years ago.

He scrubbed a hand through his hair. A twenty-hour shift in the Emergency Department left him irritable and on edge. The woman disappeared around a corner and he shut the door. He didn't have to follow her. She lived in the building. He might not know her name or which apartment, but he'd seen her lots of times before. Someone with her fiery golden eyes and her head of curly hair could never go unnoticed.

Next time, he'd warm her up first. Introduce himself. Apologize. *Yeah, definitely apologize.* She could be the key to finally finding answers. He glanced to his left and right. Not that he'd ever caught a vision of the ghost that followed him almost constantly. But he could hope. He shifted to the right again and paused. No cold mass of air that he usually felt when the ghost was near. The hairs on his arms weren't standing up. Had the ghost followed the gorgeous redhead with the pierced nose? The spirit didn't leave him often, but when it did, he always wondered where it went.

Hunter headed for the elevator, rubbing his tired eyes. He stabbed the button. *Good. Some time alone.* Maybe he'd even have the luxury of three or four straight hours of uninterrupted sleep.

The doors swished open and he stepped inside. Things were getting worse every day with this spirit. She wouldn't even let him sleep. Was his wife haunting him—making him pay because he should have been with her that fateful night an eighteen-wheeler had run a red light and killed her on impact? He'd tried to talk to the ghost. Talked to it as if it were his wife. He apologized...begged for forgiveness. But he never got any real clues that it was really her.

The night of her death, he'd stayed at work for one more operation. One more patient. It was always one more patient with him. And he'd lost that patient, too. A high-schooler who never made it to graduation. Two deaths that night. His ghost could be any one of dozens of people he'd fought to save...and lost.

The doors opened to the eighth floor and Hunter stepped out. What had started as small incidents—smacking a few pills from his hand when he'd attempted to dull the pain of losing his wife—had escalated into a feeling of never being alone. Made it tough to sleep. Like someone was always staring at him. And, cold spots. Stuff in his apartment moved to different places. Restless noises in the middle of the night. Someone pacing. Just enough to creep him out and keep him on edge. A feeling that followed him to the hospital, where similarly strange things happened.

He'd turned himself in to his chief. Explained he'd been drinking and taking a few self-prescribed meds. After some therapy, they'd allowed him back. On probation. With weekly drug tests. But he'd never told anyone about his ghost companion. His job was his life now. The only thing that kept him going. But in order to fully concentrate, to give his job one-hundred percent, he needed the otherworldly companion to go.

He unlocked the door and stepped inside. No cold. No feeling of being watched.

Hunter tossed his keys on the mahogany table by the door. They hit a little too hard, and bumped a small vase over the edge of the table, crashing it onto the ceramic floor.

He'd deal with it later. Sleep now. Clean up later.

Might as well take advantage of some ghost-free time...while he had it.

ભ

Veronica used her hip to open the lobby door, since she carried two brown bags of groceries in her arms. As suddenly as the thunderstorm had approached, it disappeared. Hot afternoon sun beamed in through the windows and warmed the back of her damp shirt.

After a quick glance around the empty expansive entry, she relaxed her shoulders. The dark-haired man was nowhere in sight. Good. That would give her more time to decide if, or how, she might help him.

This level of the building housed the pool, the workout room, and some storage rooms. With her elbow, she jabbed the elevator button. Easier than trekking up a flight of steps. Not that she didn't need the exercise.

Once in the elevator, she smiled and thought of how she'd spend the afternoon involved in one of her favorite activities. Cooking. Well, with this Baltimore heat, not so much cooking. More like chopping and creating. Homemade salsa and a few healthy bowls of gazpacho would get her shorts to fit right at the waistband again.

The smile dropped from her face as she spotted the football player crouched beside her apartment door, his elbows on his knees, head on his palms. *Great. How does he know where I live?*

Hiking the bags up to get a better grip, she moved forward. He was dead already. She could help him. No chance of getting sucked into a situation like she'd been with police. No holding a pacifier and feeling the exact moment the life of a baby slipped away. Now that she'd taken a walk, gotten some distance from the current situation, she understood. Ghosts, she could handle. A pounding headache would be the price she'd have to pay, but in any case, since he knew where Veronica lived, she'd have to deal with him.

"What are you doing here?" she asked.

He glanced up slowly as she approached, his face drawn.

Why wasn't he moving on? Had he just died today? Unfinished business? Most spirits crossed easily after death, stepping from one world to the next with no help. So what was keeping this kid here?

"Will you help me cross over to the next world?" he asked, his voice gravelly, as if he hadn't used it in a long time. Even he looked surprised at the sound and his large hand flew to his neck as if checking his vocal chords.

Poor kid. So young to be dead. But this situation was different. Not like the kidnapped woman whose scarf she'd held. That woman had been buried alive, only for police to find her after she'd died. Yeah, she'd helped police find victims they might not have found. But she also had seen things she couldn't un-see. What good were her so-called powers if she couldn't get to dying people before they died?

"Let me see what I can do. Stay out here, though. I've set my apartment up to keep out spirits." The crushed brick dust, and White Light of the Goddess she'd put around her place had done the trick so far.

He stood, stretching at least six feet tall, towering over her. "You'll help me?" His brows knit together, as if he didn't trust her. She didn't know much about football, but he had probably intimidated players on opposing teams.

She laid a hand on his upper arm. Cold. So cold she snapped her hand off right away. "I'm going to try to help you. I don't know if I can. I'm not...well, I'm not trained in this, or anything. It's just something that...." How did she explain a stupid gift forced on her—and that she'd learned from experience? "I'm going to unpack my groceries. I have an idea of how to help you."

She stepped inside and heard a bump behind her and turned in time to see him back away from her open doorway.

"What is that? Why can't I get in? It's the same thing that happens when I try to leave this world for the next." His voice was stronger now.

"It's a shield. No ghosts in my apartment. Ever. That's my rule."

He reached out with his palm and tested the entryway. Looking for a weakness?

"The vortex on the eighth floor? You've tried it?" she asked. She knew about the spot there. For no reason she could figure out, spirits, both good and bad, could cross over from that particular area. It was a place she liked to stay clear of because evil entities could latch on to her if she wasn't careful. Stories about a woman who'd killed her husband and his mistress by setting them on fire in that hallway in the early 1900s only added to her discomfort.

He crossed his muscular arms on his chest and nodded. More sadness.

"How long have you been dead?" *May as well tell it like it is.* He knew he was dead, right? Some spirits didn't.

"I died in the summer. Fall, winter, and spring came. And another summer. Now it's summer again." His shoulders slumped as if the load was too much to carry any longer.

Two years? *Holy crap.* The longer a spirit remained earthbound, the harder it was to cross over. After the two-year mark, they often began to lose their connection with their human life and turn darker...more dangerous.

"Give me one minute. Then we'll take a walk."

His face instantly lit with a huge smile, white teeth that contrasted the dark of his skin.

Inside, Veronica set the bags on the granite countertop. She could still say no. She could still walk away from this. She glanced toward the door, where he stood clasping his hands, looking so damned hopeful.

She pulled out her cell, punched in a message, and hit send. "Before we go, I want to make sure the coast is clear up there on the eighth floor. There's a resident who is vulnerable during crossovers at that vortex. I want to give her time to leave. I know you've tried that vortex, but maybe if I'm with you it'll help. It's worth a try."

Her phone beeped with a return message from Angie. *I'm at the movies. All clear. Good luck.*

Thanks! She sent the text and glanced at the kid.

Five minutes of her time. That's all it would be. She'd walk with him, make sure he stayed to the right side of the vortex, where he could cross over. If he didn't make it to the other world after that, they'd have to figure out something else.

"Come on. Let's go." With a last glance at the bags of groceries she'd never unpacked, she jammed her keys in her shorts pocket and closed the door behind her. "We're taking the steps. I need the exercise."

Inside the stairwell, he took the stairs two at a time, waiting for her on the second floor.

"Show-off," she said.

He grinned.

"What's your name, anyway?" She marched upward, wishing she'd worn tennis shoes instead of flip-flops.

He raced past her to the top. "Wade Montgomery. I've forgotten a lot of things, but not my name."

Well-spoken guy. Educated. How had he died? Baltimore streets could be deadly for teenagers, with the gangs, drugs, and the temptation to make money doing illegal activities. But this kid didn't seem like a drop-out or a criminal. Knowing his name could help them figure out a reason for his inability to cross over. A good start.

Veronica started to breathe a little heavier and walk a little slower by the time she hit the seventh floor. She needed to spend less time strolling around taking photos and more time hitting the paths for runs.

"Why are we trying the eighth floor again? I've already tried that. I've watched other people walk through it and disappear. But when I try, it's like an invisible wall. Like your doorway." He tilted his head and lowered his brows.

"Let's see what happens if I'm with you." They had to give it a shot. Maybe he'd been on the wrong side of the hallway. But Veronica's heart sank. No. More likely he had something yet to do before he crossed over.

Guilt tugged at her gut as she started the last flight of steps. She'd been beside herself with grief months ago after she and the police had found the dead baby in a dumpster. The image of that infant kept her awake at night. And it was one of those nights when Stanley—a current ghost on the other side and former tenant of the eighth floor—had visited her and persuaded her to take a vacation. She'd been entertaining the thought about going to the neighborhood pool and letting water fill her lungs in an attempt to rid herself of the powers she'd acquired when she'd almost drowned.

She hadn't wanted to die. Only to lose her "gift". If drowning had caused her problem, maybe having it happen again would relieve her of it? She wouldn't have had the guts to follow through on that plan, and she knew it, but still...the thought of never having to feel the guilt of finding someone too late was tempting.

And just that morning, she'd helped Stanley's wife cross over. She'd had unfinished business, too.

Wade walked through the door at the eighth floor and waited for her.

"Oh, big deal. You can walk through things." She stepped from the cement landing onto the carpeted hallway.

He glanced at the end of the hall at the area where ghosts could cross from this world into the next. The entire apartment building was haunted—as was much of Baltimore—but the eighth floor of this building had more supernatural activity than most. Chills ran down her spine at the thought of dying by fire.

"Do you see it?" She eyed a cloudy spot at the end of the hall. "The vortex?"

He nodded and bit his lower lip as he stared in that direction. Poor kid. Alone for almost two years. Nobody to talk to, nobody to help him.

"It doesn't hurt, you know." She moved closer, laid her hand on his cool skin.

"Okay." His voice broke on the word and his hands shook.

The vortex bent and flexed as if in a breeze. As if waiting for Wade. "Stay to the right side. There's a stronger pull there. Hug the wall." Veronica pressed her lips together. *Please let this work. Bring this kid some peace.*

His jaw flexed and with a final glance at Veronica, he forged forward, taking long strides toward the swirling mass of air. He must have been a formidable football player. Once the kid set his mind on something, good luck to anyone who stood in his way.

He moved closer to the end of the hall and straightened his shoulders as if bracing for battle. His jersey, sporting the number five, hugged a strong body and his cleats were silent as he moved along the carpet.

Fisting his hands at his sides, he stopped and lowered his head. All he needed was a helmet and he would have been ready for a scrimmage. Ten feet to go. He sprinted the distance.

Veronica's heart raced.

A low growl emanated from the end of hall and the left side of the vortex flickered orange and red. Like a fire.

"More to the right! More to the right!" she shouted. Whatever was on that left side of the passageway was getting stronger.

Wade stopped and jerked backward. *Shit.* He'd avoided the left side, but the right side wouldn't let him in, either. It must be the invisible wall he'd mentioned. Which meant there was something keeping him here besides his own will, or any physical barriers. He had something left to do before he'd be allowed to cross over.

With narrowed eyes, Wade marched closer, and turned toward a door. "I just want to go home. Only problem is...I don't know where that is anymore." He stalked through the entryway of 803.

Maybe he needed time alone. He knew where to find her. She turned to go back down the hallway, but stopped at the sound of banging pots and pans inside apartment 803. Those sounds were followed quickly by a holler.

Wade was getting stronger, probably because of his connection to her. He could speak now, but she guessed she was the only one who could hear him. And apparently he could touch things, throw them. Must drive the man he haunted crazy.

She could walk away, let the man deal with it by himself. But he'd looked so damned tired. She raised her hand and knocked.

Locks clicked and the door opened. She stood face to face with the dark-haired, blue-eyed man from the lobby. He was shirtless, clad only in a loose pair of gray sweatpants cut off into shorts. Her eyes dropped from his rumpled hair to his muscular chest and broad shoulders.

Movement tore her gaze away. Wade, with his right hand wrenched back, ready to throw something, stood behind him.

"No!" She threw her body against the man's, pressing him against the wall as an object traveled through the air toward them.

Chapter Two

*H*unter's shoulder blade bit into his foyer wall behind him. A ripe orange whizzed past the woman's gorgeous head of hair and hit the doorframe with a thud. Noises and cold were escalating to a...citrus attack?

Her petite body pinned him to the wall. Damn sexy. The fabric of her cotton T-shirt brushed against his bare chest. She smelled like rain and her clothes were still a little damp from the storm. The coolness almost singed against the sudden heat that built inside him. What it would be like to have this woman's body pressed against him under different circumstances?

"A simple hello would have done, but nice to meet you, too." He tried to keep a straight face but couldn't stop his lips from lifting.

They both glanced toward the kitchen area, where the orange had come from. "Stop throwing stuff!" she said. She faced Hunter. "I just reacted, that's all. I saw the ghost was throwing something at you and I didn't know what it was at first. I'm Veronica." She pushed off him and he missed her warmth instantly. "Great to see you're one of *those*."

"I'm Hunter. What do you mean 'one of those'?" Part of him wanted to risk another citrus attack so she would press against him again.

"The type who covers your fear with sarcasm. Has this ghost been with you for two years?" She marched toward his kitchen, where the ghost likely stood.

Hmm. Sarcasm? And here I thought I'd been charming. "Not quite two years, but almost." About the same time he'd lost his wife.

Like a schoolteacher correcting a student, she put her hands on her hips and then shook her pointer finger at a spot in the kitchen. "You're making things worse, not better. Just because you've discovered your ability to throw again doesn't mean you use it against somebody."

The smile fell from Hunter's lips and he walked toward the woman. "You can talk to her?"

She frowned. "Not her. *Him.*"

A weight lifted from his heart. "Thank God. It's not Dianna, then." He grabbed the edge of the counter with both hands and closed his eyes, relief flooding his system. His knees shook. For so long, he'd worried that his wife blamed him, haunted him.

His eyes opened. If it wasn't Dianna, who the hell was it? "Who is he?"

Veronica glanced up. This was a tall damn ghost. At least six feet. "He's a bored teenager, but not a dangerous one. At least not yet." She pressed her lips together, as if unsure about how to continue.

"What do you mean not yet?" So there *was* something to fear? He hadn't been overreacting?

"It's complicated. Maybe you were the last one who touched him before he died. He feels a connection to you."

A patient? "I'm an Emergency Department doc over at University Hospital. I wish I could save every patient, but I can't." He stuck his hands in the pockets of his cut-off sweatpants.

She leaned a slim hip against the counter. "Does the name Wade Montgomery ring a bell?" Her golden-eyed gaze bore into his, questioning him.

He swallowed hard, picturing the strong boy's limp body on his operating table. Hunter had tried the paddles, tried everything he'd ever learned as the young football player's life leaked away, the result of an undiagnosed heart condition. Nothing had worked. He'd pronounced the boy dead merely an hour after he'd been unloaded from the ambulance.

"Yeah." His voice came out a croak. "I remember him." His eyes stung with unshed tears, but he wouldn't cry. "He died the same night as my wife." Even after all this time, he still hated saying the word aloud. *Died.* So permanent. Something that happened in his hospital, not to the people he loved. Grief didn't go away in two years. It lessened, but it sure as hell didn't go away.

Hunter glanced to the spot where this ghost stood. "I'm so sorry." He could have added more. Could have explained how the nurses practically had to rip him away when their last-ditch efforts hadn't worked. He had wanted to keep trying even though everyone knew it was futile. Sure, he'd lost plenty of patients over the years. But losing kids was the hardest.

Veronica tilted her head at the invisible-to-him ghost and nodded. "He says he doesn't blame you." Her face softened. "I'm sorry about your wife."

"Thanks." He appreciated the sentiment, but his mind whirled with the other information she'd imparted. "Wade isn't dangerous...yet. What does that mean?" Hunter took a deep breath. This woman brought hope to this ridiculous situation. But what did she mean by "yet"?

For so long, catching the hushed tones and awkward looks from nurses when he walked by, he'd worried he was crazy. He'd also feared he could lose his medical license because others would think him crazy for believing he was being haunted. How could he be a good doctor when he lived in constant fear the ghost might interfere while treating a patient? Unplugging equipment, making pens float behind a patient's head, or tossing papers on the floor? Now, he might have finally found the one person who could help him.

Veronica glanced at the spot where the ghost stood, and shook her pink-tipped pointer finger at him as if telling him to behave. "Let me start at the beginning. I'm actually a photographer by profession. One who's able to talk to ghosts...." She broke eye contact as if she didn't want to continue, but lifted her chin and gazed at him. "Able to talk to ghosts and, if I hold something that belongs to them, feel things from living people who are in distress."

"You've had this gift your entire life?"

"Gift?" She crossed her arms. "No. I've been cursed with this ever since I almost drowned ten years ago."

Drowning? This was one badass woman. A survivor. His hope lifted. "Well, I'm feeling very lucky that we ran into you in the lobby earlier…." Something—his doctor sixth sense, maybe—made him glance down. Blood dripped off the side of her left foot where a four-inch piece of glass stuck out of her skin. "Shit. Sorry. I forgot about that damn broken vase." Out of habit, he'd stuck his feet into a pair of loafers when he'd awakened to the banging pots and pans.

She followed his glance and furrowed her brows. "I didn't even feel it."

Draping Veronica's arm around his shoulders, he supported her weight, grabbed a roll of paper towels from the counter, and led her around the sharp mess. Slowly, he lowered her to a wooden dining room chair and slid another seat out for himself. Positioning his knees in front of her, he pulled her flip-flop covered foot to his lap.

He focused on the clear piece of glass. "Might need a stitch or two. I'm going to prop it up and get my first-aid kit." Hunter shifted to the side, transferred her ankle onto the chair, and rose.

She leaned forward. Her curly hair swung to the sides of her face, curtaining her gorgeous features and golden eyes. "Oh for crying out loud. It's a piece of glass. I'll pull it out and put on a bandage."

"Listen, I'm a doctor. You should—"

She leaned forward, plucked out the piece of glass, and pressed a paper towel against her foot.

Hunter had opened his mouth to protest, but she was done before he could get a word out. "Let me at least get you antiseptic and a bandage."

"Thanks." She squinted at the spot in the kitchen where the ghost had stood earlier. "It's fine. Nothing to worry about." She glanced at Hunter. "Problem is…." She pressed her lips together and stared behind his head. "I'm not sure I can help you with this ghost."

"Let me get the first-aid kit, then we'll talk." He left the room. God, he finally had a chance to do something about this ghost and now Veronica looked like she wanted to leave. Was this danger she'd spoken of scaring her away?

This was his chance to finally move on, put this ghost behind him. For now, he'd concentrate on healing an injury. That was *his* expertise.

He returned to the room, where she sat with arms crossed. Taking a seat in front of her, he motioned for her to lift her foot to his lap.

She winced when he dabbed disinfectant on her cut, but only for a second. "Something is keeping him from crossing over. If you figure that out, you can help him move on."

With care, he leaned in closer to look at the cut. Not as bad as he'd first thought. Pulling a butterfly bandage from the kit, he said, "That doesn't sound dangerous."

Her foot stiffened in his hand and he glanced up. Her entire body had gone rigid.

"You said Wade's been haunting you for two years now?" she whispered.

"Yes." An anniversary he would never forget. The night Dianna died. He squeezed the cut together and adhered the bandage, keeping his hands on her skin. The only way to be sure she understood was to lay it all out, let her know what he stood to lose if this ghost stuck by him.

"I need your help. The only thing that keeps me sane since losing my wife is my work. And if I can't shake this ghost, I'm going to lose my license."

Her eyes widened, and with a quick check toward the kitchen, she leaned forward. Her secretive posture made him lean forward, too.

"If ghosts don't cross over in two years, sometimes they lose all sense of their time on earth as a human. The younger the ghost when he died, the faster it happens," she whispered.

Hunter frowned. "So we have two weeks to help him remember who he was? That's what will help him move on?" Crossing over? The other side? At this point, he'd believe anything if it got rid of the ghost.

"Not that simple." She glanced toward the kitchen again and kept her voice at a whisper. "If he doesn't cross over, there's a chance he could become darker...forget about his human years. Not every ghost who doesn't cross turns bad, but there's no predicting which ones it will happen to. Instead of throwing oranges, he could throw knives...or worse."

ॐ

Veronica wanted to run out Hunter's door and keep running, all the way down to her apartment where her own personal therapy—cooking—awaited. But it was too late to back out. Wade knew her. If he lost his sense of good, he'd know where to find her. She'd be as haunted as Hunter, but by a meaner ghost than this version of Wade.

Hunter stared with parted lips. "He'd try to kill me?"

"Maybe. Eventually." She'd never seen it, had only read about it when she'd researched ghosts that didn't cross over.

Like the still shots she took that made it into her coffee table photography books, another image burned in her skull. The baby...the kidnapped teenager...the missing mother. All people she hadn't been able to help. She'd held the pacifier and felt the baby's pain. Felt the cold steel walls of the dumpster and the scent of rotting trash around her. What if she couldn't help Wade cross over before he changed? She failed as a psychic, obviously, when she hadn't reached those victims in time. What if the same thing happened when she tried to help Wade? What if one of Hunter's patients died because Wade turned to the dark side?

Her fingers shook as her fears began to consume her. Hunter's strong, warm hand covered hers.

"I know it can't be easy to do what you do." His whisper was husky and warm.

Veronica had been on her own for a long time and didn't need anyone taking care of her. Especially not some hot guy who probably had twenty girls on speed-dial. A doctor. From experience, she knew what that meant. God complex. Like her rock-star father who believed relationships didn't need to be monogamous. Hunter, and all doctors, had to have confidence to do what they did. That very same confidence made them think rules were for others. The same way rock stars thought they could get away with anything.

She worked her hands free of his and leaned back, crossing her arms. "What do you mean you could lose your job?"

Wade moved out from behind the counter and studied Hunter as if waiting for the answer, too.

Hunter dragged a hand through his dark hair. Late afternoon

sunlight drizzled in through the windows, shadowing his face and his piercing blue eyes. "I—I had a bit of a drug and alcohol problem after my wife died."

Wade snorted across the room, but of course she was the only one who heard him. To Hunter, she said, "Go on."

He heaved a sigh. "I'm on probation at work and basically, I will be for a long time. Maybe forever. I get to keep my job as long as I submit to drug testing."

Veronica shrugged. Not great that he'd hit the pills, but big deal...he and the hospital were handling it. "So what does a ghost have to do with that?"

He shook his head and leaned both hands on his knees. Large hands. Meticulous hands that knew what to do to cure people. Hands that likely knew ways to make a woman feel pleasure....

Damn. Concentrate!

"I've had some close calls." He glanced at a spot near the counter where Wade had stood earlier. Only now, Wade was pacing by the front door. But Hunter couldn't see him, could only guess where the ghost was.

"The cold spots...the worry that a ghost is going to do something to startle me while I'm operating...well, I'm afraid it will break my concentration. And the worry keeps me up at night. As much as the kid's pacing and pranks."

"What else am I supposed to do? Ghosts don't sleep." Wade stood upright, frowning. "I tried to visit my mom at first, but that was too sad. I thought about trailing my old friends around, too, but I forgot where to find them. And I felt some sort of connection to Doc Hunter. Like I *had* to stay near him for some reason."

"Okay, let me hear the doc's side of things," Veronica said. Hunter narrowed his eyes, confusion written on his face. "Wade doesn't know what to do at night because ghosts don't sleep."

Hunter threw his hands up, stood, and paced the dining room rug. "Hey, I would've turned on the TV for him or something. If only I'd known."

Veronica got a good, long look at his back muscles as he turned to pace toward the bedroom area, and at his pecs as he whirled to pace back toward her. Strong, sinewy muscles and a patch of dark hair that formed a V and trailed into his shorts. He worked out. Maybe she should start using the gym on the first floor more. Maybe she'd run into him....

No. Bad enough she felt compelled to help him with this ghost. Her lousy track record with this sort of guy would be her reminder. No hot guys with God complexes. It always ended badly.

"I'm happy to pay you for your time. Just help me get rid...help this ghost move on or whatever it is he needs to do." Hunter sat in the chair again and propped her heels on his lap.

Using a good amount of willpower, she resisted the urge to yank her feet away. The move was too intimate. His skin was too hot. Pulling away again would show him he was affecting her, right? She wouldn't give him the satisfaction.

"Please?" He tilted his head and grinned, a sideways smile that revealed a dimple. *Oh shit. Not a dimple.* Hard to resist a man with a dimple. *Oh yeah?* Well, she'd stand firm against this one. Problem was, his problem was now her problem. And they had thirteen days to figure it out. Together.

Shifting in her chair to break the spell he had on her, she said, "I don't need your money. I have a job. I told you, I don't make my living as a psychic-medium." The police had offered her money, too. A stipend, they'd called it. But she couldn't accept money for failing to find a victim alive. "And my apartment is a perk of the job. I'm the photo editor of Maryland Fishing Magazine." Yeah, she'd gotten lucky. A wealthy local businessman who had no family. Fishing—and his fishing magazine—were his passion and he'd fallen in love with her photography. And he happened to have a vacant downtown apartment. Overpaid for the job? Yes. Complaining? No.

"If you don't need money, what do you need? Box seats at the Lyric? A press pass for the Orioles bench? I have contacts...I could hook you up." He massaged her uninjured foot and she wanted to moan in pleasure. She needed food. And a long, long nap. The stirrings that radiated from her toes through her body told her she needed something else, though.

"I don't need anything from you." Especially not those skillful hands on her body.

"I save lives." He glanced toward the counter where Wade had stood earlier. "Well, most of the time." Letting go of her foot, he leaned back. "My job is all I have."

She sighed. If she helped him figure out how to get Wade to cross over, they'd both be free. "Thirteen days is all we have. I'll help you. If he doesn't cross over by then, we're in trouble."

A smile split his face and he shot out of his chair and stood beside her. His warm lips pressed against hers as he clasped both her hands. Instead of pulling away, she leaned into the kiss.

Common sense returned. With a quick twist of her body, she slid out of the chair and bolted toward the door.

Chapter Three

The image of Veronica's startled face interrupted Hunter's thoughts whenever he had a spare minute or two in the ED. Her golden eyes had opened wide and her lips—those luscious, ripe lips he'd helped himself to in a moment of relief and excitement—had opened and closed wordlessly.

The first woman he'd kissed since Dianna's death. The first one he'd wanted to kiss in almost two years. Had he betrayed his deceased wife? Guilt poked at his gut and he pushed it away. After all this time he was entitled to move on, wasn't he?

Veronica had practically pushed him over in her dash for the door. At least he'd had the sense to get her phone number before she left.

What the hell had he been thinking?

He hadn't. That was the problem. Everything culminated at once: learning the identity of the spirit, the dangerous apparition Wade could become, and a possible way to get rid of his ghostly companion once and for all. Not to mention the fact that a casually sexy woman—the type who didn't know she was beautiful, which made her even more so—had made him lose his freaking mind for an instant.

His lips curved into a smile and he wondered when he could make a mistake like that again.

Hunter pushed the curtain to one of the ED cubicles aside. Tearing a prescription off his pad, he handed it to the teenaged girl's mother.

"No more trampolines for a while."

"Oh, heck no," the forty-something woman said with a sideways glance at her daughter. "My husband's taking it apart right now."

The hairs on Hunter's arm and back of neck stood. Behind the mother and daughter, a plug for the IV pump that wasn't in use unplugged itself. No, not by itself. *Wade.* An invisible force twirled the cord and its plug like a lasso.

The woman frowned. "Dr. Anderson? Are you okay?"

The plug landed soundlessly on the floor. Thank God the machine hadn't been in use. "Fine. Busy, that's all. Have a nice day." He whirled and pulled the curtain aside, almost plowing into a nurse outside the room. "Who's our next visitor?"

"Room three. Dr. Rochester said he'll take over after that."

One of the whisperers, as he called them. Nurses who stopped talking when he neared. Not paranoia. Staff who gossiped about the way he jumped at shadows and the deep depression he fell into after his wife's death. They were waiting for him to slip. How much more could he hide from everyone? How many times could he keep from reacting when Wade played his pranks? And how the hell much more dangerous would things get if Wade didn't cross over before the two-year anniversary of his death?

The nurse raised her brow at him. "You okay? You look kind of pale."

"I'm fine, thanks. Another long day. Who do we have in room three?" He wiped the back of his hand across his suddenly sweating forehead.

She tapped the clipboard with her pen. "You've got a frequent flyer. Back pain."

Frequent flyer was their name for people who habitually used or abused the ED...treated it like a physician's office. Often, they didn't have a medical expert they trusted, sometimes they didn't have transportation, or once in a while, they just wanted attention for a minor ailment. They always ended up on the bottom of the triage list, meaning a wait of two to three hours before they saw a doctor. Worse yet, they clogged the ED system and often enough, were only looking for drugs.

"Got it, thanks." Hunter headed for room three, flipping through the chart.

He hesitated outside, waiting for the cold or the goose bumps.

Nothing.

Maybe Wade was done for the day. Maybe today was the day they'd figure out how to help the ghost cross over and Hunter would never have to worry about looking crazy at work again. His mind shifted to Veronica, his one hope with this situation. No woman in the past two years had triggered that soul-deep longing in him. The need to see her again burned like a hot coal, overpowering the pangs of guilt about betraying Dianna.

His shift was almost over. He yanked out his phone and texted Veronica. She needed to be updated on Wade's latest prank. Now, for his chance to get to know this woman better as she helped him move on with his life.

଼ଷ

Veronica scooped the chopped tomatoes into the food processor, plopped the lid on top, and pressed the button. The loud whir took over the kitchen and drowned out her thoughts as much as the scent of fresh parsley.

She'd chopped her way through at least two pounds of tomatoes, a few onions, peppers, and cucumbers. Even needed another trip to the store for avocados, all in an effort to keep herself from thinking about Hunter's brazen move.

Was it her imagination, or did her lips still tingle? Maybe she should have told him she couldn't help him. The fact he'd kissed her was proof he was the type who took what he wanted, right? Maybe she should put more garlic in the gazpacho to keep him at a distance when they met in an hour.

She ladled the fragrant soup into a bowl, carried it to her small kitchen table and savored each bite of the spicy treat. Hunter. A good-looking guy. Just like the good-looking surgeon who had claimed to love her and when she let her guard down and allowed herself care about him, she found out about the other women he was seeing. Or the one before him who didn't admit until three months into their relationship that he was also dating two other women.

She wiped her hands on a dishtowel and glanced around the clean kitchen. Maybe she should put on some makeup.

No. No signals that she could be interested in Hunter. She wouldn't change out of her old T-shirt and faded jean shorts, either. Her job was to help Wade move on, to figure out his life, and then Hunter would just be a guy she'd wave to as she passed him in the lobby. She'd help him keep his medical license. After all, the world needed doctors. And she sure as hell didn't need anyone haunting her. For her sake and Hunter's sake, Wade had to move on.

After the kiss yesterday, the thought of being alone with Hunter in his apartment made her gut squeeze. It wasn't like they could meet in public, though. Not if she was going to be the middleman between Hunter and Wade. They couldn't exactly sit in a restaurant, at a table for three, while she chatted with an empty chair. And her apartment was off-limits to ghosts. She had to have one place where she was free of them.

That left Hunter's. The room where they'd been when he'd pressed those hot lips against hers, throwing her insides into a raging storm where lust roared and common sense battled to maintain control.

With a sigh, she shoved a notepad, some pens, and her laptop into her knapsack, shrugged the pack on her shoulder, and walked out her door. Wade leaned against the faded hallway wallpaper, a shy look on his face. He stepped forward, brows raised and questioning.

"That doctor tried to save your life. You haven't been very nice to him," she said.

"I know."

"You should leave him alone. Especially at work."

He shrugged. "I'll try."

She nodded her chin toward the end of the hall. "We're riding up to Doc Hunter's apartment together, then?" She could've interviewed Wade by herself, but Hunter wanted to be part of the questioning, and having his help would probably yield a better outcome anyway, so she hadn't objected.

A smile cracked Wade's face as he fell in line beside her. She'd had enough exercise today, so they rode to the eighth floor in silence and when the doors opened, Wade stood to the side to let her out first. Manners. If they could figure out how to get him to cross over, this would be a positive experience. She'd finally use these stupid abilities for something good. No nightmares after this one. Just a feeling of accomplishment. She rapped on Hunter's door.

He appeared, looking better than any man should after a twelve-hour shift. No bags under his blue eyes. No slumped shoulders. In his creased khaki shorts and stretched-across-broad-shoulders collared black shirt, he looked ready to play a game of golf. Or go on a date.

Her heart sank. Maybe he did have a date after their meeting tonight. Some gorgeous woman, likely. Maybe a nurse from the hospital. Or another doctor.

"Hey, thanks again for coming. I realized our meeting coincided with dinner time, so I picked up crab cakes from Phillips Seafood on the way home. Hope that's okay." He moved to the side so she could enter, and the scent of something spicy drifted toward her nose. She'd just eaten. Still, her stomach rumbled. If there was one thing she couldn't resist, it was a Baltimore crab cake.

Evening sun filtered through his windows that overlooked the Inner Harbor. All they needed was a set of candles on the table and a little romantic music, and this would be the perfect setting for a date.

Wade moved beside her. *Oh yeah...all that and to rid ourselves of a ghost.*

"Can you tell him I'm sorry?" Wade's voice was gravelly, but strong.

Veronica moved behind one of the mahogany chairs in the dining room-slash-living room combination area. "Can we bring another seat for Wade? He wants me to tell you he's sorry." There. At least it wouldn't seem like a date. Not with three of them.

"That's great, Wade. I appreciate it. Sure, let me grab one." Hunter pulled a green-and-white striped upholstered chair from the living room.

"Iced tea? Soda?" he asked, transferring two Styrofoam containers to the small table. "Sorry. I don't keep anything harder around." He glanced at the upholstered cushion where Wade's bulky body sat.

"Alcohol and I don't get along."

"Iced tea is great." She slid her knapsack to the floor and took a seat.

Hunter brought two glasses of tea and sat across from her, opening his Styrofoam box and grabbing a fork. He frowned, looked at her untouched container. "Should I get us real plates? I'm used to eating out of—"

She had to laugh at the devastated look on his face. He really was on edge, afraid of doing something wrong. Is this what it was like for him at the hospital? Always worrying someone was going to take something he did or said the wrong way and he'd get fired?

"Loosen up." Veronica cracked open the box and the savory scent of Maryland blue crab and steaming French fries curled toward her nose. "We're here to work. No need to go to any trouble." Hungry or not, she plucked out a fry, and took a bite. "I eat out of carry-out containers all the time."

He smiled and grabbed one of his fries, shaking it at her. "Good to know I can be myself." He stuffed it in his mouth.

This was getting too friendly. She wiped her fingers on a napkin, and bent to pull out a spiral notebook with a pen shoved into the curled wire. She faced Wade, who sat erect with his hands on his massive football-pants-covered thighs and flipped the spiral open. "Okay, full name is Wade Montgomery. Do you know where you lived? Your parents' names? We can find out a lot about you online, or in the doc's records, but I'm curious...how much of your time on earth do you remember?"

"I played football for South High School." Wade frowned and his shoulders slumped forward. "I used to know more about myself, but I-I, well, I forget a lot now."

Veronica nodded. "It happens. The longer you're here, the less you're tied to your old world. I want to find out what's keeping you from crossing over." She faced Hunter and repeated Wade's answer since he couldn't hear Wade speak.

The skin between Hunter's dark brows creased and he nodded at the chair where Wade sat.

"It'll be easy to find your parents. Why don't we start with what you can remember?" She gave into the temptation of the delicious-smelling crab cake and forked a bite, taking the creamy, savory mixture into her mouth and letting the textures and taste dance on her tongue.

Hunter took a bite of his crab cake, all the while watching her hand on the pad of paper. He pushed his chair back. "Duh. Why didn't I think to plug Wade's name into a search engine?" He tugged a laptop off the kitchen counter, plunked it on the table next to his dinner.

"I remember the football practice. I'd just sacked the quarterback to end the offensive possession. It was practice, but the coach had just told me I was going to be a starter that year. I was pumped up." Wade's eyes got a faraway look. Maybe this was a moment he'd rerun over and over again since he'd died, in some kind of effort to make sense of it all.

Quietly, she repeated what he said so Hunter would follow the conversation. Hunter took his fingers off the keyboard and stared at the chair that, to him, was empty. But he had to feel Wade's presence, and maybe he even felt the emotion and tension of the moment, too.

"Good, Wade. You're doing great. What next?" Veronica kept her voice low, unobtrusive.

"Time for the special teams players and the punter to take the field. I was running off the field, but then...everything blurred." He glanced at Veronica, his eyes questioning. She sat still with lips pressed together. This wasn't a time to interrupt him or update Hunter on what was being said. Wade needed this memory to come out as clearly as he could if they were going to help him.

"It had only rained a little bit, but all of a sudden, it was like I was running in deep mud. Every step was so hard. My chest hurt. Like a fire burning from the inside out. I clutched at it, and my feet stopped working. My knees gave out." Tears shimmered in his eyes.

Veronica reached out to put a hand on his shaking one.

He stood and started pacing the area behind the chair. "Time did something weird. I was lying on the field, with my team around me. Then I was watching myself...standing next to my body. Suddenly, I was in an operating room. Lights. Doctors and nurses." He turned to face Hunter. "This doctor."

Veronica repeated what Wade told her. Hunter's eyes grew wide.

"Do you remember the doctors and nurses while you were on the table, or were you off the operating table then?" Veronica asked.

Wade frowned and concentrated for a moment. "Next to it. Doc Hunter was shouting, sweating...moving around fast."

Veronica glanced at Hunter. He'd been working hard to save Wade's life, but Wade was already dead.

"I tried to talk to them. I screamed at the top of my lungs. Nobody would listen." Tears streamed down Wade's cocoa-colored cheeks and he fisted his hands at his sides. "A long beep. Doc Hunter wouldn't stop working on me. The others—dressed in their blue or green gowns and hats, hiding behind matching masks—backed away from the table. They just watched him. Didn't even try." Tears dripped on his uniform shirt and he fought to catch his ghostly breath. "He pronounced me dead and I got cold. So cold."

"A minute later, a nurse hurried in and told Doc Hunter his wife had been in an accident." Wade stared at the mauve carpeting. He crossed his arms on his chest as if chilled. As if coming out of a trance, he folded into the chair, elbows on the table, and his head in his palms.

Veronica blinked and quickly summarized the story for Hunter.

"I had to follow protocol." Hunter's eyes shimmered. "I had to pronounce him dead, but my hands wouldn't stop trying to bring him back."

Shit. She knew what that felt like. Knew that feeling of helplessness. When you could only do so much, and then you had to walk away, knowing your best wasn't good enough.

Chapter Four

*H*unter's heart beat triple-time at the memory of the night his wife had died, but damned if he'd let anyone in his apartment know it. He'd head to the gym later and pound a punching bag for a few hours. The emotions of that night still stung like a knife to the chest. He'd lost his wife...the happiest part of his life. With eight siblings, he was used to being around people. Coming home to an empty house after his wife died had felt so lonely. So different.

At least now he knew the ghost's identity. Being able to communicate with him through Veronica was a gift. Maybe together they really could figure this out. He'd wanted to save Wade so badly. Every patient was important, but young people...well, they had so much more living to do.

In spite of his heavy heart, he smiled when he glanced at the redheaded beauty across from him. Her diamond stud sparkled in the light and she focused those unusual golden eyes to the chair next to her where Wade sat, but Hunter couldn't see what she saw. She kept her voice low and friendly.

"Wade, Hunter had to follow hospital procedure. There was nothing else he could do." She reached to the table as if covering the boy's hands with hers. "You've never talked to anyone else in this world?" she asked quietly.

Hunter straightened, suddenly very interested in the answer. What would that be like? Roaming around for years unheard? "I've heard some grunts...some garbled sounds from him."

Veronica raised her brows and shifted her gaze to Hunter and back to the empty chair. "I'm sorry you went through all that, Wade."

Poor kid. His life had been taken way too early, and then he'd been living in silence.

Veronica sat back in her chair and perched her bare feet, toe tips painted bright pink, in front of her, hugging her knees to her chest. So casual and at home. So damn sexy. Hunter shook the thought away. *Inappropriate.*

"Okay if we move on to some more questions?" she asked.

Wade must have agreed because she smiled and tilted her head at the chair. At least the guy was calm enough to sit still and stop throwing things now. Hunter relaxed his shoulders for what felt like the first time in years.

"Okay, here's the deal. Spirits are supposed to move on. Once they do, they can come back to this world if they want. I call them happy wanderers, but they have to cross over first. Often, the ghosts who don't cross over turn mean. You've tried to move on—you know, our trip to the vortex in the hallway—but couldn't." She narrowed those golden eyes at the empty chair as if trying to figure something out. Her expression drew Hunter in, made him want to move closer to her because there was such honesty, such compassion there.

"Which means," she continued, "you're not a happy wanderer. You're either stuck here because something you believe is keeping you here, or something you don't even know about is tethering you to this world. We have to figure out what it is."

She glanced at Hunter and he almost jumped. *Busted.* He'd been studying her lips, admiring the smooth curve of her collar bone. Even in a simple T-shirt and shorts, she exuded beauty and confidence. One taste of her lips was never going to be enough. But maybe it had to be. This wasn't the type of woman who trusted easily. He'd already lost one woman he'd given his heart to. He had to avoid the grief of losing someone again.

With a small frown at Hunter, she turned her attention back to Wade. "Is there something you're afraid of on the other side? Once I helped a prostitute move into the light. She'd been afraid to go...afraid that she'd be punished on the other side." Sliding her feet back to the carpeted floor, she leaned forward toward Wade. "Is there something you did while you were alive that you think you'll be punished for? Because it's not like that, Wade. There's forgiveness in the next world. More than this world, even."

She raised her brows and glanced at Hunter. "Sorry. I keep forgetting you can't hear him. He says his mother made him go to church, study hard, and play sports. He didn't have time to do too many things other than that."

Hunter smiled, remembering Wade's mom. He'd met her before heading into surgery. She'd been devastated. In shock. And she'd been surrounded by a horde of supportive friends and family. Wade had been a good kid. She'd sent Hunter a thank you note a few weeks later. Thanked him for working so hard on her son. People didn't usually do that. Too wrapped up in their own grief to think of anyone else but themselves and their immediate family. Come to think of it...it might have been the only time someone had ever thanked him after a family member died. Sure, he got lots of handshakes and thanks after helping to save a life, but losing a patient...that was different.

Veronica faced Wade again. "Unfinished business? Something that didn't get done while you were alive? I know you don't remember a lot from your life, but think hard. Sometimes, the reason a spirit can't cross over is because they think they can't leave before they take care of something."

She glanced at Hunter. "He says he can't think of anything." Veronica let out a long breath and closed her eyes for a few seconds before opening them again and facing Wade. "You must have a job to do here in this world before you can move on."

Relief flooded Hunter's veins. Veronica ignited a flicker of hope inside him that maybe...just maybe...things could return to normal.

Problem was, being so close to her ignited something else entirely. And knowing they'd be spending a lot of time together did crazy things to his insides.

ೞ

Veronica couldn't hold back a smile. Wade's youthful eyes lit with hope. Hunter leaned closer, enthralled with a conversation he could only hear half of.

"What sort of job?" Wade's voice was growing stronger the more he used it.

She reached out and covered his big hand with hers on the table. "I don't know what it is you have to do. Since you don't remember much of anything from your life, we'll have to find out everything we can about you. See if we can figure it out from there."

She glanced at Hunter. His expression didn't give away much. Did he believe her? Was his slightly raised brow a sign that he thought this was all some sort of game? Sighing, she turned back to Wade. "You need to stay away from Doc Hunter's work."

Wade narrowed his eyes and shoved back from the table, pulling his hand from hers in the process and squaring his shoulders. Six feet six inches of ghostly muscle and an attitude to match. This kid went from docile to angry in a heartbeat.

"Go ahead. Figure it all out. I heard what you said what might happen to me in thirteen days. Maybe this is all a way to get rid of me. Maybe you're like sending me to hell or something." His gaze darted around the room as if looking for an escape.

Veronica stood and faced him, a full foot shorter. "We're trying to help you."

Hunter stood and pushed between them as if protecting her and sensing that Wade had grown angry. "This is between you and me, bud. If you're going to haunt me, go ahead. Leave this lady out of it. But let me tell you this: I do my damndest every day to save lives, make people healthier, make their quality of life better. Being a doctor is all I've ever wanted to be. Your presence rattles me and puts people's lives at risk."

Hunter couldn't have known it, but his expression mirrored Wade's. Narrowed eyes, frown, and chin thrust forward.

"Is that what you wanted to hear? Fine. You get to me, dude. And you're going to make me lose my job. That means the world will be out one doctor who cares." He threw his hands up in the air and then grasped Veronica's elbow lightly, shifted to the side. She wanted to tell him she could take care of herself, especially when it came to handling ghosts, but suddenly her mouth was dry. She could count on two fingers the number of people who had ever come to her defense like that: her best friend and her nanny.

Wade tilted his head and studied Hunter.

"What's he saying? Is he going to throw something at me?" Hunter kept his eyes on the area in front of him.

Wade relaxed his stance and rolled his eyes.

"No. He looks calm." She hoped it was true.

"I'm out of here," Wade said. "The family in apartment 612 gets all the good cable channels, and their kid likes the same programs I do."

Not an apology or an agreement, but heck, the kid was a teenager. What did she expect? She laid a hand on top of Hunter's hand on her elbow. "He wants some alone time." Nodding her head to the left, she indicated they should move. Not that Wade couldn't walk right through them, but they could at least pretend they were being supportive.

In a flash, Wade moved past them and through the closed door. The air grew suddenly warmer and Veronica slipped out of Hunter's grasp, suddenly feeling too close to him. "Freedom from your ghost. For now."

"Thank you." He clasped his hands as if not sure what to do with them. Hands that saved lives. Hands that would probably make a woman feel very cherished. She cleared her throat to chase away the thought. Wade wasn't the only one who needed some time alone.

"Yeah, sure." This was going to be one heck of a long week if her mind kept jumping where it shouldn't go. *Focus. Ghosts. Crossing over. That's it.*

"What's the plan? I have no idea what helping a ghost cross over entails, but investigating his life...that's something I can help with." His blue eyes caught the sunlight that cast through the window. Mesmerizing eyes. She could so easily get caught in that trap. But only average guys for her. Average guys with good hearts.

"I think I can probably handle most of this myself," Veronica said. Hunter wanted to be part of the interview with Wade, but now that they'd finished that part of the evening, it was time to leave. "Probably a computer search first. See what we can find out about his time on earth. And we'll go from there. Maybe check out his school, talk to people who knew him." She had a computer. She could easily do it on her own. She *should* do this by herself. She'd just wanted to interview the kid first, so she wouldn't make pre-judgments.

"Hey, I'll bet the football team at his high school practices even through summer. We could go to a practice, chat with a few of his friends, or a coach." His eyes widened. "I'm supposed to have two days off before I'm back in the ED."

Hunter was being appreciative, that was all. She was helping rid him of a ghost that got in the way of his career and he was being thankful. Why not accept his help? For the kid, right? He deserved the chance to move on. The sooner the better.

"Let's go to my apartment. If he changes his mind about leaving us alone, he can't get in there. I've done things to keep ghosts out of there." She grabbed her bag and hiked it up her shoulder. She *could* protect Hunter's apartment from ghosts, too. But for now, they'd work on helping Wade cross over.

"Your apartment is a ghost-free zone?" He grinned. "Can I move in?"

Chapter Five

*G*reat. *Real smooth*. Hunter had finally gotten this beautiful woman to help him and then he'd invited himself to live with her. *Way to scare a chick away*.

At least he got to admire her long legs and shapely ass as he followed her down the hall to her apartment. Her good looks took over his brain, but knowing his ghost might finally be gone made him almost heady with endorphins. Or maybe it was her.

She keyed her apartment open and walked in, moving to the side so he could enter.

Inside, he viewed the same basic setup as his apartment, but she'd certainly put her touch on things. Beginning with the smell. Most ladies he knew burned candles, or used air fresheners. Veronica's apartment smelled of food. Good food. Like a good restaurant or a farmers' market. That was the scent. Did that come in a candle? Not likely.

Like his, her apartment had wall-to-wall carpeting, but she'd added throw rugs. Browns, greens, and a few muted reds. And the red couch looked comfortable enough for a long nap. With her.

He cleared his throat and focused on a nearby tabletop with photos. "Nice place. You're good with colors."

"I should be." She closed the door and crossed the room to a desk where she unloaded her laptop from her knapsack, and plopped on the sofa. "Photographers are trained in the subtleties of color."

He nodded and focused on her as she set the computer on the coffee table and concentrated on typing. What the hell was her story? Investigating the ghost was one thing. Investigating her would be...interesting. With powers like hers, she should open a psychic shop. Forecast the weather. Something like that. But she wanted to ignore the fact that she had this talent? Why?

"Come on." She patted the spot beside her on the sofa. "I don't bite." She grinned and tilted her head. "Not today, anyway."

An image of her teeth biting her lip as he ran a hand up her slender waist and inside her shirt had his pants growing tighter. He lifted a framed photo to direct the blood flow elsewhere. "Who's this? Sister?" A close-up of a dark-haired woman with a huge smile and her head close to Veronica's beamed from a frame.

Veronica glanced up and smiled. "Jeanne. My best friend. More like a sister. We were at the park that day. So much fun." Her face lit up when she talked about her friend. Like she finally let her guard down. Aha. So that was the secret to breaking through her exterior.

"Cute." *Cute? Really?* What happened to his vocabulary around this woman? He was a doctor, for crying out loud. Messy handwriting, big words, a few even in Latin...the whole nine yards. Yet cute fit her. He covered a laugh with a cough when he thought how the serious set of her mouth indicated she'd probably hate being called cute.

"You okay? Want some water or something?" She leaned back and stretched her arms over her head, pulling her thin T-shirt up her flat stomach. Revealing a pierced belly button. A little silver speck of jewelry that pulled his gaze to places his gaze should not go.

"You know," he said, crossing the distance between them and sitting next to her, still staring at her midriff. "Those piercings are dangerous. Do you know how many of them get infected? I have to surgically remove at least one every...."

She yanked her shirt over her belly and laid a palm over her shirt, as if protecting her body. The color of her golden eyes darkened at least two shades. Angry eyes.

"Sorry." He smacked a palm to his head. "Doctor instinct. Lectures.

Healthy living. I'm sorry. Really. I'm running on just a few hours sleep combined with the high of finally almost being rid of this ghost." Even though he wanted to lay a hand on her upper thigh, he knew it would piss her off even more, be too intimate. He folded his hands between his bent knees and stared at them. "Stupid of me. I sound like your father, not your friend."

"Seriously?" She snapped the laptop shut and lifted her chin. "My father is an asshole and I'll pierce any part of my body I feel like piercing." Instead of bolting away like he thought she might, she leaned closer, almost nose to nose with him. "My father is Kyle Jansen."

She smelled like fresh apples and he wanted to pull her closer, but the anger in her gaze kept him perfectly still. He blinked. "*The* Kyle Jansen?"

"Yep. Has-been rock star who still cheats on my mom with her full knowledge with every bimbo he can." She sank into the couch with arms crossed on her chest and stared at him as if waiting for him to be star-struck.

She hated her dad, huh? Well, he'd never been a Kyle Jansen fan. "His music sucks."

Her eyes widened and her lips quivered with the beginnings of a smile, but she pressed them together and hid the move as soon as it lingered.

"In fact he sucks so bad, I used to throw darts at his poster. His music is so awful that I throw up when it comes on the radio. His—"

She swatted him on his shoulder and a smile split her face. "Stop it. I know what you're doing and it won't work. You're an idiot."

He nodded. Relief passed through him, even greater than it had when Wade left. How was it possible he cared about what this woman thought of him more than he cared about being haunted by the crazy, angry ghost who'd been haunting him for years?

"I am an idiot. The biggest idiot ever. If you want me to pierce something for you, to prove I'm an idiot, I have some sterilized instruments upstairs in my apartment." Her tongue poked against her cheek, signaling a laugh that wanted to erupt. Suddenly, he really wanted to be the one who could make her laugh. "Maybe I could do your lower lip?"

Her short laugh erupted. A sweet, melodic sound that filled the small apartment.

His gaze stayed on that full mouth and he lifted his fingers closer, compelled to touch her. She stared at him with wide eyes as he traced the corner of her mouth lightly with his finger. "I'm a liar. I could never tarnish something as beautiful as this."

Christ. What a line. Where had those words come from? But he meant it.

Her breath was hot against his finger as he traced the line of her lower lip. Her gaze held his. His stomach growled again, breaking the spell, and she blinked and leaned against the sofa.

"You know what? We never had dessert," she said.

He had room for dessert. *But not the food kind.* He swallowed to quell his appetite for her. "Uh...how about I make an ice cream run? Then we'll get to work." Enough of this temptation. He needed to get away from her, from this pull she had on his body and emotions.

She slapped her palms on her bare thighs—thighs he'd been tempted to place a hand on only seconds earlier—and stood.

"Who needs carry out when I've got the ingredients for chocolate mousse and can have it ready in twenty minutes with your help?" Without a backward glance, she strode to the kitchen—toward safer territory—and opened a cupboard.

Still reeling from her closeness, Hunter stood slowly. Could he trust himself near her?

She glanced over her shoulder. "You know how to grate chocolate?"

A beautiful woman who could talk to ghosts and cooked. Was there anything this woman couldn't do?

○

Veronica carried her bowl to the round antique table covered with a bright, cherry-motif tablecloth, and sat. A working dessert. Nothing romantic about that.

Then why the hell does this feel like a date? A good one, at that. Hunter was too comfortable to be around. They'd chopped, grated, and laughed their way through the mousse preparation. After years of being haunted by a ghost, he probably felt giddy with relief at the thought of finally being rid of it.

Not romance. Not even friendship. Gratitude.

Hunter lowered his bowl to the table and sat in the ladder-back chair across from her. He glanced around the room and moved the napkin to his lap. "I had an interior decorator fix up my apartment, but yours looks much better than mine."

She shrugged and spooned a bite of the indulgent chocolate dessert. "I had fun doing it."

He took a huge scoop of his mousse, leaving some on the outside of his lip. On purpose? Some sort of weird trick he used on dates to draw attention to his kissable mouth?

Wouldn't work on her. She ignored his damn sloppy eating, took a bite of her chocolate, and pulled the pad of paper and pen she'd set there earlier closer. "So, let's make a list."

He wiped his mouth, finally removing the mousse. Only now that she stared at his mouth again, she noticed a very sexy shadow of dark hair on his upper lip. Apparently, he'd worked a long shift at the hospital and hadn't had time to shave.

"A list of what?"

Focusing on the pad of paper again, she clicked the pen. "Things a high-schooler might be involved in that we could find out more about."

Nodding, he took another bite, moaned, and closed his eyes. Maybe she should let him eat his dessert in peace. Nah. Too intimate to sit and eat. And stare at each other. While he made sounds similar to what he probably made in bed.

"We already said football." She scribbled on the pad.

After a drink of his water, he said, "Yeah, football. Church, school." He lifted a dark brow. "Do you think he was a Scout?"

Good idea. She made a note.

"Social networking," he said.

She glanced at him. "I don't network socially."

His chuckle created crinkles around the corners of his eyes. Felt pretty good to be the one to make him laugh like that because he was a handsome guy when serious. With a smile, he was almost deadly good-looking. But what the hell was so funny?

"You're not on Facebook? Twitter?"

She leaned back in her chair and shook her head. "You mean you are?" He didn't seem the type. Not the type to put all his information out there for the world to see, anyway.

"Under my first and middle name. Don't want my patients finding out about my caffeine addiction. They might fire me." He took another huge spoonful of the dessert. The memory of how his hands had skillfully moved the chocolate across the grater made her blink to erase it before strange fantasies of his hands on her could go any further. "I have seven brothers and sisters who live locally, twelve nephews and nieces, and a bunch of cousins in California. That's why I use social networking."

Made sense. She had a website for her photography, and her editor was pushing her to start blogging, but so far she'd been able to avoid any Internet relations with the public. Still, his idea made a lot of sense. Teens all had social sites these days.

"Good idea." She wrote the sites on the list and glanced up at him. "What's it like? Having a family like that?"

"A family like what?"

Maybe she should stop the conversation right now. No use baring her soul to him. But he made her comfortable, and she really wanted to know. Had always wanted to live in a nice, safe world like his. "A family that cares about each other." The words tumbled out softly, as if tired of being held inside.

His brows furrowed and he lowered his spoon to his plate and left it there. Pushing his mousse aside, he leaned forward on both elbows, his face crossing the imaginary center line dividing them on the table. "It's overwhelming at times." He kept his voice soft, kept his blue-eyed gaze on her. "Especially growing up. I was never alone, never had enough space."

Veronica pressed her lips together. They couldn't have been more opposite. She'd grown up feeling alone almost all the time and always had too much space. Veronica's parents made no effort to hide the fact that she had been an unwanted pregnancy. An intrusion in their rock-n-roll lives. But her best friend Jeanne was better than a sister. They'd

318

grown up together, and basically shared Jeanne's mother. Sure, Veronica had her own mother. Mindy. She'd never called her mom. The mother who couldn't leave her rock-star husband's side, not even when he toured for months at a time.

Many psychologist appointments later, Veronica appreciated that at least Mindy had cared enough to find a kick-ass caretaker for her daughter.

"But," he beamed and sat back, enabling Veronica to blow out the breath she hadn't realized she'd been holding. "I wouldn't have it any other way. Sheer chaos when we're together for Sunday dinners and holidays. It's the reason I really want my own family one day. My siblings are my best friends and safety net." A shadow crossed his face.

His family must have helped him deal with his wife's death and his subsequent battle with drugs and alcohol. Had he told any of them about being haunted by a ghost?

"Hey!" His face lit and he reached forward, invading her space again, and grabbing both her hands. "You have to come to Sunday dinner this weekend."

"Sure...uh...I'll have to check my work schedule...." She glanced at the pad of paper, wanting to change the subject, but glanced back up at him, suddenly needing to know the extent of how all of this affected him. "Does your family know about Wade? About being haunted?"

He shook his head and pulled his plate in front of him, suddenly very interested in his almost-empty bowl again. Nice to know he could play the avoidance game, too. With a mouth full of mousse, he couldn't answer. Good. More time for questions. She couldn't help it. She wanted to know more about him.

"Does anyone know, Hunter? Have you talked to anyone about having a ghost shadow?" Her insides swirled into a knot. She knew all about the way it felt to keep secrets. Very few people knew about her gift—local police, Jeanne, and Miss Valerie—and she liked to keep it that way.

He shook his head and scooped the last bit of dessert from his bowl. She pushed her dish toward him. Her appetite had fled, so he may as well enjoy it. Damn, this man could eat!

"I think I'm finally full, but thanks." He leaned back in his chair, arms crossed on his broad chest, and stared at her. "That was delicious." His biceps flexed, drawing her attention to his muscles.

She glanced back at his face. The power of silence.

He shifted in his chair, looked away for a few seconds, before meeting her gaze again. "No. My family doesn't believe in the supernatural. We're a family of professionals. Lawyers, doctors, scientists. They'd want proof and I don't have the energy to prove, or disprove, a ghost. I would have been fired for sure if I talked about being haunted by a ghost at the hospital."

"You need to talk to people about this sort of thing." She pushed out of her chair and walked to the counter, needing a glass of wine. "Want a glass?" She poured merlot into a glass.

"I don't drink, remember?"

"Oh, sorry." She stopped pouring, and pushed the glass to the side of the counter.

"That doesn't mean you can't." The corners of his mouth turned up in a small smile that made his eyes sparkle.

"Good." She grabbed the glass and plopped in her seat.

"So I need to talk about ghosts, huh?" He leaned forward again, making her glad there was a table between them. A physical barrier to prevent him from getting any closer, tempting her with those bedroom eyes, broad shoulders, and sexy mouth. "Okay, well, I'm talking to you. There." He raised his palms in the air to signal his completion of the task.

"Fine. Okay. You're cured. I'll sign off on your case. You happy? Let's get back to this list and get searching the Internet. We're wasting time here." She took a long sip of her wine.

"Not so fast...." His gaze pinned her. "What about you? Sounds like you don't have family you're close to. Do you have someone to share your secrets with?" The air between them practically sizzled with his question.

She waved him off. "Of course I do. My best friend knows. Heck, even the local police know about—" *Oh shit*. No, she didn't want to go *there*.

He frowned and the smile dropped from his face. His eyes widened. "You help the police, don't you?"

An image of the baby girl lying in the cold dumpster screamed into her mind. She emptied her wine glass in one swallow and slammed it to the table. "I don't want to talk about it. We have thirteen days to figure this out and the clock is ticking. Do you want to get rid of this ghost or not?"

ርጽ

Hunter peered at the laptop screen as Veronica typed. They'd moved from the dining room to the comfortable living room sofa, but the mood had turned from friendly to professional.

Fine. He'd let her have her way for now. That's all he needed anyway, wasn't it? Their relationship was professional.

"There you go." She slid the laptop toward him. "Type in your information and password. I won't look." She turned her head the opposite direction.

He chuckled. "I trust you." After a few clicks on the keyboard, his Facebook page appeared. "Okay, it's safe to look now, but don't judge me by my profile picture." A photo of him with his nephew at the Orioles game. Why on earth had he let his niece talk him into face paint that day?

Veronica leaned in and burst out laughing. Reward enough for orange and black paint. He'd have to thank his niece. Veronica's laughter filled the room with happiness. Her eyes crinkled almost shut, and she leaned back against the couch, relaxing.

"That's not what I expected. I had no idea you had a fun side."

"Hey! I think I'm insulted." Damn, this banter was too easy with her. She wanted to keep it professional, wanted to keep up the giant protective bubble around her, so he needed to let her. If there was one thing he'd learned from his rehab it was that you couldn't make someone else let you in. His family had tried, and failed. He hadn't succeeded until he was ready to climb out of the abyss himself, no matter how ready everyone else was for him to recover.

He leaned forward. Keeping it light might help. "I will now remove the insulting picture by typing Wade's name in the search bar."

She leaned forward, probably more interested in the results than keeping Hunter at a distance. The apple scent of her tickled his nose, making him want to hold the inhale, hold a part of her inside him. He exhaled, reluctantly letting her go.

"Hmmm, what's this?" He clicked on the photo of Wade Montgomery from Baltimore.

"Looks like a memorial site...some sort of tribute." She leaned closer. He'd waited years for this moment...years to find out about the ghost who haunted him. Yet he found himself staring at the redheaded woman next to him as she peered at the screen. What drove her? Who did she have to turn to? And why the hell did he care so much?

ભ

Veronica closed her apartment door after Hunter left and leaned against it. They had a folder of information about Wade now. Photos, friends' names, newspaper articles about his civic and athletic achievements. All good progress in the quest to help Wade cross over, and to get Hunter to stop pestering her.

Except, in the course of the last twenty-four hours, she'd somehow started to like his pestering.

She strolled into the kitchen, opened the dishwasher and donned a pair of pink latex gloves. Hunter had offered to help clean up, but they'd shared enough domestic responsibilities for one night. She'd chased him out and insisted on doing the work herself. Besides, after two hours on the Internet, he'd looked tired enough to fall on the floor and sleep.

She loaded two glasses into the washer, frowning as she wondered when the last time was she'd had a man in her apartment. Not so long ago, right? Before Malcolm—the cheating surgeon who'd prided himself on more affairs in a year than days. He didn't count. Men like Hunter were all about the one-night stand, all about fulfilling their own needs. All about themselves.

Veronica scrubbed the mousse pot with more vigor than it needed, putting her right bicep into the move. Besides, if she wanted to have sex with Hunter, she could do it once they solved this mystery and helped Wade cross over. Just one time together in the sack and that would be it. As long as they both knew the plan up front, he'd probably go for it. She hadn't met a guy yet who turned down the chance for easy sex and no strings.

Hunter would be no different. Sure, he talked the talk about family. Family meant a lot to him. She could never expect to know how to be part of one. Sure, Jeanne and Miss Val were like family in many ways, but not the kind of family Hunter had: a mom...dad...kids...sibling rivalry. Normal stuff. Stuff other people had, not her. She scrubbed harder, wondering if the steel pot bottom would be thinner when she was done with it.

A knock on the door stopped her fast, circular motions. Setting the pot on the drain board and blotting her gloved hands on a towel, she headed for the door. Who would be knocking at ten o'clock at night?

She peered through the peephole. Hunter grinned back at her, his face warped like a funhouse mirror reflection. She turned the locks and opened the door, not at all happy about her heart rate increasing at the sight of him.

"I'm sorry, I forgot something." He stepped inside.

She glanced toward the sofa, trying to spot something he'd left. "What did you—"

"This." He stepped closer and lowered his lips to hers in a soft touch that traveled from her mouth all the way to her core.

Chapter Six

*H*unter closed the passenger side door of his car after Wade crawled into the back seat while Veronica sat in the front. The sound echoed in the apartment garage. He'd taken a risk last night when he'd returned to Veronica's apartment to kiss her, but he'd had to do it. Desire drove him.

Earlier that day, when he'd phoned her, he'd tried to pass his impulsive kiss off as fatigue-driven lust.

Her reaction to his excuse? "You should get more sleep," she'd said.

But she kept her promise to go with him to investigate the details of Wade's life. They were heading to football practice at his high school and to visit with the boy's mom. Good thing Wade was with them, because it kept them from having a potentially very awkward conversation.

Hunter strode around the car and slid behind the wheel. Veronica's red hair was clipped up today, with a few loose tendrils hanging around her face, and she wore a brown scoop-neck T-shirt and beige shorts that showed off her long legs. Tennis shoes. Simple, yet still elegant somehow. She was pretty, that was it. What man wouldn't respond to that? *Normal. Perfectly normal.*

Leaning forward, he started the ignition. "I had the best sleep I've had in two years thanks to you."

"Oh?" She raised a brow.

"No weird noises. No cold masses of air." He risked a glance into the rear-view mirror, but of course he couldn't see Wade's reaction. He backed out of the spot and maneuvered through the garage.

"Glad to hear it." Veronica leaned forward and pushed the button for his radio. "Okay if I pick the station?" Fast, loud hard rock music filled the car.

"Sure," he hollered. At least he wouldn't have to worry about making conversation on the drive to the high school.

His heart and head pounded to the beat a few miles later as he pulled into the parking lot. "Want to sit and listen to the rest of this song?" he yelled. She'd stared out her window the entire time, tapping her tennis shoe to the fast beat.

With a smile, she leaned forward, turned off the music, and opened her door. She pulled her seat forward, apparently to let Wade out. The silence almost deafened him. Or maybe it was a delayed reaction to the loud-ass music.

Veronica stood in front of his car, her eyes shielded from the sun with her hand, and peered around the barren high school and surrounding grounds.

South High. The two-story brick building had to be at least fifty years old. Outer walls with green fiberglass panels and brick with smooth ceramic facing dated the building, making it look old and neglected. Rusted and caged air-conditioning units jutted out of windows, resembling sores.

"Looks like the football field is over there," Veronica said.

He locked the car and joined her. She smelled of peaches and was almost a full head shorter. But he would never underestimate this woman. Not with her attitude and determination.

The summer sun beat down as they followed a well-worn path dotted with trash and smashed beer cans behind the school. Sweat broke out on his brow, but Veronica looked cool and comfortable. A good-sized stadium, but not in the best shape. Even the scoreboard was the old-fashioned type where they had to climb a ladder to change the numbers.

The sound of a high-pitched whistle blowing in the distance

carried up the hill, and two groups of football players—one dressed in white and one in red—peppered the area between the goalposts.

"Wade!" Veronica shouted, her head whipping toward the grassy hill that led to the field.

"What is it?" Hunter asked.

Veronica pressed her hand against Hunter's hard chest. Even with his mind whirling with worry, her touch sent his body into overdrive.

She glanced at the hill again. "He's charging toward that field like he's determined to do something."

ɔ3

Veronica and Hunter hurried down the hill and toward the stands, chasing Wade. What if the football field or the players jogged a memory for Wade? A bad memory? What was he capable of doing? Veronica switched her attention to the dented and bent metal bleachers. Wade dashed around them, down the brown grass, and stopped at a chain-link fence near the track to stare at the football field. He rested his lower arms on the fence and glanced back at Veronica and Hunter, smiling.

Relief flooded through Veronica and she slowed and faced Hunter, shielding her eyes from the sun with her palm. "He stopped at the fence and he's smiling. Maybe this is one of his happiest memories."

"Or one of his last." Hunter's voice cracking on the last word.

"Let's check out this practice." He rested a hand on her lower back. A simple gesture. Downright chivalric. So why did shivers of pleasure shoot from her toes to her scalp at his touch? She just hadn't been with a man in a long time, so she was definitely over-reacting to being around a hot guy. *No big deal.*

At the edge of the stands, they paused. "I'm not sure if this even qualifies as a stadium," Hunter said.

Half the bleachers were missing and rusted stubs of poles remained. Wade still leaned forward with his beefy elbows resting on the railing behind the players' bench.

Hunter ushered Veronica in front of him, single file down the narrow aisle of bleachers toward Wade. Hunter's hand rested on her lower back again. *Damn, I wish he'd stop touching me.*

"I wonder if the boys or coaches ever mention him," Hunter said.

Gosh, she sure hoped so. He would know he was missed, he would know people cared. "We need to get this coach talking about Wade," she whispered over her shoulder to Hunter as she sidestepped two empty beer cans.

"We'll make sure of that."

He cared about this ghost. Maybe cared the same way she did. *Humph.* She had something in common with too-hot-to-handle doctor? Something to think about.

She plunked down next to Wade on the sagging aluminum bleacher.

The kid stared at the field, where two young men crashed into each other with a loud thud and groan. "I used to love football practice." Tears swam in the boy's eyes and his mouth curved into a smile.

"These guys friends of yours?" Hunter sat and leaned forward. Veronica forgot for a moment that he couldn't see Wade, because he was looking almost directly at him.

Wade nodded. "A few. I was a senior. These guys were mostly freshmen and sophomores."

Veronica repeated the information to Hunter and then the coach blew a whistle, and instructed the players to run three laps around the football field. Good time to chat with the man.

"Is that the same guy who coached you?"

"Yeah. Coach Butch," Wade said.

"Okay." She slapped her hands on her thighs. "We're off to do some investigating. Found a few things out about you on the computer...."

Hunter stood and leaned toward Wade, his face serious. "You were a good kid, Wade. You had a great mother. I remember, her, too. We're going to figure this out. I promise."

Wade nodded, keeping his eyes on the football field. "Thanks." He blinked and tears rolled down his dark cheeks. Veronica rested a hand on his thick arm. "He says 'thanks'," she said.

Hunter led the way down to the field. Veronica took long strides to keep up with him, admiring the way his strong calves and leg muscles bunched and flexed as he hurried across the brown grass toward the portable table covered with sports drinks. Their target stood just beyond that with a half-dozen other men in red T-shirts.

"Coach Butch?" Hunter asked.

Veronica was happy to play wingman in this situation. First of all, she didn't know much about football. Secondly, time for Hunter to take the lead since she was the go-to ghost person. She stood quietly next to Hunter, observing the tall, muscular coach who scared her a little just by his standing close to her. His face was a little redder than it should be. Summer heat would be brutal during workouts, and his expression—pissed off at the world—made her want to turn and run away. He must not be having a good practice.

"Yep, that's me." Butch lifted a cup of water and chugged it, took off his red ball cap, mopped his sunburned bald head with a towel, and picked up another cup. "What ya need?"

"Wade Montgomery," Hunter said.

The coach choked on his water and spit it out, slamming his cup to the table. He faced the other coaches. "Head to the shade, will you? Make sure they hydrate. Get ready to lecture those three guys who want to be starting quarterback. They need to prove they want it."

The men nodded and transferred coolers and water to a hand-pulled wagon and headed toward a small patch of shade outside of the track.

"What about Wade?" His eyes narrowed and he glanced at Veronica for the first time. "You lawyers or something? We've already been cleared of any wrongdoing. That heart thing that happened...well, it was a shame, but it had gone undiagnosed. Happened to a boy running track in Indiana last year too—"

Hunter shook his head. "No. Nothing like that. I'm the doctor who tried to treat him after his heart gave out. I'm...well, I'm trying to get some closure. Hey, listen. Do you have a doctor lined up for the sidelines this fall for games?"

The man let out choked laugh. "This is the city, man. We share an athletic trainer for all sports. He tries to stay on the sidelines, but it don't always work that way. Most of the kids' parents are blue-collar shift workers. We hardly fill the stands halfway on game day."

"If you'll answer some questions about Wade, I'd be happy to arrange my schedule this fall, to be your sideline doctor. For home games."

The man lifted a brow and studied Hunter, then folded his hairy arms on his barrel chest. The sound of cleats on asphalt approached as the players huffed and puffed past them on the track. "One more lap, then grab some water and sit in the shade. We're rerunning that drill in fifteen minutes and it'd better be right this time."

He hollered so loud that Veronica wanted to hold her ears, but resisted the urge.

"Deal." Coach stuck out his hand.

Hunter flashed a smile and shook hands. "I'm Hunter and this is my friend, Veronica."

Coach Butch nodded at Hunter and than turned to Veronica. "You're not a lawyer?"

"Nope." She shook his sweaty hand. He shifted his attention back to Hunter.

"So tell me about Wade." Hunter glanced toward the bleachers, where Wade had been sitting earlier. Veronica wished she could tell him that Wade had moved, that he could hear their conversation, but she couldn't say anything in front of the coach.

Butch lifted a cup, and offered it to Hunter, who accepted it. "Thanks."

The coach held one out to Veronica, too. "Thanks," she said, taking the water.

He took another one for himself and turned toward the empty football field. "It happened right here, almost two years ago." His mouth drooped at the sides, a sadness filling his face. Maybe she'd misjudged this guy. He ran the team hard, dealt with men and boys all day, and probably wasn't comfortable around women. Could this be a soft side he didn't show much?

"He was fine the first two hours of practice...played defensive tackle. You know, like Michael Oher? *The Blind Side*? He loved that movie. Was a huge Oher fan." He nodded as if seeing the practice in his head as he watched the field. "Wade was a good player. Probably would have had some college offers by the end of the season. Good grades.

But...." He narrowed his eyes.

Hunter glanced at Veronica and she lifted her brows, signaling she didn't understand where he was going, either. "But what?" Hunter asked.

Butch turned toward Hunter, his earlier mask back in place on his face. The horde of football players, slower now, traipsed past on the track, huffing and puffing. "Get to the shade now. Drink at least three cups of water, stretch out, and sit." The boys nodded as they went by. "You hear me? I need to know you heard me."

"Yes, Coach!" they chorused.

He shook his head and turned. "Wade was smart, but he was getting into the wrong crowd. Girls, especially."

From the corner of her eye, Veronica spotted Wade getting closer. *Shit.* He wasn't carrying a weapon or something was he? She stiffened as Wade approached. Hunter must have noticed a change in her demeanor, because he glanced at her, eyes wide.

She gave a small nod, hoping she was right to appease his fear. When had they gotten to the point where they understood each other's nonverbal signals?

Hunter crossed his arms, revealing those strong biceps. He could have been a football player, probably. Not the guy who pushed the other guys around, but the one who threw the ball and got protected. Yeah, she'd like to see him in those tight football pants.

Wade stood next to Veronica. She could feel the tension radiating from him. Curiosity? Or had his rage returned? But she couldn't risk talking to him. The coach was too close.

"He must not have liked me," Wade stated.

She could only give him a slight nod, hoping he understood she was on his side and nothing the coach could say would sway her opinion of him.

"What do you mean, girls?" Hunter asked.

Butch shrugged. "A distraction. I know the guys need a good boink every now and then, but relationships...dating drama.... I tell them go ahead, have a good time sticking your dick in the girls, but don't let them get in your head."

Veronica's knee wobbled, she held it so tight to keep from kicking the coach in the balls. She bit the inside of her mouth to clamp her lips together, hold the verbal assaults inside.

Hunter's jaw twitched. To his credit, he kept his voice level. "So Wade let a girl get in his head."

"Ah." Butch waved a dismissive hand. "More like a bunch of them. He had a thing for girls. Never had a father figure, just a mom who smothered him, so he liked girls...fell for them, ya know? Not healthy for a boy."

Veronica suddenly wanted to leave. They weren't getting anywhere. All this guy cared about was football.

"How about his friends?" Hunter glanced in the direction of the players in the shade.

The coach followed his glance. "A few. He wasn't exactly a leader, but a good follower. Some of the guys like Tyree—he's number twenty-four, and Dwayne—number forty-eight—were sophomores that year. They would have known Wade."

"Those the guys he was closest to?"

"Yeah. Far as I can remember. Listen. I gotta get back to running drills. Practice starts next week and I gotta finish picking the team."

"I appreciate your help." Hunter dug in his pocket and pulled out a card from his wallet. "If you think of anything else, or anyone else I could talk to about his social life, I'd appreciate a call. And I'm serious about being the sideline physician."

"Okay. Thanks. I'll call you." The coach nodded and turned to walk toward the group.

"Real nice guy," Veronica said, watching the man skulk across the dry grass. "How can somebody like that be in charge of a group of impressionable boys? His belly hangs over his shorts and he's beet-red. Not from the sun, I'm thinking."

"Yeah." Hunter stared after the guy, too. "Drinks a little too much and it shows."

"Wade's here," Veronica said, putting a hand on the kid's upper arm.

Hunter gazed at the spot she indicated.

"Do you remember having a girlfriend, Wade?" Veronica asked.

"No. I barely remember any of these guys. The ones I remember...I think I remember them because I started coming here every day during the rest of that football season, and every year after that for tryouts, practices, and games.

"You cheer them on at games?" The thought of Wade, sitting in the stands, happy to watch football, warmed Veronica's heart.

"What's he saying? Does he remember a girlfriend?" Hunter moved closer.

She shook her head. "No, but he remembers a couple of the guys. I think that's our next step."

"Good. That's good. We need to talk to them. I have a feeling we'll get a better picture of his life from them. Butch knew Wade's abilities on the field, but his male chauvinism kept him from seeing who Wade was," Hunter said.

Wade opened his mouth to speak, and cracked a smile. Veronica chuckled. "Hunter, I believe you just made Wade smile."

"I was tempted to ask Butch if we could talk to the players he mentioned, but something told me to hold off. Let's wait in the parking lot. See if we can track down a couple of them without the coach around. But it means postponing our visit to Wade's mom."

"Well, we're here. Hopefully she can meet us later, or tomorrow. Maybe we can take her out to dinner." She fanned herself. "Can we sit in air conditioning?"

"Yeah, air conditioning sounds good. Let's wait in my car."

He glanced to the spot where Veronica still had a hand on Wade's arm. "Wade, you want to join us?"

"No thanks. I want to watch them. They usually like to hang out in the parking lot after they shower, too. I like to listen in. Besides." He smiled again. "Ghosts don't get hot."

Veronica laughed and repeated Wade's words for Hunter.

"Okay, pal. We're in the car if you need us."

Oh great. Sitting in a small vehicle with a hot guy. Easy as pie.

Except, well, as much as she loved cooking, she'd never been able to make a pie successfully.

Chapter Seven

*H*unter blasted the air, pushing most of the vents toward Veronica. He'd phoned Wade's mother, who'd agreed to meet for dinner at a local diner. As if sitting in a small car with Veronica wasn't temptation enough, he'd be eating with her tonight, too.

Too bad the feeling wasn't mutual. As if a Plexiglas partition split the middle of their two seats, she kept as far away as possible.

"Can I ask you something?" He studied her face.

Her brow rose, and her golden gaze met his. "And if I said no?"

He shrugged. "I'd ask you anyway, probably."

Her lips quivered. God, how he wanted to be the one to put a smile on her face, get behind that aloof exterior she presented to the world. She'd dropped that mask a time or two, but not long enough to let him in. And he wanted in. Wanted in badly. All this togetherness made him yearn for more from her.

His question would either make her leave the car or it would open the door to what lay behind her mask...just a crack. A calculated risk. Even if she did storm out of the car, she'd be back. For Wade. That was one thing he could say for sure about her already. She cared, and cared a lot. Probably part of whatever her issue was.

"Your talent to see ghosts is incredible. You must be able to help a lot of people...and spirits. What happened with the police?" He kept his voice soft.

She inhaled, blew out a breath, and stared down the parking lot toward the field. "If you research it, you'll find that there's never been one proven incident where a psychic-medium has led law enforcement to anything noteworthy in a case."

He stayed silent, urging her to go on without interrupting.

She faced him with eyebrows drawn together. "However, that's not entirely true. Most of us don't want recognition for working with police, and law enforcement doesn't want the media attention when they use a psychic-medium. It's not just that I can see ghosts. I can communicate with dead people, and some sort of psychic ability enables me to sense the energy of living people if I make a connection of some kind with them."

"Like if they're a missing person, you can hold something that belonged to them and feel a connection?" Beyond cool! She found missing persons. She *was* using her skills. She just didn't run around bragging about them.

She nodded. "Exactly."

"Veronica, that's incredible. You save lives. Maybe you've saved more lives than I have." He reached out, through the invisible shield she'd put between them, to pull her hands into his.

Tears filled her beautiful eyes. One tear leaked out and flowed down her smooth face. He unlocked his grasp on her, lifted a hand to her cheek, and gently brushed away the tear with his thumb.

She swallowed, tilted her head back, and blinked her eyes. "So. What do we ask these guys when they bring their heat-stroked bodies out to this parking lot?"

Okay. Good talk. Moving on. He cleared his throat. "Let's focus on number twenty-four, Tyree, and Dwayne, number forty-eight."

"How will we recognize them? Won't they change clothes?"

"I'm hoping Wade will help us with that." Hunter pulled the lever on his seat, reclined a bit and stared out the windshield because if he looked at those full, pink lips for ten seconds more, he'd be kissing them.

"I can't believe how hot it is." She turned the vent in front of him toward her and probably had no idea how he had to restrain himself from reaching out to pull her on his lap. His car might be small, but he could find a way to do things to her.

This was crazy. He hadn't had feelings like this for a woman since...well, since Dianna. Figures. He chose the one girl he couldn't have. A girl who wanted no part of a relationship.

"They're coming up the hill now," Veronica said.

"Good." He shifted to sit and glanced out the window. "Is Wade with them?"

She nodded. "Walking right in the midst of them."

He watched her face as she tracked the group's movement inside the building. He'd known plenty of beautiful women. Married one. Dated plenty before his wife. Veronica was beautiful in a different way. Like she didn't know it, the most attractive way of all. Red, curly hair he wanted to run his fingers through. Haunting eyes that masked so many emotions and secrets. And those lips...those damned tempting lips.

"Wade's leaning against a car now. See that beat-up old white Caddy?"

Hunter shifted closer to Veronica. Not to see better, but to torture himself with her scent. "Think it's a sign? Is he telling us the car belongs to one of the two dudes we need to talk to?"

She didn't move her face, but he caught motion in her eyes when she checked his proximity in her peripheral vision. But she didn't slide away. *Progress*? He sure hoped so.

"I guess we should wait until they come out of the locker room instead of standing with Wade, huh? Might freak them out if they came out and saw us hanging around." Hunter took a long inhale of her fragrance and suddenly craved peach pie. Or a taste of Veronica. *Damn. I need out of this car, soon.* He shifted back to his side, his shorts a little snugger at the crotch.

"Here they come." Veronica opened her door and stepped out. They walked together toward the Caddy. Two tall, muscular guys wearing red football practice T-shirts sporting their numbers went to either side of the long, white car.

"Tyree? Dwayne?" Hunter hollered and flicked what he hoped was a friendly wave.

The guys looked up at the same time. A few more players walked out, some talking loudly to each other, others wearing iPods and walking along, carting big duffle bags.

"Yeah?" Tyree said, glancing up as he opened the driver's-side door and shot a glance over the roof at number forty-eight, Dwayne. They exchanged a worried look.

They either didn't trust adults or were worried about being caught about something. Hunter smiled again and placed his hand on the small of Veronica's back as they moved closer.

"I'm Hunter and this is Veronica. I knew Wade Montgomery. I'm wondering if you would talk to us about him." He and Veronica stood at the trunk, close enough to have a private conversation, but not so close as to chase these guys away. Hopefully.

Tyree's face softened and he tossed his duffle into the vehicle and shut the door. Dwayne did the same and they both moved to the back of the car.

"How did you know him?" Tyree asked. Dwayne stood beside him, arms crossed. These two would have made good bouncers at a downtown bar, if they were a few years older.

Hunter swallowed hard. "I was the doctor who tried to save him. But couldn't."

Tyree's brows went up. He shot Dwayne a look and relaxed against the trunk and faced Hunter and Veronica. "You tried everything you could to save him?"

Hunter nodded once. "Yes, and Veronica and I are hoping to find out more about him, especially his last years, because I'm starting a scholarship in his name."

Veronica's eyes widened. The idea of the scholarship had just popped into his head. It felt good. Like it had been something he'd wanted to do for a while. Maybe it would make it easier to talk with people, too. Obviously, he couldn't start a scholarship for every patient he lost, but he was a huge football fan, and making sure Wade was remembered was suddenly very important. In a strange way, he would miss the guy when he moved on to the next world.

"That's pretty cool, man. Wade was a good guy. He helped tutor me to make sure my grades were good enough to make the team, too. I sucked at biology." His jaw tightened and he glanced away for a moment, his gaze lingering on the football field down the hill.

Hunter waited silently. Veronica turned to her right and smiled. Must be where Wade was standing now. This had to make him feel good to hear he was so well remembered.

"I never hung out with him outside of school. If you want to talk to someone who knew him real good, that would be Sam Junior, his neighbor. He comes to most practices and games, but he wasn't here today…kind of our water boy. He loved football. Has Down Syndrome, didn't make the team, but coach lets him sit on the bench for games and help out with stuff. He and his sister hung out a lot with Wade."

"Think Sam Junior will be at practice tomorrow?"

The kid shrugged. "Never know. He's a football freak, so probably."

Dwayne's cell phone rang and he strolled away to take the call.

"Thanks. I appreciate it. Good to know Wade is still remembered around here." Hunter stuck out his hand to shake and Tyree accepted it and shook.

"Oh yeah. We remember Wade. He was a good guy. Most seniors— especially the starters—treated us sophomores like dirt. Not Wade." He gave a tight-lipped smile.

"We gotta split, man," Dwayne said, pocketing his phone as he walked toward them.

"Thanks again, guys," Hunter said.

"See ya," Tyree said as he and Dwayne opened their doors.

He dropped his hand from Veronica's back as they turned. Maybe she'd think it had been part of the charade to get the boys to talk. A man and a woman were less intimidating than a man alone, right? Let her think that. Even if the reality was that he wanted to touch her every time he was around her.

A compact car rounded the bend and moved slowly past them. Coach Butch stared at them through the passenger window, his cap low enough on his face to shadow his eyes.

But he drove slowly enough that Hunter could see his expression. A frown and set lips conveyed he didn't like the fact that Hunter and Veronica were still around his players.

○8

Veronica stood in front of her bathroom mirror and finger-combed her hair into place. In the epic battle of humidity versus her curls, humidity always won. At least she'd had some alone time after spending all morning by Hunter's side. They'd be meeting Wade's mom in half an hour, but she'd needed that break from Hunter. He stirred feelings that she'd rather ignore. His announcement about the scholarship surprised her. What a generous gesture. And one that would make it easier for them to talk to people who knew Wade.

Wade had climbed into the car with his friends. A spy mission? Good idea. After Veronica and Hunter had chatted with the boys about Wade, it made sense they'd talk about him more in private. Maybe Wade would get a hint about what he had to do to cross over. Maybe the coach's comment about girls meant something.

She padded into her bedroom, the shag carpeting messaging her bare feet, and stood in front of her open closet. This wasn't a date. Hell no. This was a fact-finding mission. She had to ditch her sweaty clothes. A simple yellow sundress would do.

Her cell phone chirped, indicating a text. Hunter. On his way to her door. She pecked a reply. *Meet me in the lobby.*

Getting on the elevator now. May as well stop at your floor on the way down.

She rolled her eyes even though she knew it was immature. She slipped the dress over her head, stuck her feet in flip-flops, grabbed her purse from the bed, and headed out her door and down the hallway. Fine. She'd meet him at the elevator. She didn't need some suave guy knocking on her door and escorting her.

A dinging sounded at the end of the hall and the doors slid open. Hunter stepped out, spotted her, and held the door to keep it from shutting. He was dressed in creased khaki shorts again and a crisp green shirt. His dark hair, still a little wet from his shower, curled at the collar.

Great. Just the two of them.

"You look very pretty," he said as she stepped inside.

"Thanks. I'm looking forward to meeting Mrs. Montgomery." *Keep it professional. Don't let this get to be anything more.*

"She's a nice lady. Have you heard from Wade?" he asked as the doors to the parking garage swished apart.

"No. Maybe he's still trailing his friends. Seems to me he's having fun taking on some of the investigative part of this mystery."

"Yeah, I think you've given him confidence."

She smiled, enjoying the compliment. Being able to communicate had really seemed to help Wade's confidence grow. And he was leaving Hunter alone, too. Maybe Wade would be the one to figure out what he needed to do to move on to the other side. They crossed the garage in silence and Hunter used his remote to unlock his car.

He opened her door and she slid inside. Part of her wanted to tell him she could do it herself, but it wasn't that he was treating this like a date. He just had manners, that was all. No more, no less.

Ten minutes later, they got out of the car in front of a diner at the edge of town. The scent of fried chicken and onions drifted through the door. Veronica's stomach rumbled with hunger.

A stout black woman with a stylish straw hat and a flowered dress sat on a bench in a small waiting area by the hostess stand. She eyed them and stood, her head cocked to the side.

"Mrs. Montgomery?" Hunter asked, taking a step closer to the woman and extending his hand.

"Doctor Anderson...." She said the words slowly and a smile split her wrinkled face. "You haven't changed much in two years."

He grinned and she placed both of her hands over his. "And you look as beautiful as ever. Please call me Hunter."

"And please call me Cissy. This lovely woman is your wife?"

Veronica's smile dropped from her face as her stomach plummeted. Hunter's wife. The words must pain him.

If the words stung, he masked it well. He smiled and laid a hand on Veronica's shoulder. "Cissy, this is Veronica Matthews...a friend and neighbor."

So he saw her the same way she saw him. *Good to know.* She shook hands with the lady, impressed by the woman's strong grip.

"Let's get a table and some of this great-smelling food." Hunter spoke to the hostess who led them to a booth in the corner of the crowded room.

Cissy slid on one side and Veronica on the other. Hunter glided beside her, scooting close. His bare leg rubbed against hers, sending tingles up her spine and down her core.

"It's nice that you wanted to take me to dinner, but I'm still not sure why." Cissy leaned forward, her brown-eyed gaze on Hunter.

Good thing Wade hadn't followed them to the diner. How emotional would that be for him? He'd mentioned that right after he'd died, it was too sad to see his mom. What about now? Maybe seeing her would jog a memory or two.

"I volunteered to be the sideline doctor for Wade's high school during the coming football season. Some of the guys at practice mentioned Wade." Hunter's words were soft.

Cissy's eyes grew teary. "I know you deal with a lot of patients. It's nice that you remember Wade. And very nice of you to volunteer your time with the team."

Hunter nodded several times. "He was young. Way too young to die. I'd like to start a scholarship in his name at his high school. To find the perfect recipient, I'd like to know a little more about his life."

The depth of Hunter's grief was palpable. Veronica had spent time with doctors over the years, and most were very nice. But Hunter was made for this profession. He had both skills and bedside manners, the combination rare and needed. Helping him would be the same as helping a crapload of people.

Cissy's lips curved into a smile. "What a wonderful thing for you to do. I keep his room just as it was when he left us. I grieve for him and I miss having someone to come home to, someone to look after. I miss that a lot."

Veronica reached across the table, covered the woman's hand with hers, and gave a gentle squeeze. Cissy put her other hand on top and patted, then sat back against the padded booth, moving her hands to her lap. "I'm doing fine. There's just a piece of my heart that will never be the same. I think sometimes that it might be a little easier if I had other children, but Wade was my only child. With other children, I might be able to distract myself from my grief. Now I just think of his empty room, and the fact that I'll never have grandbabies."

The server appeared with waters and menus. They took a few

minutes to choose their meals, and put the menus aside. Hunter cleared his throat and took a long drink. "Can you tell us more about Wade? About his friends? Maybe a girlfriend?"

"Oh, he liked girls all right." Cissy chuckled. "I had strict rules. No girls when I wasn't home. And when they visited, I made sure I was nearby, you know what I mean. I was a single mom, working double shifts to cover the bills. I made it to every one of his games, though."

Veronica laughed. "Sounds like you ran a tight ship."

The waitress appeared and they placed their orders.

"He had friends that were girls, too. I was proud of him for that. He looked after our neighbor boy, Sam Junior, like he was his little brother. Taught him football. Neither of them had a stick-around father, so Hunter loved spending time with Sam Junior and his sister, Tia."

Veronica and Hunter exchanged a glance. *Tia? A girlfriend?*

"So Tia...could she have been a girlfriend?" Veronica asked, leaning forward on her elbows.

Cissy waved a hand and shook her head. "Oh no. Those two were like siblings. Same age. She was good in English, my Wade was great in science and math. They studied together a lot, and Sam Junior was usually with them. It was nice for their momma and me to know our kids had company while we were at work." She raised her brows. "But the rule was, family room and kitchen. No bedroom studying. Just because they were almost as close as siblings didn't mean I'd let them take any chances."

Hunter chuckled and shot another glance at Veronica. In this case, the mother could be the last to know. They needed to talk to Sam Junior and Tia.

They made small talk until their meals arrived.

"You mentioned Wade's dad?" Hunter finally asked as they finished dessert. "Did Wade have any contact with him?"

"In jail. Murder. Wade knew. But he never wanted to visit." The woman shook her head and cut a piece of liver and onions and dipped the fork in her mashed potatoes and gravy.

Hmmm. A father he hadn't talked to in years could be also be a reason to stick around. Guilt that he'd never tried to connect with his father? Hunter looked at her yet again and Veronica read the same thought on his face.

Maybe she should tell Wade's mother that Wade was still around...as a ghost. *No...too freaky.* Could she offer them a chance to communicate one last time with each other? A gift she could give this woman: one final conversation with the son she'd lost way too soon.

But no. It had to be Wade's choice.

Even so, the thought that she might bring the woman some peace made her feel good about her ability, for the first time in a long time.

After saying goodbye to Wade's mom, they climbed into Hunter's car. "You know what?" she asked as he shut the driver's side door.

"What?" He glanced at her.

"You're a pretty nice guy." The kindness and sincerity he'd shown Wade's mother nudged at the part of her that wanted to hide from opening herself to others. Suddenly, she wanted him to know why she hadn't wanted to help him initially. It was a risk...opening herself to him, letting him in.

He started the engine and eased out of the spot. Perfect time to talk without him staring at her.

"This psychic part of my gift...." It was harder than she thought to say the words out loud.

Hunter threw her a worried look.

"Well, the ghost part—that's not too bad. I see a lot of ghosts, but if I give off a leave-me-alone vibe, they usually do."

"But the psychic part to your gift?" His brows knit as he shot her a glance and focused on the road again.

The memory sat like a tight ball in her stomach. She needed to unwind it, get it out. Say the damn words. "When I touch something that belongs to someone who is alive and in trouble, I feel a connection to them. Like they're in my head, but not enough to know what to do to help them. If they don't know where they are, it's hard for me to figure out where they are. For instance, maybe I only know they're somewhere dark and cold. I feel the cold, I sense the darkness. Then, the longer they're 'with' me, the more I can read their mind and emotions." Like a slide show, an image of the still baby with ashen lips came to mind, followed by the teen in the woods, her throat slashed from side to side.

Tears stung at the corners of her eyes. "I've always been too late to save them," she whispered.

He reached out and placed a warm hand on her leg. "We can't save everyone. We can only try our best. You brought peace to those families, though, didn't you? You found their loved ones when they might never have been found."

The setting sun cast an orange glow on the interior of his small car, hiding the tear that slipped down her cheek, she hoped.

"Maybe."

"Yeah. More than maybe. You need to give yourself credit for helping as much as you did. But for now, how about a change of pace? I'm on call tonight in the ED, but maybe we'll get lucky and it'll be a quiet night. What would you say to a brainless movie and some popcorn from the comfort of my sofa?"

Suddenly, that sounded like the perfect ending to their evening.

Chapter Eight

This is crazy. Hunter been struggling all day to keep his head straight around Veronica. The woman blasted signals. *Don't touch. Don't get too close.* Yet by inviting her back to his apartment, he'd set himself up for more torturous closeness to her.

He poured two cranberry juices. With a glance at the beige sofa where she sat, he took in her small features and the way her red curly hair fell forward over her bare shoulders as she flicked through the pay-per-view movies available. Did she have any clue how sexy that simple yellow dress was? Especially right now, with the right strap slid down a little?

As if she sensed his mesmerized stare, she fingered the fabric back into place, jolting him back to his task. "Sorry I don't have wine around. Why tempt myself, you know?"

She stood and crossed the room, leaving her flip-flops on the rug in front of his sofa. Bare feet...a thin summer dress that, if he let his mind wander, could be almost a sexy nightgown?

Good thing the counter was between them because his dick stood at full attention. Maybe he should accidentally spill some of the cranberry juice on himself to cool off.

She leaned a hip against a stool on the other side of the counter. "Addictions are tough, but it seems like you have a handle on yours."

Yeah, good erection killer.

"I think it makes you a strong person to get through an ordeal like that. I'm sure my dad's addicted to a bunch of stuff, but he...and my mom...are in denial. It's just part of the party scene for them. Drugs and alcohol are all they see around them," she said.

"How did you skip getting that gene?" he asked. She built her walls, but other than that, this gorgeous woman had her head screwed on right. One more reason he found her irresistible.

"I guess I looked at them, saw how I didn't want to be. And lucky for me, I had a nanny who really cared, and she had a daughter—my best friend Jeanne—who was always there for me. Kind of taught me that family doesn't always have to be blood relations, you know?"

Damn. She'd survived that kind of lonely childhood and her ordeals finding dead bodies, and still had such a good grip on life?

"And," she continued. "I've found my love."

His heart skipped a beat and he over-poured the juice. All this time, he'd never thought to ask about a boyfriend. Maybe someone in the military, someone overseas.

"Hunter!" She laughed, raced around the counter, and grabbed some paper towels. "If you need help, just ask."

He backed away enough to let her through to blot the mess he'd made. Still stood close enough to brush her sexy behind with his hip.

She twirled and bumped into him, biting her lip as she held his gaze for a second, then tossed the wet towels in the trash.

"You found your love?" He needed to know.

She grinned. "Photography. Coffee table books. I have my own books coming out soon. All about city living."

Relief flooded his veins and he smiled and let out a breath he hadn't realized he'd been holding. He stared at her golden eyes. "Fascinating."

They stood close. Close enough to reach out, rest his hands on her slim waist. Close enough to lean just a little forward and—

"You said something about popcorn. The kind with butter?" She snagged the two glasses of cranberry juice, tilted her head in an oh-so-sexy look, and took a step back.

"Uh, sure, yeah. Coming right up." He turned toward the cupboard to pull out a box of microwave popcorn as she rounded the counter and headed for the sofa.

"How about a horror flick?" she asked, setting the glasses on the coasters on his mahogany coffee table.

"Will there be blood and guts? 'Cause if not, count me out. I need blood and guts." He shoved the popcorn in the microwave, punched the button, and watched the bag grow.

"Oh yeah...looks like lots of blood and guts." She settled back on the sofa, focused on the remote control, and crossed her legs, spreading her yellow dress over her knees in a way that reminded him of the petals of a soft flower. He should sit in one of the side chairs, not beside her. He'd be too tempted to touch her if he was close.

The microwave beeped and he pulled out the steaming bag, opened it, and poured it into a bowl.

Who the hell am I kidding? He'd sit as close as he could.

A minute later, he set the bowl and a stack of napkins on the table and sat beside her.

"Yum, butter," she said, leaning forward to grab a few pieces.

The move gave him a chance to peek at her cleavage when her top shifted. His heart beat faster. *Still time to move into one of those side chairs, pal.*

"Okay, movie starts in two minutes. You ready for some gore?" She popped some of the kernels past those damn full pink lips, leaving a shiny coating.

"You've got...." His voice caught in his throat. Common sense took a serious hike. She faced him and he cupped her chin, leaned closer. "Something on your lips," he whispered, touching his mouth ever so gently to hers. Just a taste. A small taste of her.

She slipped her tongue through the seam of his lips and he tasted salty oil and...Veronica. His willpower melted faster than the butter on popcorn. One taste was all he thought he wanted, but his body had different ideas.

Veronica ran one hand around his shoulder and clasped the back of his neck, holding him closer, searching his mouth deeper. Her other hand splayed on his chest as she shifted toward him.

He moved his hands to her waist, savoring the feel of her hot skin beneath the thin fabric. She couldn't commit to him. He needed a woman who would commit. But right now, she needed him and he needed her, which, at least temporarily, outweighed every other reason to keep their hands off each other.

She moaned and ran her fingers through the hair at the nape of his neck, sending shivers down his spine and straight to his dick. He licked the corner of her mouth. The oil was gone, but the salty taste still remained.

"Yum is right," he moaned. "Better than popcorn." She smiled...he felt it under his tongue as he traced her lips, taking his time, wanting to remember every curve of her mouth. He hadn't wanted a woman in so long. Hadn't been sure he'd ever again feel the burning desire that pounded his body right now.

Veronica. Not just any woman. A very special woman.

Her hand traced his hairline, her lips pressed against his...he wanted her here and now. Naked, on the couch. But what he wanted wasn't as important as what she needed. This couldn't be a night of hot sex on the sofa. As much as his rock-hard cock screamed for release, he'd build this gently, make her needs a priority. Then see if they ended up in his bed.

She sucked his tongue farther inside her mouth in a sexy little move that sent his senses flying and begging for more as he tasted deeper. Bullets of pleasure shot straight to his cock.

His hands moved higher, to the top of her dress, needing to touch her bare skin. He slipped one of the straps down her shoulder and kissed her lips. "Are you...I mean do you want...I don't want to do anything that—"

She smiled at him with half-closed eyes, her nose stud glinting off the nearby lamp. Sexy. So damned sexy. Her full lips were swollen from their kissing. In one swift move, she straddled him as someone on TV screamed in terror.

His dick grew impossibly harder and he cupped her ass through her dress.

She wiggled closer, lifting her skirt as she stared down at him with golden eyes and a small smile. "Yes, I want to be with you."

He swallowed hard, staring at her before taking a hand from her firm ass and twirling a strand of her hair. "God, you're the most beautiful woman I've ever seen."

She raised a brow and kissed him, a light kiss as she wiggled against his erection while shrugging out of the other strap to reveal the curve of her breasts. "You don't have to flatter me. I've already said yes. Condoms?"

"Bedroom," he rasped, his mind picturing her pert nipples, still hiding under that damn yellow fabric.

"No time for bedroom." She shifted her body toward the floor, where her purse lay, and yanked out a condom. As she leaned, he grasped her waist to keep her in place and her crotch slid against his length, making him gasp for air.

He hadn't time to think about whether her preparedness was for him, or if she always carried condoms, because when she shifted back, she wiggled closer, sliding against his erection again. *Damn.* He might not last long enough to get his damn pants off.

Taking a deep breath, he reminded himself that this was about her...about keeping it slow. Making her see how much he cared.

Veronica stared at him and her chest rose and fell. Looping a finger at the edge of the top of her dress, he pulled the cloth down, but only an inch, and touched his lips there, kissing a trail from the top of her exposed breast to her collarbone.

She sucked in a breath and clutched the back of his head possessively, and he licked, gently sucking at her skin, needing to taste her, needing her to know that every part of her was special.

"Don't stop...go lower, please," she begged, tilting her hips against his erection and pumping.

His cock couldn't get much harder without exploding. He pulled at the fabric on both sides, revealing two of the most perfect breasts he'd ever seen.

Settling his palms under the weight of her breasts, he circled her peaked nipples gently with his thumbs, reveling in their firmness.

She sucked in a breath and trailed her fingers down his spine. His heart hammered.

"Taste me, Hunter."

Oh yeah. He wanted to taste her all right. Here. There. Everywhere. "Gladly."

While still rubbing his thumb on one nipple, he kissed his way around her other breast, slowly lapping and working toward the center. She arched back, bracing her fingers tighter into his back and grabbing a fistful of his shirt, letting him feel her passion.

Gently, he flicked his tongue on her peaked nipple. She sighed and her hot breath feathered against his cheek. He swirled his tongue around the tip, alternating small kisses with tender sucks and licks. This was Veronica...the woman he'd craved since the day he'd met her. He'd treasure every second with her, every inch of her body. Moving his mouth to her other breast, he palmed the one wet from his kisses. A perfect body. A perfect woman. If only he could make her see it.

She reached between them and moaned as she rubbed over his shorts, along his erection.

His breath hitched and he palmed her breasts again, moving his lips to her mouth, searching it with a need he hadn't felt in a long, long time.

She kissed him back and kissed the corner of his mouth. "I need...." She panted for breath.

Whatever she needed, he'd give it to her.

"I need you to take your pants off," she said. A small smile lit her face.

"You are so bossy, you know that?" He grinned. Not just fun to be around, not just sexy, not just smart...Veronica was turning out to be someone he could fall in love with.

"Just shut up and take your pants off." Her grin widened and her eyes cast a sexy glint. "Here, I'll help you." She wiggled back, not all the way off his lap, but to the edge of his knees. With her dress hiked well past her own knees. *Damn, I want to touch those thighs.*

He unhitched his belt and she worked at the button. Leaning back, he tilted his hips off the sofa enough to allow her to undo the zipper. Her fingers felt way better than any time he'd ever taken off his clothing himself.

With a tug, she yanked his shorts past his hips. His cock sprang through his red boxers. Veronica stared at his hardness, licked her lips, and reached out to clasp his dick in her hands, stroking and staring at him. "Maybe the bedroom is a better idea for what I have in mind for you."

"Okay." The word barely tumbled out as all of his energy went to his dick.

She slid off him, her sweet breasts still exposed, her dress covering the rest of her, and held out her hand to him.

He took her hand, stood, and pulled her closer for a quick kiss on her lips.

"Let me show you my bedroom," he said, still holding her hand and leading her past the kitchen and down a small hallway.

She leaned closer, snuggled against him. Progress. Her walls were coming down. He could feel it.

His cell phone rang from its perch on the kitchen counter and his chest tightened. *No. No. No. Not now.* It had to be work. Which meant he had to answer. Which doubtless meant he had to leave immediately.

Veronica eased away from him. "The hospital?"

He huffed out a breath and lifted her chin with two fingers, hoping his remorse was obvious. "Probably." With a hand that shook with need, he turned back for the kitchen and picked up the call.

Thirty seconds later, he disconnected. Veronica stood in her dress, straps back in place, her bare feet and painted-pink toenails making her look so feminine that for the first time in his life he hated being an ED doctor.

"Hotel fire. A lot of injuries. I'm really sorry."

"No, no...of course you have to go. What can I do to help you?" She glanced at his legs. "Put your pants back on for you?"

They'd been hornier than two teenagers a few minutes ago, but here she was, going with the flow. Not mad or pouty like a lot of his fellow doctors complained about their wives and girlfriends. Ready to help.

He stepped closer to her. Could afford at least a minute more before he raced to the hospital to help. "If you touch my pants area one more time, I don't think I could walk away from you." He laid a gentle kiss on her lips and turned toward the living room.

More screams emanated from the TV. "Stay and watch the movie, if you like."

She smiled and crossed the room, sliding her feet into her flip-flops and grabbing her purse. "Nah, we'll watch it another time together."

Together. He liked the sound of that. If tonight was any indication of what they could be when they got the chance to be together...he'd do anything to be with her.

Chapter Nine

*V*eronica woke to the sound of a text message the next morning. With a moan, she remembered the reason for her lethargic sleep-in. She'd drowned her sorrows in a pint of Ben and Jerry's Imagine Whirled Peace. After having almost-sex with Hunter. The ice cream had melted on her tongue, reminding her of the way she'd responded to Hunter's kisses and touch.

She glanced at the clock on her nightstand, surprised to see she'd slept until almost nine. Blinking to adjust her eyes to the daylight, she snatched her phone off the table and read the text from Hunter.

More fire victims than expected. Some carbon monoxide poisonings and smoke inhalation. I'll be at the hospital all day. Maybe all night. Sorry to bail on Sam Junior interview. Maybe tomorrow? Or do you want to go without me?

She could go without him, but Sam Junior was a boy. What if the whole "male camaraderie" thing kept him from talking? It could be their one chance at information. Better to go in together, as a team.

I've got a lot of work to do. Might be better to do the team approach. Tomorrow is fine for me if good for you.

She pressed Send and stared at the phone, feeling like a teenage girl anticipating his next text. This wasn't a date, it was a project.

Sounds good. Look forward to seeing you.

Her face heated, confirming the whole teenage girl thing. Her finger lingered over the keys, but she couldn't type the words back to him. Of course she was looking forward to seeing him.

Good luck with your patients.

She pressed Send and tossed the phone on the bed. Sentimental words didn't come easily to her. Maybe she'd never be able to show her true feelings. A life condemned to thinking about emotions and feelings, but not letting them out. Sounded lonely.

Images of Hunter assaulted her mind. His kisses affected her like no other man's had. *Why?* He was funny, smart...dedicated to his job. And possibly capable of committing to one woman. He'd been married, right?

Why did it have to be like this? Why couldn't she just accept that he was a good guy and take a chance on him?

But she knew the answer. Trust didn't come easily, and she wasn't sure she'd ever be able to completely give her heart to a man.

She kicked off her sheet, refusing to have a pity party for one. If they couldn't make progress on Wade's case today, she'd walk around Harborplace and get some shots for her next photo book. She'd taken lots of good photos of cities in Europe, but none in her new hometown. And boy, did it have some interesting places.

She showered, gobbled a low-fat yogurt for breakfast to compensate for last night's indulgence, and grabbed a few cameras and her purse. With keys in hand, she stepped outside her door and almost tripped on Wade's long legs.

"I've been waiting for you," he said.

"Oh yeah?" She locked her door and checked the hallway. Empty. She sat beside him and leaned against her door. "What's up?"

"Where's Hunter?" he asked.

"At work. A bad fire at a downtown hotel."

"He'll save them. Make them better," he said, folding his big hands on his lap and staring down.

"Glad to hear about your attitude shift. You've known him two years, and I've only known him a few days, but he seems like a good guy."

"Yeah. He is. And it's really cool that he's starting a scholarship in my name."

"I agree." At this point, she could probably convince Wade to leave Hunter alone at work. But once he hit the two-year-ghost mark, all bets would be off. The only way to end this haunting was to get Wade to the next world. "Did you ride home with those guys yesterday? Tyree and Dwayne?" she asked.

"Uh huh." He grinned, crinkling the skin around his brown eyes. "They talked about me. Said really nice things, too. About how I was always helping people and how the rest of that football season was sad for everybody."

"Wow. They must have really respected you."

He shrugged, but the smile stayed on his face.

"Did you find anything out that might help us? Something that might be keeping you from crossing over? Did they mention a girlfriend?"

Wade shook his head.

Veronica took a deep breath and let it out. "Wade, we met with your mom last night."

He faced her with creased brows, worry etched all over his young face. "I visited her once. Right after I first died." He stared at the carpeting and glanced up. "I never went back after that. She was rocking back and forth, crying into the sofa pillow. Loud sobs that sounded like a hurt animal."

Oh God. Seeing loved ones suffer. Veronica had never really thought of that part of being a ghost. "She's doing fine now, she really is. But she still misses you a lot. Still has everything in your room the way you left it." She paused for a few seconds. "Time heals. Would you like to visit her again? I could communicate what you say...let her know anything you want." She hated this gift. She could have helped people communicate with deceased loved ones, but hated using her medium powers. For any reason. But this was finally a chance to use her gift for something positive.

Tears shined in his eyes and he turned away for a minute and stared at his feet. "I want to see her. How about after we figure out what I need to cross over? Right before I leave. That way we can tell her I'm leaving for good, and that I'll be okay."

Damn, what a brave and giving young man Wade was. If she ever became a mother, she wanted a son just like him.

"Deal." She fiddled with the pull tab of her purse, feeling restless. "Your mom mentioned that once your dad went to jail, you never wanted to visit him. Do you think that's your unfinished business? Would you like to see him?" Veronica had no idea how that would work. She'd have to present herself as the visitor, and depending who was watching, it could be a pretty strange scenario to interpret a ghost's conversation to a prisoner. For Wade, she would try, though.

He shook his head. "I don't think that's it. I mean...I can't know for sure that's not what's keeping me from crossing over, but I don't remember him at all."

"You said you don't remember many people from your life, though."

"But my dad...I don't know if this makes sense, I just know I didn't want anything to do with him. And I still don't. I don't remember much, but I remember he used to hurt my mom."

Veronica shuddered, thinking of the strong, hard-working woman they'd met earlier.

"How about Sam Junior? Your neighbor? Your mom mentioned he was like your little brother."

A grin split Wade's face. "I loved hanging out with Sam Junior." He raised his chin a notch. "Taught him about football." He let out a sigh and glanced at Veronica. "It's like the more I get to know what I was like during my life, the more I'm remembering."

"Good. That's really good." Might take him longer to turn to the dark side if they couldn't figure things out within the remaining days, too.

"Sam Junior has Down Syndrome. One of the things...and this is funny, but I hope it doesn't sound disrespectful of him...." Wade cracked a knuckle. "He liked football at first because it had 'downs'. You know, first down, second down...."

"Yeah, sure. I don't think that's disrespectful. It's a way he found a connection to the game."

"Cool. Well, that kid knows football better than most people. Are you going to meet with him? And Tia?"

The mention of the girl sent off alerts in Veronica's head. Could his relationship with Tia be something that would hold him to this world? "Probably tomorrow. Want to come?"

He nodded. "Yeah. I'd like that."

What the hell? May as well try to find out more. "So was Tia...was she somebody special to you?"

He frowned and studied his cleats for a moment, fiddling with the ties, as if trying to jog a memory. He met her gaze. "We were friends. I think that's all. Same age, but she went to private school. Really smart."

Hopefully, they'd find out if there was more to the story tomorrow.

"Well, time for me to head to football practice." Wade stood and held out a hand to help Veronica from the carpeted floor.

She grasped his firm hand and he effortlessly pulled her to her feet. "Strong for a ghost, aren't you?"

He chuckled, jogged down the hallway, and through the stairway door.

Slinging her cameras over her shoulder, she planned her day around the spectacular sights around Baltimore's Inner Harbor. She'd start with the Domino Sugars sign—a reminder to all that the harbor had been built on commerce. She'd return to take a photo at night as the sign glowed red against the dark sky. The National Aquarium Baltimore, Edgar Allan Poe's house, and Westminster Hall and Burying Ground, where Poe's body rested. Now there was one ghost she'd like to chat with. A visit to Fort McHenry could warrant some good shots. Ghosts there were said to be angry, though, so she would put out a shield, advertising for ghosts to stay away. It wasn't something she did often, because it took a lot of energy. And along the way, maybe some shots of the tall ships that had sailed gracefully into the harbor on this warm summer day.

All great ways to give in to her passion for capturing a moment of beauty around her. Didn't hurt that she could get so absorbed in her work she'd forget about pining for Hunter—and his talented hands and lips.

Chapter Ten

*H*unter inhaled the rich scent of the dark Sumatran brew that flowed from his one-cup machine into the coffee mug, and stretched as he stood in his boxers beside his counter. A whopping seven hours of sleep after a twenty-four hour shift. Much as he'd wanted to call Veronica on his way home at midnight, he'd known rest was what he needed.

He reached for the mug and then took a gulp. Besides, he'd get to spend all day with Veronica. After the way they'd ended things the night before, he'd need every ounce of his energy.

Amazing, really, that he'd made it through the crazy-busy day yesterday. He'd stayed focused on his patients throughout the day, but as soon as he left the hospital, his mind shifted to Veronica. He pictured her heart-shaped ass as he walked to his car. When he looked at himself in the rear-view mirror, he half-expected to see a scorch mark left over from the power of her kisses.

Today would be about fact-finding for Wade. But tonight...well, if things went as he hoped, this could be a Friday night to remember. One with the lovely Veronica on his lap, against his body, and in his bed, where he could show her what they could be together. He'd loosened the bricks in that wall she kept so firmly around her. At least he hoped he had. Now it was time for her to let him in, to let him show her what it could be like if she opened herself to the possibility of really being with someone.

The thought of her, glancing up at him, those golden eyes twinkling with passion. A need only he could fill....

His phone rang. With a glance at the display, he answered. "How'd you know I was thinking about you?"

"Uh...well, uh, good," Veronica stammered. She cleared her throat. "I'm afraid I'm calling with some not-so-great news, though."

He set his coffee down. Calls that started like this made knots in his stomach. "What's up?" *Nothing to worry about. Wait and see.*

She expelled a breath and he heard her frustration through the phone. It made him want to hang up and go see her in person.

"My freelance photographer for the fishing magazine bailed on me today. I can't find a backup, so I have to head to the Eastern Shore to photograph this fishing tournament myself. It's the cover story for the September issue."

"Damn. What time will you be back?" Feeling a need to vent his disappointment, wishing he could speed time forward, he drummed his fingers on the counter.

"I think I could be back by early evening. Maybe we could still chat with Sam Junior and Tia. And Wade wants to come along for that. He hoped it might jolt a memory for him. Do you think there's a possibility Wade was involved with Tia? That his relationship with her could be holding him here?"

"It certainly sounds promising. We don't have any better leads right now."

"I'll keep in touch, let you know how long this will take. Unless...." Her words trailed off and he waited.

"Do you want to ride out to the shore with me? You know," she hurried on, "brainstorm some other ideas about Wade?"

He couldn't hold back the smile. "I'd like nothing better to spend the day with you, Veronica. We wouldn't even need to talk about Wade." Hunter hoped his words conveyed his enthusiasm to be with her. "Problem is, I'm on call until midnight. I have to be able to get to the hospital within thirty minutes of being paged."

"Oh. Sure. I understand. Duty calls for both of us." Her voice was strong and carried a hint of humor.

"So, tonight..." he said, purposely letting his words drift off so she'd put her own meaning into them. Hopefully a vision of the two of them starting up right where they'd left off.

"Yes. See you tonight."

They disconnected and he downed the rest of his coffee. Need for Veronica rushed through his veins. Hearing her voice did that to him. Seeing her in person was going to make him crazy. He needed to burn off some of his adrenaline. The nonstop, never-dull pace of the ED sated his desire for action. Being with Veronica would be an adrenaline rush like no other.

Between now and then, he needed to find something that took thirty minutes or less, and got rid of his burning desire to do something wild. He knew just the thing. Bungee jumping. Maybe he'd jump twice, just to lose himself in the physical sensation of something besides the feel of holding Veronica's body against his.

ଔ

Veronica slid into her late-model Civic, smelling a little like fish and sporting a sunburned nose from a day along the piers in Ocean City. She'd met some great fishermen and women, though, and caught some awesome shots, several of which would make good cover art.

She glanced at the dashboard for a time check, and smiled when she realized she'd be home by seven, early enough to spend some time with Hunter and talk to Sam Junior and Tia, too. Leaning forward, she cranked the engine and turned the air conditioner on, letting the cool air whisk the sweat off her bare arms. With a sigh, she pulled out her phone to check for messages.

Three missed calls. Two from Hunter, one from her mom. She punched the button to listen to Hunter's first message and the smile fell from her face. He'd been called into the hospital for an emergency. A bad accident on the beltway had sent dozens of victims to the hospital. Damn. Sad news, but the clock was ticking. Even if she had to work by herself, they had to get to the bottom of Wade's inability to cross over.

But there was a second message. Maybe things had gone faster than he'd thought, and he was through at the hospital.

His warm voice cut through the phone as she listened to his message. "I'm working fast here. Technically, I'm off at midnight. Too late to meet with Sam Junior and his sister, but not too late for us to get together if you're up for it. I'll call you when I get a break."

One of the fishermen carrying a trophy from the tournament walked by and waved. She waved back.

So many obstacles kept coming between her and Hunter. A sign? She was a psychic-medium. Damn if it ever helped her figure out her own life, though. Hunter's work kept him busy and unavailable. Good or bad? In her mind...good. She loved her "me" time. Loved being alone more than she liked being around people.

How was being with Hunter going to be any different than the others she'd been with? The ones who always wanted more. The ones who needed more than her...more women.

A three-hour drive home meant she had plenty of time for a phone conversation with her mom. She donned her Bluetooth, returned her mom's call without even listening to the message, and backed out of her parking spot.

"Hi, honey!" Her mother's voice came through loud and clear. "We're in the Bahamas."

"That's great, Mindy. Having fun?" Veronica loved her mom, but didn't want to be anything like her. Her mom's love for Kyle, Veronica's dad, blinded her to all of his affairs. Or she pretended to be ignorant of them, anyway. She accepted them as part of who he was, never believing she alone could be what he wanted.

"So your daddy is out with some promoting folks...talking about a new reality show, and I'm going to buy one of those fun chick flicks on the TV. Maybe another bottle of champagne, too."

For an hour, Veronica listened to her mom grow a little drunker, and a little sadder, although she kept the lilt to her voice. The demeanor she showed the world that meant "Kyle and I are in love, we're a couple." She couldn't even let the mask fall with her own daughter.

There had to be more to love. Had to be. Veronica would never pine after a man who couldn't give his all to her. She clutched the steering wheel tight as she drove over the Bay Bridge.

Her phone rang again. Hunter. Her mother's words echoed in Veronica's mind. She didn't sit around waiting for a man. Sure, he was out there saving lives. Which basically gave him hero status with the public, his patients, and probably his staff. Rock-star status. His hands might have been the ones that had heated her desire two nights ago, but that was a physical thing. She didn't need a date. She didn't need Hunter. What she needed was a night on the town. Something fun and flirty. Then, she'd be able to focus on whatever else needed to be done with Wade.

She was not her mother. She would only take from men what she needed, knowing they weren't capable of more.

ॐ

Hunter stalked through the automatic doors from the ED and into the moonless, humid evening. Midnight. He'd left three messages for Veronica. Turned out bungee jumping—and patching up twenty-some car victims—hadn't gotten her out of his system.

Maybe she was busy. Maybe she'd been in an accident. The thought sent shivers down his back. Too many memories there. He shouldn't let his mind consider that possibility.

He unlocked his car and leaned against the roof. He didn't drink any more, but a bar—loud talking and a crowd to get lost in—sounded good right now.

Twenty minutes later, he strolled into a local joint, slid onto a vacant barstool in the darkened room, and ordered a ginger ale.

His gaze searched the bar. He was surrounded by young men in long, baggy shorts and women in short, short skirts wearing sultry smiles and flipping long hair over their shoulders as they chatted with their heads tilted.

So many beautiful women, but none compared to Veronica. The way she wore her loose, red curls so casually, the way her golden eyes lit up when she smiled. The full, pink lips that made him want to pull her close and taste them each time he saw her....

The bartender slid his drink toward him and Hunter glanced

across the room as the front door opened. *No. Couldn't be.* As if he'd conjured her, Veronica stepped into the bar, glancing around for a quick second, and then as if sensing him, smiling as her gaze landed on him.

No woman should look so beautiful wearing a simple, dark-green scoop neck T-shirt, jeans, and flip flops. She stared across the room and then looked back toward the door as if she was contemplating leaving. She'd ignored his calls and now wanted to leave because she'd spotted him? He hadn't even told her where he'd be. It had been a last-minute decision to stop here.

Hunter's mouth went dry as she picked her way through the crowd, oblivious of the men whose gazes followed her until she stood in front of him.

"Wow, you really are psychic, aren't you?"

Her lips lifted into a smile and she leaned an elbow on the bar. His gaze slipped down her curves, and he noticed the subtle way her waist dipped in above her jeans, the way her bottom fit so well in his palms.

"You didn't return my calls." He lifted his ginger ale from the bar to keep his hands busy. To keep them from wrapping around her and pulling her near. She made no attempt to get closer. "I'm glad you're here." He took a sip of his soda to prevent any more words from tumbling out of his mouth. *I've been thinking of you ever since the other night... I can't sleep without dreaming of you....* He signaled for the bartender. "What are you drinking?"

"I figured I'd call you tomorrow. Ginger ale looks good."

Ignoring the way she changed the subject, he repeated the order to the bartender. "Here." He slid off the stool and motioned to it. "Have a seat."

"Thanks. How was your shift at the hospital?" She wiggled onto the cushioned seat.

So they were going to do the small-talk thing. All he could think about was their last time together, the way it had all felt so right. But he could do small talk. For a little while, anyway.

"Good, good." Hunter moved close, tempting himself by leaning next to her ear. He could pretend the loud noise was his reason for invading her personal space. "ED was almost calm today." Not really.

But the adrenaline rush from the bungee jump had done nothing for him, and the ED shift hadn't been its usual rush, either. The only thing that would sate his appetite right now was to be with Veronica.

And here she was. He had to find a way to convince her they could be together. Make another chink in that wall of hers. But how? When he didn't even understand what had made her build that wall in the first place?

Hunter leaned against the bar, purposefully letting his leg brush against hers. "So how was the fishing tournament?" The bartender delivered Veronica's soda and Hunter passed it to her, lingering when her fingers brushed against hers.

Flashes of energy, faster than the bungee jump rush, harder than the tense moments in the ED today, coursed through his veins.

Veronica met his gaze and studied him for a moment before her serious expression changed into a smile and she laughed. The welcome sound warmed his heart. "Let's just say it's a good thing I took a shower before coming out tonight. Things got a little smelly." She took a sip of her drink and glanced around the bar. "Thanks for asking."

A drop of the soda remained on her upper lip and it was all Hunter could do not to lean over and kiss it away. *Not yet. Give her a little time. Don't blow it by moving too fast.*

"Not to sound cliché," she said, "but do you come here often?"

He chuckled and looked around at the historic hotel bar, built in the 1770s. "Not really, but it's on the way home from the hospital. I'm surprised you'd come to a place like this. It's purported to be haunted."

Veronica glanced around and shrugged. "I know this place. It's haunted by old ghosts, but none that are angry as far as I know. Most of them come back for visits. They're not mad at anybody or anything." She took a sip of her drink and laid it on the bar. "Sometimes I search for ghosts—you know, like ghosts from the past I'd actually like to meet—but they don't show themselves."

Her face lit as if picturing these ghosts. Now this was a first. Something he never would have guessed. "Yeah? Like who?"

"Well." She glanced down, almost embarrassed, and then met his gaze. "Like the other day, I was taking photos around the city. I stopped at Westminster Hall—"

"Edgar Allan Poe's burial grounds." He smiled. "I love the place. So historic and pertinent. Such mystery."

She smiled and grabbed both of his hands. "I know! And I hung out, taking pictures, sitting and opening myself to him for over an hour." Veronica stuck out her pretty bottom lip in a mock pout. "But he never showed."

Hunter swallowed hard and stared at her. A man could only take so much. He leaned closer, pressed his lips to the corner of her mouth with the barest of touches. The second their skin connected, he lost control. She slid her hands to his shoulders, crushing his mouth to hers. Her nails dug into his shoulder blades, increasing his desire, letting him feel her passion. Passion wasn't timid. He laid his palms on the sides of her soft face and drew away, eyes still closed, holding the taste of her, wanting more, but knowing they were in public.

If only he could find his voice to invite her back to his place. Right now, his heart pounded too hard, his cock twitched with desire, and his head spun with need for this beautiful woman. But she still gave off a hesitant vibe.

He opened his eyes and saw his passion reflected in her golden eyes. Still holding her face in his hands, he let his thumbs caress the corners of her mouth. "I really love your lips."

She smiled, turning her head enough to kiss his hand. Her eyes widened, and she stared over his shoulder.

Hunter stiffened and checked behind him, seeing nothing. "Wade?" He glanced at Veronica.

"No," she whispered, her smile widening. She stood, draping an arm around Hunter's waist, and faced the area behind him. "Mr. Poe, so nice to meet you."

The hairs on Hunter's arm stood and the area around them turned cold. "Is he...is he a bad ghost or a good one?" Hunter whispered, ready to pull his body between Poe's and Veronica's in case the man—*ghost*— was dangerous.

Veronica laughed and her eyes stayed glued to the empty space. "He says thanks for the compliment, but he's not really known as a troublemaker."

What must that be like? To see someone who'd been gone from

this world for so long? She claimed to hate this power, didn't see it as a gift, but wow...the impressive things she could see.

She laughed again. "No, sir. We're sticking to ginger ale tonight, but thanks for the suggestion and have fun."

Hunter watched, not wanting to interfere, as Veronica's gaze swept to the other side of the bar as if following someone. She turned to Hunter, held both of his hands in hers as they stood close. "That was incredible. He recommended the house scotch, said he needed to check on some friends, and then tipped his hat and bowed, saying to have a fun night together."

"One of those happy wanderers?" Hunter smiled.

She was breathless. Her chest rose and fell with excitement. Seeing her happy like this gave him hope. Those walls. Those damn walls. Maybe Edgar Allan Poe was helping with those walls.

"Yes, he is definitely wandering. Happily," she said.

Hunter drew her close, burying his nose in her curls, inhaling the scent of peach shampoo that traveled through his entire system, all the way to his hardening cock.

"Well," he whispered in her ear. "You know what they say about famous poets."

She lifted her face and stood on tiptoes to kiss his lips. "No, what do they say?"

He cupped her chin. "Beats me. I just like his idea of having a fun night together." He laid a twenty-spot on the bar and jerked his head toward the door in an unspoken invitation.

Veronica smiled, took his hand, and led him out of the bar, swishing her sweet, heart-shaped ass in front of him, luring him with the promise of what was to come.

Chapter Eleven

*A*lthough it had only been ten minutes, the drive home felt like the longest of Veronica's life. He'd asked about her day and put his body between hers and Poe's when he'd suspected a possible threat. Maybe she'd misjudged him. Her body buzzed with anticipation for Hunter's touch. Seeing him there, the coincidence of him being at the one spot she'd picked tonight.... Not coincidence. Fate.

She used her fob to lock her car and the sound echoed around the apartment parking garage as Hunter's car beeped in an echo.

He wore a dark T-shirt that showed off his blue eyes and hair in the sexiest way. She'd gone out to find company tonight, but now she knew. It wasn't just anybody she needed. It was Hunter. Irritating to admit. Time to stop over-thinking and let herself enjoy. Just like she'd enjoyed that moment with Poe.

Hunter slipped an arm around her waist and guided her toward the elevator. She snuggled against him, letting herself give in to the feeling of being desired and protected by his embrace. They stepped inside, and his hand slipped lower, cradling her ass on the outside of her jeans.

She swirled toward him, fisted his shirt in her hands, and crushed her lips to his. Let him see how much she wanted him.

Too quickly, the elevator dinged, signaling the first floor. The doors opened to an empty hallway. With her hands still bunched in his shirt, she grinned and guided him out of the elevator and let go, smacking his butt with one hand as she ran past him to her apartment.

"If I'd known ginger ale made you so feisty, I would have brought you a case a long time ago." Hunter sent a crooked grin her way as he caught up to her and rubbed the small of her back, sending shivers of pleasure up and down her body as she keyed open her entry.

While she closed the door behind them, she tossed her purse and keys on the side table, and turned to face him. His blue eyes beamed with an intensity she felt, too. With a sigh, she took in his expansive chest and the way his black T-shirt clung to his muscular build. It made her want to rip it from collar to hem.

"Oh, it's not the ginger ale." She kicked off her flip-flops while holding his gaze and thought about dragging this out...building the passion until it was unbearable and then unleashing it. "It's your hot body."

Veronica closed the distance between them, and skimmed her hands up the front of his shirt, needing to feel his skin. So hot it almost burned against her palms. With a playful shove, she pressed him against the door, and he grasped her waist, then bent to capture her lips. Moaning at the heat that traveled through her marrow, she swept her tongue against his, wishing she could make this night last forever.

His warm tongue explored the inside of her mouth, teasing, tempting...before tracing a line around her lips.

"You're the most beautiful woman I've ever known, Veronica." Hot breath caressed her ear and his hands cupped her bottom and squeezed. "Let me show you how much I've wanted you since the first time I saw you."

She crushed her hips against him in answer, suddenly unable to find her voice. Her body shook with need, and not just for anyone. For Hunter. For the man who made her feel normal...alive...understood.

As if she weighed no more than a stuffed animal, he lifted her. She wrapped her legs around his waist, laughing and arching her back as she threw her arms around his neck to hold on. "I can walk, you know."

"Mmmm," he murmured, burying a kiss at the base of her neck. "I like this method of transportation much better."

As they walked, she bounced against him, her crotch rubbing

against his lengthy erection, with each step inducing a glorious ache between her legs. "Well, uh, since you're pretty much driving me crazy here, have it your way."

Pulling her even closer, he headed past the kitchen, down the small hallway, and into her bedroom. At last, they stood by her brass bed with the antique ivory quilt. "I like the sound of that invitation."

Slowly, tenderly, he effortlessly shifted her to one hip as if she weighed half as much as she did. In the dim light from the hallway, his muscles bunched and expanded, his strength enveloping her.

With a tug, he pulled the quilt and sheet aside, scooped her into both arms, and laid her down gently, as if she were a treasure.

She wanted to pull him atop her, feel his weight cover her. Wanted him to take her somewhere she'd never been. Fast and hard.

But the mattress shifted as he sat beside her, reminding her that there might only be one time for them and she wanted it to last. After lying next to her, he scooped an arm under her body and rolled her toward him. He enveloped her with his other arm, bringing the front of her body to the front of his. His erection pressed against her, making her crave every inch of him inside her, now.

He might be taking the lead, but she would make sure he knew what she wanted, too. She arched her hips against him, grinding against his hard cock. Very hard cock. She moaned and found his mouth and as he pulled her tighter, she clawed at the back of his shirt, pulling the fabric up, until his abs and back were both bare.

With a final flick of her tongue, she pulled away and he shifted to let her tug off his shirt. The bare chest she'd admired earlier in the week, the same chest she'd yearned to touch, now spread before her in its muscular glory. She smiled, pushed him to his back, and straddled him. Slowly, she ran her hands up his taut belly, lingering on his strong pecs, and then cupped his jaw in her hands before bending to kiss his mouth.

He groaned and ran his hands inside her shirt. "No fair. I'm topless and you're not."

She tugged her shirt over her head and shook out her hair, leaning forward, teasing him. Sitting on him, clad only in her black lace bra and jeans, feeling his erection press against her, made her ache for him. Her hands trembled and she drew in a shaky breath. "Better?"

"Almost." With a flick of his hand, the clasp of her bra came undone. She laughed and shrugged out of it and he tossed it to the floor, cupping her breasts in his warm palms.

His thumbs stroked the area around her nipples, slowly growing closer to her peaks. Veronica closed her eyes, letting the feel of his powerful fingers take over her senses.

"Come closer." He slid his hands from her breasts, up her sides, and pulled her against him.

His heart hammered and her breasts pressed against his bare chest. The vibration raced from the tip of her head to the spot between her legs. His cock pressed against her crotch, intensifying her need for him. Every damn inch of her craved his touch, every muscle and joint shook with anticipation. He was different. She could trust him. This could work.

Swiftly, he rolled to the side, holding her close, and straddled her. Gazing up, she caught him grinning, and ran a hand through his dark hair, letting the thick strands slowly graze her fingertips.

Skilled fingers made their way to the waistband of her jeans. He paused, resting his hand against her skin, and bent to lay a trail of kisses on her belly, while bringing his hands back to her breasts, kneading, stroking, until she arched her hips and he loosened the zipper, yanked off her jeans, and tossed them off the bed.

Veronica's heart pounded with anticipation. Her skin burned with desire. Every place he touched, he left her wanting more, needing him.

He kneeled between her legs, taking a knee in each hand, spreading her. Cool air washed across her most intimate areas. She was open...vulnerable...clad only in a thin lace thong.

Hunter's dark hair stood in disarray, the effect of her hands combing through his locks earlier. Even in the shadowy light, she knew he was waiting for a signal from her, that what they were doing was okay.

"I want you, Hunter," she said, reaching for his face with her hands. "I want all of you, and I don't want you to hold back."

A low groan emanated from his throat and he crawled up her body, resting on one arm as he kissed her lips. His hand dipped inside her underpants, and she gasped as his slickened fingers opened her folds, circling her most sensitive area. She cried out and clutched the sheet and his fingers trailed lower, sliding inside, filling her.

Cool air replaced his warm hand as he pulled her panties down her legs, dragging the lacy fabric past her feet.

His warm breath fanned the sensitive area at the top of first her right, then her left thigh, and she reached down to grasp his head, bring him closer to her heat. To hell with restraint and self-control. She needed to feel his mouth on her. Now.

With a moan, he pulled her hips to the edge of the bed, hooking her knees over his shoulders. His warm fingers spread her skin, and his breath touched her clit, just before his tongue did. He made small circles at first, small and slow flicks that sent her hands to his hair, holding him tight. She gasped for breath as he swept his tongue over her clit.

Sweat pooled on her neck as passion ripped from head to toe.

"Mmm," he moaned, the vibration setting off sensations that fired through her body and out her fingers like shooting stars. "I love the taste of you."

Every nerve cell danced, every piece of her was charged with electricity. Everything about Hunter excited her, from his smile to his endless energy...to the way his tongue and fingers found the exact spots that made her crazy with desire.

The aching between her legs gave way to a shot of intense pleasure that sped to her core as Hunter's hands moved to her ass, and squeezed. That small movement sent his tongue deeper, lit into her like a thousand fireflies glowing in the night. She dug her hands into his strong shoulders, riding out the orgasm that blast through her, for what seemed like minutes, as brilliant colors filled the darkness behind her closed eyes.

"Hunter," she gasped. Veronica lay panting on the sheet, his head resting on her thigh as she stroked his hair, unable to move any other part of her body. At least for now.

"I...." She fought to catch her breath. "Wow...."

"You're amazing, Veronica." Hunter slid his hands under her knees. Instead of laying her down on the bed, sidling next to her as she thought he might, he lifted her body against his chest, tugged the quilt off the bottom of the bed, and then lowered them both to the floor.

When his erection pressed against her stomach, she buried the sudden urge to nuzzle against his neck and coo. After an orgasm that wracked her brain and body, she wouldn't have thought one minute would be enough time to reignite the fire, but his cock did the trick.

"Want to see some out-of-this-world powers?" she teased, running her hand between their bodies, snapping the button on his jeans in search of his thick length.

Ë

It wouldn't take a psychic to figure out Hunter's needs right now. Veronica's hot, taut body, clad in lacy underwear, had been too much to resist. He'd planned to take it slow, make it last, make love to her for a long, long time. Her body had other ideas as she'd taken everything he'd offered. God, he loved how she'd done that. No reservations, no holding back. She'd let him take her. Those walls were coming down and he would make sure she never regretted that she'd risked it all with him.

His cock longed for relief, but at the same time, he yearned to hold Veronica against him, to stall the desire for just a moment to be close to her. That wasn't how it used to be with a woman. Often, he'd been a man driven by passion and desire. A man who seized the moment. But Hunter wanted so much more than a moment with Veronica.

Her hand slid between their bodies as they lay on the quilt on her bedroom floor and he eased his hold on her just a little, skimming his hands down her spine. She kissed the base of his neck, sucking gently as she grasped his cock in her hand and stroked.

"Damn, lady," he whispered into her ear. "You do crazy things to me."

He felt her smile against his chest. "Oh no. You haven't seen crazy yet."

With the swiftness of a cat, she shifted position, pinning his shoulders to the floor.

"You'd make a hell of a wrestler, you know that?" Hunter

swallowed a chuckle as Veronica yanked down his jeans and boxers and then wiggled her ass close to his cock, skimming the tip just enough to torture, but not offer release.

"Uh huh. And maybe we'll do a best two-out-of-three match." Her words were husky as she nipped his earlobe, his jaw line, and then the base of his throat before spreading her palms on his chest.

He cleared his throat. "Wallet. Front right pocket. There's a condom."

She grinned, pulled out the leather billfold, and tossed it to him. "I'm not the kind of girl who searches someone's private stuff."

"I beg to differ. You're doing a damn good job searching my privates." Chuckling, Hunter pulled out the condom, threw his wallet to the floor, and grasped the foil packet.

Veronica snatched it from him, opened it with her teeth, and blew the wrapper to the floor. "I am, however, the type of woman who wants to take her time rolling this thin protection over the most sensitive and swollen part of your body."

Dim light speared into the room, casting shadows, allowing him to see Veronica's shapely outline as she lifted herself off him, turning her body toward his feet. Slowly, torturously, she rolled on the condom. She squatted, giving him a perfect view of her round ass as she teased him, practically floating above his cock, promising...but not taking anything as she rolled the condom on him.

She smiled over her shoulder, her long, red hair fanning down her back, ending at the shapeliest ass he'd ever seen, and she lowered herself and rubbed her slick folds along his shaft.

He grunted and twitched, needing to feel her around him, needing to fill her. So close. So goddamned close to having all of her. She leaned forward with the balance of an acrobat and stroked between his legs, massaging his balls as she sank onto him.

He lifted his hips, a strong thrust that made her cry out as she pressed deeper and grabbed his upper thighs. Holding her butt, guiding her, he watched as she bounced up and down on him with abandon. Nobody he'd ever been with had been like this. There was only one Veronica. And he needed her like nothing he'd ever needed before.

Her folds stroked and massaged his dick as her body rocked up and down, taking him deeper. She let out a small moan. The sight of her, the knowledge that she was turned on all over again by his dick inside her.... He held her tight against him, needing to feel her skin, as much of as her as possible, as he ground into her softness, taking her, letting her take him.

"Yes, Hunter!" she cried out.

His name off her lips sent him over the edge. He couldn't keep a lid on this desire any longer. His body stiffened as his cock slid deeper, his hips thrust farther, and he shuddered, holding tight to the woman on top of him, the one who'd brought out this need. She satisfied him in so many ways.

Chapter Twelve

*V*eronica inhaled the sweet, musky scent of Hunter before opening her eyes to the sunlight that filtered through the curtains. His strong arms held her securely, as they had through the entire night while they'd slept on the thick carpet and quilt. Neither one of them had wanted to move. Or maybe they hadn't had the energy to move after the second time they'd made love.

"Are you always this beautiful first thing in the morning?" His stubbled cheek brushed her forehead and she lifted her face in search of his mouth. His warm, firm lips reminded her of the way they'd roamed her body last night.

"Are you always so...." She reached between them to his erection. "So, *ready* in the morning?

He chuckled, slid a hand down her stomach, and inched his fingers to the moist spot between her legs.

Ten minutes later, they lay side by side, panting and smiling. Veronica leaned on one elbow, completely at ease in her nakedness, and let her gaze run from his dark hair, to his curved lips, past his strong chest that rose and fell from their lovemaking, to the rest of his spectacular body.

The guy was a freaking god. Not a centimeter of flab. Perfect. The kind of guy she avoided. But not this time. Not this guy.

"Well." He cupped her chin in his palm. "As much as I'd love to have you stare at my naked body all day...." He let his gaze drift to her breasts as they rubbed his chest. "Or stare at your naked body all day...I have to head to the hospital for a few hours to finish some paperwork before we meet with Sam Junior and Tia."

Damn, the guy sure did work a lot. She could relate. Work was what kept her sane. Maybe it was his sanity, too.

Hunter leaned close, pressed a kiss on her lips and stood, holding out a hand to pull her to her feet.

"Want some coffee, or breakfast first?" Veronica wasn't used to men spending the night, especially one she was starting to fall for.

What? No. Not falling for him. Lust. This was about lust and longing. Sex. He was sexy. She needed sex.

"Ahhh, coffee. Yes, please." He handed over her lacy underwear from last night and she rolled her eyes, tossed them to the corner, and stepped into her jeans. Let him think about that while he was at work. Let him wonder if she ever put underwear back on when she met up with him later.

He brewed the pot of coffee while she gathered mugs, milk, and sugar. So weird. This togetherness. She swirled, still holding a little pitcher of milk, spilling some on the floor as she turned. "I don't usually do this, you know."

Hunter raised a brow as the fragrant liquid dripped into the pot, filling the kitchen with the strong scent of java. "You don't usually have coffee in the morning?"

Veronica narrowed her eyes, but the edges of her mouth quivered. She had a feeling he knew exactly what she was saying, but he wasn't going to make it easy for her. Fine by her.

She tossed a paper towel on the floor to blot the mess, scooped it up, and threw it in the nearby trash. "I told you I don't have a lot of respect for my dad."

Hunter nodded, his face turning solemn.

"He's freakin' married." She slapped her hands against the sides of her jeans in emphasis. "Yet he sleeps with other women all the time. And my mother turns a blind eye to it all. In the name of love."

He closed the distance between them, took her hands in his. "Sounds like their problem, not yours."

Veronica liked the sound of that. Liked that he believed it. "I've dated a few too many guys like him to trust my own judgment."

"You can trust me," he said, lowering his hands to her waist and meeting her gaze. Such honesty in those blue eyes, such passion. She could let go and believe, right? It would be okay. She had to trust someone sometime. Why not Hunter? The man who helped so many others? The man who thrived on saving lives for a living?

She leaned against him, feeling a measure of relief she'd never allowed herself before.

"I wish I didn't have to go to the hospital today," he murmured, his chest vibrating with his words, bringing a sense of comfort.

She placed her palms on his shirt and pushed back with a smile. "Hey, I have things to do, too. You gotta get out of here so I can things done in time to meet with Wade's neighbors." She frowned. "Speaking of which...where has he been lately?" She stared toward the door. "Wonder if he's out there waiting."

"I haven't felt any cold spots...haven't had anything weird happen at my place or the hospital." He filled a mug and handed it to her. "Cream? Sugar?"

"Black," she said, accepting the mug.

"I like mine sweet," Hunter said, swatting her butt before turning to pour sugar and milk into his mug and then filling it with coffee. He took a long gulp. "Mind if I take this to go?" He wiggled his brows. "I can hold the mug hostage to force you to come to my place tonight to pick it up."

Veronica laughed, suddenly aware she hadn't laughed so much in one week in such a long time. Longer than she could remember. "Or, I could make breakfast for dinner. Blueberry pancakes and bacon."

"Mmm." He hugged her close with one arm and kissed the corner of her mouth. "A woman after my heart and my stomach. I love breakfast for dinner."

He'd probably meant his words casually, but she froze. His heart? No. This was all moving too fast.

"See you around three? Want me to pick you up or meet you there at Sam Junior's?" He made his way to the front door.

She forced a smile. "I'll meet you there. I have some errands to run anyway." Distance would help her figure this out, wouldn't it? Time away from him while he worked and she cooked her way out of the sex-induced stupor that made her think crazy thoughts about Hunter. And separate cars meant less forced togetherness, too. At least until she could sort out what was real and what was not.

ख

An hour later, Veronica closed her apartment door behind her, invigorated by a long shower and an afternoon of cooking ahead of her. If she was going to have junk food for dinner, she'd better head to the store and get some healthy salad ingredients so she could fill up on vegetables for lunch.

"Veronica." A soft voice made her spin to her right and the hairs on her arm stood.

A beautiful woman—no, a beautiful dark-haired ghost, wearing pearls over a fitted black dress—smiled and tilted her head.

"Who—what do you—"

"My name is Dianna."

Hunter's wife. Veronica's hand flew to her mouth.

"I'm sorry," the woman said, her voice soft, her smile genuine. "I didn't mean to scare you. It's just...well, thank you for making Hunter happy. He is a wonderful man and you make a great couple."

The hallway turned warmer, and the woman was gone. Veronica's heart pounded. She could tell herself she'd imagined the whole thing, but she knew better. Happiness warred with guilt. Dianna had died, still loving Hunter. Her time with Hunter had ended. Veronica was at the beginning of—well, something—with Hunter.

What did it mean that Dianna's ghost had appeared? Did it mean she was one of the rare ghosts who could cross from the hereafter to the human world at will? Did it mean Dianna had been hanging around quietly, waiting for Hunter to find happiness? And that Veronica was Hunter's happiness, so she'd just disappeared into the next world?

But the last idea didn't make sense. If Dianna's ghost haunted this world, wouldn't she have tried to stop Wade from bothering Hunter? Was it possible Dianna only had enough spiritual energy to appear to

Veronica? Maybe she should have embraced her powers more, sought answers from other psychic-mediums. Avoiding her gift made it harder to understand.

A shadow shifted at the end of the hallway and Wade waved and moved toward her.

"Where have you been?" she asked, meeting him in the middle of the corridor.

He grinned. "Following the guys."

"Did you find anything out about your past?" she asked, strolling toward the door leading to the steps.

He shook his head. "Nah. They didn't talk about me or the old days. But they talked a lot about football and that was fun."

"Want to walk with me to the store? I need veggies. Don't be offended if I don't talk to you, though." She winked at him. "Can't have the public thinking I'm talking to air."

"Sure." Wade laughed and held the door open and stood to the side to let her through instead of walking through it like he'd done every other time.

"You're getting stronger in this world," she said.

"I know. I thought about picking up the football and throwing it at the receiver yesterday."

Veronica's eyes widened as she reached the bottom step and Wade opened the door to the lobby level. All clear, nobody close enough to notice an entryway opening by itself or her talking to someone nobody else could see. "But you didn't, right?"

He chuckled. "No. I sat on my hands."

Wade had started out as a pesky ghost, bothering Hunter to the point where he hadn't slept well and feared distraction at work. In the short time Wade had been able to communicate with living beings, he'd changed. Now he was probably more like the kid he'd been when he'd died.

Veronica whispered out of the side of her mouth. "Was Sam Junior at practice yesterday?"

Wade nodded. "Yeah, I remember him better now. And his sister. We all spent a lot of time together."

"Hunter arranged to sit down with Sam Junior and Tia at three.

It'd be great to have you there. If you guys were close, they might say something that rings a bell for you but doesn't register for us."

They walked onto the busy city sidewalk into the heat and morning sunshine.

Wade faced her. "Do you think we'll ever figure out what's keeping me here?"

She moved to the side to let hurrying pedestrians pass, and nodded. "We'll keep working until we do." She laid a hand on Wade's upper arm, suddenly not caring who thought she was crazy as she stood near the building talking to herself. This gift had to have a purpose, and she'd be damn sure she used it for all it was worth. Besides, they only had a week before Wade could turn dangerous.

Forty-five minutes later, with her mind still focused on what she was missing about Wade's time on earth, she stood at her kitchen counter chopping tomatoes as if on auto-pilot. The wooden cutting board in her kitchen knocked with each cut until she tossed the fragrant vegetable in with the spinach and onions. A little diced red pepper, and her salad would be complete.

Wade had opted to hang out at the football field until later, hoping to catch some friends in an impromptu practice session. She had to give him an A for effort, but his method wasn't yielding any answers. At least it kept him busy and granted Hunter some ghost-free time at the hospital.

Pain shot up her arm and she cried out as blood oozed from her fingertip. Oh come on. She knew how to chop like a freaking professional. She never cut herself. Cringing, she whirled and grabbed a paper towel, wrapping it tight around the tip of her left middle finger.

Carefully, she peeled the towel back, almost afraid to look. A lot of blood pooled on the wooden cutting board.

Gritting her teeth, she stared at the still-bleeding gash. Not a clean cut. She must have yanked her finger back instinctively as she'd sliced it. Shuddering, she wrapped it again, holding it high above her head to stop the blood flow, and headed to her bathroom for the first-aid kit.

A thorough cleaning, antiseptic, and taped-on gauze pad didn't halt the bleeding. She held her hand high over her head and stared at herself in the bathroom mirror.

Hunter would tell her she needed the Emergency Department. Well, he'd told her that when she'd stepped on glass, too and her foot had been fine.

But her finger throbbed. Why take a chance? She could even ask for him. That way she'd feel less stupid if it wasn't serious enough for a hospital visit. And she could tell him about seeing Dianna.

Or not. Why bring old love into things?

In spite of the two layers of gauze and first-aid tape wound tight around her injury, blood drizzled to Veronica's wrist as she pulled her Civic into a spot in the ED parking lot.

Well, at least she wasn't overreacting. It was still bleeding. Probably not a good sign.

So why was she more nervous about seeing Hunter than she was about any potential lingering injury to her hand? They'd crossed that line, that was why. They weren't just neighbors, they were lovers and this would be the first time they'd see each other in public after making love.

She shrugged off the thought and hurried across the air-conditioned lobby. After signing in, she took a seat in a brown vinyl chair, holding her hand above her head. The bleeding had slowed, but not stopped.

A shadowy figure moved in the corner of the waiting room and Veronica narrowed her eyes. *Not now.* Hospitals were full of ghosts and she was not in the mood to deal with any. Concentrating hard, she communicated to all of them that they were not to approach her. Sometimes it worked, sometimes it didn't. Some ghosts ignored pleas for peace and some respected it.

The shadowy figures paced, but didn't approach her.

To distract herself, she glanced around the room. A mother held a crying little boy on a seat near Veronica. An elderly man sat in a wheelchair with one very swollen leg propped up. Across the room, a uniformed man slid a long, rectangular mop quietly across the tiled and sterile floor.

A woman came out and called a name and the man in the wheelchair rolled toward the registration desk. Veronica knew all about triage, and a cut finger wasn't a priority. May as well settle herself for a bit of a wait.

No sooner than she shifted her position to get more comfortable, than the uniformed woman called her name.

Veronica followed her, through automatic doors that swished open, and the woman guided her to a peach curtained area with an examining table. They passed more ghosts, who glanced at Veronica, but didn't approach. Leaning on a portable computer with wheels, the woman asked a dozen questions, smiled, and then put a blood pressure cuff on Veronica.

"Can I request Dr. Hunter Anderson? He's my neighbor." The cuff tightened around her arm.

"Sure, I'll let him know," the woman said, squinting at the machine and typing numbers into her computer. Thirty seconds later, she was gone.

Veronica relaxed into the stiff paper on the cushioned table and held her hand out. No more bleeding, but her finger throbbed against the bandages. Maybe she should take them off.

Whispering voices outside the curtain caught her attention and she held her breath, trying to quiet the area so she could hear better.

"Sure, wouldn't we all like Dr. Hunter to take care of us," a woman said.

"Yeah, he can take care of me in the supply closet if he wants." Different voice, still female.

Veronica stiffened. They were making fun of her request to see Hunter? Was he the staff hottie with a reputation for hook-ups at work?

Veronica's breath caught in her throat and all the pain from her finger disappeared. And reappeared in her chest.

She'd been so stupid. So fucking stupid to think Hunter was any different. He wasn't a one-woman sort of guy. How could he be? Guys who looked like him, with his charm, had a phone address book full of beautiful women he could call on in a moment's notice.

She swung her legs off the examining table and grabbed her purse from the counter. A butterfly bandage was all she'd needed. Not stitches. But this hadn't been a wasted trip. She knew why Hunter spent so much time at work now.

Whipping the curtain open, she came face to face with Hunter. He grinned and his blue eyes lit up. "Veronica—great to see you. What are you—"

"I—I have to go. I'll stop on my way out to pay what I owe. See you at three." She tried to brush past him, but he caught her upper arm. His warm hand on her skin scorched her senses because she knew she wouldn't be feeling his touch again. Not the way she wanted to, anyway.

"Wait. What happened to your finger?"

Fine. He wouldn't let her leave without an explanation. She'd give him one. "I cut it while slicing vegetables." She glanced over his shoulder at the two nearby nurses' aides who busied themselves with paperwork. "And another thing. I saw Dianna this morning. Outside my apartment. She gave us her blessing. But really, there's nothing to bless, is there?"

Chapter Thirteen

*H*unter leaned his elbows onto his office desk, cradling his head in his palms, his white doctor's coat parting as he stared at the oblong box on with a bow on it. Meant as a thank you gesture. Instead, it was poison that laughed at him, mocked his control.

A bottle of his favorite whiskey from a patient whose life he'd saved. Turns out, he owned a liquor store.

He sighed. *Really*? He should laugh. Usually he would. But the look on Veronica's face—and he knew what put that look there once he spotted the two nurses' assistants. The ones who liked to gossip more than work. He wasn't her father. Had never—and would never—date anyone from the hospital.

But to Veronica, it had to be a slap in the face. She'd started to trust him, believe he was different.

He stared at the foil box, almost tasting the smooth, soothing burn of the liquor. He'd been stupid. Believed he could change Veronica's mind about men, and in the process he'd opened himself again to the worst possible pain: Losing someone he cared about.

He stroked a finger over the raised foil on the box and tugged at the blue bow on top. Dianna had appeared to Veronica? Did that mean she was one of the happy wanderers Veronica had mentioned? The hurt of losing his wife slammed back as if it were that night again.

He was stronger now, though. He'd made it through those lonely months and worked his way through the guilt of not being there. Yes, he'd been weak and used prescription drugs and alcohol. They hadn't eased the pain. Masked it. But didn't take it away.

He pushed away from his desk and took a deep breath. Wade would be moving on soon. Veronica would likely move out of his life. All he needed was his work. Always a rush. Caring took so much energy.

Turning away from the liquor bottle showed he had strength. Maybe he had enough strength to fight for Veronica, too.

He might not have been able to fight to keep his wife with him, but he sure as fuck wasn't going to let Veronica go without a battle. She had no idea how hard he was willing to fight. But he wouldn't scare her away. There was time. He'd take it slow.

He grabbed the box from his desk and strode to the door. The two busybody nurses' aides could probably use some spirits for their weekend drinks.

❦

Veronica swallowed hard and stood when Hunter pulled behind her car and parked. She'd half-expected him to be a no-show, but really...they were here to solve his ghost problem, so he had to come.

Wade stood next to her, so at least there was a diversion. Not that their conversation with Sam Junior and Tia wouldn't be enough of a distraction.

Hunter stepped closer. He'd changed from his dressier work clothes into casual shorts and a black polo that made his hair disappear into the collar. Suddenly, she wanted to run her hand along his neck, pull his hair out.

"How's the cut?" He glanced at her bandaged finger.

"Not bad. Some gauze and tape did the trick." Not the complete truth. She'd needed to wrap a few layers around it to keep the blood from leaking out, and it still throbbed. Still, it hurt less than knowing the man she'd been starting to fall for had a harem of women at the hospital.

"Good. Let me know if you want me to take a look at it." He tilted his head toward an old brick townhouse to the left of Cissy

Montgomery's place. Wade's former residence. "This the house?"

Wade's mom was at work, so they'd waited on his front steps. Veronica had hoped being at his former home would bring back memories for Wade. Instead, he'd commented the neighborhood was a little familiar, but nothing more.

"Yep, this one." She glanced at Wade. "Wade's here, too. He's hoping what these two say will jog his memory."

Hunter nodded and followed her up the crooked, cracked sidewalk to the brick townhouse with a small cement porch enclosed by a sturdy iron rail.

Mrs. Beck, a woman in her early fifties sporting a hotel uniform and wearing a stylish scarf that showed off her dark skin, smiled and opened the outer door as if she'd been waiting.

"Ms. Matthews, Dr. Anderson," she said, shaking each of their hands as they moved inside the cozy living room that smelled like oranges.

"Oh, please call me Veronica, Mrs. Beck. Thanks so much for taking time to meet with us." Wade stayed one step behind her, keeping between her and Hunter.

"Yes, that goes for me too. And please call me Hunter."

"Only if you call me Lydia. I have to be at work in twenty minutes, but Wade's momma—Cissy—she says it's okay that you're here when I'm not. Tia's twenty, but she's still a young lady, and I'm pretty protective of her."

"Sounds like you're a smart mama," Veronica said.

Lydia waved them down a narrow hallway decorated on both sides with pictures of two children, a boy and a girl as they progressed through the years. "I've made some iced tea. It's cooler in the kitchen. We don't have air conditioning but the ceiling fan does a mighty good job of keeping things cool as long as I don't turn the stove on."

Two young adults sat across from each other at a shined and polished kitchen table. Tia—who sported dark hair pulled back into a low pony tail, glanced up from a laptop where she was typing.

"Tia's taking an online class to get ahead for next semester." Lydia's shoulders straightened. "She's on the dean's list at college."

Tia smiled and waved and Veronica waved back and then focused her attention on the young man—boy, really—who sat across from his sister. He glared at them with narrowed eyes as he leaned back and folded his arms on his chest.

Lydia gestured to the two empty seats on either side of her children and then walked to the cupboard. "Since you're trying to find out about Wade's life, let me start because I have to go soon." She marched to the refrigerator, retrieved a pitcher of tea, and filled the two glasses she'd pulled out.

"We'd appreciate that," Hunter said, sitting to Sam Junior's right.

Lydia placed the glasses in front of them, and sighed. "Such a sad time when Wade died. He was a good kid. And his momma was such a good mother. I think it's great that you're interviewing people who knew him so you can determine the scholarship winners who are most like him."

Veronica glanced toward Wade, who stood behind Sam Junior, staring at him.

"Good at football," Sam Junior said. He wore a red shirt with a football logo and had hair trimmed close to his scalp.

"And good at helping others." Lydia placed a hand on Sam Junior's shoulder and smiled. "He took my Sammy under his wing after his daddy left us. Tutored him—tutored Tia in math, too—" Lydia shook her head. "I think the Lord needed another angel, that's why He took our Wade."

Lydia's cell phone beeped and she wiped a tear from her eye. "That's my alarm. Need to head to work." She kissed the top of Sam Junior's head and blew Tia a kiss. "In bed at a decent time and lock the doors after Mr. Hunter and Ms. Veronica leave, okay?"

Tia nodded and Sam Junior groaned.

A few seconds later, the front screen door slammed shut.

"Nice that you're starting a scholarship in Wade's name. Not many kids from his school get to go to college." Tia shut her computer and looked from Veronica to Hunter, blushing when Hunter smiled at her.

Yeah, yeah. Dr. Hottie crush.

Wade walked around the table and leaned closer to study Tia. Her eyes widened and she rubbed her hands on her bare upper arms and shivered.

"I spent a lot of time with her," Wade said, a smile splitting his face. "She made me laugh."

Veronica pressed her lips together to keep from responding, part of her wishing she could pass Hunter a note, let him know what Wade was saying. Maybe this was it. Maybe something between Tia and Wade was keeping Wade tethered to this world. Maybe he loved her and had to let her go so she could live her life.

Veronica raised her finger the slightest amount, letting Hunter know she'd take the lead this time. He lifted his tea and took a long drink, showing he understood. Veronica's heart skipped a beat. They got each other.

They just couldn't *have* each other.

"Wade had a lot of friends—"

"I was his best friend," Sam Junior said.

"I've heard that from a lot of people." Veronica smiled and glanced at Tia. She needed to really concentrate on Tia's reaction to the next question. Spot any gestures, anything she might try to hide. "How about a girlfriend? Did Wade have a girlfriend?"

Tia's gaze shifted to the floor and she pressed her lips together as she shook her head. "No, his mom wouldn't let him date."

Oh yeah...something definitely going on there. This could be a matter of Wade letting go of the girl he loved. Not easy, but once she knew how to help him....

Sam Junior chuckled. "Wade had a secret girlfriend."

Wade whirled, shifting his attention from Tia to his young friend, and he frowned.

Hunter leaned toward Sam Junior "Secret?" he asked.

Tia glared at her brother. "If it's a secret, Sammy, you need to keep it a secret."

Veronica wanted to pull the girl in for a hug. Two years and she still cared so much? Lucky guy. This kid was only twenty and she'd already experienced a deeper love than Veronica had at age twenty-eight.

"I'm not telling a secret." He scraped his chair back on the tile floor and strolled to the back door where a worn and tattered camouflage backpack lay.

Veronica exchanged a look with Hunter and then risked a glace at Wade who stared at Sam Junior

"What are you doing?" Tia bolted from her chair to the spot where Sam Junior stood.

Sam Junior unzipped a small compartment, pulling out a necklace. A simple black cord with a small pewter peace sign. Sam Junior held it in the air like a prized possession. "His lucky charm. His girlfriend gave it to him."

"Put it away. It's not yours," Tia said.

"My necklace," Wade said.

Hunter and Veronica crossed the room and Veronica reached out to touch the peace sign as it dangled in Sam Junior's hand. Instead of cool pewter on her finger, sudden pain—like a fist—slammed at Veronica's upper arm. She gasped and her head ached as if it were full of shaking, exploding rocks.

Sam Junior let go of the necklace and it puddled into Veronica's palm. Her airwaves constricted, she fought to catch her breath. Black— a darkness so thick she could feel it—swarmed through her head. Pain ricocheted around her skull as she fell to the floor with the necklace clasped in her hand.

ೞ

Hunter grabbed Veronica's shoulders before her head connected with the linoleum.

"What's wrong? What's the matter? Should I call nine-one-one?" Tia's eyes were wide and she pulled her cell phone out of her shorts with hands that shook so hard, her phone dropped to the floor.

Sam Junior stared at Veronica.

"Not yet. I think she needs some air, not an ambulance." He laid her down gently, felt for the pulse in her neck. Fast, but not a medical emergency. Cold air circulated around him. Wade. Damn how he wished he could communicate with Wade, see if the kid knew what was going on.

Hunter lifted the black cord from Veronica's hand to examine it, one hand stroking Veronica's scalp, willing her to come back while he studied the peace sign trinket that hung from the necklace. She blinked against the bright sunlight streaming in through the back door.

"Veronica?" He leaned forward, his face close to hers. Cool air surrounded them again and he sensed Wade hovering.

"Something…." she whispered, her voice hoarse. "That necklace…somebody is in trouble and hurt. We need to find her."

He stared at the pewter peace sign and at the two kids whose worried gazes pinned him. As soon as he'd taken the jewelry from Veronica, she'd become more alert. Did she realize it? Better move her, away from prying eyes and ears so they could talk.

He held her wrist, checked her pulse again. Normal. "Okay, let's get you outside. I think you need some fresh air. Can you sit?"

She nodded. "Tia," she whispered. "Is this your necklace?"

Tia pressed her lips together and shook her head.

"Do you know whose it is?" Veronica's gaze moved from the girl to the black cord in Hunter's hand.

Tia stared at the ground, silent.

"Do you mind if we borrow the necklace tonight?" Hunter asked, holding Veronica's elbow as she maneuvered to her feet. Was she affected by this pendant more than she was letting on? Maybe she was forgetting that she hated him.

"It's mine." Sam Junior reached out for the necklace. "Wade asked me to keep it for him during the game."

Tia snatched it from him. "It's not yours, you were just holding it." She handed it to Hunter with a concerned expression.

Sam Junior crossed his arms and glared at his sister.

"Let me get Veronica outside now." He draped her arm over his shoulder, and she clasped her arm around his waist and together they staggered to the front door. She'd hardly wanted to be around him, earlier, much less be touched by him. Her willingness to cling to him now knotted his gut with worry.

After a quick goodbye to the kids, he took the car keys Veronica offered and lowered her to the front seat, reclining it. Her hands flew to her head and she moaned.

"The necklace," she whispered so slightly that he had to lean closer. "I'm connected to the person who wore it. We have to find out. I don't think it's Tia...she's not in pain. Whoever that necklace belongs to—whoever Wade's girlfriend was—she's in trouble and we need to find her. Soon."

Just as he figured. That's why her symptoms had lessened when he'd snatched the strand away. Was this what happened when she helped the police find missing people? She went through the same hell the victims were going through? He had to end this and end it quickly.

"Is Wade here? Can he help?" Hunter straightened, looked around the sidewalk. Cool air surrounded his hand, opening his fingers and the necklace pulled from his hand to hang in mid-air.

"Wade's next to you," Veronica said. "Good job, Wade. What do you feel?" After a pause, Veronica shook her head. "It's okay. Try to think about it. Picture a girl...." She turned her attention to Hunter. "Hunter, you need to go back to that door. Use every ounce of charm you have and woo Tia into telling you what she knows. Smile. Do that sexy eye thing you do to get your way. Charm her into telling you."

He raised a brow. Sexy eye thing? All the things she supposedly hated about him and now she wanted him to use them. "That's creepy. The girl's only twenty."

"She's got a major crush on you. Do it."

With a glance toward the front door, he laid a hand on Veronica's shoulder. She looked better. Her face had more color now. "You sure you're okay?"

She nodded her head toward the front door. "Go."

Pretty demanding for someone who'd just fainted. Telling it like it was, telling him exactly how she felt. Did she know how rare that was? How damned refreshing?

He turned and then raced up the steps. After two quick raps on the door, Tia opened it.

He grinned and kept his voice soft. "Tia. I need your help. Please." Sexy eyes? What the hell had she meant? He tilted his head down just a little, feeling like a puppy dog begging for a treat. "Who is she? Where does she live?" He sighed. *Fuck charming.* This girl had to understand how important this was. "Her life might be in danger. You could save it. We couldn't save Wade, only memorialize him. Tia...let's save this girl."

Tears filled the girl's brown eyes and she bit her bottom lip for a few seconds. "Jasmine. The coach's daughter. He took the bus to see her, and she took the bus in from her part of town to see Wade sometimes. I'm not sure where she lives. Somewhere near Arundel Mills Mall. I saw her there once when I went to the movies."

The coach's daughter? The way that man felt about women? Had to be tough to be his daughter. Recognition dawned. Red face. Alcoholic. The disrespect his obviously had for women. They had to find her and find her now.

"Thanks, Tia. You did the right thing." He turned and raced down the steps, almost tripping on the cracked pavement. Arundel Mills Mall was south of the city. About a thirty-minute drive. What was the quickest way to find the coach's address?

Should he call the police? And tell them what? I think somebody might be getting beat up? He didn't have an address to phone in an anonymous report. She might not even be at her house. Better not risk the one shot they had to finding this girl and getting her safe. He'd Google the address when they got closer to Arundel Mills.

He slid into Veronica's driver's seat, started the engine, and sped down the street. "Wade dated Coach Butch's daughter. Her name is Jasmine."

"What? That chauvinistic idiot has a daughter?" Veronica gasped and started coughing and put a hand to her throat. "It's like...like someone's trying to strangle me."

What the hell? Why was she being affected physically again? "Where's the necklace? You're not holding it, are you?"

She coughed again, as if fighting for air, and pointed at the console where the necklace lay. He snatched it, shoved it in his left pocket, as far away from her as possible, but still within reach.

"Where does he live?" She croaked out the words, her voice hoarse.

He pressed the pedal down and glanced over his shoulder into the back seat. "Wade, does the name Jasmine sound familiar? You used to take the bus to see her. Somewhere by Arundel Mills Mall."

Veronica moaned and blinked several times. "Shit. Something bad is happening to this girl. I'm hurting all over. Like I'm covered in bruises." She shifted and faced the back seat as if listening, and then nodded. "Okay. Do it."

The car turned suddenly warmer. "Did he remember her? Does he know where she lives?"

Veronica leaned back and held her forearm over her eyes. The sun had moved behind some dark clouds, but she wasn't shielding her eyes. She was in obvious pain.

"He said holding the necklace made him remember a little bit, but not everything. He's transporting himself to the Arundel Mills area and he's going to walk around. See if it jogs his memory. Oh—" She flinched and her head bobbed back against the seat and then lolled to the side.

Pressing the pedal even farther to the floor, speeding ticket be damned, he reached out his right hand and felt for the pulse in her neck. Racing.

"Hurry, Wade," he whispered. "There might not be much time." Whatever it took, he'd be there for whatever Veronica needed and keep her safe.

Wouldn't he?

Chapter Fourteen

*V*eronica's head pounded and her bones and muscles ached as Hunter turned the corner. Dark clouds hovered above them, and spits of drizzle peppered the windshield. How long had she been out?

Hunter stared through the glass, his posture erect and alert as he guided her car through a neighborhood, looking on both sides as if searching for an address.

Wade leaned forward from the back seat. "I found her. I found Jasmine. I tried to help her, but I can't." His words came out rushed and he looked like he wanted to cry. "All I could do was stand there, unseen, unfelt, while her father tossed her in the corner like she was nothing. I tried to throw a lamp at him, but I couldn't. My hands were shaking too much."

"It's okay, Wade. Maybe you used up too much of your energy to get to her house." She blinked against the pain in her head. They had to get there in time. Had to. This gift was good for nothing if they got to Jasmine after.... She couldn't even finish the thought, but her pain told her this beating wouldn't stop until the girl was dead. Unless they saved her. "When you're upset, you might not be able to hold items. Good job finding her."

He nodded and sat forward, imitating Hunter's body position. Well, if Wade were to imitate a man, he couldn't have picked a better one than Hunter. Reliable, driven.... *Cripes*. It sounded like she was describing a good set of tires. Compassionate and honest. Why didn't she give him credit for that? Her mind flashed to the aides' conversation. Whom should she believe? The man who'd shown he would be there for her and for others? Or the gossipy staff who talked too loud? As soon as this was over, she had to apologize.

"Almost there," Hunter said, reaching out to lay a warm hand on her upper leg. The strength of his hand lessened her pain.

"Wait…. How do you know where you're going?" She glanced back at Wade again. "Did I wake up? Did you tell me the address and I said it aloud?"

Wade's gaze remained on the houses outside the window. "You were out cold. I used your phone and texted him the address. I think you were right about the energy thing. Once I calmed down, I could hold things again."

"He got your phone and texted me. Smart kid," Hunter said.

A flash of lightning lit the dark sky, followed by a boom of thunder. Her headache weakened. Maybe Jasmine was getting a reprieve. "Good job, Wade. Did you guys call the police?"

"They're on the way. I told them I got an anonymous tip that a man was beating his daughter." Hunter moved his hand to the steering wheel as water splashed against the windshield and lightning lit the late-afternoon sky again. She missed his warmth immediately. What would it be like to rely on that touch, rely on him?

Hunter turned on the wipers. Ahead on the right, red and blue lights shimmered like glaring dots through the rain. Four patrol cars were parked at different angles in the driveway next to a gray house with red shutters.

The football player faded through the car door and bolted down the street at a full run.

"Wade's going toward the house."

"I figured." Hunter maneuvered the car to a spot by one of the squad cars. "Stay here. Let me see what's happening." He gazed at her and used his sexy eye look. "Please. Stay here. Stay safe."

"Yeah. Fat chance." *Ha. Good try.* Now that he knew he possessed secret weapon, he'd try to use it all the time. But not to sleep with lots of women. To help. He'd used it to get Tia to talk. Just now, he'd used it in an effort to keep her safe. She smiled. Yeah, she'd figure it all out later. At that moment, her head cleared and her body felt stiff, but not hurt. The pain was easing.

She dashed through the drizzle, her dark T-shirt plastering to her skin within seconds of exiting the car. Hunter splashed in the rain beside her and they got to Tia's front porch.

A uniformed policeman blocked the doorway. "Step back, folks."

Veronica peeked around him, rubbing her eyes to keep the cold rain from blinding her. One cop was unrolling yellow crime scene tape in a small living room just past the front door.

Veronica swayed on her feet. The pain was gone. The connection was gone. Which had to mean....

Oh God.

She was too late. Again.

⃝ℬ

Hunter clasped Veronica's elbow. An ambulance pulled up to the curb. Medics scrambled to get out their equipment.

"Officer, we're friends of the family. Can you tell us what's going on?" Hunter held tight to Veronica. Was she feeling more pain from the victim? Was that why she was suddenly unsteady again?

"I fucking found her like this. I didn't do a damn thing." Coach Butch's voice boomed from the living room.

Found her like what? Was Jasmine alive? Where the hell was Wade?

"I'm an emergency medicine doctor. Can I help?" Hunter flashed his hospital badge. He glanced behind the cop, but saw only a group of uniformed cops.

"I'll let the EMTs know. You need to step aside. Too dangerous right now." The cop directed them out of the doorway and the medics hurried up the porch steps. "This man's a doctor and he's offered his help, if needed. You'll need to wait 'til we secure the area," the cop said. The cop turned his attention to the inside of the house, his hand on his weapon as if anticipating trouble.

"Come on. Over here." Hunter guided Veronica to a spot on the porch by a window.

"Oh my God. That must be Jasmine, slumped in a corner. Wade's stooping next to her," Veronica whispered.

Hunter peered through the window. Cops had Butch on his stomach, handcuffed, and a petite girl with blond hair lay unconscious—or possibly dead against the wall—one eye bruised and swollen shut, and blood on her head.

Cool air surrounded them and Veronica gasped.

"We've got to tell the cops." She yanked Hunter's arm and ran for the front door.

"Tell the cops what?" Hunter asked. She'd gone from weak to strong enough to pull him across the porch.

"Officer," Veronica said. "Please. Send someone into the bedroom closet. Behind the suitcases. I'm a psychic-medium and I've worked with Lieutenant Joe Snyder from the Baltimore Police. I have his number if you want to call him, but you've got to check that closet now."

The officer frowned and took out a notepad. "What's your name?"

"My name is Veronica Matthews and this is Hunter Anderson. We're friends of the girl." She glanced toward the corner where Jasmine lay. "Just please send someone to that closet."

"Stay here," he ordered, and then took a few steps inside to talk to another officer.

"What's going on?" Hunter asked.

"I have no idea. Wade asked me to tell the cop to check the closet and then he disappeared."

The officer glanced at them, but didn't ban them from the doorway.

Two officers pulled Butch to his feet. "You have the right to remain silent...." The officer continued reading the coach his rights and Butch glared at the man and his gaze shifted to the side as the officer who'd gone to check on the closet returned.

He carried a child. A child who calmly sucked her thumb and stared over the officer's shoulder.

"A child. Wade has a child," Veronica whispered. "He's talking to her, and it's almost like she's hearing him."

"Wade's?" Hunter asked. "He had a baby with Jasmine? You think that's why he couldn't cross over?"

"It makes sense. A baby would bond him in a way that could hold him to earth. His connection to Jasmine must have been a strong one."

"Damn half-breed," Butch sputtered, his face reddening as he fought to break away from the officers toward the child, who looked to be about two. "From a damn slut."

"Get him out of here," one of the officers said.

Veronica and Hunter moved to the side as two officers escorted Butch through his front door.

When Butch spotted them, he narrowed his eyes and struggled against the men holding him. "You two. None of your goddamned business. This was a family matter."

Hunter stood in front of Veronica. Butch was in handcuffs with two strong police officers holding him, but he didn't even want her to see a man like this. Standing between Veronica and anything that could hurt her was suddenly very, very important to him.

"Do you want to add resisting arrest to your charges, sir?" the officer asked.

Butch gritted his jaw and shut his mouth. The two men led him to a patrol car.

"Ma'am, sir?" The officer who'd been guarding the door beckoned them inside.

"You knew about the child in the closet because you're a psychic?"

Veronica glanced at a spot near the child and smiled. "Her name is Mia. Yes, I'm a psychic-medium who has worked with police before. We knew Jasmine would protect her child."

"We'll need to get statements from both of you."

Hunter nodded and took Veronica's hand. "No problem. Can you tell us if Jasmine's going to be okay?"

The cop glanced toward the paramedics. "How is she, guys?"

A young redhead medic snapped a neck brace into place and glanced up. "Likely a concussion. Some bruises. We'll check for internal bleeding at the hospital, but her vitals are good."

Hunter breathed a sigh of relief. Veronica squeezed his hand tight and smiled. They'd done it. Veronica and Wade had gotten them here in time.

"So." The officer glanced at his notepad. "Ms. Matthews...Dr. Anderson. What exactly was your part in all of this?"

CB

Any other time, Veronica would have hated being in a hospital. Too many ghosts.

But leaning against the air conditioning vent in Jasmine's hospital room, watching Wade's mom hold her two-year-old granddaughter while Wade cooed and made goofy faces at the baby was worth having encounters with ghosts every five minutes.

"Thank you, Dr. Anderson, Veronica," Jasmine said from her bed. "You saved me and you saved Mia."

"Don't you worry, honey." Cissy jiggled her leg up and down and Mia giggled, holding her new pink teddy bear the hospital had given her. "And don't you worry about a place for the two of you, either. Wade's bedroom is yours. He might not have known you were pregnant when he passed, but he would have wanted to take care of you." She kissed the child's cheek. "So, since he's not here, I'll take care of you."

A tear dripped down Jasmine's swollen face and she reached out, laying her hand on the bed. Cissy covered it with one of hers, and grinned.

"Well," Veronica started. May as well get this over with. "Actually, Wade is here." She let her words hang in the air.

Cissy gasped and her eyes widened and then she glanced at Jasmine.

"He's with us, isn't he? He spoke to me when I was unconscious. I told his mom." Cissy squeezed Jasmine's hand. "He told me everything would be okay. I thought it was a dream at first, but it wasn't, was it?"

Veronica shook her head. "I have the ability to talk to spirits. Wade led us to you."

Jasmine smiled. "I told him he had a daughter...and that Mia was behind some suitcases in the closet." Her gaze moved to Hunter and then to Wade's mom. "You don't think I'm crazy, do you? That I heard

Wade when I was in danger? Do you believe me? Do you hear him, too?"

Veronica smiled and leaned closer to Hunter as he slipped an arm around her waist. He'd been with her since the day she'd met Wade, and knew what this journey had taken from her. Heck, he'd had so much stolen from him the past two years. Somehow, through their experience with Wade, they'd bonded. She was getting more and more comfortable around Hunter. Actually missing him when he wasn't around. So easy to trust him, so easy to know she could lean on him. And she wasn't a bit sure she liked that feeling.

"I think Wade was there for you when you needed him most." She glanced at Wade, who stood by his mother. It was time for him to cross over. Just when he'd reconnected with his family, he'd have to leave them. "He loves all three of you so much." It felt good to know all of this had happened because of her psychic-medium gift. Her guilt about earlier failures, and fear about letting people down, were lessoned when she'd helped save Wade's girlfriend and baby. Maybe she wouldn't succeed every time, but if she didn't try, she'd never know.

"Where is he?" Cissy asked.

"To your right. Smiling down at you and Mia. And he glances at Jasmine a lot, too. I've known him a little over a week, and I've never seen him smile more than I have today."

"He's going to leave us now, though, isn't he?" Wade's mother asked.

"I'm afraid so. He's done what he stayed here to do, and he needs to move to the next world now. If he tried to stay, he'd probably lose all of his memories quickly. He'd be a lost soul." A lump formed in her throat. Who would have thought the big lug of a football player with an attitude would have grown on her like this? Tears stung her eyes.

"I already told Mia what I wanted to say." He winked at the little girl and she smiled back and then hid her face in Cissy's shoulder. "Told her to be good for her momma and grandma, and to work hard in school."

Kids were so much more open to spiritual interactions. The girl probably thought he was human.

"I want to say something to my mom and to Jasmine, though."

Wade glanced at Veronica and she stepped forward, closer to the bed.

Hunter gazed at her, pride evident on his face. Not disbelief or annoyance that she had this gift, but pride.

"Wade wants to tell you both something," Veronica said, glancing from Jasmine to Wade's mom.

He moved in front of his mom's chair and stooped, placing a hand over Jasmine's and his mom's on the bed.

"Oh," his mom said.

Jasmine's eyes opened wide.

"Mom, I was so lucky to have you as my mother. You sacrificed and took good care of me. You taught me to do the right thing, and I usually did." Wade blinked hard.

Veronica repeated his words.

"I love you and thank you for being you. Thank you for taking in Jasmine and Mia."

Again, Veronica repeated everything, but it was harder speaking past the growing lump in her throat.

Wade stood and kissed Jasmine's cheek. She pulled in a quick breath.

"He just kissed you." Veronica said.

Jasmine smiled.

"I'm sorry you were alone for two years, sorry I wasn't there to help you with Mia. She's beautiful. You'll find love again. What we had was special, and I was lucky to have it with you. But I know you'll find it again. I love you."

Veronica repeated his words and tears flowed freely down Jasmine's face.

Wade pinched the bridge of his nose and closed his eyes. Then he opened them, and faced Veronica. "Let's do this now before I change my mind."

∞

Veronica paced the hall carpeting in front of Hunter's closed apartment door. One o'clock in the morning and she was wired instead of exhausted. They should all be tired after the day they'd had. Wade and Hunter stood nearby. The tension built inside her. Would it work this time? Because if this wasn't it—if this wasn't the reason Wade hadn't been able to cross over, then she had no idea what would be.

"We're almost ready." Veronica glanced at Wade, who leaned against the faded hallway wallpaper. He grinned.

"This vortex—" Hunter blinked and shook his head. "I can't believe I'm using words like that. As if I know what I'm talking about. But is it safe?"

I can only hope it's safe. The negative force—it might have something to do with that murder that happened up here—is making the left side stronger. Not in a good way, either."

Hunter scrubbed his jaw with a hand, a worried expression on his face.

"Remember, you had to deal with me for two years. That makes you an expert, I'd say." Wade shot Hunter an apologetic look.

Veronica laughed. Leave it to Wade to calm the moment. If only Hunter could see the sorry look on his face. "Wade says you *are* an expert because you had to put up with him for so long.

Hunter smiled. God, she was really getting used to that smile. His touch calmed her nerves, made her feel less alone. His words made her feel loved. And his hands...well, she couldn't let her mind go *there* right now or she might never have the brain space to help Wade get where he was going.

"Ah, it wasn't so bad," Hunter said.

"Really? Want to forget this whole crossover thing and keep him with you?" She winked at Wade.

"Uh, well...." Hunter moved beside her and put an arm around her waist. "No use keeping him here when he needs to be somewhere else."

Veronica and Wade chuckled.

"Can you tell him I'm sorry for pestering him all that time? I really was a pain in the ass. I see that now." Wade shifted his weight from foot to foot, obviously anxious to get this done.

Veronica smiled. "Wade's sorry he pestered you. He says he was a pain in the ass."

"Ha, you were," he said. "But I enjoyed getting to know who you were and getting to know your family. We'll check in with your mom,

Jasmine, and Mia, you know. Birthdays...holidays...we're considering ourselves part of the family. That's what you gave us."

Veronica's pulse raced at the mention of her and Hunter as part of a family. That was the problem. That was how she was thinking of him now. Part of her. And it scared the shit out of her.

Wade beamed at Hunter's words.

At the end of the hallway, a door opened and a tall man walked down the hallway. "Here he comes," Veronica said. She didn't know if it would help Wade or not, she might as well go with her gut. The eighth floor had more haunted activity than any place she'd been to in Baltimore. And some of the eighth-floor residents had experience with crossovers.

"Rob," Veronica said, shaking hands with the handsome brown-haired man from apartment 807. "Angie's secure on the other side of town again?"

He nodded. "One of these days we'll tell you why, but I appreciate the heads-up on the vortex being used, because for now, I feel better knowing she's safely somewhere else."

Rob and his fiancée Angie liked to be warned when she accessed the vortex with a spirit. She didn't know why, but she respected their wish.

Veronica nodded, knowing he had his reasons for thinking his wife was endangered by the vortex. "This is Hunter Anderson."

The men shook hands and offered pleasantries.

"I think we've met on the elevator," Hunter said. "Nice to see you again."

"And Wade is our friend by the door there. He's crossing over tonight. He's a bright young football player who died during a game two years ago. He helped save his daughter's and girlfriend's lives."

"Impressive." Rob glanced toward the spot where Wade stood.

Halfway down the hall, a door clicked open and a couple exited, hand in hand.

Veronica smiled and waved as Missy—a beautiful local disc jockey with long, brown hair—and Blake, a cop, marched toward them, hand in hand. Veronica's heart skipped a beat at the thought of her and Hunter ever looking so much in love. *No. Too fast, too much.*

"Hey, Veronica," they said in unison.

Earlier, when she'd explained about having other neighbors who were familiar with the vortex present at the crossover, Hunter had realized he knew several of them from the apartment workout room.

"This is Missy," Blake said to Hunter.

"And I know you can't see him, but Wade's right here. Like I just told Rob, he's a really great kid who died too soon, and he stayed to take care of his family. But tonight, we're hoping your presence helps him move on."

"Good luck, Wade. We're pulling for you," Missy said, smiling at the spot Veronica indicated.

Wade wrung his hands. This had to be like ripping off a bandage. Quick. Now.

"This is it, Wade." Veronica moved in front of him. "As you cross to the other side, you might see somebody who's been gone a while. Somebody who loves you—like a grandma or grandpa." She looked over her shoulder. "Or even a sweet older couple—Betty and Stanley—who used to live in this building."

He nodded and glanced at the end of the hall.

"It won't hurt, Wade. And it won't be scary." She reached up to give him a hug, her forearms barely making it around his huge shoulder pads. He hugged her tight and then released her.

"Ready?" she asked.

He straightened his shoulders, pulled himself to his full height, and with two long strides, stood in the center of the hallway facing the end with the vortex.

"Good-bye," Wade said, turning to look at Hunter, and then the other apartment residents.

"He says 'good-bye,'" Veronica repeated to the four observers.

They offered goodbyes and luck.

Wade turned to face the end of the hall again, his right foot bent in front in a "line of scrimmage" stance. Ready to go.

"Stay to the right side, Wade. We're lucky we got to know you." Tears stung Veronica's eyes.

Wade took off, arms pumping, feet thumping the floor. In his red jersey and football pants, he looked like a kid running sprints. Instead, he was a kid running toward the unknown. She could only hope it would be as terrific as he was.

The hairs on Veronica's arms rose and the end of the hallway became blurry, as if the air were moving. Hunter shifted close to her and took her shaking hand. "It has to work," she said.

"It will." He squeezed her hand.

That squeeze, that confidence in her—more than she had in herself—was the reason she was falling for Hunter.

Wade didn't break stride. He was almost to the spot. Veronica sucked in a breath.

Fire. On the left side of the vortex. It looked so real she was amazed the heat didn't fill the hall. *Oh God, no.* A charred arm reached out from the flames. Reached for the football player.

"All the way to the right!" she screamed.

The right side wobbled like a funhouse mirror.

And then Wade was gone.

"He made it!" she cried.

He made it. Veronica took stock as her breathing slowed. Now she had another spirit to learn about. And, if she could learn how to help the murder victims, maybe the evil side of the vortex would close.

She didn't need to avoid her gift. She could embrace it and make things better. In this world and the next.

Epilogue

One month later

$\mathcal{T}$he referee blew his whistle and Veronica glanced around. She wished she had a clue about football now that she'd probably be attending more games with Hunter, but she had no idea why the players from both teams were running off the field.

Hunter put a hand on her knee. "It's halftime. We're up."

Veronica grabbed the chain-link fence in front of her and stood, glad to be off the aluminum bleacher that had put her butt to sleep. Front row or not, these seats at the high school football field were uncomfortable. Wade's mom, Jasmine, and Mia also stood.

Led by Hunter, who grasped her hand, they crossed the track on the way to the makeshift podium being assembled midfield.

Mia's soft little hand slipped into Veronica's. She looked adorable in an oversized football jersey. Number five.

In the weeks since Wade's crossing, Veronica and Hunter had kept their promise to Wade. They'd visited the Montgomery household once a week, often staying for a home-cooked meal. Eating as a family reminded Veronica of days in the past when she'd yearned for a family to sit down with, to have dinner with.

Spending time with Wade's family made her more comfortable with the whole idea of leaning on people...letting them lean on her. And trusting. Hunter had shown her over and over again how trustworthy he was, and showered her with attention. He was a one-woman man, and she saw that now. He'd made it very clear he was interested in being with her, and only her. But she'd been scared to trust. At least back then.

So how did she let him know that had changed? How could she let him know she felt like he did? That she was ready to risk her heart?

The principal did a quick sound check on the microphone and the Friday evening football crowd grew quiet.

"Time for our four announcements," Hunter said as they approached the stage.

Four? What did I miss? Three announcements, right?

"And without further delay, I give you our team doctor, Dr. Hunter Anderson."

The crowd politely applauded and Hunter stepped to the mic. "Wow. Heck of a game so far."

His voice was strong and confident. Damn. This guy could do anything with style. She'd never been prouder of him than this moment. A warm September breeze ruffled tufts of his dark hair and he grinned at the spectators.

"Tonight we'd like to honor a very special young man with a very special presentation. Wade Montgomery was a football player who gave it his all—in the classroom, at home, and on the football field." Hunter held out his arm and motioned for Wade's mother to step closer.

She stood beside him with tears brimming.

"Tonight, we'd like to announce that we're establishing a full, in-state college scholarship to a South High student each year. The Wade Montgomery Scholarship." Hunter paused as the crowd cheered.

When they quieted, he laid a hand around Cissy's shoulder and placed his other hand over the microphone. "Go ahead, Cissy. You tell them."

She cleared her throat and stood taller, reminding Veronica of the way Wade had done the same thing when it was time for him to cross over. Even two months later, Veronica missed that kid.

Cissy held up Wade's jersey. "As of today, Wade Montgomery's jersey—number five—will be retired."

The crowd cheered and a whistle that rang out louder than everything else caught Veronica's attention. She glanced toward the sound and smiled as she caught Sam Junior and his sister, each with two fingers in their mouths, whistling and smiling.

Cissy smiled and handed the jersey to Jasmine, who blushed and held the jersey to her heart—pressing it against the peace-sign necklace she wore on the outside of her own version of Wade's jersey. Hunter had them specially made for Cissy, Jasmine, and Mia.

"Last...." Hunter leaned toward the microphone as Cissy stepped aside. "Look to the east side of the field for a moment...." He pointed to the right.

Veronica smiled as five hundred people turned to face the direction he pointed.

"If you'll all help me count backward from three." He held up three fingers. "Three...two...one..." The crowd shouted with him and a tarp fell to the ground as two players tugged at ropes.

"South High—your new scoreboard," Hunter announced. He beamed with pride, knowing it was something that might give the team confidence, give them something schools in many other districts had as a matter of course. The crowd cheered louder.

The screen flashed on and a photo of Wade, his smiling face, in his football uniform, filled the screen. Veronica pressed her lips together to keep them from quivering. How could she miss someone she'd only known a little over a week?

She knew the answer. He hadn't just been a wonderful kid, he'd been the reason she found Hunter.

"And," Hunter said as the cheers died down. "We've already enlisted some local businesses to run ads on the scoreboard. A great way for the team to make some extra money for uniforms and new equipment." He glanced at Veronica and swallowed. "So without further delay...." His voice shook. Gone was the perfectly assured speaker, and in his place stood some guy with stage fright.

Veronica frowned.

"Your first scoreboard ad." Hunter stared to the right with wide eyes.

Veronica followed his gaze. Flashing red letters ran across the screen: *Veronica, I love you. Will you marry me? <3 Hunter*

She stood absolutely motionless, disbelieving.

Cissy elbowed her. "That's you, honey."

Veronica's pulse raced. He was asking her to spend her life with him. Telling her in front of all of these people that she was the one he wanted.

She turned to face him, looked into his light blue eyes that were wide and staring back at her. He tugged a black box out of his pocket, opened it, and bent to one knee.

She couldn't speak, could only nod her head several times. Yes, she'd spend the rest of her life with him. He was like the other side of her she'd always been looking for. The part of her she never let herself be. Except around him.

Hunter stood, and she threw her arms around his shoulders and stood on tiptoes to kiss his lips. He held her tight and the crowd cheered.

Cissy laughed. "Well look at that," she said.

Veronica's heart pounded and she couldn't stop smiling. She turned toward the scoreboard again and the words flashed: *She said yes!*

She raised a brow and peered up at Hunter. "How'd you know I was going to say yes?"

He shrugged. "I didn't."

"So what was Plan B message?" His warm hand in hers made her forget they stood in front of five hundred strangers.

"If you said no, I would have asked you again in five minutes. And if you said no then, I'd ask you again five minutes later.... Well, you get my drift."

The principal stepped to the microphone. "Well, I think this was the best halftime ever." The crowd cheered again.

"Oh no, he's so wrong," Hunter whispered in her ear. "The best halftime celebration ever is just beginning. Now we go back to my place where I can show you exactly what you can expect from me as we score one touchdown after another."

Holding hands, they left the podium. Veronica had never felt so loved. Friends, a family—even if they weren't blood-related—and the